Death

in an

Evil Place

Antony
Norman

Matador
9 Priory Business Park,
Wistow Road, Kibworth Beauchamp,
Leicestershire. LE8 0RX
Tel: 0116 279 2299
Email: books@troubador.co.uk
Web: www.troubador.co.uk/matador
Twitter: @matadorbooks

ISBN 978 1785893 667

British Library Cataloguing in Publication Data.
A catalogue record for this book is available from the British Library.

Printed and bound by CPI Group (UK) Ltd, Croydon, CR0 4YY
Typeset in 11pt Times by Troubador Publishing Ltd, Leicester, UK

Matador is an imprint of Troubador Publishing Ltd

Acknowledgements

Roughly in chronological order, I would like to thank:

My daughter Jay, who read the first draft and survived;

Dr Alan Tricker, who read a later version and encouraged me to do better;

Alan's wife, Carole, herself a published author, who edited what I had thought was the final text. But wasn't.

And lastly, to my dear wife Moira for her amazing patience.

1

Rural Lancashire 1992

It was hatred at first sight. I was standing in a gravelled forecourt looking up at a massive Victorian stone-built house. Shrouded in a November fog it loomed at me, dark, silent and threatening. Suddenly, I shivered. It was cold. But it wasn't that cold. I hated the place.

It was chance, blind chance that had brought me here – the classic cold turkey. I'd spent the day touring our customers among the hill farms. I was on my way back to the works when, approaching the narrow bridge over the beck, a heavy lorry loaded with animal feed came looming out of the mist. He wasn't giving way; I moved onto the verge and waited while he lumbered past. As I pulled back onto the road I spotted a small paint-blistered sign half hidden on the overgrown grass verge opposite. But for the delay at the bridge I would never have noticed it: *Fellbeck*. It pointed down a track rutted with tractor tyre marks – a farm. There was still time for a call.

Fellbeck was not on my calling list – I didn't know the place existed. I knew the beck: it flowed down from the fell country towards the Ribble. Today it had an evil look – oily, black, slipping along malignant in the cold mist.

I followed the track alongside the river bank. After a couple of hundred yards, the beck took a sharp right turn. The track conformed and ran me into a solid grey wall of fog. Shit! I braked and switched on the fog lights. They didn't help much, the beams reflecting straight back at me. I was lucky: if the fog bank had been lying a few yards further back I could have missed the bend and motored smartly into the water.

It was a first gear crawl now, I could barely see past the end of the bonnet – an old-fashioned pea souper – I thought fogs like this were extinct. A long dead farmer had planted a line of elms along the river bank – bare winter trees crept past in silent procession – it was enough to keep the car on the track. My eyes were smarting but there was nowhere to stop and rest. Suddenly, another bend to the right, this time away from the water and the worst was over. The fog thinned to a mist and the track opened out onto a large gravel forecourt at the far end of which stood the house.

I pulled up on the edge of the forecourt, switched off, removed my nose from the windscreen, sat back and shut my eyes for what seemed to be moments. When I opened them the smarting had subsided. I grabbed my briefcase from the passenger seat and climbed out. Looking back the way I had come, the track disappeared into a solid grey curtain. I was in a closed space, trapped between the heavy grey bulk of the house and the fog all round.

I turned towards the house. It was screened all round by elm trees; a cold, dark, secretive place. Heavy lintels topped blind black-faced windows; no lights showed. The track, which must lead on to the farmyard, disappeared down the right hand side of the house, as if the owner, devil porter-like, sat and controlled everything that came and went. A mock-Palladian porch with four thick fluted pillars gave the entrance an austere look. On the pediment an oval shield was carved into the stone: *ED* surrounded by laurel leaves and beneath that, the date, *1878*. Somewhere at the rear a horse whinnied.

I set off towards the front door. A dog started to bark, a slow mournful woof... woof... woof. A door banged rhythmically as a loose shed door might blow in the wind if there was a wind; the mist hung motionless.

The front door was a solid affair in nailed oak, varnish clung in patches to the woodwork. I grabbed the iron bell pull and hauled downwards. It was rusty but it worked, a bell clanged inside. I was surprised by the instant response – a light appeared in the fanlight above the door followed by quick, purposeful steps on a hard floor, the turn of a heavy lock, the door flew open.

'I'd almost given you up...' the greeting faded. The man in the doorway stood staring past my shoulder, away up the fog-bound drive.

I pulled out a business card, my last, and handed it over, 'I've been seeing Bolton up at Sunnyside...' (*Get on with it Hardy*) I take it you're the farmer here?'

'Did you pass anyone in the lane? Walking?'

'No, just as well. The fog's so thick I could have run them over.'

'Really?' the farmer made to hand my card back.

'No, keep it.'

He gave me a blank stare and pushed the card into his jacket pocket. 'You're sure? Fog, you say?'

Could he not see for himself? 'Look, if you can spare me five minutes.'

The farmer dragged his thoughts away from his missing visitor, 'A brief word then.' His voice was a resonant baritone, educated – nothing of the local accent. He offered his hand, 'Adams'. It was a strong grip; the man did work of some sort around the place – he could be worth talking to. Adams led the way into the hall. Instead of switching on more lights, he turned off the transom light leaving only the feeble daylight filtering down through the stained glass. The entrance hall was large and in shadow. On the right was a wide oak staircase leading up to ...darkness. In front, a wide corridor disappeared into the black hole of the interior. I followed Adams blindly down the passage until he opened the first door on the left. I walked in anticipating the usual farmhouse muddle – a big desk covered in piles of paperwork, smells of damp sheepdog from the hearthrug and boiling hen food from the kitchen.

It was not what I expected: a dark brown dado ran round the walls topped by paintwork in a brownish cream. The heavy carved plasterwork on the ceiling – devils chasing cherubs – was grey with muck of ages and wood smoke. It was a big room with two large windows giving onto the courtyard. Three more were spaced down the long wall overlooking the beck. The wall opposite housed a fine stone fireplace. A log fire was laid but not lit. The room struck cold. By way of furniture it contained a pair of high-backed chairs either side of the fireplace and between them a settee set back. A couple of occasional tables and three or four heavy wooden chairs stood around the walls. A large oil painting hung above the fireplace, dominating the room. Adams switched on a pair of feeble wall lights on either side of the picture revealing the subject – a Victorian farmer, black bowler, black jacket buttoned up to the neck, leather-gaitered legs set aggressively apart, stick in hand – the master standing before his mansion.

My host was drawing heavy red curtains, shutting out what remained of the daylight and closing the room in. He moved silently like an assassin. I stepped up to take a closer look at the portrait. He was a big man with powerful, heavy features, a great beak of a nose and a massive jaw accentuated by grey mutton chop whiskers. His eyes were piercing black, deep-set in a weather-beaten, hard lined face. Brutal years had frozen his expression into a scowl, the stick was not only for support. This man got what he wanted, never mind how. The evidence was behind him – the big house, a nervous groom respectfully to one side holding a black hunter. In the background, fields dotted white with sheep swept steeply uphill to a terrace of workers' cottages lining the ridge where John Bolton's Sunnyside now stood. A brass plate screwed to the bottom of the picture frame rounded off the story – Ezra Dawson, 1814-1891 – so that was him; ED – builder of this house completed in 1878. The evil that men do...

'Impressive picture,' I told Adams. I did not mean that exactly. It changed the whole atmosphere of the room from gloomy to menacing.

'My great uncle', the farmer switched on a standard lamp behind the fireside chair on my side. It cast a patch of light over the chair, the only bright light in the place. 'Sit down,' he said, 'tell me why you've come.' He moved to the chair opposite and sat. I wasn't buying that, instead of my backside, I set my brief case on the chair, withdrew a glossy leaflet and handed it over, 'Ditchfield Packaging'.

He turned the sheet over with little interest. 'I can't offer you tea, Mr Hardy.'

He had read my card, after all. 'I had a cup with Bolton.'

'Bolton?'

'John Bolton – next farm to yours, top of the hill – Sunnyside.'

'Really?' What did that mean? News that he had a neighbour called Bolton, or surprise that he supplied tea? He looked all wrong for a moorland farmer – tweed jacket, pressed trousers, stiff collar and tie – smartened up for his visitor? I guessed he was in his early forties; spoke like a gent, looked like a bandit – a handsome bandit – broad across the cheekbones, with a straight nose and a high forehead. His complexion was smooth and swarthy, no red chapped cheeks from the fell wind. A dark moustache curled down either side of the top lip, thick but well trimmed. He didn't resemble his great uncle. Ezra was an English bastard, no doubt about that. This man looked like a Turk. The eyes were tawny, gold-flecked, hooded, killer's eyes – unsettling.

'Are you a large concern, Mr Hardy?' I told him about a hundred and fifty employees. 'Strange. I've never heard of you.'

I shifted the brief case and sat, 'You make silage?' The

5

farmer fixed tawny eyes on mine, saying nothing. 'Winter feed for sheep.'

'There are a couple of timber silos on the land. I believe they were used for silage in my uncle's time but not since the war. I've never considered it.'

It was an opening of sorts, 'Silage went out of favour postwar because of the labour shortage. Now we've developed products that make it less labour intensive. I was at the Lisle estate earlier today (*name-dropping Hardy, how public school is that?*) they're heavily into it.' Reaction – a tawny stare. 'I can arrange for one of our advisers to contact you, there are DEFRA leaflets that would help you to get started.' I got up. I didn't like this freezing place or its owner.

Adams sat looking up at me, eyes narrowed, suspicion on his bandit features, 'DEFRA?'

'Ministry of Agriculture, hill farms aren't suitable for hay, they want to encourage silage.'

The farmer was on his feet. 'Government? What business is it of theirs what I choose to do on my own land?' I followed him to the front door. 'If you want your man to get in touch instruct him to write, will you? I don't deal on the telephone.' He opened the door for me and stood staring up the drive. It was all but dark. I stepped out.

'You could give me your mobile number?'

'Mobile?' (*Skip it*). 'Thanks for your advice, Mr Hardy.' Not hard to spot the irony – supercilious bugger, 'if you're going in the Coldedge direction you may meet someone on foot coming this way...'

'I'll be careful to give them room.'

'That would be so kind.'

'We'll be in touch, Mr ...er,' I'm not that bad at names, I just wanted to be sure of my man.

'Ostrick', the door closed, the lock turned. Ostrick? But he'd said "Adams" at first. It must have been Adam, his first name – Adam Ostrick – an unusual name. Why had he given his Christian name? He wasn't the first names type – anything but. It didn't make sense, nothing did, and overlaying everything I couldn't shake off a vague feeling of menace; something was going on in that house. Whatever it was, I wasn't taking part.

I looked back at Fellbeck: brooding, isolated, evil – what a place for murder! 'Last time I see you, bugger,' I told it. Empty defiance, that turned out to be, but I wasn't to know until years later.

I walked to the car, no sound from the horse, the dog or the shed door. I hauled out my mobile – no signal. I was at the bottom of a steep-sided valley with the massive farmhouse blocking the southern side.

I drove across the yard and into the fog bank, dead slow, nervous in case there really was someone. I didn't want to meet whoever was in that fog. At first it was as thick as before then, quite soon, it started to thin. A few more yards and it was no more than a mist. There was no one walking along the track or on the Coldedge road. I needed a pint.

2

Ditchfield 1992

The Garibaldi was loudly crowded with young office workers from the new estate so I stayed at the bar. Wilkinson came in and joined me.

'What's to do Hardy? Look as if you've met a ghost!' Should I tell him? We go back to primary school, me and Wilkinson, I told him.

It was on his business territory – he would know the place. He didn't, 'There's remains of a track there but no sign that I can remember.' He called to his van driver. Alec was on his way out of the pub; he came back. Peter said, 'Fellbeck – farm on th' Braxtonby road out of Coldedge, know it?'

'A big stone house half a mile downstream of the bridge, you can't see it from the road,' I added.

'Empty, has been for years – derelict, likely. See you Monday, Pete.'

'Now then,' said Wilkinson, 'this farmer, what's his name?'

'Ostrick.'

'Ostrich? What sort of name is that?'

Wilkinson turned serious, 'Ken, I think you walked into something we're not meant to see. Keep it between us two and no harm done. Don't go back. Whatever you do, don't go back.'

'I shouldn't have bothered you with it,' I admitted, 'I feel a bit soft now.'

'Well don't. I wouldn't go there on my own and in that fog.

8

There's places up there... places where the trees don't grow. Have you not noticed?'

'Rubbish,' said the wife after she got it out of me, 'that Ostrick is never a farmer – a speculator more like – he's bought the place to develop it and it's driving him off his head. He'll end up shooting himself. Keep away.'

I had a bad night and woke feeling lousy. I crawled out of bed, staggered to the bathroom and stuck the thermometer under my tongue – 102. 'Flu! I went back to bed. The wife was supportive, 'Stay there, you. I don't want it, I've got things to do.' She moved into the spare room.

I stayed in bed until Sunday afternoon; by Monday I was fit enough for work. I'd got the better of the flu but I was haunted by the Fellbeck episode: it cut the ground from under me. Who was I? Ken Hardy, a practical engineer and down to earth northern business man interviewing a farmer who looks like something out of the thirties and talks as though he's living in the past, in a house that the locals say has been empty for years.

Worst of all, I couldn't leave it alone. Doreen's crazy speculator theory didn't hold water nor did I accept Wilkinson's view that the episode was supernatural. I don't do supernatural, I don't lecture ghosts about silage and I don't shake hands with beings from parallel universes. But I couldn't deny what I had seen and heard. Or what I had felt.

It hung around me all day until on the drive home an explanation struck. On Friday afternoon I had been incubating a dose of 'flu. When I closed my eyes outside Fellbeck to relieve the smarting I'd fallen asleep without realising it. I never went inside the house; I never met the owner. Alec said the place was empty, had been for years, deserted.

It was a feverish dream and I could prove it. I put my hand in my pocket to check my last remaining business card. It wasn't there.

I had given it to Ostrick.

3

Ditchfield 1998

It was the job that dragged me back to reality. The market went into one of its boom periods, sales shot up like forced rhubarb and business was a scramble to satisfy the customers. I had no time or patience for speculation about the supernatural. By the time the boom petered out Fellbeck was safely parked in the past. Five years later brother-in-law George threw a spanner in the works. He dropped dead.

It was an evening in May. I drove home feeling unusually relaxed. It had rained most of the day before brightening up at knocking-off time. I came over the moor top under a big sky dotted with floating cathedrals of white nimbo-cumulus. The plain of the Fylde stretched sunlit below me all the way to Blackpool, the tower and the line of darker blue that was the sea. 'The north! Beat that!' I told them – the unfortunates trapped south of the Mersey.

As if catching the mood, the wife swaggered down the drive to meet me.

Doreen was not dressed for gardening or cookery. 'We've nothing in the house,' she said, 'bread and pull it, or eat out.' Fish and chips were rejected; we would try the new Italian.

Conversation was on the stilted side at first. Then, carbonara disposed of, 'Kenneth, I'm worried about you. You don't look well. You're stressed out, I can always tell. You've been overdoing it for years. If you want my opinion it started with that Fellbeck business *(she's saved that one up)*. That was stress. *And* it put you in bed which is not like you. It's time to relax before it's too late – it'll do you good.'

I didn't want to be done good to. Relaxing makes me nervous. Feebly, I mentioned this. It got me nowhere, 'Right, leave it to me,' said the wife, 'I'm not having us finishing up like our kid and George.' She meant her elder sister, Brenda and husband (defunct).

As I saw it, things weren't like that at all. George had happily worried away at his carpet business for years until Brenda got to work on him. He gave in and sold up. They moved to a villa on the Costa del Sunstroke – sweaty, dusty, boring and pointless – a modern development inhabited exclusively by sweaty, dusty, boring and pointless ex-pats. Two years of living the dream and floating in buckets of sangria left George three stone heavier and brought on his heart attack – a massive one that knocked him off his bar stool before he'd quite finished his after-breakfast brandy (large).

I protested, 'It wasn't stress that killed George, it was boredom. Worrying about money was life to George. When that was taken away he didn't know what to do with himself. I don't worry about money, that's Scotty's job, he likes worrying about money. I worry about the factory; I can't take the factory to Spain. What am I going to do when I get there?'

'Well anyway,' said the wife, 'I've decided (*so do as you're told, Hardy, you'll feel better*). Brenda has invited me to stay.'

'She's lonely.'

'Is she 'eckerslike? She loves it.'

Like the Roman at Cannae I had neglected to anticipate the encircling movement, 'Then?'

'Wait and see', said the wife grasping her victory glass of Geographica. 'You've done enough, Kenneth. It's time to hand over to someone younger.'

'The only way I would hand on to someone new would be to sell out and walk away.'

'Well then,' said the wife, ruthlessly.

'I can't – not just like that. Ditchfield Packaging isn't a public company. I can't sell my shares on the stock market and push off. It has to be done by agreement with the others. There's McIver and me with forty five percent each and Aldershaw (our law man) with the rest. It's all laid down in the company articles. Anyway, even if I could, I wouldn't do that to Scotty. He founded the firm. He was the one that spotted the opportunity, organised the finance so we could get started and then kept us right in the early days when we could easily have gone under. If it hadn't been for McIver I'd have slogged on with a dead-end job at Raistrick and Brown until they went bust and I got the sack.'

Facts failed to impress, 'You'll sort something out between the three of you,' Doreen said and moved on to the digestivo.

★

The following Monday I drove to the airport drop-off point: 'Back in six weeks,' she told me 'sooner if it's a no-no.'

'It won't be. You'd settle for the workhouse if it had guaranteed sun.'

I drove out of the airport. It was too early for my appointment; I had half an hour to kill. I spotted a caff with a chalked board outside: *Tea, Coffee, Soup Filled Roll's, All Day Brekfast*. Inside, the windows streamed with condensation, the floor tiles were slippery, plastic tabletops well greasy. Perfect: nostalgia set in. I ordered a large black coffee, no sugar, cold milk on the side.

'You mean like tea?' asked the big blonde.

'But coffee.'

'Anythink tweet?'

I was not tempted by the All Day Brekfast or the Soup Filled Roll's. I settled for a bacon sandwich. Crouched by the streaming window I watched the traffic jostling anxiously onto the motorway. It brought back my early days on the road – red Cortina in the fast lane, stress-related stomach ache.

Hewitt's were our oldest customers. It was unusual nowadays for Aaron Hewitt to invite me in person. Without being reminded, he pushed a cheque across the desk. That was a bad sign. Next he produced a bundle of potato bags, 'What do you think of these?' I'd seen bags from the Far East before: smudgy print – "Selected Patotoes" – seams that split if you looked at them. These were tough, nicely printed, perfectly good bags. I said so.

'I know,' Aaron said, 'from China'. Then he told me the price.

★

Dr Jones entered my weight into his computer. 'You've put on two kilos.

How much are you drinking per week?'

'No more than my doctor.' The computer wasn't having that; numbers and no messing. I mentally tallied the score for last week, divided by two and rounded down. The computer was willing to believe me but my doctor wasn't. I suspected that the figure he entered included a correction.

'How many eggs a week?' God, they're not still asking that one? Three eggs a week means death plus ten percent on the premium.

It was the annual company health check. 'Right,' said Bill Jones, 'let's have a second look at the blood pressure'. I looked out the window whilst the cuff squeezed my bicep and then slowly relaxed. 'A hundred and eighty over ninety five – as before.' I thought it sounded high. 'It is high, much too high. I'll give you a prescription.'

'Will that sort it out?'

'No. It'll give you time to sort yourself out. Exercise –you should be taking a brisk one hour walk at least four times a week.

Work – what are you doing, sixty hours a week still?' I thought that was about right. 'Take on some more help, delegate, ease off.'

'I can't imagine anything more stressful than passing on my business to a young genius and then sitting back to watch him wreck it.'

'You could copyright that for carving on gravestones. What does Doreen think?'

'Doreen says I've done enough. She wants me to sell up and retire.'

Bill Jones said, 'Speaking as a friend, she's right.'

'And as a doctor?'

'If you're sensible now, you're good for another twenty years. If not, I won't be answerable. Start reducing your working hours, think seriously about selling out, cut the alcohol by half, exercise and get some weight off.'

'Am I talking to Bill Jones here, or the political wing of the BMA?'

'Yes,' said my GP, 'last appointment for the day over; fancy a pint?'

The late George, the blood pressure, Hewitt's Chinese bags, how was I to break it to McIver?

On Friday morning Dorothy said, 'Mr McIver's compliments, Mr Hardy, and would you take a cup of coffee with him?' McIver crouched ape-like in his top floor office with a commanding view over the roofs of Ditchfield. Although it was early, the office air was already thick with smoke. Tracey, McIver's blonde secretary of the moment followed me in, set the coffee on the desk and swayed out, closing the door behind her.

McIver sniffed, looked at me like a monkey and said, 'I've had a call from Livesey at APC.' He meant Amalgamated Polythene Converters plc, biggest in Britain, founded and run by Stefan Kovacs. 'Livesey wants to know if we're interested in a bid. I said we'd think about it and let them ken. What do you think?'

'What's the offer?'

'Net asset value – the thick end of ten million – I might improve on it.'

I took a sip of McIver's coffee, shuddered and told him about Aaron Hewitt's Chinese bags. 'But that won't bother APC. If Stefan was serious about supermarket bags he'd set up his own factory in south China. Our agricultural business will be what he's after. How do you feel?'

McIver's reply was exactly what I didn't expect, 'I'm ready, have been for a wee whiley. *(And dropped a hint to Livesey?)*. I have ambitions Kenneth beyond polythene bags and I'll need capital.' My partner wore the daunting expression of a McIver on the make. He picked up the phone, 'APC, Tracey. Mr Livesey.'

4

The wife found the villa of my nightmares on a south-facing slope of the Costa del Sol, ruthlessly slashed our asking price and sold the matrimonial home before the August rains set in. 'What about me?' I demanded, 'Scotty's near to shaking hands on the sale with APC. I'll have to stay on for two years to meet our guarantees and train their people. You're not expecting me to live in a B and B?'

I need not have bothered: she had fixed it with Paula, our younger daughter. Paula had married Tom Harrison, Ditchfield lawyer and ex rugby-playing thug. Tom and his partner, Niall Potts, had moved upmarket from their backstreet premises to York Terrace only to find that after computerisation it was too big. What I didn't know was that Paula had spotted an opportunity and converted the surplus space into a pair of flats for let. 'It'll suit you down the ground,' the wife instructed. 'You'll be over Tom's offices with your own private entrance and your own keys so you can come and go.'

'You mean I won't be under house arrest?'

'Paula's let the top flat to a young single teacher. He takes over at the beginning of September, quiet, guaranteed no trouble', the wife said. 'I'm right suited; I can get on with meeting new people, socialising, which you hate. Meantime, you relax in Ditchfield.' *(No comment)*.

At the airport drop-off she handed me a wicker travelling basket, said an extended and moist farewell to the contents, a quick dry one to me and disappeared into Departures. I was on the wrong end of a hostile glare from the cat.

I drove to my new address. I met my new neighbour on the stairs as I struggled up bearing an angry cat plus an armful of items of a personal and confidential nature. Appreciating the situation, he relieved me of the cat basket and led the way up to my front door. Inside the flat, which had been left open for their convenience, the removal men stood around in postures both heroic and expectant having distributed my furniture more or less randomly. I applied the usual inducement for them to leave.

'I'm Chris Berry, I've just moved into the flat upstairs. Could I give you a hand to sort things out?' He could, he could also feed the cat.

While we shoved the furniture around I got to grips with his cv, 'You mean, aged 36 you've abandoned a career in electronics engineering and moved from Royal Berkshire to teach science at St. Cuthbert's, Ditchfield, North East Lancs?' He had. Having sorted out the furniture, I moved on to saucepans, toaster, microwave and the like. Chris watched and fidgeted. Another job was needed here.

'Does electronic engineering include setting up my computer?'

'Anything except mend the telly.'

'Well you know where it is.' He disappeared into the room I planned to use as my study. Half an hour later he emerged.

'It's all working: computer, printer, scanner. Modem connected and implemented.' I expressed relief. 'It takes for ever to boot up,' he said, 'will it be alright if I plug in some extra RAM?'

By the time Chris had done that and demonstrated the improvement I was experiencing a thirst. 'Superb, come on,' I said and guided him unresisting to the public bar of the Duke where he took his debut sip of Ditchfield's finest.

'It's a little on the sharp side.'

'Of course it is – compared; it demands an educated palate. In time, you'll grow to like it. This new career of yours, when do you start?'

'Thursday.'

'This is Monday – what's the rush?'

'I'm hoping to have a chat with Meyer, my new boss, head of science. I'd like to sort out one or two issues with him before term starts.'

'Issues? Didn't come to blows, did you?' He denied that.

'But,' Chris admitted, 'I was partly to blame.'

'Go on. How?'

'When I arrived for the interviews, I was sent on a guided tour with one of the senior girls. Dawn had dropped science at the first opportunity. "Nobody likes Meyer", she said.

'When I arrived at Science, Meyer was in his office having a chat with Mrs Patterson – the hot favourite. Meanwhile, I had tea with Gloria, the lab technician. She briefed me on Meyer's management style. "Likes things done his way, fair play to him – he got two Oxford scholarships last year."'

I wanted to get to the point. 'So where did things go wrong?'

'From the start,' Chris said. 'The moment I got into his office, Meyer brought up my lack of experience. I said I'd had twelve years in real world hi-tech industry followed by one year PGCE with a distinction on teaching practice. Then he wanted my assessment of science teaching at St. Cuthbert's.'

'Good question after half an hour in the place. What did you say?'

'I wondered whether more could be done to stimulate interest in the lower streams. He just glared and said nothing. Then I volunteered to concentrate on that area for my first couple of years.'

'I bet he loved that – you were telling him he's only doing half a job.'

Chris grinned ruefully, 'It was a waste of time. He'd decided; he wanted Mrs Patterson; the interview was just going through the motions.'

'But, having fallen flat at the starting gun, our hero comes from behind and breaks the tape ahead of the field. How?'

Chris took a deep breath, another sip of his beer, pulled a face and went on. 'After the Meyer disaster, I joined the three other hopefuls in the holding tank. It was like a small cell painted battleship grey with two tiny windows high up. "Let's hope they get on with it", said Joe Greening. He was 22, fresh from University. He was playing in a county trial in Manchester; he didn't want to hang about.

He got his wish. A blonde girl appeared at the door, "Mr Greening?"

Joe jumped up, "Here we go then." He didn't come back. Instead the blonde came to invite Mrs Patterson. She dropped her paperback into her bag, inspected herself in her mirror, stood, smoothed herself down and left with a consoling smile at the rest of us.

"I think I'm next," said Paul Ritson. He had been sitting pale-faced saying nothing. "I can't take it any more where I am: sink comprehensive out of control. If I don't get this I'm getting out. Meyer's looking for experience. Patterson has that but being a Church school, they'll want a man for science." Mrs Patterson was back after twenty minutes, still smiling.

"Mr Ritson?" The odds-on favourite got up shakily, dodged his chair as it tried to trip him up, wiped his palms on his handkerchief, took a deep breath and stumbled out. Mrs Patterson looked up from her book, "He's a dead duck before he gets in there."

Ritson came back, grey faced. I followed the guide up the corridor to a large, dignified room with bay windows.'

I summarised the state of play, 'So at this point the favourite is six lengths ahead and the rest of the field nowhere.'

Chris paused for another sip. My glass was empty, his was barely half way down. 'Hang on,' I said, 'let's see what can be done about that.' I came back from the bar with my pint and a half for my pupil, which I teemed into the remains of his pint. 'Try that,' I urged, 'you've now got half and half bitter and lager: a blend currently fashionable with progressive members of the fifteen to twenty-five age group.' Obediently, he took another sip. 'Come on Chris', I said, 'we're waiting for the denoument.'

Without obvious regret he put down his glass and resumed, 'The selection panel was sitting at a long table facing a single empty chair. A tall, good looking, silver haired man got to his feet. I took him for the headmaster.

"Good afternoon Mr Berry, my name is Lancaster, I'm deputy head here. If I may introduce the rest of the panel, Canon Jeffreys is chairman of the governors." Jeffreys in shining clerical grey and dog collar looked like an unsuccessful pugilist. He raised his big battered face for a brief nod. "Next to him, Mr Wormald, headmaster." The headmaster was a small ratty looking specimen with a pock marked face and a badly trimmed moustache. The large middle aged woman to Wormald's left was Miss Bridger from the Local Authority. "Mr Meyer, our head of science you've already met."'

'Too right you had.'

Chris gave me a lop-sided grin and went on.'It wasn't a comfortable interview, Meyer made no attempt to conceal his hostility and Miss Bridger, for the local authority, seemed to take a personal dislike. I stumbled through to the end and went back to the holding tank.

The deputy head appeared at the door, "We've finished the formal interviews and we hope to announce an appointment shortly. Mrs Patterson?"'

'So that seemed to be that?' I said. 'Clearly it wasn't.'

'Ritson had cheered up, he'd had a chat with Mrs Patterson. She'd given him an idea – getting out of classroom teaching. Five minutes later the door opened, Lancaster's head reappeared. "Mr Berry? Could you come please? Mr Ritson… sorry… please let us have a note of your expences."

The selection committee were standing in a bunch. "Mr Berry," said the Canon, "the board have agreed to offer you the position of junior science teacher subject to your taking up the post on the first day of the academic year, 7th September."

You mean Mrs Patterson turned it down?

Lancaster was standing at my shoulder, "Let's say that we couldn't reach agreement on all points.'"

'Couldn't reach agreement on one point,' I said, 'the favourite takes the last jump ahead of the field and then runs off the course. She wanted more money – a move up to the next pay scale – quite right too. You were cheaper.'

'Whatever, that's how it turned out,' Chris said.

'And Meyer?'

'Narked.'

'Is that why you want to meet Meyer before term starts?' Chris nodded. 'If you want my advice, forged from a life in management, forget it. Clock in on Thursday morning, say as little as possible, keep your head down and show what you can do. When you get to know the place you'll find that everyone falls out with Meyer sooner or later.'

'That's what Caroline said.'

'Who's she? Another science teacher?'

Chris had turned a pinker shade of pale, 'No, she's head of drama.'

5

Chris's complexion was saying it all, 'And how did you happen across this brilliant head of drama?' He was going to tell me, any road.

'I got as far as the school gates. Caroline pulled up in a big black four-by-four and offered me a lift into town. We both had time to kill. My train wasn't for an hour and she was waiting to pick up her husband. She said he was speaking at a conference in Carlisle – *New Thinking in Business* – he was last on the programme with *Towards the Spiritual Boardroom.*'

(Great start, she's married to a New Age nutter). 'Then what?'

'Caroline knew a wine bar near the station.'

'Not Julio's? Ditchfield's one and only gay bar? You're a better man than me.'

'Caroline promised I'd be safe with her. She seemed to know Julio pretty well. She pulled his leg over a row he'd had with his partner – seemed to centre around Julio's new hairdo. After that she wanted to know why I decided to move into teaching? That was the last thing I wanted to talk about... my failed marriage.'

'But it was exactly what she wanted to hear about. So do I.'

Chris gave me a rueful grin, 'I'd been married to Claudia for five years, we bought a flat, I thought everything was fine – my mistake. I was up to the neck in work. Claudia the same, she's in television merchandising – late meetings, deadlines, lunches, crises, tantrums mainly about nothing much, I thought. We hardly met except on Sundays. One evening Claudia didn't come home from work. I had an early start so I turned in. Next morning I still had the bed to myself. She'd made a career move into her boss's flat. I carried on for a year, worked crazy hours, thought that would be the answer, but it wasn't. Deep down I suppose I was hoping she'd come back. Then her solicitor wrote: Claudia wanted a quickie divorce. I agreed, struggled on at work for another year. That was no use, I needed a change. I read an article about the shortage of science teachers and applied for a teaching course.'

'What did Caroline think of that?'

'She asked how that went down with the interview board. I said "mixed" – the Local Authority woman practically accused me of wife abuse. That made Caroline laugh, what did I expect, making out it was all Claudia's fickle fault?'

"I don't believe a word of it," Caroline said, "I bet you were an absolute brute – serial sex on the kitchen table – poor Claudia."

I was wondering what the fascinating Caroline was up to, 'Then what?'

'Then her mobile rang, it was Martyn *(with a "y")* "Poor little thing," Caroline said, "all alone at the station."'

'So she headed for the exit dutiful wife-like?'

'Yes. Julio called to her from behind the bar, "Bye darling, come again when you can stop!" Caroline turned, swirling her skirt and sketched him a curtsey. "Superb!" shouted Julio. Caroline winked at me and went.

Julio came to the table, gave it a wipe and picked up Caroline's glass, still half full. "What a waste," he said.' *(Perhaps he meant the wine).*

I thought I knew the answer, 'Warning you not to take her seriously?'

Chris shrugged, 'Forget it, I got the job! That's what counts.'

I was not convinced about that either.

★

I didn't see much of Chris after that. He was head down in his new career, bent on breaking pots. Then, at the end of his second term – back end of March – having mysteriously failed to come home the night before, he showed up in a state of some excitement.

'Ken, I'm in love,' he said, 'with Caroline Enderby. Remember her?'

'The drama lady that chatted you up in Julio's bar. How do you know this is serious; not a one-nighter that got out of hand?'

'I don't. I won't know about Caroline until I see her after Easter. She might go off the idea.' He then moped around the place looking moonstruck. After a week of this carry-on I dragged him into the Duke and suggested he find something to occupy his mind. He started designing small websites for local businesses. By proxy, I had awakened Ditchfield to the www.

*

A month later I was climbing the stairs. Chris was waiting on my landing with a bag of books at his feet. He was stood standing with a look on his face suggestive of floating above the ground. That did not look right healthy, so I asked, 'What's to do, Chris?'

'I had such a strange day, yesterday,' he said. I took him in, sat him down in my kitchen, poured him a beer and invited him to tell.

He did, 'It was half past five, I was in the prep room catching up on some marking?' That was his usual after-school routine. He couldn't get used to knocking off at four thirty like the others. 'I got this peculiar telephone call?' He'd picked up the Australian habit of making statements that sounded like questions. Like all smart ideas from abroad it had infected the media, then the young and finally gone nation-wide; except to me *(Old and pig headed, you, Hardy)*.

'You got a phone call. What about it?'

'The caller said, "Benson is my name, I was recommended to speak to you." It wasn't a nice voice to listen to. It was dry and it grated as though he had an iron throat with loose sand in it. He sounded like a time waster.

He rambled on until finally I got him to the point; he would send a list of two dozen names and addresses together with sixty pounds in cash to be collected from the school reception desk. I was to leave a sealed envelope addressed "C J Benson Esq., to be collected" at the desk containing six sets of printed address labels and a programme which he could use to print more for himself – a simple database application.'

'All right, this Benson sounds a bit eccentric but what else was so peculiar about his call?'

'How did he get on to me?'

'He'd seen your small ad in the local rag.'

'But,' Chris said, 'the advertisement only gives my mobile number? But Benson came through on the prep room outside line. How did he know where I work?' That was a real question, not an Ozzie statement.

Chris went on, 'Thirty seconds after I got rid of Benson, my mobile rang. It was Caroline, excited. She said Martyn had rung, from Cardiff, "He's been doing a seminar – *Other Ways of Knowing*. It went down so well that they've extended it for in-depth discussion. He's staying overnight."'

I interrupted: 'Giving you two the perfect opportunity for your own seminar. But you said, sorry darling I'm washing my hair this evening...'

'Very funny Ken,' said Chris, 'I rushed through the rest of the marking, drove back here, quick shower and change, jumped back in the car... Coming up the drive to Heywood I realised I was twenty minutes early. Caroline had said seven. She'd hinted at a surprise, but I thought "something special" meant supper. No problem, I carried on round to the back, walked into the kitchen, took a dog nose out of my crotch and called out. There was a rustling on the stairs. Caroline came flaming down the hall in red silky satin and fury to match. "Cue jumping wrecker!" I was early. I was sorry. I said so.

"Snivelling apologies are not the point. I had it all planned: high romance – *grande toilette*, make-up, *parfum*, the lot. Now look at me: dishevelled trollop, no shoes, no knickers!"'

Threatening to get personal, was this, but there was more and Chris was sharing it, 'I turned her round, grabbed her round the waist, put my other hand on her breast and felt her nipple harden, 'no bra either,' I said and kissed the back of her neck, 'You're a beautiful trollop and I love you.'

Caroline sighed, "I see, romance cancelled: play as cast." She slipped away and walked to the foot of the stairs, the long red skirt clinging and swaying around her legs. She pulled the elastic band from her hair letting it fall over her shoulders and stood, with her back to the newel post, like a Greek *caratyd*. "Come along Mellors, I don't suppose you've washed your hands but never mind."'

Getting out of order, was this. I needed to slow things down, 'What's a caratyd when it's at home?'

Chris waved that aside, 'A pillar carved in the shape of a young girl. The Ancient Greeks had them all over the place. She started up the stairs, one hand lifting her long skirt. Strange, nowadays you have to get used to teaching a class full of teenage girls in school uniform microskirts and I was getting aroused by the sight of Caroline's ankle. She led the way into the guest bedroom, the one we had used our first time.'

It was time for the parental control button, 'Hold your horses, Chris, am I old enough for this? We're at the bedroom door. I've a vague idea what happened next.'

'No you haven't,' said Chris, 'what happened next was a disaster.'

'Sounds like my first attempt. I was a teenage private in the

Canal Zone. "Nice try sonny," she said, "shame your fucking horse bolted."'

'No, Caroline took it as a kind of a compliment.'

'Next thing you were in the cookhouse?'

'Next thing, she was on top, "Lady missionary position", she whispered, "I'm in charge, no escape, resistance is useless. Lie still and think of Jesus."

At the end she suddenly flushed all over right up into her hair. She cried out and collapsed on me. I was still with her, unfinished, still hard.

Hey! Wait for me Lady Chatterley.

"Christopher! Do be careful, I've only just come! Oh you *bugger*, oh god, oh god. *No! Don't stop!* Oh god, oh love. *Harder!* Love, what love, oh bloody hell!" and she flushed all over again.'

'Disgoosting,' I told him, 'I hope you apologised.'

He was wearing a sloppy sort of grin, 'She said, "Of course it hurt, monster. It was volcanic – seven point eight on the Richter scale. You were amazing. Are you feeling better now darling?"

Absolutely first rate darling.'

'Not the typical Ditchfield experience as I remember it,' I admitted. *(Out of date you, Hardy. Nowadays it would be just, "having good sex").*

'Caroline got up, "Feeding time at the zoo." She threw on a faded dressing gown, threw my trousers at me and ran downstairs singing, "a screw, a screw, a first rate screw, I have had with you, Manrico…"

When I caught up she was mixing batter in the kitchen, who's this Manrico person?

"No one you know. Fifteenth century Spanish tragedy – the musical. Start on the chips."

We ate supper, took fat old Bonny for a waddle in the dark and sat down to finish the beer.

"You and me, Chris – where are we going?"'

'A good question by the lass,' I said, 'at least one of you realises it won't go on like that for ever. Testing, was she?'

'I reminded her of what we'd agreed. Wait a year, we said, to make sure and be fair to everybody. That's another ten months. Can you do it?

"If you can, I suppose."

What if our cover gets blown in the *Ditchfield Express*. Think of the headlines – *Sexy Teacher Misses Period. Drama in Class.*

Caroline laughed, "If only! I'm going to start a secret stash at your place. A change of underwear, I refuse to go into work smelling of sex."

Where shall we live? I don't see you in a suburban semi; mowing the lawn on Friday evenings, washing the car on Sunday mornings. That leaves sophisticated city flat or rural hideaway with water coming through the roof.

"Do you mind if I want children?"

Think how brilliant they'll be with you for a mum.

"Unbearable. First chance, we kick them out and settle to a peaceful old age with clematis round the door. That's settled then," Caroline said, "let's get the map out."

Later we fell into bed. Caroline cuddled up, "Have you come down from heaven to me, or am I in heaven with you?"

What's that?

"I told you, a Spanish tragedy."

Forget tragedy; this is a love story. No answer, she was asleep.

The sun woke us early. Caroline hadn't closed the curtains. "Have you heard that a man is at his most potent at sunrise?" she asked. After that we must have gone back to sleep until her alarm went off. Work! Up, shower and shave. At breakfast I had a thought. I dreaded the answer but I had to ask.

Suppose Martyn wakes up early, what happens then?

"He fucking meditates," said Caroline and poured the coffee.'

Neither of us said any more until Chris seemed to snap out of his fairytale and said, 'Sorry Ken. You didn't need to hear all that...'

But what had got into him? Berry wasn't a teenager burning to disclose his personal life to a million others on the internet. Why did he imagine a connection between the two phone calls: first Benson, then Caroline?

I didn't waste time speculating. Next morning I rang Cardiff University and got through to the Philosophy faculty secretary. I told a tale about what a wow Enderby's seminar had been, how tempted I'd been to turn up on spec and how disappointed to have missed it.

That got a laugh in Wales, '*Other Ways of Knowing*? Sold out, over ran, you say? It was over and done with inside a couple of hours. Pity you couldn't manage Mr Hardy, you'd have made up the audience to a round half dozen, you see. I'd have given him a proper room instead of the broom cupboard.'

Enderby was up to something. He'd stopped over, not for an extended disputation with fellow philosophers, but a spiritual sex romp in Wrexham or Warrington or wherever. I would never have guessed Martyn had it in him.

I didn't mention it to Chris. Later another possibility came to mind – Martyn was up to something quite different – he was setting a trap. I wasn't in a position to know, but it carried a sense of foreboding.

6

On a Friday evening the following September, Chris Berry came gallumphing up the stairs. I'd left my front door open. He stuck his head in and called out. I shouted from the kitchen to come in, which he did, dumping a bulging briefcase and a loose pile of exercise books on the table.

I made with the welcome, 'Haven't seen you for weeks, have a beer.'

He asked how things were. 'Boring. The new director is dying to get me out of his factory so he can mess things up his way. It's like National Service – counting the days to demob – twelve months until APC finalise their take over.'

'Then retire?'

'Not if it means joining the ex-pats. Now you're here, you may as well stop for supper – I've been getting creative with my Ditchfield fine dining cuisine. Wild rabbit run over by a number 47 bus and enhanced with hand-picked building site herbs. How was the vacation?'

Chris opened his beer bottle and took care to use the glass provided. *(Who says education is futile?)* 'It started badly, remember? Martyn took Caroline off to the Bahamas for sun, sea and how's your father? We had our first row. I went to see my parents. Then Claudia's parents invited me over.'

'Unusual isn't it – inviting the ex-son-in-law – what for?'

'For tea, why not? They never seemed to blame me for the break-up.'

'I see. You asked how Claudia was? They said everything

was absolutely super and how were you? So you said absolutely super and Caroline never got a mention.'

'Come off it Ken. Four years ago Claudia walked out, we're divorced and she's living with her boss. When there's time to spare from growing his new business they'll get married.'

I was sceptical, 'Or not. His plan was to get pretty little Claudia into bed with her customer contacts and no knickers. He's now got in-depth awareness of her limitations. For her part, although on the dim side of gormless, Claudia has realised that she's about to be binned like a well-pooped pamper. The parents were doing a recce for a Berry comeback.'

'Don't put money on it,' he said, 'Before I met Caroline I'd realised that the marriage had never worked. One flat is cheaper than two – that says it all.'

'After that, you were back here on your tod while I was in Montana seeing Evelyn and huntin' bars in the forest with Cy. Gee, it was tough – shootin' 'em, skinnin' 'em, eatin' 'em raw. Fortunately we never met one. What about you?'

Chris finished his first bottle and started a second, 'I could have been stuck, but a website job turned up that kept me going. It arrived by hand the day before we broke up.' He produced a fat brown envelope.

I turned the envelope over. It was addressed in spiky black ink, to "C Berry Esq., The Science Laboratory, St Cuthbert's Senior School, Preston Road, Ditchfield." and sealed with red sealing wax impressed "CB" in flowery lettering. '"CB" – Chris Berry,' I said, 'you sent it to yourself '.

'CB stands for Crackpot Benson, the one with the scratchy voice. This time, he wants a website. This is content for it – just for starters. Remember the list of names and addresses for his labels job – London addresses but no post codes? If you look at the website some of them are listed as contributors but I've only got Benson's input so far.'

They didn't mean anything to me then – just names.

Chris went on, 'I typed up his manuscript and coded it for the web. I'll leave you the original if you're interested. Then it was back to fretting about Caroline. She should have been back. She had gone missing.'

'Why not phone her?'

'*Verboten*. We agreed at the beginning – Caroline phones me. There was nothing to be done but wait. Then, the last day of August, she phoned.'

'You still had a week of holiday left. Didn't spend it in bed, did you?'

'Caroline had a plan. We took off into the wilds: moors, fells, walking in the rain and staying at country pubs...'

'...And making love,' I said romantically, 'how are things now?'

Chris showed me a photo of Caroline standing against a dry-stone wall, hair blowing, laughing into the wind, drop dead lovely, 'Just like that.'

I questioned whether being that much in love was good for you – exhausting and liable to end up with poison for two. That didn't go down right well, so I asked how the new term was looking.

'Same again,' Chris said, 'I've no idea why Meyer's made such a thing out of the row we had last March, but that's his problem. I've survived my probationary year, I'm permanent staff.'

The lad still hadn't cottoned on to why he'd been appointed over Meyer's head – a ploy by higher management – but I wasn't getting into that.

'Perhaps he resents you sleeping with Drama.'

'He doesn't know. And if he did, so what?'

After Chris had gone I took his envelope into the sitting room and sat down to read. It was hard going for a Friday night: old fashioned spiky gothic crammed onto yellowing heavy gauge foolscap. I struggled through the first couple of pages then gave up and locked it in the filing cabinet.

It was November, late in the afternoon, 'You're a surprise!' I said, 'Don't stand there posing. Put wood in th'oyle.'

Caroline closed my front door and stood with her hands behind her. 'How do I look?' Her smile was small and on the mocking side of come hither. I wasn't sure who was the one being mocked.

'Disturbing, why do you ask?'

'I mean in this.' She was wearing a 1970s shiny plastic mac, Laura Ashley green, hard belted – seriously retro. 'I found it at the back of the wardrobe. I haven't worn it for years. I got it in a second hand shop when I started Drama school. Mummy said I looked tarty in it.'

'Mummies are always right,' I said, 'hang it up before it does any more damage. And come through, I'm wetting the tea.'

'It's only while I'm waiting for Chris. It's freezing up in his flat and I don't know how to turn the heating on.'

That sounded suspicious. Caroline could turn anything on if she wanted to. I fetched another cup from the kitchen, cracked open the front door so that I would hear when Chris arrived and went back to the sitting room. Caroline had fitted herself into one corner of my settee and the cat had fitted himself onto her lap. They made a striking couple: he in skin tight black fur while she wore a red polo neck sweater with a pale green paisley pattern scarf dangling round her neck. Her leggings fitted with never a wrinkle, her boots were knee high. She caught me looking and grinned. I said, 'Are you going on a sub-arctic expedition or what?'

'We've a meeting at Preston – teachers' discussion group. Then Chris has to visit a client out in the sticks about a website design.' She patted the settee beside her. 'Don't sit at the other end of the room, Ken. I need to talk.'

(That was it?) I obeyed and got a glare from the cat. Caroline didn't hang about, 'How committed do you think Chris is?'

'He's never cooling off?'

'I'm talking permanent relationships – living together.'

'What's brought this on?'

'We don't seem to talk about it now. We used to, you know, like lovers do?' I mentioned Granada, with a thousand guitars playing softly in the rain. I got her boot on my shin. She was serious.

'Why are you telling me this, Caroline? Apart from Chris being my neighbour, it's nothing to do with me.' *(Apart from his disclosure in May).*

'You're the only friend who's likely to talk sense.'

'Look, in September I asked Chris how things were. He showed me a snap of you taken on the moors and said "like that".' Caroline knew the photo I meant. She said it showed how she felt about him, not the other way round.

I wasn't having that, 'Come on Caroline, tragic doesn't suit you. I can tell you one thing: he hates weekends when he doesn't get to see you. The way he cheers up at eight o'clock on a Monday morning is indecent. He runs downstairs whistling, regardless that it's stair-rodding it outside and the rest of Ditchfield is sober, hung over and suicidal. Doesn't that tell you?'

Caroline didn't think it did, 'I'm not talking about sex – that's wonderful, it always has been – I mean commitment: "till death us do part", that sort – do you think Chris is committed?'

I was out of my depth. The cat started washing its feet. 'Let's be honest,' I said, 'I don't know, I've never asked him. As for my personal experience, things have changed. In my day commitment came with the baggage. You fancied a girl, you chatted her up, you lured her into the back seat of the banger, you started to make progress... Then it was, "Stop it you daft thing, you're subverting my suspenders". After that, *il ne passera pas* until you'd convinced her Mam of your honourable intentions. Next thing, you were married with a wife, three kids and a mortgage. That was commitment, fifties style. Then the sixties arrived with the pill.'

I was talking about another world. I don't think Caroline believed me. I tried again, 'When did you decide that this was *really, really it*?'

'In Julio's wine bar the day he got the job. I didn't think he was interested then but I waited and finally got him to Heywood.'

'Poor little thing. And had your wicked way?'

Caroline ignored that, 'It was heaven until last July when I told him about the Bahamas and we had our first row.'

'Chris drew the obvious conclusion.'

'He thought that Martyn's plan was to turn the marriage around with a second honeymoon in a Caribbean paradise and me consenting all the way. It was nothing like that: it was a creative writing session on his new book, *Spiritual Aspects of Remote Viewing*. He scribbled and I typed. I tried to convince Chris. If only he knew Martyn, he'd have believed me.

Guess what we did for our honeymoon – a walking tour in the Languedoc. The country's lovely but Martyn wanted to visit the Cathar caves, he was writing a monograph on medieval dualism.'

'Medieval what?'

'Instead of one God, the Cathars believed that the world was divided between a loving God and an evil Satan.'

'That would never have worked – split responsibilities.' The cat stopped washing and gave me a dualist glare.

'The king of France condemned the Cathars as heretics and started to exterminate them. The survivors hid in caves. The biggest goes right into the mountain – total darkness. We went in, pressed the time switch and the lights went out. "Woo-hoo!" I thought. Well, it was a honeymoon.'

'And then?'

'Nothing. Martyn went off into a profound meditative state.

(Like when he wakes up early?). I sat there for twenty minutes all alone in the dark.'

'Spooky.'

'At first, it was, then it was boring, finally I was having trouble staying awake. When the lights came on Martyn was sitting in his medieval saint attitude: eyes turned upward, right hand raised, fingers pointing to heaven, spiritual expression.' Caroline demonstrated.

I laughed, 'Looks bloody silly to me.'

'That's because you're a reductionist materialist cynic. Martyn got up and strode out of the cave, whilst I trotted along behind. He didn't speak a word to me for ages. Then he said that it was the most intense life-changing spiritual experience of his life, the shining way to a new understanding.'

'Beats me why you fell for him in the first place.'

'I thought Martyn was the shining way,' Caroline said. 'After drama school nothing great happened: walk-ons, small parts and the odd soap cameo. Auditions, auditions, finally a real break – a super part in a touring production. It was a nineteen twenties thriller about a ghost train, updated with new effects and dead scary. It went a storm, full houses: great crits.'

'What were you, the damsel in distress?'

'Not likely – I don't do fragile – I was the *femme fatale:* a sexy spy smuggling arms to revolutionaries under the noses of the police. I got a glamorous red evening dress, I still have it. We played Birmingham, Nottingham, Sheffield and arrived at the Leeds Playhouse. After the first night at Leeds I stepped out of the stage door and this huge Ozzie farmer walked into me. He was looking the other way – sheep walking. He was ever so nice about it, took me to dinner to apologise for treading on my foot. Next morning I couldn't get my shoe on, it was a fractured metatarsal – eight weeks in plaster. They wouldn't let me do *femme fatale* in a wheelchair. The understudy took over, she got rave reviews as they always do and went on to the West End.

I got rid of the plaster and then got nothing. My agent said I'd been labelled "unreliable". I ended up working in a West End wine bar.'

Caroline paused to stroke the cat's tail – loud purrs (*Creep! He hates it really*). 'Early one evening, Martyn walked in. The bar was empty, he was teaching a summer course at one of the London colleges. We talked a bit, next day he phoned the bar and asked me out. He wanted to tell me about his new philosophy. I was lonely and bored – it sounded wonderful. Three weeks later he proposed. He wanted me to give up the stage. I didn't fancy the lady of the manor part – full time baby machine, unpaid cook and floor scrubber but Martyn had an old school friend, *(Like they do)* who was related to a bishop, who might put in a word at St Cuthbert's. I landed a job teaching drama.'

'Stately home in the country with Prince Charming and job laid on?'

'Not just that,' Caroline protested, 'we had some lovely times to begin with, but they died out.'

'Why?'

She had stopped looking me in the eye, 'You're not going to believe this,' she told the cat, 'Martyn started to change.' She looked up. Caroline wasn't the girly sort but she was on the verge of tears. 'Isn't that what they always say – the guilty ones – "he changed"?'

'When did it start? I mean when did it start to go wrong?'

'I believe it began in that bloody cave. Not that the sex was superb, Martyn doesn't do *petit mort*. To him, sex is a spiritual experience. We entertained a lot at first. It wasn't all New Age then. Martyn was "fringe" but not "loony fringe". He didn't take himself too seriously; we had a lot of fun. Then he started inviting people of another sort, far-out, near-fanatics, some of them on drugs. It was turning into an activist campaign group, plotting, but for what? The last straw was a philosophy lecturer. He went on all evening about "the soul" then he followed me into the kitchen, said that come the revolution women would be held in common and tried to touch me up.'

'What did you do, scream?'

'Kneed him in the balls, hard. He was sick in the sink and had an early night.' I told Martyn I wasn't having that sort in the house. He said I was denying him his destiny. He stopped bringing them home so I don't know who he sees nowadays – some sort of spiritual clique. You think I'm exaggerating?'

'No. I've heard Martyn lecture – the manic bit – I know what you mean.'

Caroline started playing with Timmy's ears – more loud purrs (*Rat! Just wait, you*). 'To begin with, with Martyn's lifestyle – lectures, seminars, conferences, workshops, always travelling – it was a marriage with a lot of space in it and it worked surprisingly well. Now we've started having rows, quite poisonous rows. Sometimes he frightens me; imagine that – Martyn! I'm never sure which Martyn I'm talking to. He won't give straight answers. When I ask what he's up to, he says it was my decision to stay out. Then he's the old Martyn again and in a way that's worse. Don't laugh Ken, I'm scared.'

I wasn't laughing, 'Are you afraid of him turning violent?'

Caroline was having none of that, 'Resort to violence? What, Martyn?'

'Surely he suspects? He must have realised you're seeing someone?'

'No. Martyn's a feminist, Ken. He knows bugger-all about women.'

'So you want out of the marriage but now you're worried because Chris isn't talking permanent relationships any more?'

Caroline stopped messing up the cat and looked reproachful. 'Stop it, Ken. At the start I said to give it a year until next April. That would mean sticking it for another four months. I can't do it. I'm looking for tea and sympathy and what do I get? Tea and interrogation.'

It was time to get off the fence, 'Caroline, you are a dozy trout. You know that?' She sniffed and denied it. I was remorseless, 'Look, Chris's divorce has gone through. He's free but he's giving you space to make your own decision. Tell Chris what you've just told me. Where's Martyn tonight?'

'He's at Skipton.'

'Staying overnight?'

'Yes. It's the AGROW annual gathering and dinner. He doesn't want to drive back afterwards.'

'AGROW? As in aggression?'

'Action Group for the Re-Spiritualisation of the West. It's about alternative philosophy and re-establishing the supremacy of the feminine.'

'I thought the West was already feminised. Is AGROW that sinister?'

'No, it isn't sinister – just a bit silly. It's the old Martyn: spirituality, love and peace, the sacred feminine.'

'And a handy cover for something that he's fanatical about?'

'I think that's what it's turned into. It's what I'm scared of.'

'All right, here's the plan: stay with Chris tonight and sort yourselves out. Tomorrow, have a word with Tom's partner. Niall Potts is Tom's specialist in property, family law, divorce. I'll fix it for you to see him after school...'

'That's kind Ken, but I'll do it my way. I'll face Martyn and then organise a lawyer for myself – someone well away from the Enderby network.'

(That's you told, Hardy). 'This client that Chris has to see after your teachers' meeting, is he called Benson?'

'I think that's what he said. Chris said it was a farmhouse out Braxtonby way.' At that moment the street door banged – Chris. I got up.

'Kenneth,' she was looking up at me, 'I'm not going back to Martyn. It's over. If Chris isn't ready I'll find a flat and fend for myself until he is.'

'That's the style. I'll leave my door on the latch in case it's plan B.'

She got up, 'Kiss for luck?' She offered her face at an ambiguous angle; I was uncertain whether she expected a quick peck on the cheek or a full frontal so I kissed her on the nose. She grinned and squeezed my hand.

Chris was halfway up the second flight when I called him back, 'Come here this minute. She's in my sitting room telling me all her private business.'

He said, 'Hang on,' continued to his own door, dumped his pile of books and came down. Caroline was already at the door, silk scarf at her throat, belting herself into her mac – actresses are efficient at quick changes.

It was 5.45, or just after when the lovers chattered down the stairs to the street door. Chris had his hand on the latch, I called after them, 'Chris, what's the name of Benson's house?'

Chris looked over his shoulder, 'Fellbeck!' They were gone. I poured a large whisky to celebrate a problem solved for the gorgeous Caroline. *(Fellbeck?)*. I dialled Chris's mobile number. He was switched off. Why not? He was with Caroline. Why would he need phone calls?

I put my supper in the oven and attended to the cat. In view of his treacherous behaviour the reverse procedure crossed my mind.

After supper I went back to the Board Meeting papers. It was hard to concentrate because there was something else on my mind. Seven years ago almost to the day – November 1992 – Fellbeck. *(Don't be so bloody daft, Hardy. Benson's bought it. He's a harmless eccentric. Doing it up. Possibly)*. I tried Chris's mobile for the last time – still switched off. Leave it – pointless to worry about nothing – I poured myself another whisky.

★

The phone woke me with a start, 'Ken?'. The voice was blank, toneless.

'Ken! It's me, it's Chris. I'm in trouble.'

'What's to do? Where are you?'

'Ditchfield Police Station. It's Caroline. I need a lawyer,' his voice started to shake. He was on the point of breaking down, 'Can you get Tom? Get Tom, quick. *Please! They think it was me… They think I did it!* '

7

I was awake now. I tried to sound reassuring, 'I'll get Tom. He'll sort it out. Ring off now. Don't say anything, not to the police, not to anyone. Wait until Tom comes.' I put the phone down. I looked at my watch, gone eleven.

I dialled Tom's home number, 'He's in a hell of state, Tom. I think there's been an accident and Caroline's hurt and the police are trying to pin the blame on him. I didn't ask details, I thought the police were probably listening. I told him to say nothing until you get there.'

Tom was positive, 'That's the style Ken. Are you off to bed?'

'Not yet.' No point in trying to sleep now.

'Probably nothing much will happen tonight. I'll let you know.'

I put the phone down, shuffled through to the kitchen to put the kettle on. I went for a book, *War and Peace*. That should keep me awake. It didn't.

★

Spring had come to Ditchfield: brief, bright sunshine clouding over for the next downpour. I was in the High Street. As warning drops hit the pavement I caught the rich dark brown aroma of roasting coffee. *Déjà vu*. This shop used to roast coffee beans behind the counter. Every time the door opened, the aroma flowed out into the street and the customers flowed in. Good thinking, they had gone back to in-house roasting. The rain came on in earnest. Pausing to push on the coffee shop door, I caught sight of a pretty girl on the opposite pavement. She was talking to a couple of smart suits crowding under her umbrella.

The shop was full of people and cigarette smoke. All the places were taken except one: a table for two in the corner. I claimed it and sat down.

'Excuse me!' It was the girl from across the road. She was carrying an umbrella and wearing a green macintosh cape that made a sharp rustle as she moved. 'Do you mind if I sit here? All the other seats seem to be taken.'

Did I mind? 'Delighted,' I said. She was in her twenties: fine forehead, delicate cheekbones, dark hair curled and cut short, immaculate makeup. She went off to the coat rack taking her umbrella, a slender figure outlined under the cape. The waitress arrived and I ordered coffee for two.

My table companion was back in a twin set and pleated tweed skirt with country shoes. She looked like a lady from a 1950s *Country Life* cover. 'Gosh, what a day!'

'Well you're equipped for it.'

'That old thing? It belongs to the company. When I saw the weather, I pinched it for the day. It's the Green Room mac; we all use it for popping out. It slips over anything, keeps the rain off your shoulders.' She had old-fashioned shoulders, not too wide, sort of Audrey Hepburn.

'Green Room? You're an actress, then?' She agreed. 'I spotted you across the road. You were talking to a couple of fans.'

'Fans?' she laughed, 'they wanted to know the way to the station.'

The waitress came with the coffees. 'Did you want anything to eat?' She didn't, but did I mind if she smoked? 'No, it doesn't bother me. I used to but I gave up.'

'Strong!' Perhaps she meant the coffee; she had leaned forward to stir in the sugar. I caught her scent, a discreet perfume

43

mingled with mild cigarette and a whiff of warm macintosh. 'Everyone smokes in the theatre; you spend so much time hanging about we all do it for something to do.'

'No choice for me. I'm in an inflammable business; we're forced to ban smoking in the factory for safety. I couldn't sack the workers for doing what I did in the office so I gave up.' I got a quizzical look as if concern for the workers' feelings was unusual.

We introduced ourselves. 'Jenny Finch,' she said. I asked what she was doing in Ditchfield where there was no theatre. 'Visiting,' Jenny said, 'no show tonight so I took the opportunity.'

'Show? What show is that?'

'*The Ghost Train* – it's a touring production. We were in Sheffield last week now we've a three-week run in Leeds – opening tomorrow. We get a day off when the play moves on while the stage crew are fitting up.'

'What's it about?'

'It's a revival of a play that was in London in the twenties.' (*Twenties?*) That accounted for the dated outfit – she'd borrowed the costume as well. 'A thriller about a group of passengers stranded for the night at a railway station in the wilds of Cornwall. The old stationmaster's out of his mind. He warns them that the phantom train will come thundering through at midnight carrying the ghosts of the passengers killed in a railway disaster. So turn your faces to the wall my dears, because to look upon the ghost train means death.'

'Wow! But it turns out that…'

'You've guessed!'

'And what part do you play? Are you the damsel in distress?'

She dismissed that – no such luck. It isn't a ghost train at all, it's a gang of criminals smuggling guns to revolutionaries and I'm the villainous spy sent to pull the wool over the passengers' eyes.'

'And when you're not doing Dietrich in Leeds you're in Ditchfield. Have you got family here?'

Jenny's mood changed, 'No, this is a friend who farms out in the country near Coldedge.' She stubbed out her cigarette, seemed to consider for a moment and then, as can happen with chance strangers, went on. 'Vernon's an actor too, a damn good one – that's his stage name. We met in rep. At first I thought it was just a backstage romance. We both did. Then it got serious. Everything was fine until Vernon's uncle who ran the family estate died and Vernon was the only one able to take it over. You see, he was brought up on the farm; he didn't go on the stage until after the war, so he knows the business. It was supposed to be temporary until they got a manager in, but the right man never turned up and after a year, Vernon started to get the farming bug. I suppose it was in his veins all along. So things changed.'

'What's the deal now?'

Jenny dropped her eyes, hiding the troubled look. 'We agreed that I would give the theatre another couple of years and then, unless my big break had come along, I would give up, marry Vernon and settle down to raise kids and chickens.' I had some trouble imagining a welly-booted Jenny sloshing through mud to the hen house.

'Now you've got the big break?'

'No. It's worse, much worse.'

I tried to help, 'It's been three years. Now you've met someone else or you can't face giving up the theatre or you'd hate living in the sticks.'

She was not taking any help. 'We've changed. No, Vernon's changed. I know that sounds like an excuse, putting the blame on him but it isn't. I don't know whether it's the isolation, or that house. It's uncanny, perhaps it's the way the house is designed – it's huge, Victorian, big rooms and every room has two doors. I get a feeling going into an empty room that someone has just gone out through the other door. It's as though there's another presence in the house. I've heard Vernon talking to someone.

Not talking to himself – two voices. He won't tell me but I'm afraid that he's gone in for the occult. Most of the time he's all right and then... I told him I can't stand the place why not sell up and find a farm somewhere else? He flew into a passion, this place was his destiny, I thought he was going to hit me. We made it up afterwards, but later I thought about it and I've decided. Now I've got to go and break it to him.'

It seemed to me that she was making hard work of it. 'Jenny, why put yourself through all this? Why not write or phone? Arrange to meet somewhere neutral – a hotel in Ditchfield – why go all that way?'

'That would be rotten and cowardly, wouldn't it? A betrayal; I think he still loves me.'

'The name "Vernon" doesn't ring a bell. I do business around there. What's his real name?'

She caught sight of my watch. 'Is that the time? I've a bus to catch. I missed it last time and had to get the afternoon one. It was foggy and I ended up walking all the way from the village.'

She was digging in her handbag for her purse. 'No,' I said, 'coffee's on me. Look, why don't I give you a lift out there?'

She accepted the first offer, but not the second, 'No, that's very kind but it really wouldn't do.' I was about to say that I could drop her off out of sight of the house but she was away to the coat rack, threw the green cape rustling around her shoulders, picked up her umbrella, blew me a kiss and was gone. The rain was on again.

8

The phone was ringing again, it was two am. Tom said, 'I'll have to be quick; I'm in the car park. They haven't charged him, I don't expect it tonight. As soon as he's been charged, they'll be into the flat taking it apart. (*A bit extreme for a road accident?*) I've phoned Niall. He'll be with you in ten minutes. The police have got Chris's laptop. He had it with him in the car. I want to get his PC, so we get first look at that – even things up a bit.'

By now I was awake, 'The PC will have everything. Chris uses it as a backup for his laptop.'

'That's great Ken. Could you show Niall where everything is and give him a lift? Thanks.' Tom rang off.

I picked up my coat; it was damp, I must have been out to the bin, muddied my shoes as well. I couldn't remember. I unlocked the front door and waited in the porch. Niall Potts arrived minutes later. The partners made an odd pair – Niall six inches shorter than Tom, nine stone wringing wet, curly headed, short sighted and studious-looking. Tom did all the heavy criminal stuff, he liked a scrap. Niall hated courts, didn't like fights, not that they never happened with his divorce work. He arrived, tripping over the steps because he was wiping raindrops off his spectacles. Having sensed my presence he put them back on to identify me – and reassumed his diffident, chubby-faced owlish persona. He fetched the master key from the office and we opened up Chris's flat. I took him to the computer and started pulling out plugs. 'I'll leave the connection to the modem here and we'd better leave the printer as well,' I told Niall, 'otherwise they'll spot something's missing.'

Niall made a grab for the computer, I stopped him. 'Hang on a minute,' I said, 'I want to have a quick look round just in case.'

'Be quick then,' Niall was jumpy as though he was the suspect the police were after. I was looking for a photo of Caroline. I was spoilt for choice; they were all over the flat. I took the one out of the kitchen and stuck it in my pocket, frame and all. It was a larger print of the one taken on the moors. I reckoned that was the most recent. 'What do you want that for?' Niall asked.

'It might come in handy for Tom. '

We picked up the loot and carted it down the two flights of stairs. 'We'll put everything in the archive store,' Niall said, 'sort it out later.'

I went to bed, not to sleep. For one thing, after the dossing around I'd done that evening, I wasn't tired. For another, I was wound up about Chris and Caroline. Was it a road accident? Was she hurt? Why were the police aiming to charge Chris? What with? I was getting nowhere. Leave it!

That was some dream, I was quite taken with Jenny Finch. She and Caroline: both actresses in a thriller about a ghost train...

★

For once, I was late for work. I took a turn round the factory and stuck my nose into Ed Willis's office. 'Nothing we can't handle, Ken.' I went back to the office and drank coffee. 'Haven't forgotten there's a Board Meeting at two o'clock, Mr Hardy?' Dorothy reminded me. I spent the rest of the morning finishing my report for the Board.

APC's driver arrived from Head Office bringing Stefan

Kovacs – the boss – and Jack Livesey. They'd driven up from Watford that morning. Livesey was Stefan's Finance Director, a company accountant; enough said, nothing to like or dislike about Jack. I did like Kovacs. It was unusual for him to come up for Ditchfield Board meetings. I thought it would liven up the proceedings. Stefan was a Hungarian Czech or the other way about. During the Prague uprising he took the opportunity to get out and started a business in London trading plastics scrap from the back of a van. Now he owned the biggest plastics manufacturing group in Europe. I got the massive handshake and a big grin, 'Things all right Ken? How's Doreen?' (They'd only met once).

The meeting went through at a fair gallop – routine monthly Board stuff. I couldn't see why Stefan had bothered to make the trip. When the meeting broke up I found out. 'Hang on a minute, Ken,' he said.

Stefan lowered his mass back into the chairman's seat. 'Ken,' he said, 'I really like the way this takeover has gone. You and Scott McIver take most of the credit for the way you've run this company and you personally for the work you've put into getting Ed Willis and the sales team up the scratch,' (sic).

That was a long speech for Stefan. 'About the deal,' he went on, 'we agreed that McIver would stay on for six months to see your accounting system amalgamated into ours. That's done, so Scott's away living the life of the Riley. In your case, we reckoned two years for you to teach my people your business. You've done it in fifteen months.'

'I don't like the way this is going', I said, 'you're not going to offer me a job at Head Office?'

Stefan emitted a mid-European guffaw, 'Was you ten years younger, I bloody would.' Stefan stopped laughing and went back to business. What it amounted to was that for the remaining nine months of my contract, he wanted me out of the works, 'Act in an advisory capacity, don't come into the factory unless there's something serious.'

'The way Ed's shaping, that's not even a part-time job.'

'There'll be other things. First, I want you to do feasibility studies on two projects that I'm working round. I need practical thinking. Some travel, you can do the rest from your desk at home. I don't want 100-page reports. Like Churchill had the right idea, "pray let me have your plan for winning the war on the back of a postcard". Existing salary and pension arrangements, you'll do it?'

In the car park, Stefan said, 'Give the works switchboard instructions to pass all phone calls for you to Ed Willis. Send your expenses direct to Jack.'

That was it: ten months on full pay and not over-much to do. I went back up to the office, briefed Dorothy and then started sorting out the filing.

When I got back to York Terrace it was nearly six; the lights were out. It was an early finish for Tom but Niall was usually away at five o'clock. I got to the front door just as Tom came flying out as though breaking away from a maul and nearly knocked me flat. 'Sorry Ken, got to get back.'

'Tom, what's this all about? What are they aiming to charge him with?'

'Murder of Caroline Enderby.'

9

I went up to the flat, numb. My friend was charged with the murder of the girl he loved to distraction – the girl who loved him back – the girl who sat in my lounge to tell me her troubles and then went away to be killed. I could drink myself senseless – there was another bottle of scotch in the kitchen cabinet. It stayed there. I sat in the dark, slept on and off. By break of day I had decided: I didn't believe this and I was not standing for it.

I spent the morning clearing my office. Then I rang Ed Willis and asked him to come up. 'Today's the day. All this is now yours, my son,' I told him and took him out to lunch. So ended my career as a manufacturer of credit and renown, I might even have got emotional about it, but for one other thing.

My son-in-law was sitting at his desk doing his barn door imitation. In normal times Tom is the very model of a former rugby forward – outgoing, sociable, especially when shoving your face into the mud. He gets on well with senile magistrates, incompetent policemen and friendly robbers. He wins his fair share of cases on behalf of the latter and many a burglar he's restored to his friends and his relations. He brightened up when I appeared through his door due, I thought, to the prospect of a break from the pile of papers confronting him. He asked how things were.

'The company want me out of the road until the takeover is completed. I've got ten months to fill in a part-time advisory capacity. You?'

'Moderate. After the police took him in on Tuesday night, Chris made a short statement. He thought that all he needed to do was explain to Sgt Foster what had happened and they'd send him home. When they started asking questions he realised that he was in trouble and phoned you. DI Evans arrived immediately after me and started interviewing Chris. After I'd said "you don't have to answer that Mr Berry" half a dozen times, they arrested him on suspicion and kept him in. This morning Chris gave me a detailed statement which doesn't differ in essentials from what he said to Foster so there may be no harm done. They spent the rest of the day interrogating him.'

'How did that go?'

'He stood up to it pretty well in the circumstances. They tried to get a confession out of him but he stuck to his statement.'

'That's good, isn't it?'

'Not that good. They're certain they've got their man. I expect them to charge him tomorrow.'

'What then, Magistrates Court?'

'Yes. I'll try for bail, but there's no chance of that. It'll go for trial at the Crown Court.'

'With Harrison and Potts for the defence?' Tom didn't seem ecstatic about the prospect. I found that disappointing, 'A high profile murder case like this will put the firm on the map, won't it?'

'Yes and no,' Tom said, 'if we put up a good defence, even if we lose, that's good. If the prosecution wipe the floor with us, it's not. Country gobbins out of their league they'll say.'

'Tom, speaking personally, do you think he did it?'

That got me a stern rebuke, 'I can't answer that Ken as you know very well. But if he had done it, one would expect him to have acted differently.'

'All right, what's the police case?'

'Apart from their confidence regarding his guilt, it's early days yet. We haven't any Scene of Crime findings and they haven't found the murder weapon. In due course we'll get the Prosecution Case Statement. Meantime they've decided that it's a crime of passion arising out of a lovers' quarrel. It's easy for them: a standard scenario, boxes sitting there waiting to be ticked.'

'When Chris phoned me,' I said, 'he was in shock. It didn't sound like remorse to me, horror more like, and disbelief.'

'The police interpret that as he'd *done* something too terrible to believe.'

'His original statement? I did warn him.'

'I know Ken. He'd already blurted it before they let him phone you.'

Tom was looking older than forty, strained, drawn round the eyes. 'You could do with an early night.' With which massive advice I left him to it.

★

Next morning I cleared out my spare room for an office. Then I made some coffee and thought about Chris's predicament. What with starting a new career, falling out with his boss, designing websites and making love to Caroline, Chris had not made much impression on Ditchfield society. Apart from me, who knew anything about him? That couldn't be good.

I walked into town and ordered some bits of office furniture, then returned to York Terrace for a word with the seat of power – the partnership secretary. Pam is efficient, all-knowing, considerate and of repellent appearance. I suspect that our Paula had something to do with her appointment. I asked about an extra phone for my flat, she said to leave it to her because she knew how to get it connected quick sharp. 'Mr Harrison asked me to give you this,' she handed me a sealed brown envelope addressed, "K Hardy Esq, Private and Confidential." 'Read and return'.

I asked about Tom's whereabouts. Pam said that he'd gone off early to the station. 'He didn't know when he'd be back, best leave it till tomorrow, I'll let him know.' I went upstairs and opened the envelope. It was a copy of Chris's statement.

It began with what I took to be the standard format then moved on to his relationship with Caroline – how it had begun the previous March, how they had been meeting whenever they could and how they had done everything to keep the affair quiet until they were both ready to make it public and permanent. It fitted what Chris and more recently, Caroline had told me. Details of the fatal evening followed...

We attended a teachers' meeting in the outskirts of Preston until about 8pm on Tuesday 23rd November. I had an appointment to meet Mr Benson at 8.30 pm. I had been working on a website design for him. He wanted me to demonstrate the design and discuss further developments. He made the arrangements by his usual method – an after-hours telephone call to the science department at St Cuthbert's. His call was early in November – I don't remember the exact date. I was alone in the department when the call came through. I had no means of contacting him because he never gave an address or phone number.

Caroline left her car at my flat where she planned to stay overnight. After the meeting, we followed the directions that Mr. Benson had sent by post to the school – block capitals on paper torn from a plain note pad – I didn't keep it. The address was a farmhouse called Fellbeck about two miles from Coldedge. The road was unfamiliar to both of us and visibility was bad due to mist and drizzle. After some difficulty, we found the Fellbeck sign at the roadside just after 8.30. I followed the farm track alongside the stream until we came to a gravel forecourt in front of the house. In the car headlights, it appeared to be a large stone building. I remember a porch with stone columns at the front door. The place was in darkness. I got out of the car taking the small torch from the glove pocket with me.

I didn't see any farm buildings. I remember hearing a faint sound that I took to be a petrol engine coming from behind the house. I guessed it was a small generator of some kind. Caroline joined me, suddenly she shivered. She said, 'Let's make it short, I want to get back, I've something to tell you.' She caught hold of my free hand while I tugged on the bell pull.

A light came on above the door. I switched my torch off and put it in my coat pocket. A man opened the door. He looked middle aged, average height, although a trifle stooped, with grey hair hanging almost to his shoulders. He had heavy horn-rimmed spectacles. I don't remember any other details because the hall light behind him was dim and yellowish. There was another dim light in the corridor which led towards the back of the house. I remember Caroline moving closer to me as if she was nervous. He was wearing a sort of short dressing gown, quilted like an old-fashioned smoking jacket and a cravat. He introduced himself as 'Benson' and said 'Mr Berry? Come in, I'm expecting you.' We shook hands. He was wearing lightweight cotton gloves. He said, 'Excuse the gloves, I wear them on account of eczema.'

I recognised him as Benson by the quality of his voice on the telephone and his formal way of speaking. He didn't say anything to Caroline. The place was warmer than I'd expected for an old house. He showed us into the hall, which was paved with large flagstones.

A woman of about the same age, with short grey hair appeared through a door at the far end of the corridor. She was on the tall side for a woman. I remember that she was smiling as she came towards us. Benson introduced her as 'Mrs Watts, my housekeeper.'

Mrs Watts was pleasant and seemed friendlier than her employer. She took Caroline's free hand and addressed her as 'Mrs Berry'. Caroline liked that, she gave my hand a quick squeeze then let go and seemed to relax. Mrs Watts suggested to Caroline that they should go and sit in the lounge where she had a 'nice log fire' burning.

'I'm sorry we're in such a state,' Mrs Watts apologised, 'Mr Benson bought the house recently. The electrics aren't finished so we're on temporary lights. We've had builders and carpenters doing alterations and you know what a mess they make.' She exchanged a knowing smile with Caroline on the subject of workmen and their habits. She opened the door to a small closet under the stairs. 'For now, this is where Mr Benson keeps his horrid machine,' she said, 'as you can see there's only room for one chair there. The gentlemen can play their computer games and then join us in the sitting room. Meanwhile we'll have a chat and a cup of tea in front of the fire.'

I noticed the sound of an aircraft approaching. I remember thinking it might be a flight from Leeds-Bradford en route to Belfast. Mrs Watts offered to take my coat saying I'd be too warm, which was right. I pulled the CD out of my pocket and handed my jacket to her; Caroline said 'see you in ten,' and followed Mrs Watts down the passage. They went into the sitting room through a door on the left. I saw that Mrs Watts had turned on the lights because they shone out through the doorway. She said something I didn't catch because the aircraft noise was now loud and getting louder then the door closed firmly. Benson touched my arm to direct my attention to the computer and pulled out the bentwood chair for me to sit down. That was the last time I saw Caroline alive. If only I'd told her to wait with me...

There followed a note by Tom to the effect that at this point Mr Berry was overcome and was unable to continue. After a short break, he felt able to go on.

The aircraft noise was very loud now. It wasn't a civilian flight, more like something military. It was like a pair of Tornados coming low along the river valley. Benson shouted something about 'low flying exercises'. For a few seconds, the noise was deafening. I stuck my hands over my ears and waited for the aircraft to pass over before powering up the computer.

The computer room looked as though it might have been a walk-in cupboard under the main staircase – there wasn't even a desk lamp. The monitor, keyboard and mouse were on a trestle table, the computer itself, a modern Viglen PC, was on the floor alongside. When the PC finished booting up I put the CD into the drive slot. I waited for that to start up and then copied the website design onto Benson's PC.

I opened the homepage and watched my graphics resolving which took perhaps twenty seconds. I turned to Benson to ask him whether he liked the display. He wasn't there. I assumed he'd gone to reassure the women about the aircraft noise so I waited, perhaps a minute, for him to come back. Then without warning, all the lights went out and the computer shut down. It was a power failure. I was in total darkness.

I stood up, shouted for Benson, got no reply and tripped over the chair. I felt my way out into the passage. I couldn't see or hear anything and I was cursing because Mrs Watts had taken my torch away inside my coat pocket. I shouted for Benson again and once more there was no answer. I started to feel alarmed and called out for Caroline – nothing. I felt around and worked my way down the passage until I found the door on the left. It was shut. I turned the handle and tried to open the door but it wouldn't budge. I was angry now, what was going on? I pushed hard. It was a solid oak door but there was a small amount of give, the door didn't seem to be locked or bolted. I thought it must be jammed. I yelled again for Caroline – nothing. I drew back and shoulder charged at the door. It took several tries because of the dark and because I had to hold the handle down at the same time as shoving at the door. Then the door flew open and I followed it, tripped over something lying on the floor and fell flat.

I got up and stood for a moment. The only light came from

the fireplace and there was not much of that. The flames were dying down and there was a high-backed armchair, one of a pair, partly blocking my view. I moved closer and made out a shape on the hearthrug. It looked like someone asleep. I ran forward. It was Caroline, lying on her back with her face turned towards the fire. I called out her name, knelt down at her side. She didn't move. Then in the flickering light, I saw why: there was a great gash across her throat, there was blood all over her coat and sweater and soaking the hearthrug. Blood was trickling from her throat. Her eyes were open but the pupils were fixed, staring. I tried to find a pulse. I asked her to squeeze my hand if she could hear me. There was nothing. Caroline was dead. I took her in my arms; I held her and sobbed out her name. I touched her face and told her I loved her, she was warm...it seemed all wrong that she was limp and lifeless.

There was another note here by Tom saying that Chris had to break off again to recover himself. Then he went on...

I don't know how long I stayed there. I wanted to cry but there was a dry ache in my eyes, mouth, throat and nothing came. It seemed like hours, perhaps only a few minutes. I didn't think to check the time. Then I realised what I had to do – get the police. First, I had to find my jacket. I made out a shape behind me – a settee. It was facing the fireplace, four or five yards back from the pair of armchairs. I pushed myself up on the brass fender, went to the settee and felt about until I found my jacket draped over the back. I got my torch out of the pocket, switched on and went back to Caroline. The wound in her throat was horrible. There was blood all over her and over me. I knelt by her side again and I closed her eyes and kissed them. I found a loose blanket on the settee. I used it to cover her.

I took my mobile out of my jacket pocket and switched it on – no signal. I would have to go outside, but where were Benson and Mrs Watts? I flashed my torch around. I found a door in the corner of the room leading towards the back of the house. It was locked. I went back to the passage door. The thing that had tripped me up turned out to be a wooden folding chair. It must have been wedged under the door handle. There was a door facing on the opposite side of the corridor, locked. I walked down the corridor to the door that Mrs Watts had appeared from and another to the left of that – both locked. I went back to the entrance hall and up the wide staircase. I tried the first two doors I came to, they were unlocked but the rooms were empty and smelling of dust and damp. My torch battery was starting to fail. I could do nothing without a proper light and I was getting shaky in that silent place so I went downstairs to the front door. The door was unlocked – no sign of a key – as I stepped outside I heard a dull thudding sound coming from the darkness behind me. I couldn't take any more. I slammed the door to stop the noise, ran to the car, shut myself in and tried to pull myself together. I tried the mobile again – still no signal. For all I knew the murderers were still inside. There was nothing they could do to hurt Caroline now and I had to get the police. I was shaking but I fumbled the key into the ignition, started the car, turned it round and drove through the mist to the bridge. I stopped there, tried the mobile again – no signal. I could see why – the river ran along the bottom of a steep sided valley. If I turned right, it would take me across the bridge and uphill on the other side to Coldedge. If there was still no signal there would be a phone box or a pub or I could knock someone up. I set off. I was driving like a zombie, talking to myself. Once or twice, I nearly went into the ditch on corners and had to slam the brakes on. I don't remember seeing any lights until I came to the village. I checked the mobile and found I had a signal. I parked in the main street and phoned the police.

I did my best to explain what had happened. The operator said that they had a patrol in the area. I was to wait in my car until they arrived. She said that my call was timed at 9.28pm. I sat waiting trying not to think until suddenly I was dazzled

59

by headlights. It was a police 4x4 with two young constables. I didn't check the time but it seemed a long time since my 999 call. I told the officers that I had gone with my girl friend to keep an appointment at Fellbeck with a man called Benson and that Caroline had gone to another room to wait with a woman called Mrs Watts while I was working on his computer. A few minutes later, I had found her murdered. They said they knew where Fellbeck was and didn't need any directions. They put me in the back of the vehicle. I was sitting behind the driver. I couldn't see where we were going. It was dark and misty and the driver's headrest blocked the view. The officer was driving fast so I gave up and lapsed into a daze until the patrol car stopped in front of the house.

I told the officers that I couldn't see a key when I left the house so I'd closed the door and left it like that. The driver tried the door and said it was locked. He tried the windows at the front of the house which also seemed to be locked. Then he disappeared round the corner of the house and I heard the screech of a sash window being opened so he must have found one that was unlocked. Then a key turned in the door and the policeman opened the door. 'Key was lying on the mat,' he told his mate, 'must have locked the door from the outside and then posted it through the letter box.'

The other officer looked hard at me, 'That's what happened, isn't it?' He sounded angry.

'No,' I said 'I told you, the door was unlocked when I left. Benson or somebody must have still been in the house.'

I got no answer to that but from that moment the police seemed hostile. The driver was called Bob Cartwright, the other was called Tace, he seemed to be the senior of the two. He said to Cartwright that they should take me inside. I realised that Cartwright had climbed in through one of the sitting room windows and he must have already seen Caroline's body. The house lights were not working but the police torches were much more powerful than mine. As we walked up the hall, Tace asked where I was when I last saw Caroline. I showed them the closet space. The table was folded against the wall with the chair I had used. There was no sign of the computer, keyboard or monitor. I said Benson must have taken them. 'Been a busy lad hasn't he?' said Tace sarcastically. Then they wanted to see where I had found Caroline so I took them to the sitting room. Her body was lying where I had left her, covered with the blanket. As far as I could tell, she had not been moved. 'Let's have a look, Bob', said Tace. PC Cartwright folded back the rug and Tace confirmed that she was dead. There was a big patch of blood on the hearthrug and what looked like handprints in blood on the brass fender. I said that they could be mine. I might have rested my hand on it to steady myself, I couldn't remember.

'Didn't even bother to wash your hands after, did you?' Tace said.

I told the policemen about the lights going out and how I'd felt my way to the sitting room door and forced it open. I looked round for the broken chair that had been used to block the door. There was no sign of it. The fire had died down to embers. PC Cartwright took off his glove and put his hand down to test the ashes, 'still hot', he said to his mate. Tace came over and confirmed, 'hasn't been out long', he said. The room felt cold. The officers got me to sit on the settee while they went to the door and had a low-voiced conversation ending with the driver saying 'OK Trev'. He went out, I supposed to radio for back up. Tace began asking me about the murder weapon and writing in his notebook. Had I got it? Where did I see it last? Did I know where it was? 'Threw it in the beck, did you?' Then he asked what time I'd found the body. I said I didn't know for certain but estimated ten minutes to nine, perhaps a couple of minutes either way. How did I account for the time between finding the body and phoning the police at 9.28? I said 'shock' and searching round the house to see if the murderers were still there. Bob Cartwright came back and said that a vehicle was on its way to take me to the station.

When I got to the station, Sergeant Foster took me into an interview room and said I should make a statement. He seemed friendly and I agreed, partly because of Tace's attitude. I wanted to put the record straight. A woman constable came in and they switched on the tape recorder. I was feeling terrible by this time, shaking again and couldn't stop. I couldn't get my thoughts in order and I kept breaking down. Then the questions started. Mainly they were about Caroline and me. Was she trying to call it off or was it me? We'd had a row about something, hadn't we? Even in the state I was in it was obvious what they were getting at. So I said I wouldn't answer any more questions without my solicitor present. They let me phone Mr Hardy. Then I sat and said nothing until Mr Harrison arrived.

There followed a note by Tom: could Mr Berry remember what happened to the front door key after Benson admitted them.

'I can't remember, I don't suppose I was noticing.'

'Did Benson re-lock the door?'

'I don't remember him doing that.'

'What did he do with the key? Did he leave it in the lock?'

'He may have just dropped it into the pocket of his jacket. When I left the house to fetch the police, the front door was unlocked and there was no sign of the key.'

Chris had been framed. I believed that if no one else did.

10

The following morning I recorded a rare sighting of Potts. He had emerged to usher a nicely dressed but rather plain lady towards the front door. She was tearful, he was all solicitude. 'Don't distress yourself, Mrs. McCarthy. I'll have words with the other side and press for an improved settlement.' Mrs. McCarthy allowed herself to cheer up marginally at the prospect of money, blew her nose delicately and clattered out on high heels. The dastardly McCarthy was in for an expensive day. Niall turned away and beamed at me through his thick lenses. 'Morning Ken. What can we do for you – quicky divorce?' (*What had Potts got to be so bloody cheerful about?*)

He had a few minutes to spare before his next victim. I followed him past reception, the waiting room, Tom's office, the interview room, Pam Fisher's office, the small room used by the cleaner, Dawn's room (Niall's secretary) – and finally reached his office. I followed Potts inside, carefully closed the door, and addressed the lawyer with some freedom, 'Like a fucking mole, you – no one ever sees you, apart from the odd client.'

Potts regarded me sternly, 'I work better, I find, away from noise, chatter and unnecessary interruptions.' (*Like this*).

I attempted to explain, 'Last Tuesday evening, Chris had an appointment to meet Benson...'

Niall knew what was coming, 'He took Caroline Enderby with him. She was murdered and the police are about to charge him. What's that?'

Thick lenses notwithstanding, Niall had spotted the brown

envelope in my hand, 'It's the manuscript delivered to Chris by Benson. Chris passed it on to me in September. He said that he'd transcribed it to his PC during the holiday. All I did at the time was to skim the first couple of pages. Then I gave up because the handwriting is hard to decipher; it's been in my filing cabinet ever since. I want to read it properly before I pass it on to Tom. It'll be a lot easier to read from Chris's copy on the PC. While I'm about it I could see if there's anything else on his hard drive that Tom ought to know about.'

Niall pointed me to the door behind his desk. 'It's all in the archive store next to the server, help yourself.'

'How do I leave without bursting in on you consoling a big blonde on the couch?'

'Make a few thumps on the door then enter. If I am with a client say, "You shouldn't have any more bother with that server, Mr. Potts, but if you do, switch into warp drive and it'll be right." Then leave.'

I went into the back room, booted Chris's computer and wondered how I was going to find the Benson file. It turned out to be easy; Chris kept a separate folder for each customer. I opened the Benson folder and found two files, one called 'index', which was the homepage for the proposed website and the other, 'Dawson'. I opened the Dawson file and started to read. Immediately, a name jumped out at me, *Fellbeck*. I read on to the finish then clicked the homepage. It had some nicely sinister graphics of London's East End in Charles Dawson's time when Jack the Ripper had stalked his victims down dark alleys. There was also a list of other potential contributors: Chapman, Creamer, Druitt, Kelly, Kosminski, Ostrog and more. The names meant nothing but they brought to mind the label project that had been the start of the Benson business. I found a folder labelled 'Database' and inside, that, 'Benson-labels'. Listed with their addresses were the same names: Chapman, Creamer... no postcodes. I copied the Benson files onto a CD.

I spent half an hour going through the other folders. They contained website designs for Ditchfield worthies; there was nothing of interest to Tom. There was a folder called 'Diary' which I opened. Most of the documents were appointments, notes of telephone calls – nothing there. As a precaution I copied the "Diary" to a separate CD and shut down. Then I banged on the door and marched into Niall's office.

Niall was not wrestling with a handsome woman. He was not wrestling at all, which was wise because this client resembled a nightclub bouncer. Instead, he was dispensing parting words and paper hankies. The client made a moist exit; I stayed. 'I was expecting a cubbyhole with two computers. It's like Abanazer's cave – acres of filing racks.'

'It's the partnership archive,' said the mole, '1980's style, one day everything will be digital, but meantime we keep the old paper records in suspended folders. They go back to when our predecessor, old Jefferson Whalley, owned the business.'

I went up to the flat and copied the CDs onto my computer. I printed out two copies of the Benson document. It was clear that this had been the bait that lured Chris and Caroline to the fatal meeting. I had a gut feeling that it contained the key to the whole business – if I could spot it.

At half past four, Pam rang and said Tom was available; I laid Chris's statement on his desk. 'Have you read it?' Tom asked, 'What do you think?'

'I think it's a straightforward account of what happened, which is why as you said, there are no substantial differences between this and what he volunteered to the police at first. If he'd been telling a tale it would have improved overnight.' Tom was non-committal, I pressed on, 'he and Caroline were lured to Fellbeck by this character calling himself Benson. Whilst Chris was engaged elsewhere with Benson's computer, Caroline was taken off to the sitting room and murdered by Benson, Mrs.

Watts the housekeeper, or someone else entirely. Meanwhile Chris was distracted by a loud noise like low flying aircraft followed by a power failure. It's pretty clear what the police think. I doubt if they've thought anything since the two bright sparks in uniform solved the crime at the scene in five minutes flat. They've convinced themselves that Chris flew into a rage with Caroline, murdered her brutally and disposed of the murder weapon... probably in the beck.'

Tom broke in, 'It's a common scenario for murders of this sort.'

'... and Chris then thought up this complicated Benson conspiracy story while in a state of shock? Anything new?'

'They've brought in DCI Kent from HQ as chief investigating officer, and shifted DI Evans sideways.' I asked his opinion of Kent. 'Strictly in the family, he's a lean and hungry bugger, sharp as shit and twice as nasty (*not like Tom to speak thus unlawyerly*). He cross-examined Chris today. It was hard work: he's a master at implying something out of nothing.'

'I know,' I admitted, 'I taught him. How did Chris cope?'

'He batted the straight balls back and I blocked the twisters. In the end, Kent gave up and charged him with murder. We'll appear at the Magistrates Court on Monday.' I said that Tom was looking more relaxed. 'I am. It means the end of the interrogation tactics. They'll have to get down to it, and build a case from the evidence, then we'll see them in court and fight it out.'

'What about the Benson connection? What do they think of that?'

'They're grinning all over their faces about that.'

I pushed the envelope containing the Benson document across Tom's desk. 'Here's your first piece of solid evidence for the defence. They'll be grinning on the other side of their faces after they've seen this,' I said and went on to explain. I concluded, 'the original's quite hard to read but Chris transcribed it onto his PC. I've printed it out, it's in the envelope with the manuscript original. It proves the existence of the man Benson who, according to Chris, lured him to Fellbeck and murdered Caroline.'

'It might, unless Chris manufactured the document himself.'

'Wait until you've read it. I'll write you a note on the Benson background as I had it from Chris. I spent a couple of hours this morning in Niall's archive store going through all the stuff on Chris's hard drive. Apart from Benson there's nothing of interest. Chris gave the original manuscript to me in September, for interest. It's been locked in my filing cabinet ever since.'

Tom put on a pair of white gloves and eased the manuscript out of its envelope. 'Doesn't look likely that Chris could have manufactured this himself, does it? Niall's the documents man; let's see what he thinks.' He restored the manuscript to its envelope, then turned the package over and looked at the impression on the red wax seal. 'CB', he said, 'standing for what, Cardew Benson?'

'Yes, also for Christopher Berry. I've never seen Chris wearing a signet ring but someone might have given him one. If he has one, would he be daft enough to use it on the seal?'

'It's a point though,' Tom said, 'the prosecution are bound to use it, unless we can identify Benson.'

'Have a read of the document, it makes a lively bedtime story,' I promised, 'for maximum effect, read it at midnight during a thunderstorm by the light of a guttering candle.'

Tom tidied the case papers into a folder, got up and locked it into his safe. 'Ken,' he said, 'you've cheered me up. This case might turn out to be more fun than I thought. Fancy a pint?' Coming from a trained lawyer it was a bit of a daft question, until he went further. 'Why not stay for supper afterwards? I don't expect you'll be feeling too cosy in the flat at the moment. You can have the spare room and come back in with me in the morning.'

'Sound!' I slotted off to get my overnight stuff. Tom phoned to warn Paula and order an extra helping of swill.

We stopped off at the pub by the green in Tom's village, called "The French Defence". Nothing to do with chess – the sign showed a moustachioed and top-hatted cricketer executing a wild swing at a ball which was in the process of demolishing his stumps. I hoped it was not a premonition of the fixture in court. The bar was almost empty. I got a couple of pints in. 'What's next? Post mortem?'

'That's automatic. I expect a copy of the pathologist's report next week.'

'What will that tell us?'

'Cause of death, basically, she had her throat cut.'

'That's what settles it as far as I'm concerned,' I said, 'Chris couldn't do that to save his life.'

Tom was determined to stick to the facts, 'We should also find out if there were any other injuries, caused by self-defence or restraint for example.'

'How about other things that might be evidence? Recent sexual activity, were there any signs of violence in that connection? If the prosecution line is that this was a crime of passion it could be relevant, couldn't it?'

'I'll have a quiet word with Evans at court on Monday and ask what they've requested as part of the post mortem. If we're not happy, the defendant can ask for a second post mortem with his own doctor present. It isn't cheap, especially if forensics are involved. We'll wait for the pathologist's report. Right,' said Tom, 'we'll just have the one we came for and then you'll want to see the animals before bedtime.' He meant my granddaughters aged three and five. The advantage of being a grandparent is that you can hand them back when they've finished using you to practice their karate chops.

11

On Saturday morning, Tom drove me back to York Terrace. 'Now they've charged Chris, are the cops going to be climbing all over his flat this morning?' Tom thought they might leave it until Monday. 'Why?'

'Because if there's going to be boots up and down my stairs all morning, I'll probably make myself scarce.' I went up to the flat and unpacked my bag. Then I tapped on Niall's office door and received something between a grunt and a squeak in reply. I went in and found Niall poking around mole-like on his massive partner's desk; eight foot by six and littered with papers. It was a strange sight, 'what are you up to?'

Niall looked in my direction and screwed up his eyes as if it would improve his vision. 'Ken,' he said, having recognised my voice, 'Good morning. Can you see my spectacles?'

I advanced, 'they're on top of your in-tray,' I told him.

'Which is…?'

'Far left hand corner.'

Niall stretched out a hand, made contact, put his specs on and blinked owlishly at me. 'Normal service restored,' I said, 'why mess about with those when you could have contact lenses?'

'I have enough trouble finding these. Imagine crawling round the bedroom at seven in the morning looking for tiny transparent lenses.'

'Virginia would help.'

Niall begged leave to doubt it. 'Virginia would never agree to creep about the bedroom carpet in her nightie. She'd suspect my motives.' I was doubtful. 'Kenneth,' said Niall in his best courtroom voice, 'for those of us still virile it's like Chinese elections – have one everly morning. You've forgotten.' Having put the witness in his place, Niall enquired how he could assist.

I handed him a printout of the Benson document. 'I think this is strong evidence in support of Chris's case.'

'The prosecution will say that Chris wrote the original document himself – it's a fake intended to mislead. When they find Chris's fingerprints all over it they'll claim that as evidence.'

'But we know that he transcribed it onto his PC for use on Benson's proposed website. If there weren't any prints they'd say "cunning swine – practising to deceive by wearing gloves". Let's leave that until you've looked at the original. It's in Tom's safe; I think he'd like your opinion on the provenance. If Chris wrote it, it dates from August at the latest. It's been in my filing cabinet since early September. What sort of crime of passion is three months in the planning whilst conducting a love affair with the intended victim? How long have we until your next tearstained lion tamer arrives?'

'He's late.' Niall wiped his thick lenses, blinking several times in my approximate direction, then he put his specs back on and gave me an intimidating stare from magnified eyes. Being a short sighted solicitor has its advantages so long as you know how to handle the props. 'What it amounts to,' he said, 'is find Benson and you've cracked the case.'

I was not falling for that – no lachrymose labourer, me. 'Then tell me, who am I looking for? What sort of a lad is this Benson? Where is he likely to live? What's his job, if any? What are his interests, apart from composing fake Victorian romances and murdering women? Which pub does he drink in?'

Niall did not bother to remove his spectacles to that one, 'Let's have a chat next week.'

'Sorry to spoil your weekend,' I said, 'but it will be a respite for the lovely Virginia.'

Potts gave me the sort of hard stare you might expect from an irritable teddy bear, 'She'll want to send you a thank you card.'

I've been thrown out of one or two lawyers' offices during my business career but this was a real crusher – teach me not to be facetious. I slunk along the corridor, arriving on cue to follow a pair of plods upstairs. I entered my flat while they went on to clog dance on my ceiling (checking for loose floorboards in Chris's flat?). After an hour the noise from above gave way to clatterings on the stairs. I watched from my sitting room window whilst the lads slammed the rear doors of their Transit and drove off.

Pam was starting to shut up shop for the weekend. 'Have they finished? I bet you could hear them from your office.'

'One of them put his head in and said that they were done.'

'I hate to think what sort of mess they've left,' I said, 'fancy popping up to have a look before you go?' That struck a housewifely chord with Pam, she agreed. The flat struck cold as soon as she got the door open – exactly as Caroline had said. The state of the apartment put morbid memories out of mind; it looked as though it had been turned over by bombed-out baboons.

Chris must have left his pile of exercise books waiting to be marked on the kitchen table. The police had turned the children's books inside out and dropped them, one at a time, in a heap on the floor. At first, it looked like senseless vandalism until it occurred to me that they were looking for evidence of improper goings-on between Chris and his pupils. I wasn't right pleased.

Everywhere was the same, even the bathroom, with the contents of the wall cabinet scattered on the floor – looking for drugs, I supposed. The room that Chris used as an office had been taken apart: files, books, computer discs, tapes, all gone. The filing cabinet stood with both drawers gaping open

– impossible to tell what had been taken from the folders. Scattered on the floor were the contents of the upturned drawers: ballpoint pens, pencils, paper clips, a stapler, a paper punch and the assorted bits and pieces found in every office. The shelf for computer books was bare. The manuals had been held open by the covers, shaken to see what dropped out and dumped on the carpet to join the rest of the debris. The printer stood alone, unvandalised. It was comforting that the PC was safe in Niall's archive store.

'I'm not leaving it like this,' I said, 'no way is Chris coming home to this shambles. The kids' homework books need to go back to the school for the teacher who's taking over Chris's classes. I'll see to that next week.'

Pam suggested setting on the office cleaner.

I said, 'I've a fair idea where he keeps things. If I get things back into some sort of order, I might be able to deduce what they've taken which could be useful for Mr. Harrison. Why not leave me the key for the weekend? I'll sort out the mess and slip it under your office door for Monday morning.'

Pam saw the sense in that. She had the key off the ring and was away downstairs to start her weekend shopping before I could say 'Metro'. I fetched my camera then moved through the flat photographing the wreckage. Clearing up took longer than I expected. I started with the kitchen. I picked up 3A's homework books and stacked them on the kitchen table. Then I replaced the kitchen cutlery in its drawer and went on from there. After the kitchen, I moved into the lounge. Chris's books were all over the floor having been treated the same as the office manuals. His reading matter was run of the mill relaxation therapy – murder mysteries, SAS action thrillers, plenty of healthy violence. I found three paperbacks about Jack the Ripper, well thumbed. The police hadn't thought them significant or they would have taken them as exhibits, especially if they'd known about the Benson document. I decided to take possession in case they came back. The photo of Caroline that I'd rescued on Tuesday night was safely in my place, others of Caroline had been removed from their frames – looking for notes or messages I supposed. After I had paired up frames and photos, one empty frame remained. I guessed that was a snap of Caroline that they'd taken for the media. His family photos were intact.

I searched especially for a signet ring and a stick of sealing wax. I found neither – the police would have no reason to confiscate them until they knew about the Benson document, making it still more unlikely that Chris had manufactured it himself. Equally, there was no thick black ink, no ink well, no old-fashioned steel nib pens for calligraphy. The only paper I found was modern 80 gsm A4, no heavy legal foolscap – yellowed or otherwise – no thick brown foolscap envelopes. In short, if Chris faked the Benson manuscript he didn't do it in his flat.

It took most of the afternoon to restore order and clean up. Apart from the office stuff, I couldn't think of anything else that might have been taken, except personal correspondence. I was confident that none of that related to Chris's affair with Caroline. They'd probably taken pay slips, bank statements, invoices for website work – so what? Perhaps if the murder charge failed they would get him for tax evasion like Al Capone. By the time I had finished I had calmed down. I was more depressed than angry. I showered, went for a pint and talked football with the intellectuals at the Duke.

12

I got in to see Tom on Monday afternoon. 'Remanded until next week,' he said. I laid out my photos on his desk. 'What was that before a bomb hit it?'

'Chris's flat after the cops had turned it over. I spent most of Saturday afternoon cleaning up after them.' I told him what I had not found – any evidence that Chris had manufactured the Benson document himself, even if he was capable of writing the narrative, executing the calligraphy and so on.'

Tom passed the photos back, 'not pleased, are you?'

'I was bloody cross at the time,' I admitted, 'but it was a wake-up as far as the cops are concerned. This isn't a search for the truth; it's about convicting Chris. "We've solved the case. Don't confuse us with facts."'

Tom grinned at me. 'Sit down a minute Ken.' That sounded like a good idea. I got a short dissertation on the adversarial system of criminal justice in England compared with what the rest of the EU (poor devils) had to put up with. 'But it's got its faults – the police are always under pressure so sometimes they jump to conclusions and then stick to them like shit to a blanket. I think they've overdone it this time. Kent could end up regretting it.'

'It isn't a level pitch is it? The police have the resources but they're not going to spend time looking for evidence that they think is irrelevant or hostile. The defence has few resources, so they have to make a case out of the crumbs dropped on the mat.'

'What is there to stop the defence grubbing around for

evidence of their own? There are criminal defence agencies that take on that kind of work.'

'How many detectives can you pay for on Legal Aid?'

Tom wasn't giving anything away, 'The application has gone forward.'

'In this case, is a detective agency what you need?'

'Why not?'

'According to my researches (*in paperback novels*), these agencies are staffed by retired police detectives. I expect they're great on contacts – digging out odds and ends of gossip from ex-colleagues and slipping the odd tenner to seedy ex-cons for information received. I don't believe this case will be cracked by sidling up to a low life informer, bent copper or whoever. It isn't about the criminal underworld or police corruption or drugs. Something strange has gone on here, nothing to do with prostitution or extortion or gang warfare. I think it could be a bit indigestible for an ex-police detective.'

'What are you suggesting Ken?'

'Me. I'm on the spot, I'm local, I know the protagonists. I have motivation, time on my hands and I don't want payment – expences are up to you. I've got 30 years experience in industry at board level so I won't do anything daft.' Tom rated it a possibility. I wasn't leaving it there. (*Close that deal!*) 'I can start now. When will the trial come up at the Crown Court?'

'Probably the end of April.'

'Give me until Christmas, three weeks and let's see if I can make progress. I'll keep you informed, I'll warn you before approaching a suspect and give you a written report on each interview.'

'Where would you start?'

'The person calling himself Benson – Niall said "Find Benson and we've cracked the case". I think he's right, but we need an idea of what sort of chap we're looking for. Perhaps Niall could go through the Benson text; see if he can assemble a profile? Otherwise it'll be a drag because we'll have to trawl through all the phone books or electoral rolls in North East Lancs for Benson, Cs, just in case that's his real name; and what if he isn't local?'

'I could offer some help – manhandling the directories, making lists and so on.' Tom picked up his phone. 'Pam, could you send Jason in? Yes, ok just five minutes more.' He put the phone down, 'There's a gang of worried bank robbers in the waiting room. Let's make it short. What else can you pursue?'

'Gloria. Gloria Davis, she's the technician in the Science Department at St. Cuthbert's. Benson's method of communication was to phone Chris after hours at the school. After five, he could get straight through to the department. If Chris wasn't there when Benson rang and Gloria picked the call up...'

'...Gloria has spoken to Benson?'

'There's a good chance. Benson has a distinctive voice with a grating tone to it. In his statement, he says that Benson opened the door at Fellbeck. He recognised him by his voice at Fellbeck. If Gloria confirms, I don't fancy being inside Nigel's underpants when he hears.'

A knock on the door and a striking figure appeared: six foot two and eyes of blue with a golden fleece on top. (If this has a brain it's dangerous). Tom introduced us. 'Ken, this is Jason Goode, our trainee. He's on work experience until next September. After that, if he behaves himself, he's off to University. This is Mr. Hardy, Jason. He's taking on confidential investigative work for us on the Berry case. I want you to help, it will be good experience.'

Jason's jaw dropped, 'The murder Mr. Harrison? When do we start?'

I got up. 'Now; Mr. Harrison needs his office so we'll go elsewhere.' Jason was already on his way to the door.

Tom called us back. 'Jason, any information that you acquire on this project is confidential to you, Mr. Hardy and me. Bear in mind, this is a murder enquiry and a man's life is at stake; no one else is to know, I mean no one. We don't hang people for murder any more but by the time they've done life in Strangeways they might just as well be dead. Don't misunderstand me: if I suspect something has leaked, you're out.'

The charming smile vanished. Jason confirmed that he understood.

'Right Jason,' I said, 'get your coat'. I took him out to the car. 'Can you drive?' Jason said he'd passed first time a year ago. He hadn't driven anything as big as the Mercedes. The only way to find out was to set him on. I passed him the keys, 'Once you get used to the size most people find a big car is easier.' I showed him reverse gear and he inched out of the parking space, slipped into forward gear, stalled the engine with a jolt and turned a pretty shade of pink. 'No Jason, that's fifth gear. First is here.'

We eased into the street, out of town, and set off for Coldedge. Jason relaxed and began to drive quite nicely. That is the problem with the young. They know nowt to begin with but set them on and they learn like lightning: it makes you sick. It was time to brief the lad. 'Now this job here,' I told him, 'is a preliminary recce of the scene of crime and the surroundings. It's not foggy for once, but it'll be dark before five, so we haven't got long.'

'Won't the police be there?' Jason asked.

'Yes. I'll be surprised if the SOC lads have finished already. But I want to have a scout round the outside. The reason for letting you drive is so I can have a look *en passant*.' We drove through the village of Coldedge and turned left towards Preston. After just short of a mile the road forked left for Preston. I told him to carry straight on towards Braxtonby. We were dropping steeply now to the valley bottom and the bridge over the beck. 'Maximum twenty now,' I told him as the bridge came into view. We crossed over and I spotted three cops wading about in the water.

'What are they looking for?'

'The murder weapon, I'll bet. This is day six, if they haven't found it yet... not breaking any pots, are they?' The entrance to the farm lane was marked off with police tape. The *Fellbeck* sign was gone. A constable stood guard to see that no one sneaked in. Bored, he gave us a grin as we passed.

'I thought there'd be press photographers and TV cameras all over the place,' Jason said.

'They lost interest long since. What you see here is the murder investigation. That was last week's news. This week it's the court proceedings.'

'Where next?' Jason asked.

'Keep on up the hill, careful on the blind bends, at the top there's a gate on the left to a farm called Sunnyside. We're going to start our enquiries with the neighbours. The farmer's called John Bolton.' Jason spotted the Sunnyside entrance and drew up. I got out and opened the gate for Jason to drive in. 'Now,' I said, climbing back in, 'always close farm gates, otherwise you won't get invited back. We'll have a quick word with Bolton, and see if we can walk down his field to Fellbeck. I know the layout from the front, if the place isn't swarming with cops, I want to spy out the lie of the land round the back.' Jason parked up in front of the house. 'If Alison, John's daughter, is around get her to show you the farmyard while I have a nose to nose with her dad.'

Jason said, 'You can't see Fellbeck from here.'

'Because Sunnyside is built back from the brow of the hill. They might see something from the upstairs windows.' I remembered the painting of Ezra Dawson at Fellbeck: supposing it was real, the artist had used a bit of licence when he showed the workers' cottages lined up along the brow.

'If I get her on her own, is there anything I should ask Alison?' Jason wanted to know.

'Did she notice any activity around Fellbeck on Tuesday? Did she hear any low flying aircraft? Jets flying at zero-zero feet up the valley are a regular complaint round here. The timing's important for the aircraft noise; it would have to be between 8.30 and 9 o'clock in the evening.'

A good-looking girl of eighteen – nice figure, slim, curly blonde hair opened the door to us. This was Alison. Normally Alison was chatty, this time she said nothing. She was stood standing with her mouth half open. As Wooster might have put it, she presented all the symptoms of a young maiden on first clapping eyes on her demon lover. More specifically, her pupils expanded to twice their previous diameter whilst her well-budded breasts jutted like chapel hat pegs through her denim shirt.

'Hi', said the demon lover.

'Hi,' quavered Alison. The golden couple then stood gawping at one another. We hadn't got all day: it was necessary to intervene.

'Hullo, Alison,' I said in my voice reserved for other people's budgies.

Alison jumped, almost out of her jeans, closed her mouth and opened it again. 'Mr. Hardy! Sorry, I didn't see you.' (*Quite.*)

'Is your dad about? I want a quick word with him – business.'

'He's just come in for his tea, Mr. Hardy.' Alison stood to one side, 'he'll be pleased to see you'. (*Not half as pleased as she was to see Jason*) 'Why don't you go through to the kitchen?'

'This is Jason Goode, my assistant,' I said, 'my business with your dad doesn't concern him... show him the piglets, he'll like them – they have interests in common.'

Jason woke up (just as I was about to hack his shin) and expressed a desire to know all about farmyards and matters associated. 'Ten minutes,' I said. Surely, they couldn't do much damage to one another in ten minutes? John Bolton was sitting by the kitchen range complete with mug. 'No thanks, John, I've just had one,' I sat and explained my position, 'I'm semi-retired from Ditchfield Packaging now, meantime I'm helping out the defence team on the Fellbeck murder case.'

'You mean you're a private detective, Hardy?'

'No I'm not.' I was firm about that. 'I'm a volunteer, unpaid, helping in a paralegal capacity by gathering information. I'm not stating that the police have got it arse about, but my money's on it. I expect you've had them round?'

'Aye,' said John Bolton, 'a couple of young lads came last Thursday. Where was I and doing what on Tuesday night apart from murdering young women? I told them I was in front of the telly in company with the missis, Alison, and a sheepdog. I told them what happened on *East Enders* – they were interested in that. I was in bed and asleep by ten as normal.'

'And you didn't see or hear anything – except a pair of RAF Tornadoes going past the bedroom windows at 500 knots just before nine?'

John paused to reflect, 'We do get low level flying exercises, but never this time of year. When they do come over it shakes the whole house. No chance of missing it, TV or no TV.'

'Did the police ask about aircraft?' John said they didn't. 'John,' I said, 'the big meadow in front that runs down to Fellbeck: is it yours?'

'Good as; officially the home field's still part of the Fellbeck estate, but I've rented it since Alison was a nip.'

'Who do you pay rent to – the estate direct?'

'No, house and land are owned by the Dawson family trust. That's run by old Jarvis Dawson, great grandson of the founder, he had a legal practice in London. When he retired, he went to live abroad. Since then I've dealt through the agents, Helmsley and Jordan at Braxtonby.'

I asked John's permission to walk down the field to the house, 'Just for a gander at the layout. When we came across the bridge, we saw the police wading about in the beck.'

'Likely,' John agreed, 'they've been swarming around Fellbeck since Wednesday morning. I don't know whether they've finished yet, but they've had a mobile generator, three or four vans and all sorts.' At the front? I supposed. 'That's right,' said John, 'but they've got their plastic tape all round. There was a right set-to when I wanted feed out of the barn. "Bugger your crime scene," I told them, "my pigs want their dinner". We compromised.'

'Their generator,' I said, 'was that at the back?' John said no, it was outside the front door. 'No mains power supply to the house?'

'Cut off years back I reckon.' I thanked John and went to round up the young couple. They were not talking piglets; they had lapsed into teenage pop gabble so I only understood the occasional word. Alison had found a pair of wellies for her new friend, size 18 they looked. I read somewhere that when a species evolves towards extinction its feet get bigger. I did not mention this for fear of stimulating the survival instinct. Instead, we walked down the hill towards Fellbeck. There was still enough daylight, the sky had cleared for the first time in weeks and we were in for a frost. I wanted to see if there was police activity in the courtyard in front of the house.

We veered left coming down the hill to get a look at the front. In summer the elm trees growing round the front yard would have blocked the view. Now, with the trees bare it was obvious that the courtyard was empty, no vehicles, no police guard on the front door. The team at the bridge was half a mile away out of sight behind the hill. 'I want to see round the back', I said, so we turned right and carried on down.

The farmyard was separated from the meadow by a stone wall, the top decorated with police tape. The back entrance to the farmyard was by a five-barred gate in reasonably good order. I was surprised to see the grass churned up by broad vehicle tracks running from the yard gate alongside the beck to another gate in the distance.

'That's the main Preston Road yonder,' Alison explained. 'The tracks are delivery trucks and you can see where our tractor has been up and down. We have stuff in bulk delivered to the road gate, cart it across to the yard and stack it in the barn – animal feed, fertiliser. If it's a big delivery and not too muddy the driver sometimes brings it across into the yard here.'

'When did you last have a delivery truck in?'

Alison said 'Last Monday, the 22nd'. She was sure of that, 'it was a new driver, I took the padlock off the road gate for him because he hadn't been told where to find the key.'

We had arrived at the farmyard gate. 'Could you stay there?' I asked Alison, 'give us a whistle if you see anybody.' The gate wasn't locked but it was tangled up with the police tape. I climbed over and dropped into the yard.

'Isn't this illegal? Jason asked, 'crossing a police line?'

'We are the law,' I said, 'they're the police.' *(You've just made that up, Hardy)*. Jason vaulted the gate and grinned at Alison – little show-off. The yard was in poor condition with weeds growing through the cracks in the concrete. I wanted to have a look at the back door. Jason didn't need to know so I sent him to search inside the barn.

'What am I looking for?'

'Animal droppings. You know what horse poo looks like?' Jason thought he did. 'Depends what it's been eating,' I advised, 'if uncertain, look around for hoof prints. Don't taste it.' Jason disappeared inside. Having got him safely out of the way I went to look at the back door of the house. It was solid enough but I could see that the lock wasn't engaged. Instead, the door was secured by a basic hasp and staple with an ancient-looking padlock. That was all I needed. I joined Jason. There were a couple of stacks of animal feed in the barn, (in Ditchfield Packaging sacks, I was pleased to see) but nothing else. The

82

floor was cobbled, old style, so there were no hoof marks. 'Nothing here,' I said, 'we'll have a quick look in the small sheds. You can tell where a dog's been because there'll be hairs sticking to the timber where it's rubbed up. And there are the toilet arrangements. Unlike cats and the Army, dogs don't dig latrines.' There were no dog traces, (*no horse, no dog)* just bits and bats – a rusty bike frame and a few old tools. 'Nothing here,' I said and turned away.

'Just a minute, Mr Hardy,' the boy detective had spotted something. I went back and found him standing over a small pile of logs, all cut to length. I turned them over. I was expecting to find the grey armour plated wood lice creatures that live in damp places – "pigs" we used to call them. There were no pigs, the logs were dry, I guessed they had only been lying for a few days. 'A funny place for Mr Bolton to keep his firewood,' Jason said.

He was right, but according to Chris's statement there had been a log fire in the Fellbeck sitting room on the night of the murder.

'Before we go,' I said to Jason, 'I expect your mobile is newer than mine, see if you can raise the office.' He couldn't – "no signal".

'Find anything?' Alison asked. I said nothing, apart from a few logs. 'Not ours, we don't keep anything in the sheds,' she said, 'probably been there for years.' I didn't comment, we started on the hard climb up to Sunnyside. 'Did you hear anything on Tuesday night? Like a portable generator – the same sort of thing as the police have been using?'

She said 'No, I went in for supper about half past five. It was well dark by then.' I asked if Fellbeck was visible from their upper windows. 'Only the upstairs windows at Fellbeck,' she said.'

'You didn't see any activity there on Tuesday night?' she didn't, 'have you ever seen lights there?'

'There used to be a bit of bother with squatters, hippies and the like getting in.' I asked if her dad had reported it. 'He would have, but it never came to anything – by morning they were always gone.'

'Why do you think that was?'

'The old people reckon Fellbeck's haunted. Just a tale but I wouldn't want to spend a night there, whether or not.' It was a long slog uphill back to Sunnyside, by the time I'd got my breath back, changed out of wellies and said goodbye to John and his Missis it was dropping dark.

Jason turned the Merc round Clarkson-style, (*Alison was watching*) and we got back on the road. 'Take it easy back into Coldedge,' I instructed, 'drop me outside the Black Sheep, that's the pub in the High Street. Drive back to Ditchfield and park the car, put the key through the letter box and I'll see you tomorrow. You can write a short report – just what we found out at Sunnyside and what conclusions you reached.' Jason drew up outside the pub. I got out. 'Off you go,' I told him, 'I'll get the bus back. I want to do a bit of local research.'

'Can't I help?'

'No. You've done enough damage to village maidens for one day.'

'Thanks for letting me come, Mr. Hardy, it's been really interesting.' I didn't enquire whether he referred to his legal training or his trousers. The Black Sheep was an unpretentious village pub with old-fashioned beer pumps, not too many because real ale needs drinking up while it's fresh. The place was quiet – it was early yet. The landlord was called Vic; he pulled me a pint of Marston and asked what I was doing in Coldedge.

'I was hoping to take a look at the empty house – Fellbeck,' I said, 'it turned out to be swarming with cops in waders. They wouldn't let me in, not even for ready money, they said it was a crime scene.'

'Fair play, they've a job to do,' said the landlord, 'where've you been lately?' I told him I'd been away down south (*I had: fifteen miles south at Ditchfield*). Vic was ready with a briefing, 'there was a murder there last Tuesday night. Young woman found with her throat cut. They've got the feller, a schoolteacher. Crack is they were having an affair and it all went wrong.'

'What's your interest in Fellbeck, then?' asked the boiler suit alongside. His name was Walt; I told him that I was thinking of buying it. 'Can't think why,' said Walt, 'it hasn't been lived in for years, not regular, anyhow.' I explained that I was selling my business and was looking to get out of town and start a retirement project. 'I think it might be developed to make a centre for tourists, hill walkers, people like that.' Walt thought it might, so long as the customers were partial to ghosts. I rejected the temptation to try the tale about milk. Never tell jokes on your first visit, you might be talking to the resident comedian.

'If you want to know about Fellbeck, you could have a word with Dick.' Vic pointed out an old man sitting on his own in the corner. Sixty plus years of hard labour had reduced Dick to a shadow but his eyes were bright when he spotted me looking at him. I asked whether he would take a drink off me.

Vic raised his voice, 'Dick! There's a young man here asking if you'll take a drink with him.' I bought a refill for myself and a half for Dick – 'he only ever drinks halves', the landlord told me – Walt politely declined. I asked about buses to Ditchfield. 'You've had that, now,' Vic said. 'I can get you a taxi for twenty.'

'No rush,' I said, 'I've got this to down first.' I took the glasses across to Dick and introduced myself. 'I'm interested in the property at Fellbeck,' I told him, 'I was wondering if you could tell me something about it. I'd been told it was derelict but it doesn't look that way from the outside. The roof looks sound and the windows have glass in them. How is it that a place like that has stood empty for years?'

'You'd have to ask th'owners about that,' said Dick, 'there's been talk of it being bought, but it never came to owt. It always had a bad name did Fellbeck, ever since my great grandfather's time. It were his first place as head shepherd until he got out and went to work for Parkin at Braxtonby.'

'That wouldn't have been Wilf Barber? Would you be Dick Barber?'

'I am that!' Dick exclaimed. 'How did you guess?' (*Because I'd skimmed through the Benson document*). Recognition at last, old Dick launched into his story, 'See, the Fellbeck estate was started by old Ezra Dawson, well over an 'undred and fifty years back. He knocked down the old farmhouse and built new – three times the size, best quality mason work, carved lintels gentry-style, expense no object. There was money in farming then and Ezra knew how to make it. He were a nasty bugger... big man round here, big in the church and th'council, local magistrate, nobody could touch him. Worked his men to death, worked his own wife to death. She suffered with consumption and Ezra wouldn't have a doctor to her. Some said he murdered her, suffocated her with a pillow. It couldn't be proved one way or t'other. Drove his eldest son off the farm. The lad walked out one night – never seen again. After Ezra died the youngest, Edward took over. He were a different proposition altogether but the bad name stuck and the place went downhill. After the first war, some of the land was sold off. Then there was the murder.'

'You mean, before the murder last week?'

'Aye, sixty years back or more.' I asked if Dick could remember when. He frowned to aid calculation. 'It were a couple of years after I got my first proper start as shepherd's lad – farm up th'back road.' Could Dick say what year that would have been? 'It must have been 1933 or 4; not 35, definite, might have been about this time of year.'

'Do you remember what happened?'

'I can that. It was an odd sort of day, not cold, there were these heavy downpours with thunder on and off and sun in between.' Dick took a reminiscent sup of his beer and his eyes clouded over. I was afraid he was going to lose the thread so I prompted him. He came back with a start and set down his glass. 'See, after work that night I was biking home and I was caught in the worst cloudburst of the lot, rain was jumping six inches off the road. I got home like a drownded rat. Mam said I would catch me death and nowt else would do but I had to go in th' bath in front of th' kitchen range. No sooner was I in it but our neighbour, Mrs. Crossley, came rushing in to say there'd been a 'orrible murder at Fellbeck, young woman found with her throat slashed. Well, Crossley's missus was a good looking lass and she'd only a thin dress on. She'd got caught in th'rain too, and it clung to her – showed her to some advantage an' all. And there was me, stark naked in the bath. She stopped dead, hand over her mouth – I were just that age and she was barely 19 herself and at sight of her, wringing wet, I were like a pink periscope sticking up above th'waves. I met her up th'back field, following Sunday. She were my first. Poor lass, her husband was no good, impotent y'see. At th' finish he was killed at Alamein and she married a Yank.'

That was Dick's favourite memory of November 1933 or 4, and why not? I tried to get him back to the point. 'Did they find who did it?'

Dick sniffed and wiped his nose reminiscently on the back of his hand. 'Not likely, I were saying nowt, nor was she,' said he with a wink. I rephrased the question.

'Th' farmer. After old Edward Dawson died, his nephew came to take Fellbeck on. He'd been there happen four years. This young woman used to come visiting now and then. Folks said they were planning to wed. On this same day, late afternoon, the foreman went to the house with an errand, found the place deserted, back door wide open, nobody in th' kitchen. He went through into th'ouse, called out, no answer. It struck him that something was wrong, sitting room door was open, he looked in and there was th' lass, dead on the sitting room floor with her throat opened to the bone.

Police had to be called and they found th' farmer hanging in the barn. It was clear what had happened. After that, the owners tried putting tenants in but that wouldn't do. Word got round that the place had a curse on it, haunted, that sort of daft thing. When war broke out I was called up and when I came back on embarkation leave th' place had been requisitioned for the duration and most of the land parcelled out.'

Dick laughed at a thought that struck him, 'They had Italian prisoners billeted at Fellbeck – working on the farms around. One night the whole lot of them decamped and ran all the way up to Coldedge police station. They handed themselves in and swore they wouldn't go back on account of it being haunted – spent the rest of the war sleeping in barns. When Italians got shot of Mussolini and changed sides, RAF started flying back them that was willing to fight Nazis. Some from here volunteered but the plane crashed in France – killed the lot. Well,' said Dick, 'folk are daft, said it was because they'd seen the ghost at Fellbeck.' He sniffed, 'Didn't explain the pilot and crew getting killed did it? The ones that stayed here, nowt happened to them, regardless they'd seen th' ghost or not. A couple of Italians stayed on after th'war and married Coldedge women.' Dick grinned, 'A fate worse than death any road.'

It was a daft question, but I couldn't resist asking, 'This ghost, who was it supposed to be? Ezra Dawson?'

'Nay a woman; it was said she appeared walking happen a pitch length or two ahead of you. If she disappeared, you were all right. If she turned round and looked at you, you'd be dead in a twelvemonth – a girl dressed in green.'

'Taxi for Mr Hardy?' The shout came from the doorway. I emptied my glass, thanked Dick for his company, and got up.

I left my glass on the bar with a quid to pay one on for Dick, whenever. I didn't talk on the drive home except to ask the driver whether anyone local had heard aircraft flying low on Tuesday evening. 'No, never this time of year. They stopped that in 1944. They sent a flight of three Meteors on a low flying exercise, winter, a foggy night – straight into th'fellside – all killed. But that was wartime on course.'

13

Talking with old Dick Barber at the Black Sheep, I'd got away with a quick skim of Chris's transcript. That was not good enough for serious discussion of the evidence with Tom. I settled down to read.

The Benson document was a biography of Charles Dawson, the eldest son of Ezra Dawson, farmer of Fellbeck, Coldedge, County of Lancaster. It began with his brutal childhood. His father took him away from the village school and set him on at the farm as an unpaid labourer. No Ditchfield Grammar School for him. Charles struggled for approval and got nothing but blows.

When he could take no more, he ran away from home and joined Attwood's Strolling Players: a wandering troupe that he'd met by chance. Morrison Attwood, actor, promoter, impresario and manager of the troupe set about giving Charles a rough and ready training in the acting trade. After three years, Attwood cast Charles opposite his pretty daughter Lucy and they promptly fell in love. It didn't last; Lucy's parents sent her away to join a professional repertory theatre. Charles gave up the strolling life and went to try his luck with a Birmingham professional theatre. By his 20th birthday he was holding his own with the "stars" that came slumming from the West End. He caught the train to London: Mr. Charles Dawson, actor.

The story caught up with Charles Dawson now actor-manager of a theatre in the East End struggling to fend off bankruptcy. The narrative came to a violent and catastrophic end with Dawson's death in a dangerous stunt on stage.

I read the document twice from beginning to end. Frankly, I was no wiser at the finish. What mattered, as far as I could see was not the story itself but the use Benson had made of it.

Next morning Jason arrived with his report on the Sunnyside visit neatly typed. I glanced through it and found that he had picked up the main points. 'Good, sit down a minute. What school were you at?'

'St Cuthbert's'.

'You left in July this year? How well did you know Mrs Enderby?'

'Hardly at all, the year she came I was in the fifth form working for my five A's. After that it was the sixth, no time for drama.'

'Was she popular with the kids generally?'

'Not especially, apart from the ones who were stage-struck.'

'No gossip about her?'

'There was a daft rumour when I was in the first year sixth. Just before the end of the summer term she'd been seen in a pub in Preston with Mr Meyer, wink, wink. The sort of thing a leaver might invent. I think it was against Meyer rather than her, he was seriously unpopular.'

'Did anything come of it?'

'No,' said Jason, 'it was like hey lads hey, heard the latest? Two days later it had died.'

I got down to business, 'Right, if we can track down a man called Benson we can crack the case.' I explained why. 'Let's set the parameters as C. Benson (male), location maximum thirty miles from Ditchfield and listed in the telephone directory, or the electoral roll.' Jason pointed out that this took in a big area, Greater Manchester for example. 'I think C Benson lives somewhere rural, let's start with the telephone directories. He might be a farmer or a country lawyer. For starters we want a list of C Bensons with addresses and phone numbers. Pam will have the local directory in her office. You'll get the others in the town reference library. If one of the library staff asks what you're doing, say that you're an assistant with a local solicitor and you're searching in connection with an unclaimed inheritance. Better say it's a small one, we don't want them excited.'

Jason was keen to get on. 'While you're at the reference library, you could do something else.' He sat down again. 'This may not be the first murder at Fellbeck. I need to find the newspaper reports on the earlier case. They could give us a lead. Ask if they keep the *Ditchfield Express* back numbers in the archives.' Jason was on his feet. I didn't want him raising too much dust in the archives, not yet. 'Hold your horses,' I cautioned, 'see how far you can get in the office. Then go into the library and list all the C Bensons from the other directories. After that, speak to someone in the reference department and ask if they have the *Ditchfield Express* for 1933 to 1935. If they have, ask what the procedure is. You can say you're enquiring on behalf of a local historian and you can give my name and address. And think on,' I emphasised, 'Do not mention murders.'

'Do you think the Enderby murder might be some sort of copycat?'

'I don't know, Jason. The police don't want to know but we do.' It sounded pompous, 'Slot off, look in at midday and report. If I'm not here, put a note through the door.'

'Super!' said Jason and went. A beautiful young woman lies mutilated on a mortuary slab. Her lover is locked in a remand cell out of his mind with grief and shock. What has sensitive, idealistic and untarnished youth to say about that? "Super!"

I went to interrogate Potts, 'I expect you want to talk about the Benson document,' he said, 'well I haven't got time today, appointments wall to wall.' More tears on the carpet? I would never have suspected Ditchfield of such heights of emotion. I suggested meeting after hours.

'Say quarter to six?' he relented, 'I'm in town last thing, 5.45 at Julio's. Do you know it?' I did.

I moved to the seat of power. 'Not much chance of Tom today,' Pam said, 'how about this time tomorrow?'

'Tell him I expect to report massive progress.' Pam was so excited that she offered a "definite maybe" – ten minutes maximum. Also, my public phone line would be installed in the flat tomorrow.

I took a walk to the High Street. Wragby's, the electrical retailers, were still in business for big screen televisions, mobile phones and all the modern tat. Lance, thespian founder of the firm, had joined the Ditchfield underground twenty years back. The seventies had knocked the stuffing out of him: wife swapping had gone out at the same time as marriage and trade turned rough, Lance retired. One of his sons had inherited the business, he seemed to be making a do. I asked young Mr. Wragby if they hired out large audio equipment, powerful, the sort of thing a pop group might use.

Wragby junior wanted to know how powerful, 'We don't handle the really big stuff. What about two-fifty watts, run off a 13 amp socket?'

'It's information I'm after just now, a legal matter.' Wragby's expression moved into wary mode. 'All I need to know is did you hire out an audio set of about that size covering the period 23rd and 24th of November.' Wragby relaxed a bit and went to get the diary.

'No,' he said, 'it's the wrong end of the week. Professionals have their own equipment, most of the letting out is to people having weddings, private parties, hen nights. That means weekends. We're not the only ones round here, you could try elsewhere.' I thanked him, forbore to upset his feelings with a fiver and left. Another research job for Jason, I thought.

Jason returned at midday with C Bensons neatly listed. 'I got on really well,' he congratulated himself, 'out as far as

Greater Manchester going west, Huddersfield east, Lancaster and Bolton.' That was the easy part. The next job was to contact them all to find out how many had scratchy voices; that was going to be the killer. 'The library can help with the newspaper archives if you phone the department and make an appointment.' He gave me a slip with the phone number.

I sent him off to refuel. The cat expressed a similar interest. I reminded him that he had already eaten breakfast. I understood how he felt, but comfort eating was not the solution. After that I got out the tin opener.

I collected a small tool kit, the camera, an extra torch and gloves. I also equipped myself with the Irish blackthorn from the broom cupboard. Years back, we had bought it as a curiosity in Wicklow. I was not seriously expecting to need the services of a cudgel at Fellbeck but the mere feel of it does wonders for a nervous disposition.

When Jason returned, I briefed him for the afternoon. 'Now, game for an afternoon of cold calling? Sit here and start ringing these numbers. Ask to speak to Mr. C Benson. If he's out at work or something, ask when best to contact him. If you do get to speak to him, we're looking for a reasonably educated voice with a peculiar, scratchy tone to it. You should be able to spot that straightaway.'

'What's my excuse for ringing him,' Jason wanted to know.

We cooked up a narrative based on a fictitious insurance company who thought that Mr. Benson had a small policy with them that has just matured.

'If he's an honest Bensonian he'll deny the whole thing so you apologise for the error and ring off. If he's fly, he'll claim that he has such a policy. If that happens, ask him his date of birth and then the number of the policy.'

'I'd better use the code for withholding the caller's number, hadn't I?'

More evidence for the presence of brain cells! I agreed,

'That should keep you busy for a while. It'll probably take you all this afternoon at least. Write up your report, drop the catch on the door and I'll see you tomorrow.'

14

I got in the car and headed for Fellbeck. There were no cops wading in the beck, the tape had gone from the farm track and there was no fog like the one on my first visit but I hated this place, no error. There was no police presence at the house either. I continued along the track up the right hand side of the house. I drove into the yard, turned round and backed into the barn where the Merc was well out of sight from the Preston road.

I walked back and checked at the front of the house. The front door was locked. I walked round to the back on the beck side of the house trying the windows as the constable had done. They were all locked. The soft ground on that side of the house was well trampled with big boots two thirds of the way along; after that, nothing. When I got to the back of the house I stood back for a moment surveying it. Whereas the posh end of the house had immaculate stonework and massive windows, the masonry at the working end was rough and uneven as if the stones had been salvaged from an older and inferior structure. The windows were less than half the size. 'Nothing in that,' I thought, 'par for the course on the average stately home.'

At the back door, I pulled on gloves and got out my screwdriver. There was a simple hinged hasp that closed over a staple and was secured by a padlock. The staple was screwed to the doorpost. All four screws were visible, I only had to remove them to open the door. All four came out readily in fact, a bit too readily. Someone else had passed that way not long ago. The door handle and the hinges had also received a squirt of lubrication – murderer's own WD-40? I took my tool bag and torch in one hand, shillelagh in the other and stepped inside. I stood for a moment. The place was grave-silent and cold – colder in than out. I was in what had been the scullery with a big stone sink and an ancient wooden drainer. The small window over the sink was slarted with muck of ages so when I closed the back door the space was quite dim. I thought of opening the back door again then realised it would be seen from the road, so I left it.

I switched my torch on and hunted for the mains box. It was inside a wooden cupboard on the wall. It was the old cast iron type and rusty. The supply looked as if it had been disconnected and sealed off by the Electricity Board years back. I got the fuse box open. The fuses were present and correct – the old ceramic type with fuse wire. Bolton had said that the police parked their generator at the front door. Benson could have parked his at the back and wired the supply into the fuse box. For his quick blackout, all he needed to do was throw the main switch.

The door from the scullery into the main hallway was unlocked, there was no key. This was where Mrs. Watts had appeared. The corridor was almost dark but by shining my torch, I could see that it ran all the way up the house to the front door. I walked up the passage to the point where it opened out to form the entrance hall. There was some light in that area coming through the fanlight and the window opposite the foot of the stairs. The front door was locked; no key. I assumed that all keys had gone for fingerprinting.

I stood in the hall. It was exactly as I remembered. No feverish dream: I really did pay a call on Adam Ostrick six years ago. What did that do for my confidence? *(Don't stand frightening yourself, Hardy. Get on!)*

The door of the closet where Benson's computer had been was open. The space was tiny and windowless. A folded trestle table stood against the back wall. Alongside was a cheap bentwood chair, the sort found in church halls all across the land. There was no power point for Benson's computer and no light switch. By torch light I couldn't see where a high power loudspeaker might have been hidden. In the passage, I found a power socket screwed to the skirting board – the old 15 amp round pin type – handy for Mrs Watts's vacuum cleaner. I took flash photos of the computer closet, the hall and the main passage.

That left the sitting room where Chris had found Caroline's body. After forensics had crawled all over it, what could I expect to find? I started back down the passage. The sitting room door was open a crack. This was the hard one. I stopped for two deep breaths, I hadn't come here to be dufted, I pushed the door wide open and walked straight in. To my surprise I felt relieved. After fumbling about in the semi dark of the scullery and the hallway, there was light from three big sash windows overlooking the beck and two more giving onto the courtyard. It was all as I remembered from my 1992 "visit". I was nervous all over again.

I turned back to look at the door. There were marks around the handle but none of them new enough to be caused by Chris forcing the door. He had said that the chair blocking it had been flimsy. The floor was bare but the boards were of good quality – no recent scratch marks, no sign of a chair. I walked to the fireplace where Caroline's body had lain.

The hearthrug had gone with forensics. The same went for the blanket from the settee that Chris had put over her body. The only visible sign of what had taken place there was on the brass rail of the fender – several smears and a partial handprint in blood. The handprint was likely to be Chris's but that proved nothing given his reaction on finding the body. Why had the police left the fender behind? The fireplace was a big, imposing affair in carved stonework in proper stately home style. The fender by comparison looked cheap and undersized. This was not Ostrick's fender – I was nearly sure of that. There were no blood traces on the floorboards. All the blood must have been caught by the hearthrug.

There was an undisturbed heap of ashes in the grate and partially burnt ends of log. The log remains looked like those in the shed. The furniture was exactly as Chris had described. I went to look at the three sash windows on the long wall. The red curtains had once been of decent quality but now hung, moth-eaten. The catches were all engaged but there was mud on the sill of the middle window – where PC Cartwright had climbed in? Was leaving one window catch open deliberate? It had channelled the police into the house at the point where almost the first thing picked out by the PC's torch was Caroline's body.

It all looked more foul than frightening. I went to the door at the top corner of the sitting room; it was open – again no key. The room beyond was much bigger – five windows worth instead of three – and empty. What had gone on here? Billiards? Banquets for thirty covers? Board meetings? There were two more doors at the far end of the room replicating the sitting room arrangement. One on the right led out into the passage close to the scullery door, the other straight ahead into the kitchens, which were large, and from there into the scullery and the back door. The murderers' escape route?

For reference purposes, I decided to call the big space "the dining room". As I walked back I noticed spots scattered on the bare floorboards close to the sitting room door. When I got down for a proper look there was a scattered trail extending a few feet from the door. I photographed the trail of spots then got my penknife out and scraped at one of them. It came up easily. It was red candle wax. The one next to it was green. I bagged the samples.

The trail stopped at the door. There were no traces on the sitting room floor. It was as if someone had hurried to the door with a lighted candle in each hand, one red, one green and had become aware of the falling drips of molten wax and done something to catch them before continuing.

I went back into the sitting room and closed the connecting door behind me. The light was fading now. The room had changed. In the shadows, it was instantly sinister. Had I come here to sense something of Caroline, some sort of message? (*What are you Hardy? Psychic clairvoyant or polybag manufacturer?*) The room held nothing but a frozen memory of what had been done there – pure evil.

I came out of the sitting room leaving the door open as before. There was a similar door in the passage facing me. Again, it was unlocked, and giving onto an empty space.

I walked down the corridor and through the scullery door. I got out of the house, shut the back door and began to screw the padlock assembly back into place. At that moment I realised that I had left my shillelagh in the scullery. It could wait. No it couldn't. I took the screws out again, stepped back into the scullery and picked up the blackthorn from the draining board ... stopped and froze. There was a sound from within the house – heavy footsteps walking steadily away up the passage. I moved to the door that shut the scullery off from the main passage and stood listening. They stopped. I was shaking, I don't mind admitting, I was terrified of what might be on the other side of that door.

I took a grip on my shillelagh and something primeval came over me. I was going through that door to have it out with whoever or whatever was on the other side. I grabbed the door handle and then common sense took hold. What if it was the police? How could I explain myself? I would be well out of order – breaking and entering at a crime scene. I left by the back door, closed it quietly and ran the four screws back into place. Feeling braver now, I walked down the side of the house as far as the corner, taking care not to look into any of the windows en route. The forecourt was empty.

I put the toolkit in the car and started the engine. When I reached the high ground outside Coldedge I stopped. According to Chris's statement, Benson must have had a power supply of sorts – lights at the front door, in the passage and in the sitting room and power for the computer. After all these years, what was the state of Fellbeck's wiring? There was an easy way to find out – all I needed was the instrument for the job. I got out my mobile and phoned Tom Burns, the maintenance engineer at the works. 'Tommy? Ken Hardy here, could you do me a favour? I want to borrow a megger, the small one. It's for checking a domestic wiring job – just a couple of days.'

I drove into Ditchfield and round to the back door of the works. The steady humming from within was reassuring. Tommy Burns was in his workshop. He handed the instrument over. I promised to take care of it, remembered a personal word about Tommy's cancer-stricken wife and left. Everything was running. They didn't need me any more.

15

I marched through the front door of St Cuthbert's carrying my passport – the pile of children's homework books from Chris's flat. There was no one at reception, the building was deserted and silent apart from the sporadic banging of doors as the cleaners moved from room to room. I was banking on Gloria, the lab technician still being there. I did not want to meet Meyer – not yet. I walked to the end of the main corridor and out at the back of the main building. To my right was the entrance to the modern science block. I climbed the wide staircase designed to take a stampede of kids, six abreast, and found the laboratories. There were three or four offices in the corridor opposite, the middle one was Meyer's. I guessed that the unlabelled door opposite was the prep room. I got it open without dropping the homework books and pushed inside. I was met by a friendly black face. 'You look out of breath,' it said, 'what's to do?'

'I've been legging it round the school carrying this lot,' I said, dumping the pile on the bench, 'they're for you, well, for Mr Meyer I suppose.'

'You'd better sit down,' Gloria invited. I sat on a lab stool and explained that I was Ken Hardy, Chris Berry's neighbour. Gloria's sunny expression vanished, 'go on.'

'He was carrying this pile of books when he came home the evening of the murder. They were found in his flat.'

Gloria took the first two or three from the top of the pile and flicked through. 'That's right; he hasn't marked them yet.' She showed me. 'These are 3A's science homework books.' She went to the large departmental timetable pinned to the wall.

'3A science, Tuesday afternoon; he must have collected their homework. He did most of his marking here – liked to spread things out on the bench. I remember him coming in with these. He said something about kids getting confused over melting and dissolving because when sugar disappears in hot tea, Mam says "it's melted".'

'Took his teaching seriously?'

'I'd say so,' said Gloria, stoutly, 'when this mess gets cleared up, he'll make a bloody good teacher – there! Meyer or no Meyer,' she added.

'It must have been a shock to the whole school,' I said.'

'Place in an uproar, Mrs. Enderby dead and Mr. Berry arrested, then he's in court charged with her murder and finally they were having an affair.'

'You know him, probably better than anyone else here,' I suggested, 'do you think that Chris Berry would be capable of murder?'

Gloria was not for messing around, 'No', she said, 'I don't care what the police say. It's wrong and I'll get up in court and tell the judge to his face. Chris Berry teaches physics, nice and clean – no blood. But last year Meyer handed him Barry Walker's biology fourth years for a week – three classes, Barry was off on some course. On their timetable that week was the anatomy of the common rat. That meant killing a rat and pinning it out on a board to display the spinal column and the main organs. Kids love it, little buggers.

Could he kill a rat? Could he heck; I did it for him – three times. Even then he had to rush out to be sick. I ask you, a man that can't dissect a dead rat is supposed to have slashed his girlfriend's throat open and left her on the floor bleeding to death...?' Gloria rested her case.

'He didn't get on right well with Meyer, did he?'

Gloria sniffed, 'Who does?' she had second thoughts, 'don't misunderstand me, Meyer is brilliant with the top stream, gets them into universities all over. He's not that interested in the rest. Chris is the other way round – keeps wanting to rescue the dropouts.'

'You might expect some sort of compromise.' I went into my pocket and pulled out one of the cards I'd printed. I passed it to Gloria. 'Look', I said, 'I'm sorry, I should have told you this at first, but I was a bit short of breath. I live over Harrison and Potts the solicitors. Chris's flat is on the top floor above mine so we know each other. Tom Harrison is Chris's defence lawyer. When this happened I offered to help Chris's defence team with collecting information. So, do you mind if I ask you about a couple of other things? In confidence, it won't go any further than Harrison; you've got my word on that.'

'Try me', said Gloria, 'if I don't like it, I won't tell you.'

'How long has Meyer been here?'

'Ages of a duck,' said Gloria, 'he was here when I first came and then he went abroad for a spell. To South Africa, that's where he's from originally. When I first came, he was head of physics – that's one below head of science. He was never what you'd call sociable but he seemed to get on well enough. Then all of a sudden he packed it in and went off to South Africa.'

'Any idea why?'

'He never said. Bear in mind this is a church school. Most people thought he'd got the call and gone to teach in a Christian mission school. Then, five or six years ago, he came back as head of science. He was a different man altogether. Of course, he has the authority now, so he can do things his way. That's what he's been doing ever since.'

'How did he get on with Caroline Enderby?'

Gloria reared up straightaway, 'What's that supposed to mean?'

I grinned, hoping it looked conciliatory, 'I spoke to an ex-pupil. He hadn't done science or drama so he didn't have an axe to grind. He said that a rumour went round at the end of the summer term a couple of years back. Apparently, Meyer was seen with Mrs. Enderby in a bar in Preston. My informant thinks the tale was malicious.'

Gloria laughed, 'If the headmaster was found in bed with the Canon it might cause a stir – but Meyer and Mrs Enderby in a pub in Preston? Even the kids didn't reckon that one.'

'No basis?'

Gloria said, 'Meyer helped Mrs. Enderby out when she first came. He built bits of scenery for her productions, helped her with the lighting and that. She used to come up to science now and again. Then she stopped.' I asked why. 'Probably disagreed about something – that's Meyer, he gets on with people to a point and then falls out. He's bought a place in the sticks, started restoring it – probably had enough on his plate never mind scenery for Caroline.'

'Do you know anything about a man called "Benson"?'

'You mean the one that keeps ringing Chris up and pestering him?'

'Did you ever pick up his calls?'

'Only when Chris wasn't here. After hours the science calls come through to this phone because I'm here until five. This is where Chris sits to do his marking. If it rang he would answer it. I picked up two of Benson's calls last summer. I didn't like talking to the feller, gave me the creeps,' said Gloria, 'croaked like a crow with a sore throat, never left a message. First time, he wouldn't even give his name, just asked for Mr. Berry. I said, 'well he's not here', and put the phone down. The second time I asked him straight out if he was Mr. Benson and he said "yes".'

Good enough, I thought, at least he didn't deny it. 'I don't think you'll hear from him again. If he does phone you could say, "Mr. Berry isn't here" and then ring off. Ring me at the number on the card and let me know. Would you do that?' Gloria said she would. 'On the two occasions when you answered, can you remember where Chris was at the time? I mean was he somewhere else in the school or was he offsite altogether?'

'Now you're asking,' said Gloria, 'it's a long time back to remember a small thing like that.'

'Can you remember the dates?'

'No. I would have told Chris that Benson was asking for him...'

I persisted, 'roughly when, would you say?'

Gloria was getting flustered, 'At a guess, one in June and the other not long before the end of term – middle of July? I couldn't swear to either, mind.'

'If anything does comes to mind, will you let me know?'

'I can't stand injustice,' Gloria said, 'I cried myself to sleep on the Wednesday night after he'd been arrested.' *(So did I lass, so did I)*.

'If I've got owt to do with it, never mind getting off, it won't even come to court,' I thanked Gloria, rather profusely for me, and left.

I drove into town. Julio's bar was buzzing with trendy Ditchfield. Lance Wragby would have felt at home, I didn't. There were no curly-haired, short sighted solicitors on view, so I edged to the bar. I asked the stocky, hairy-armed barman about beer – 'bottled or Azzura on tap?' he offered. I thought Azzura was something to do with their rugby team but decided to chance it. I got a demi in a tall thin glass for twice the price of a pint of Thwaites. I found a spot on a leather two-seater and sipped until Niall came through the doors without busting his nose against the glass and located me by a process of elimination. He accepted a small white wine.

'Nice weekend? How is the lovely Virginia?'

Niall looked at his watch, 'the lovely Virginia is fine thanks and will continue that way for a further ten minutes.' He opened his briefcase and rummaged inside.

'Before we start,' I said, 'I've established that a person

calling himself Benson does exist and he has made telephone calls to the science department at St. Cuthbert's.' I told him that Gloria had taken his calls on two occasions and that her description of his voice matched what Chris had stated.

Niall was sceptical, 'That's not decisive. The defence line is that Benson set the whole thing up, lured Chris and Caroline to Fellbeck and there, with one or more accomplices, murdered Caroline. The prosecution can argue that Chris decided to murder Caroline and used Benson's document for an alibi.'

'Some alibi – guaranteed to land him on a murder charge?' I said, 'let's stick to Benson's document. What do you make of it? Do you think that Chris could have written it himself?'

'I think it's most unlikely, either the content or the calligraphy.'

'What was Benson's motive?' I wanted to know. 'Why devise a complicated scheme to murder Caroline and leave Chris carrying the can?' I supped the last of my Italian beer and decided to hang the expense and risk another. Niall declined an encore having barely started on his wine.

When I got back Niall was gazing into infinity, polishing his specs and lost in thought. Progress on his wine was negligible. I prompted him back to the subject in hand. 'Oh yes …'

I said, 'The first job that Benson gave to Chris was a set of printed address labels. Those names were the same as those listed on his website. What were the address labels for – Christmas cards? Is Benson a hoaxer or a fantasist? Or was it a ploy to get Chris hooked?'

'This isn't a smoking gun, Ken,' Niall got up, 'if I've the time, I'll perhaps look at one or two angles.' *(Or perhaps not)*. 'I wouldn't bother Tom with all this – far too speculative at the moment.'

'I'm seeing him tomorrow. Shall I just say that we're making progress?'

'If you like,' said Niall, he glanced at his watch, 'Oh God!' and dived for the exit leaving me forlorn. My theory about the

Benson document hadn't impressed Niall. It was plain that he didn't want to be involved and he was right about Tom, so that left it to me. My second Azzura was turning sour.

The bar had cleared. It was the lull between the five o'clock swill and the start of the evening business. The barman was tidying up. 'Yerate?' he asked. I said a single malt might help to rescue the taste buds. 'How did you get on with the Azzura?' I told him, he grinned, 'It's not an all night boozing beer, 'it's a sipping lager for chatting up signorinas on the terrazzo. This your first time in here? I'm Julio.' He offered a Roman paw. His accent was no more Italian than mine. Perhaps he was a descendant of one of the POWs.

'I saw you talking to Niall Potts – not about the Enderby case?'

'No,' I said, 'I'm not CID, it was about my divorce.'

'Terrible,' said Julio, 'terrible. She used to come in here. She was a lovely girl.' He leaned confidentially over the bar giving me a garlic blast. He lowered his voice, 'but she did put it around a bit. Last August...'

'Julio?' a young man had arrived at the bar with a shipping order for six. I'd had enough wine bar chit-chat. I knocked back my whisky and left.

16

'We've got the pathology report,' Tom said, 'the pathologist attended the scene of crime at 23.35 on Tuesday 23rd. He estimates time of death as between 20.00 and 22.00.

"The subject was female, in her late twenties, well nourished, exercised and in excellent health, height five feet eight inches, weight eight stone ten pounds, sexually active but no evidence of connection during the last five days."

'Not since she was last with Chris.'

Tom carried on reading, "Details of clothing…".

'That matches what she was wearing when they left my flat.'

"Cause of death: the skull exhibits a depressed fracture on the back of the head that would have incapacitated the victim causing immediate loss of consciousness. The injury severe but survivable, given the age and physical condition of the subject, assuming prompt medical attention followed by surgery. The skull fracture is consistent with a blow from a hard spherical object of five to six inches diameter, possibly a large pebble of the sort used for edging garden beds or a rounded cobble. If the victim was standing at the time the injury resulted from a blow struck from behind by a right-handed male of average strength and height. If she was seated it is also possible that the assailant was a woman.

The fatal injury – a massive wound to the throat – was inflicted almost immediately afterwards. The blood traces were consistent with the victim having been laid on the hearthrug as subsequently discovered by the police. That is, on her back with her head to the left hand end of the fireplace. The assailant, again right handed was probably kneeling on the nearside of the body, gripping the victim's face between the cheek and chin with his left hand and turning the head as the knife was drawn across the throat with his right, probably with the intention of avoiding blood spurts. The wound was inflicted with considerable force and dexterity, the knife being inserted about two inches below the ear and drawn round the throat in a single movement separating the skin, the blood vessels, windpipe and gullet and all the subcutaneous structures down to the spinal column, which was exposed. The instrument used was a sharp, strong bladed knife with a pointed tip having a blade length of five to six inches. A slaughter man's knife is a possibility and the nature and execution of the wound suggests a person familiar with the technique of animal slaughter. The wound to the throat was not survivable. There was minor bruising to facial areas consistent with the above. The assailant was wearing gloves."

'Were there any other injuries?'

Tom read on, "... no defence injuries, no tissue fragments under the fingernails, no restraint marks." He paused, and then said, 'It's clear that Caroline was taken by surprise. The only consolation is that she never knew what was happening – a blow on the back of the head and then blackout. There was minor bruising on the cheek and the chin caused by the face having been gripped between thumb and fingers of the assailant's left hand whilst he was in the act of cutting the throat."

'Horrible. When can we view the scene of the crime?'

'Now,' said Tom. 'The defence has the right to view the SOC at the police's discretion. I sent Jason to pick up a key from the agents.' He produced it from his desk drawer and waved it at me. It wasn't as big as that to the Bloody Tower, but getting on that way. 'The police have the front door key they recovered at the scene; I spoke to Evans about it. It'll be an exhibit. There were no fingerprints on it, it had been wiped.'

'We'll need torches, there's no power at Fellbeck. Alison Bolton says that the police brought their own lighting kit and parked it by the front door.' We collected gloves and other useful bits and bats.

'What's in that bag?' Tom asked. I told him to wait and see. We set off, Tom driving. On the way, I told Tom about my visit to Sunnyside with Jason. 'Neither John Bolton or his daughter, Alison heard low flying aircraft on Tuesday evening. When I asked in Coldedge, I got the same answer. Low-level training exercises are an issue locally, but they only happen in summer. It was dark and foggy: suicidal that evening. During the war they weren't fussy about safety until there was a triple crash in 1944 – three pilots written off.'

'What do we make of that?' Tom asked, 'is Chris wrong? It's hard to see how he could have been mistaken.'

'The noise was real but it wasn't a real aircraft. A recording played through an amplifier and loudspeaker could have done it. I'm getting Jason to research hirers of audio kits.'

There was a welcoming committee at Fellbeck comprising one overweight PC in wellies. 'What does he want?'

'It's usual for the police to accompany,' said Tom.

''Arrison and Potts?' asked the law. I confirmed without mentioning that, although Tom was 'Arrison, I was not Potts. The cop brandished his ID, 'PC Dunn from Coldedge, not going to be long are you? I've got a sheep stealing to attend.' That and his mud-plastered Panda confirmed that Dunn was not a sharp-nosed tec from CID. Things could have been worse.

I pointed out to Tom that the forecourt was surfaced with small gravel. If Caroline was hit with a cobble or a rounded stone, the murderers must have brought it with them. While Tom unlocked the front door, I commiserated with the local law. 'Nasty business,' I said.

'No error, every year there's more of it. Sheep spread out for miles around. How am I supposed to stop it by mysen?'

'Difficult, especially if you're pulled off the job for this sort of duty; bit of a waste of time for you, this?' PC Dunn ventured no opinion.

It was cold and gloomy inside. I pointed to the fitting in the hall ceiling, 'that's the light that came on before Benson opened the door.'

Tom reached up and removed the bulb – forty watts, 'That would have been dim in this space.'

I suggested that we went through the house in the same order as in Chris's statement. That meant starting at the computer closet. 'You couldn't swing a small conker in here,' Tom said. 'I take it the computer tower was under the table, but where was it plugged in?' I pointed to the fifteen-amp power point in the passage. That left the question of the equipment for the sound effects – where could that have been? Given that the only light in the closet came from the monitor screen, which was in his face, Chris might have failed to see the loudspeaker. I needed to test that.

I checked inside the closet, 'there's a trestle table and chair here,' I said, 'both folded up and standing against the wall. Sitting room,' I said. PC Dunn followed us as far as the door then stood leaning against the doorpost. He was not taking notes.

The bloodstained brass fender had gone. That was a relief because it explained the footsteps – nothing more ghostly than a welly-booted cop retrieving evidence. I had Dunn pencilled in for the job.

Tom was looking at the fireside chairs, 'Both have high backs,' he pointed out, 'if she was sitting there, Mrs Watts could have delivered the blow but it would have landed on the top of Caroline's head.

'Not if she was leaning forward towards the fire,' I said, 'either way you'd expect blood on the chair.'

Tom went on undeterred, 'If Caroline was standing up Mrs.

Watts couldn't have knocked Caroline out by herself. According to Chris, Benson was with him when Mrs Watts brought Caroline in here. It's looking like three murderers: Benson, Mrs. Watts and a third – a reasonably tall man, probably.'

I drew Tom's attention to the fireplace. 'What about the fire? Who lit that and when?' I pointed to the heap of ashes in the grate. 'Look at the log ends there, quite thick, aren't they? There was enough light from the fire for Chris to find Caroline's body. By the time he came back with the police the flames had died out, but the embers were still hot.'

'We'll see what forensic say.'

I was examining the carvings on the stone fireplace. 'Wasn't short of a bob, this Ezra Dawson, was he?' A pair of carved bosses had caught my eye. I got my camera out and photographed them: shallow circular domes with carved borders round the edges. I pointed it out but Tom was more interested in the floorboards. 'I thought the murderer could have cracked her head against one of these bosses,' I said, 'but they don't tally with the fracture – too large in diameter, much too flat.'

Tom had not found any bloodstains on the floorboards. 'It looks as if the hearthrug stopped all the blood.' We looked round the room, not that there was much to see. Apart from the area in front of the fireplace it was almost bare. I encouraged Tom to look at the windows and let him find the mud on one of the central windowsills. 'That's where the policeman climbed in,' he announced. I felt a bit of a fraud.

I opened the door to the next room. 'This is massive', I said, walking in, 'the sitting room has three windows on the long wall, this one has five. What do you reckon went on in here?' We followed the routes through the connecting doors to the kitchens. 'We could refer to this as the dining room,' I said. Tom had no alternative to propose. 'I bet this was the murderers' escape route. After cutting Caroline's throat they came out this way, locking the connecting door behind them.

If the access doors along the corridor were all locked, Chris had nowhere to go except upstairs or out through the front door.'

I took him back to the sitting room door, hoping that he'd notice the wax drips. He did! "Hawkeyed lawyer spots vital evidence".

I offered to bag a sample of each colour. 'Interesting to see if forensic noticed them, but I doubt if they're evidence.' I said discouragingly. I didn't speculate on their value as pointers to the murderers' motives. I thought it might be one for Niall – but was he interested?

We came out of the sitting room into the corridor. PC Dunn asked hopefully, 'Is that it then, gents?'

'Not quite,' I told him, 'say another twenty to thirty minutes, that all right officer?'

It wasn't, Dunn's honest face fell a mile. Then he brightened up: idea! 'I need a word with John Bolton about these sheep stolen from his neighbour. Happen he noticed summat. If I nip off and back here in half an hour, alright with you?' We had no wish to impede PC Dunn. He clumped off giving a fair imitation of the noises that had put the wind up me on my illegal visit.

I tried the door on the opposite wall of the passage which was unlocked like the rest. It opened into another large empty space – morning room? Study? The room was the same size as the sitting room, running parallel up to the front of the house. 'It's not exactly the same,' I said. From where we stood, the top right hand corner had been partitioned off to form the space under the stairs occupied by the computer closet. I walked up and banged on the wall. It was no more than a wooden panel. 'This is where the audio equipment might have been,' I said, 'a pair of powerful loudspeakers hard up against this partition would have made all the noise they needed to cover Benson's exit.'

'All adds to the stuff they had to move for the getaway,' Tom said. That was bothering me too.

Able to talk more freely, we took a second look at the murder room. I proposed, 'Suppose the third murderer was waiting behind the door – in the corner here with the door open? Mrs. Watts came in first and switched the lights on, Caroline followed her in and...'

Tom agreed, 'That fits what Chris saw. The third murderer grabbed her from behind, probably with his hand over her mouth and hit her on the back of the head. Mrs. Watts closed the door, "firmly", and wedged the chair under the door handle. They carried Caroline, unconscious, over to the fireplace, laid her down on the hearth rug and set about the butchery. Meanwhile, Benson was with Chris by the computer. The aircraft recording was already running, covering the sound of any scuffle in the sitting room. While Chris was busy on the computer, Benson slipped away "to reassure the ladies", actually to kill the lights. That left Chris fumbling his way to the sitting room in the dark while the murderers made themselves scarce through the connecting door which they locked behind them.' Tom's interpretation was the same as mine.

'Let's have a look at the electrics,' I said. We walked to the end of the central passage and through the door into the back scullery. 'Chris says that this door was also locked,' I reminded Tom, 'preventing him from seeing what was going off out the back. My guess is that after the murder the gang got busy outside loading the generator for the getaway.' Tom found the electricity board's distribution panel and fuse box. 'Someone's been here recently,' I said, 'there's dust over everything in this place except the fuse box lid which has been wiped clean. Why?'

I got out the megger. 'I thought we should test the wiring,' I said, 'I expect it's pretty well shot-at.' I connected to the first circuit and cranked the instrument. 'See that? That's the insulation breaking down. If you connected the mains supply to this circuit you'd blow the main fuse or set the house on fire.'

There were four circuits. The first three failed. The fourth was much better, not brilliant, but adequate. 'See, this circuit has got PVC insulation, the others are the pre-war rubber-covered stuff – well perished by now. If this is the one that feeds the 15 amp power point in the hall, we're on to something.' We went back up the hall and I took the cover off the power point. 'There you are – PVC. I cut a short length from the cable in my bag, bared the ends and inserted the loop in the live and neutral terminals. 'Could you hold that in place?' I asked Tom, 'you won't get a shock – it's only 5 volts.' Bravely, he agreed. I went back to the fuse box and put the multimeter across the circuit, *bleep*! Zero resistance. I went back to relieve Tom. 'The one half-decent circuit from the fuse box feeds this socket, possibly the downstairs lights as well. This is where Benson plugged his computer in. Just to be sure, let's try the same trick on one of the light fittings that Chris says was working.' I fetched the kitchen stool from the scullery and we tested the light fitting in the hall then the wall lights in the sitting room – all on the same circuit. 'That means that Benson only had to throw the switch on the fuse box to turn off the computer and all the lights.'

Our 30 minutes was up but there was no sign of our bold gendarme. We checked upstairs. On the first floor were five empty bedrooms and two antiquated bathrooms with Edwardian plumbing. At the far end was a door opening onto a narrow staircase leading down to the kitchens and up to the second floor housing empty storerooms and a pair of garret bedrooms for servants; the usual Victorian "back stairs" arrangement all draped in Miss Havisham-style cobwebs. There was access from the second floor up to the loft – we didn't bother.

'That's good enough for me,' I said, 'why not lock up and have a quick look outside? Give me the key and I'll get it back to the agents after.'

Tom was locking up when the Panda appeared. PC Dunn wound down his window revealing evidence of his visit to Sunnyside – egg yolk and toast crumbs round the mouth. 'All done. Thanks for your help officer.' Dunn executed a smart U-turn, narrowly missing Tom's lawyerly Lancia and left.

We walked down the side of the house to what had been the farmyard. I explained that John Bolton used the old farm buildings as a store for animal feed and fertilizer.

'If they had a mobile generator at the back door,' Tom asked, 'how did they get the power into the house?' We went to investigate. It did not take an engineer to spot the makeshift padlock arrangements on the back door.

Tom slipped a card between the lock and the door jamb. 'This door isn't locked, the proper key must be missing and the padlock was fitted instead.'

I inspected the arrangement Oscar-style, 'A pretty cheap one at that. Remove these four screws and then you can swing the padlock out of the way and open the door.' I spoke with authority based on experience, 'see the oil traces? It could have been the police but having rubbished Chris's statement on sight I doubt whether they were interested in the back of the house.'

Tom was casting around, 'You can't see Sunnyside from here, if the gang parked a van at the back door they couldn't have been seen from the house and they wouldn't even need to unload the generator and reload it afterwards.'

I said, 'Suppose the gang arrived at seven. It was dark. The Boltons had finished for the day, locked up, had their tea, and settled down in front of the telly before bedtime at nine. The murderers had an hour and a half to prepare and light the fire before Chris and Caroline showed up.'

We went back to the car. Tom got his mobile out to check with the office – no signal. 'Chris states that he couldn't get a signal from here meaning he had to drive up to Coldedge to call the police. Later, the police were able to call for backup but theirs is a different system.'

Tom drove back up the hill to Coldedge and phoned Pam. 'All hell let loose,' he said, 'I need to get straight back.' After that, he went quiet. A tour of Fellbeck was enough to shut anybody up.

'Nothing decisive either way is there?'

Tom gave a noncommittal grunt, then, 'Why not get together, say at five tomorrow afternoon and we can have a general run through the evidence? I may have some forensics results by then.'

When we got back I went in search of Jason. 'How did you get on tracing Bensons?' He showed me his list complete with results and comments. He had only been able to contact five C. Bensons during the afternoon. None sounded likely candidates and none of them had anything strange about their vocal chords. I thought he might do better on a Saturday morning. I had sent the lad on a bad errand, 'You've done very well, Jason,' I said, 'I think we'll file these results for now and try a more promising angle,' that cheered him up.

I explained, 'Could you get on to the electricity board and find out when the Fellbeck supply was cut off? Tell them it's a legal matter for Harrison and Potts and let me know if they get difficult. After that, it's off to the library again for the Yellow Pages. The murderers had to have a power supply; most likely they would have hired a small petrol generator. Go through the same areas as before for names, addresses and phone numbers of businesses that offer small mobile generators, say 250 to 500 watts.'

I phoned Gloria at St Cuthbert's, 'It's Ken Hardy here, can you speak for a moment? Have you found any clues on Chris's whereabouts when you picked up Benson's calls?' Negative, she couldn't give dates for any of Benson's calls. 'Not to worry. Who's usually on the reception desk?'

'Betty, most likely', said Gloria, 'the desk closes at four thirty then they switch to night service. Betty's the fat one.'

At St Cuthbert's I found plump Betty at reception and passed her my card, fresh from my PC: *K Hardy BSc (Eng), A.M.I.MechE, Paralegal Consultant.* I asked if she remembered the person who had delivered a packet for Mr. Berry during the summer term. 'I never got much of a look at him. When he came to deliver packets for Mr Berry, he put them down on the desk, said "for Berry" and walked out. The time he came to collect, he didn't say a lot more.' When pressed, Betty remembered he wore a jacket with the hood up, in spite of it being summer.

17

It was time to clear up old Dick Barber's story about the previous murder at Fellbeck. I phoned the library on the number Jason had given me. I got a lively sounding girl at the other end, and explained what I wanted. 'When would you like to come round?' Now, if possible. 'Just hold on a minute, love,' she sounded the sort sometimes referred to as "bubbly". I tend to interpret that as blonde curls, quick-release knickers and minimal brains but that's my chauvinist prejudice. Back came the bubbly one, 'That'll be all right. Come to the desk and ask for misdeeds in archives.' *(Wow!)*

Bubbles was on the desk when I arrived. 'Isn't he lovely?' she said, 'will he be coming again?' She meant Jason. I mentioned my own interest and Bubbles rang through to archives, 'Take a seat, misdeeds will come up.'

Miss Deedes arrived five minutes later. She was a daunting prospect, a gaunt woman in her mid-fifties with grey hair cropped military style, a beak nose which ran parallel to her jutting chin, which in turn continued in a straight line up her jaw to the back of her head. (*Definitely not "bubbly" – has to be a genius*). I explained what I was looking for – a murder near Coldedge, probably in November 1934. 'Come along, Mr. Hardy,' said the gaunt one. We descended to the bowels of the library. There rows of racks with hanging folders. 'Everything after 1960 is on microfilm,' Miss Deedes explained, 'but the earlier copies are still kept here.' She found the folders she was looking for, carried the loot to a large table and handed me a pair of latex gloves. 'I'll be up at the far end, come and find me when you've finished, or if you're in difficulties. As you're an author, I don't need to warn you to handle the copies with care.' She stalked off. I had forgotten that I was an author.

I worked through November 1934 without finding any murders, in Coldedge or elsewhere. September, October and December gave the same result – depressingly law-abiding. I found Miss Deedes and reported zero progress. 'How did you come to hear of this event?' she asked. I explained about Dick. 'Very well,' said the archivist, 'it's unlikely that Mr. Barber invented it. You've confirmed what he told you about his great grandfather from a documentary source?' In Miss Deedes' book, if it was documented it was top gen. 'He's probably mixed the dates up. Let's try the card index.' She set off and I followed at the trot. She picked out a card index box and dialled M for Murder. 'Nothing there, but "C for Coldedge" and there we are, it wasn't November 1934. It was reported in the edition of Tuesday 24th of April 1934. The murder was the previous day: Monday the 23rd.'

I was surprised that Dick had been so far out with his date. Miss Deedes asked whether he had assigned more than one event to the same day.

'Yes, a significant personal event,' I spared her the details.

Miss Deedes said, 'People do it all the time and not just the older ones. Memories seem to hang in clusters, sometimes in chronological order, and sometimes not.' She found the original newspaper articles for me. There were two on successive days, the first of the shock, horror sort with precious little information: *Double Killing at Coldedge*. The next day, after the newspaper had got to the facts, *Actress Murdered at Coldedge Farm, Farmer Found Hanged*. She also turned up the report on the subsequent inquest. 'Happy now, Mr Hardy? Sit down and feast on horrors.' She made a triumphant exit between the storage racks.

It did not take long to get the facts; coming to terms with

them was something else. The body of actress Miss Jenny Finch, an occasional visitor at Fellbeck Farm near Coldedge was discovered in the farmhouse parlour with her throat horribly slashed. Jenny's photograph hit me like a ton of bricks. It was my Jenny Finch; the actress with a lovely smile – Jenny Finch in life, Jenny who had taken coffee with me in Ditchfield and chatted about her personal problems while in reality, sixty-odd years later, I was asleep in front of the telly and Caroline was being murdered at Fellbeck. The other picture was no comfort, either: "the farmer, Mr. Nathaniel Ostrick, was found hanging from a beam in the barn, having taken his own life. No suicide note has been found but it is understood that the police are not seeking any other person in connection with the deaths. We can also reveal that Mr. Ostrick was formerly a professional actor appearing under the stage name of Vernon Adams". There he was in a fuzzy photo – the farmer with the face of a Slavic bandit. The man I had tried to interest in silage making while his mind was on his absent visitor who had missed her bus. It said why my encounter in the coffee shop was more like a spring day than November. It was the morning of 23rd April 1934. Jenny Finch died that afternoon. It meant that my meeting with Ostrick, *aka* Adams was not in November 1992. It was on the day of Jenny's previous visit in November 1933, *(I was born eight months later!)*. I was shaken, badly shaken. I sat and stared at the article in disbelief. Had I been talking to ghosts? Was I insane, psychotic or what?

I went to the report on the inquest. Jenny had suffered a serious head injury before the dreadful throat wound that had ended her life. In the pathologist's opinion she had fallen or been pushed against a hard surface probably during a violent quarrel. He favoured one of the carved bosses on the stone fireplace. It had caused a fracture of the skull, rendering her unconscious. The head injury was not necessarily fatal, but when the victim was lying on her back, her throat had been violently cut across from the left hand angle of the jaw to the opposite side exposing the spinal column. The likely murder weapon was a sharp, strong bladed pointed knife, six inches long. Despite a diligent police search, the murder weapon had not been found but there was no doubt that Mr. Ostrick was responsible for her injuries: his hands and clothing were heavily stained with Miss Finch's blood. His coat was damp suggesting he walked out to the barn in a heavy downpour.

My coat was damp on the night Caroline was murdered. Where had I been? Doing what? It was too horrible to think about. I was tempted to walk away. *(Just get on with it Hardy. Pull out now and it'll haunt you.)*

Mr Griffiths, the Fellbeck foreman gave evidence that he had heard raised voices from within the house about an hour previously. He had no doubt that Miss Finch was arguing with a man who he assumed to have been Mr. Ostrick. He remarked that the man's voice had been unlike the farmer's normal tone, being harsh and coarse-sounding, compared with Ostrick's usual way of speaking which was refined. He put this down to Mr. Ostrick being in a furious temper. There was no possibility of there being a second man at the house that afternoon. Griffiths said that he spent a couple of hours with two of the farmhands hedging and ditching along the farm lane (getting pretty wet in the process) and no one had passed that way (Unless they were hiding from the rain on the other side of the wall). Mr. Griffiths further stated that he went to the house to report that he had brought the men back on account of the weather. There was no one in the office, so he looked in at the parlour door and found the body of Miss Finch. He used the office telephone to call the police. There was no one else in the house it being the housekeeper's half day off. Mrs Watts *(Mrs Watts!)* confirmed that she had gone to the village to visit her aged mother.

That was that, I sat there gawping at the yellowed newspaper pages trying to pull myself together. I was not going to be pitched into the paranormal. (*I am not going there. I refuse. I'm an engineer not a psychic*). The trouble was that there was no engineering explanation. How could I have driven through the fog to Fellbeck and talked to a farmer who had hanged himself nearly sixty years ago? How could I dream about sitting in a coffee shop talking to a beautiful young woman on her way to be murdered by that same farmer? Had I been talking to ghosts? Had I slipped into a parallel universe that was running sixty years behind mine? Was I living two separate lives at once? Was I a reincarnation of Ostrick with a taste for murdering actresses? Worst of all, what was I doing the night Caroline was killed to end up with muddy shoes and a wet coat?

It explained the mix-up over the farmer's name. When he introduced himself he gave his professional stage name of "Adams" – a slip. Then, as I was leaving, he gave his real name: "Ostrick".

I believed that the inquest jury had got it right in 1934. Jenny had said, "I've realised it won't do," and then, "Vernon's changed". I wasn't consoled for long, had Chris "changed" and murdered Caroline? It was a waste of time speculating; the job was to prove who really had killed Caroline. It was the only way out of this mess, not just for Chris – it was for my own sanity now – most of all, I owed it to Caroline. I closed the folders and walked a touch unsteadily up the aisle to find Miss Deedes. She was sitting, solitary, like a gaunt grey troll. 'No Mr. Hardy, just leave the folders on the table. I always file them myself.' I wondered how many wretched searches for misplaced documents that routine derived from. 'Is there anything else, Mr. Hardy?'

It was enough for one day. I thanked Miss Deedes and did a shaky exit.

I went back to York Terrace meaning to write up some notes for the meeting with Tom. I met Niall at the front door. 'All right, Ken?' he asked, 'you're not looking yourself.' If Niall could spot it with his eyesight, it had to be drastic. I admitted to having experienced a bit of a shaker. 'Come along,' said Niall, 'I wouldn't normally suggest it, but you need a drink.' He took a firm hold of my arm above the elbow, which was about level with his own ear.

'Not Julio's', I said, 'he talks too much. Last time, after you'd gone he tried to pump me about the murder. How come I was talking to Mr. Potts? I told him you were handling my divorce.'

'Well aren't I?' We went to the Duke which was empty apart from a pair of professionals at the bar. I ordered a pint and a scotch chaser contrasting nicely with Niall's diet coke. I disposed of the whisky and got half the pint down, after which I felt braver. I badly needed to make sense of my afternoon with a rational explanation. I described my dream about coffee with Jenny Finch. I went on to my discoveries in the library archive and how it all tallied. I didn't mention that while I was actually having the dream Caroline was being murdered at Fellbeck. I also kept off the subject of damp overcoats.

'Hours of fun,' said Niall, 'you think you've dropped into something paranormal?'

'It makes you wonder.'

'You've been talking to ghosts?' (*And not for the first time*) 'You're afraid that in a previous existence you had something to do with the murder of Jenny Finch and by extension, Caroline Enderby. Is Ken Hardy the latest in a line of murderous reincarnations?'

'Forget reincarnation. I don't believe in it.' (*But Martyn Enderby does*).

Niall gave me the full beam stare through his extra heavy duty lenses, 'Sounds good, but could you be drifting into psychosis? Can't distinguish between hallucination and reality, can't tell sanity from delusion?'

125

That was worse, horribly like the Fellbeck encounter which Niall didn't even know about, 'Niall, I don't know.'

'So you want Nanny to give you a cosy explanation before bedtime to chase away the nasty nightmares.' Niall grinned at me. Was he serious or taking the piss? 'You're not the first to have this sort of experience.'

'Can I have another drink first?'

'If you must, no more whisky, one more pint, and leave me out,' I did as I was told, which showed how shaken I was. 'When I was a student at Manchester,' Niall began, 'just before history finals I had a vivid dream about being killed in a skirmish in the English Civil War. My point is that dreams like that get touted as evidence of previous lives, always far more exciting than the dreamer's current existence. "Launderette attendant was Pharaoh's mistress in previous life – with knowledge that she couldn't possibly have now" (unless she'd seen a Hollywood blockbuster starring Elizabeth Taylor). These paranormal claims turn out to be a hotchpotch of information that the dreamer already possessed. When I dissected my dream, that's exactly what it was. I'd been swotting the Civil War. It was all there. The clincher was that one of my windy comrades was my university room mate from first year. I recognised his skinny legs. It was nothing to do with reincarnation, parallel universes, or anything else.'

'What about my dream? Where would I have got the information?'

'Your Mam's scrapbook mainly – every woman kept one, my granny did. They pasted in all sorts of stuff – weddings, recipes for apple pie, juicy murders. You already possessed most of the information that Miss Deedes found for you by the time you were seven. Forward to the 1950s and grocers' shops roasting their own beans; pretty girls in high heels and rubber macs – pure Kingsley Amis – at the time, the routine teenage fetish.'

Potts wore a faint smile. I was tempted to stun it with my meeting with Ostrick in 1992. I rejected that idea. I'd already lived with that for seven years and I wasn't going over it again. My dose of 'flu would have to stay by way of explanation. 'Thanks, Niall, I'm not completely convinced but you've stopped the rot. I shall now go back to being a soulless materialist reductionist.'

The smile moved in the direction of mockery, 'Don't overdo it Ken,' then vanished, 'What's Jason doing tomorrow?'

'Chasing up sources for hiring mobile generators.'

'That's the style, could you let me know when he's finished?'

I had one more question, 'Suppose Caroline had divorced Martyn to marry Chris, how would her alimony settlement have left the Enderby estate?'

Niall did not want to pursue that subject, 'You're looking for a motive to pin on the bereaved husband? There might have been a pre-nuptial. If not, given that Caroline's post-nuptial sex life was not unspotted, *(How does Niall know that? Does Tom?)*, he could have got out of it practically scot-free.'

'So Martyn didn't murder his wife to preserve the Enderby millions?'

Niall drained his coke in one: not a man to be trifled with. He got up, 'Kenneth, your deductive powers are a credit to the plastics industry and a menace to polite society. Without prejudice, and between you and me in a public bar, I doubt whether Martyn Enderby's estate would raise even half a million. It would have made more sense for her to murder him...' he paused, 'don't get too personal about this, Ken. The police are right. Don't kill yourself trying to prove the opposite.' Niall went back to the office.

I stayed behind to apply my deadly deductive powers to Niall's remarks. Acting for the defence in a high profile murder case had to be the biggest event in the history of Harrison and Potts. But Niall had already made up his mind: Chris Berry was guilty. Whether or not, Tom had to put together a defence and if properly interpreted, the Benson document could be the biggest shot in Tom's locker. Niall was the antique documents man in the partnership but he was not interested. How unprofessional was that and why?

What about my own relations with Niall? Potts had largely convinced me about Jenny Finch. I had to give him credit for that, but it had nothing to do with Caroline's murder. Until that was solved, dealings with Niall had to be "hear all, see all, say nowt" – a deplorable philosophy typical of the wrong side of the Pennines where it is popular and in this case, apposite.

I was about to put the peg in when a figure I knew appeared quite plain at the public bar entrance. 'Thought you'd be here, Hardy,' it said, effortlessly banishing all paranormal speculation to the small back burner, 'supposed to be working, but discovered in the Duke giving it this.' Wilkinson's own presence was not explained.

18

An ear-splitting screech in the kitchen: *Neeeeoow!* It was not the cat with his tail in the toaster, it was the TV breakfast show presenter introducing the next item. A bit of a head this morning, how was I to know that Wilkinson would walk into the Duke?

I tried local radio – serious concern over alcoholism in Ditchfield. Jason arrived glowing with health (*does he have to?*) and fed the cat. I provided tea and invited a progress report.

'The electricity board were uncertain exactly when they disconnected Fellbeck – at least ten years ago and probably longer. Will that do?' It would, for now.

Jason produced his list of possible generator hirers. 'Work through the list,' I recommended, 'Do they deliver or does the customer collect? Did they hire a generator covering the period 22nd to 24th November and say, up to five days either side of those dates? If they have a record matching those dates, what was the name and address of the hirer?'

'They'll be asking questions before that,' Jason said.

'Probably, impress on them that this is a very serious legal matter and if that doesn't shift them, offer to get one of the partners to phone their boss. You can start now, use the partnership line, not mine. Mr Potts knows about it. This time, don't withhold our number.'

The people I planned to deal with next were not early starters. I watched the clock past nine and then rang the Skipton Tourist Information Office. 'I'm looking for a hotel in the Skipton area that offers conference facilities; a business conference for twenty to thirty people, nothing too elaborate.' The Information Office suggested four hotels. I rang round and got a possible at the Ram's Head. The receptionist started reeling off information. I interrupted, 'I got a very good report from a contact who organised a conference in Skipton last week. She didn't mention the name of the hotel and now she's gone abroad so I can't get hold of her.'

'What was the name, sir?'

'I don't know whether she placed the booking personally, she's a Ms Hoggett. *(An obvious lie, Hardy)* The name of the organisation is AGROW.'

'We did have the AGROW conference, last Tuesday. That was 23rd November, is that the one you mean? It wasn't booked by Ms Hoggett, it was Ms Partington – their secretary.'

'Sounds promising,' I said, 'I'd like to come and have a look at your facilities. Is the hotel manager around this morning, say at eleven o'clock?'

She went off the line to check. 'Hullo, Mr Hardy? Mr Ackroyd Finley would be delighted to meet you. Could you make it 11.15?' – I accepted.

That left me with time to spare. I had decided to take a chance on Miss Deedes. She didn't strike me as the sort of girl who would clype to DCI Kent in the back bar of the Rat and Parrot.

I stopped off at the Library and struck lucky with the archive department. 'I've been thinking over the information you gave me yesterday, Miss Deedes I wondered if I might trouble you a bit further.' Although remaining gaunt, she was not unwilling. Perhaps I was a welcome diversion from routine drudgery. I pulled out a copy of the address labels that Chris had produced for Benson and put the sheet in front of her. 'Do any of these names ring a bell?' Miss Deedes replied 'Yes, some of them, why?'

I took a confidential seat at her table and said, 'Could it

be a list of police suspects at the time of the Jack the Ripper murders?'

Miss Deedes was dismissive, 'The Lending Library has a complete shelf of speculation on that subject, Mr. Hardy.'

'It's a bit more than that,' I said, 'yesterday, with your help, I was able to confirm some important parallels between one of the Ripper murders and the death of Jenny Finch in 1934. It could be coincidence, it could have been a copycat murder, or there could be a direct connection with one of the suspects on this sheet.'

Miss Deedes brightened up, 'As an author, Mr. Hardy, you're planning to publish the final solution? You won't lack competition, the society painter Walter Sickert, the Duke of Clarence, the Prince of Wales, Mr Gladstone, all the best people have already been fingered... you'll find the evidence upstairs.'

'But they've been debunked already,' I said, 'this approach is completely different. I want to look into the background of the Jenny Finch murder, particularly Vernon Adams, the actor and farmer who was responsible. Was there a family connection between Ostrick and one of the Ripper suspects? Can you suggest someone local who might point me in the right direction?'

Miss Deedes promised to give my request some thought. I gave her my phone number, thanked her and climbed back up to street level.

I had my own source for identifying the names on Benson's list – the three Ripper books that I'd rescued from Chris's flat. It would make for a suitably squalid evening.

At the enquiry desk I found Jason chatting the bubbly blonde receptionist. I advanced from the rear (*dirty work, Hardy*). A miasma of testosterone hung heavy on the air. 'Hi Jason, making progress?' He jumped, turned round, and blushed a fetching shade of pink and said something on the lines of 'er yes...er...Mr. Hardy...er getting on'. (*Rotter! Never been*

young and pestered by an over-eager trouser snake, Hardy?).
I said, 'Good, I'm going out now and I may be some time, so
why not give me a knock, usual time in the morning?' I thanked
Bubbles for her kind assistance and buggered off.

Once out of town the Skipton road ran mainly through farming
country. I passed a small motel on the right then, three or four
miles further on I entered the 30 limit for Skipton and spotted
the Ram's Head – a medium sized hotel – on my left. The main
building in the Victorian style was substantial and not pretty;
perhaps built by a wealthy wool merchant. After a laborious
existence hatching consumption in Bradford he would have felt
it was his due.

There were spaces for four cars at the main entrance, one
occupied by a five-year-old grey Mondeo. The visitors' car park
was at the rear, I parked there, facing a modern single storey
extension which emitted the wartime British Restaurant aroma
of stale cabbage (boiled). The main building was fitted with an
iron fire-escape reaching the first, second and third floors which
had windows overlooking the car park. While I was parking, a
delivery van arrived, not via the hotel entrance, but up a short
lane through a belt of trees sheltering the hotel from a minor
road behind. It parked by the kitchen door and started to deliver
catering-sized packs of tomato soup (*everything home-made,
sir*) and other delicacies.

At twenty past eleven, I got out of the car and walked round
to the front door of the Ram's Head. The receptionist offered me
the leather settee and went to alert the manager. 'Mr Finley will
be with you in just a moment, Mr Hardy.'

After a suitable pause, Ackroyd Finley appeared at his door
behind reception and made measured progress to greet me. He
was in his mid-forties I suspected, but had wasted no time in
equipping himself with an oversized belly (*all that tomato soup*).
In order to maintain balance, he leant back at a substantial angle

and walked slowly with long strides. It was impressive in its way. He offered me a moist, pudgy hand and lowered himself at the opposite end of the settee. He sagged, I rose.

'That your car at the front, Mr Finley – the Mondeo?' It was. 'Nice', I said, 'plenty of power under the bonnet (*it needed plenty with Ackroyd on board*) the hotel's obviously prospering.' Clearly it wasn't if the manager had not changed his car for five years.

'We get our share,' said Finley, comfortably.

I passed him my (genuine) APC business card, suggesting that to contact me he should use the phone number pencilled in below because that was my private line. Finley studied my card with a frown as if (correctly) suspecting a deception but then shoved it into the pocket of his suit and launched into his conference sales pitch. I did not pay close attention. The shape of his head interested me more: the two halves didn't match. The back was perfectly formed suggesting high character and considerable intellect whilst the front was a podgy oval of half-baked Yorkshire pudding. Halfway back, his ears stuck out as though to mark the parting line where the back and front halves were glued together. It could not have evolved like that – Finley was impressive evidence for Intelligent Design.

When the manager's sales talk began to falter, I endangered my future relations with the great Designer by explaining that APC were looking for an alternative venue for their annual Northern sales conference. 'Salford last time,' I confided, 'a disaster, never again.' We would require conference facilities and overnight accommodation for up to twenty sales executives. Sharing in twin rooms would be acceptable with three single rooms for senior executives. I was talking in terms of a midweek booking for October next year. Finley received my information, droopy-eyed, as though doubtful of its possible relevance.

'I notice that for the AGROW function, you offered lunch

only. As a matter of fact I was led to believe that there was to be dinner.'

Finley was equal to that, 'In the event they couldn't guarantee our minimum of sixteen covers for dinner so the arrangements were changed.'

I got up, suggesting that a tour of the facilities would be useful. This caused the manager's mouth to fall open but after due consideration he took a deep breath and grunted himself into an upright position. We toured.

'We like to promote team spirit – bonding – at these conferences,' I said. 'Is there a room where we could hold an impromptu smoking concert after dinner, say between eight thirty and ten?'

Finley said that could be accommodated. He had a room that was regularly used by a local jazz group for rehearsing. It was in the basement. He took me down. 'What about audio equipment?' Finley assured me that whereas the jazz group brought their own equipment, the hotel had a local source and could provide what was needed at a reasonable rental. I received this with enthusiasm.

'As a matter of fact,' the manager confided, 'the organisation we entertained last week did take advantage of the service.'

Last week seemed to be about the limit for his memory circuits. I prompted, 'Would that have been AGROW?'

'That's it – AGROW!' It was a eureka moment and Finley was taking the credit. 'They were very decent about it. The artiste that they booked the audio equipment for had to cry off at the last moment.' The manager lowered his voice, 'health reasons you know. But the chairman…' he tailed off. I prompted again, 'Yes, Mr Enderby, undertook to meet the full charge, for the equipment *and* for the studio.' It was a studio, not just a damp and windowless basement with a mains socket: originally the Victorian coal-cellar. That was not all. '*And,* the equipment would be loaded into his four by four the following morning.

Black, four-litre turbo, you know, very stylish set of wheels and he would *personally* return to source that morning.'

'Very interesting,' I said. These were the only honest words I had spoken to poor Mr Finley in the last half hour. I walked back with him to reception, 'as a final check, I would like to spend a night in the hotel, Mr Finley, nothing like personal experience. Could you accommodate me in a single tonight together with a copy of your tariff for conference events?'

'No doubt we could,' Ackroyd Finley said gloomily. He handed me over to the receptionist, moved resolutely to his office and closed the door.

'Knows his business, Mr Finley,' I told the receptionist. She smiled in near-total disbelief. My booking did not take long to complete. While the girl was registering my plastic, I flicked back a few pages in the hotel register. 'Hope you don't mind,' I said, 'just looking to see if any of my colleagues have been here recently.' In the detective business, I thought, citizenship of a catholic county was an advantage – sins of this sort were forgiven if freely confessed, cash down in the poor box. How investigators in nonconformist Yorkshire could evade the wrath of their God (if any), was a puzzle.

'Help yourself, petal,' said the receptionist. She had clocked that I was having her on about Finley.

Petal found the entries easily enough – they were few. Ms Amelia Partington had been in room 17, Enderby in 31 and Dr Pascal Threnadie de Morzine in 24. The other names meant nothing and might not be those of AGROW members. 'Any chance of room 31?' I asked, 'I see a friend of mine took it last week and he recommended it.'

'Did he really? It's not one of our most popular, but he specially asked for it. It's top floor right at the back, overlooking the car park.'

'He said he liked it because it was quiet.' Lying became almost painless with practice. Room 31 was mine for the night.

I undertook to book in around seven and would require dinner. I sat in the car park for a few minutes and made notes. Having met the main man, I looked forward to checking out the night shift.

I drove into the historic market town of Skipton, put the car in the cash-and-flash and wandered down the High Street. I hate stopping people and asking for information. I was ashamed of this timidity until I read that it was testosterone-related. All the same, in the time it took me to find what I wanted, the wife would not only have located the main Radio and Television retailer but also checked the local weather forecast, the going price of fat lambs and the disgraceful goings-on in the Town Clerk's office. I had to manage without this additional knowledge but I did get to my destination without disclosing my private business to the citizens – a sound policy in Yorkshire. The assistant confirmed what Finley had said. I explained that I wanted an audio amplifier, speakers and mike for an event in a room say forty foot by thirty, powerful enough for young people playing heavy rock and the like. 'Definite,' said the shopman. It would plug into a domestic socket. I reckoned that equated with blowing Chris's mind in the tiny computer closet at Fellbeck. I asked to see the equipment, it was not as large as I had imagined.

After that, I entered the public bar of the Magnet expecting to find it occupied by a mob of Yorkshire Stalinists; it was empty, all but. I forced down a pint of Yorkshire bitter with a slice of pork pie. I've tasted worse.

19

When I returned to the office there was a message to ring Stefan.

'Ken,' Stefan greeted me, 'how's the semi-retirement?'

'Semi-boring.' (*Stop it, you. You'll end up with no friends except Wilkinson*). It wasn't clear how, but experience so far suggested that any involvement with the law made habitual lying inevitable.

'Good,' said Stefan. He had a couple of jobs for me. The first was quite small. 'I've got a tonne of CMI's new wonder plastic to evaluate. I'll send it up to Ditchfield along with their specifications. How long will it take you to run trials on it?' I reckoned two or three days assuming Ed could fit in time on some of the machines – another day to write up a report.

'Good,' said Stefan, 'shall we say next week?' We said next week. 'The second one's more substantial. I'm looking at investment opportunities in sub-Saharan Africa. My team have pencilled in three companies as possible business partners.' He meant takeover victims. 'I want you to go out and have a look. Say a week for each, what about February?'

'Hang on,' I protested, 'what about the politics and the legal set up in these places and the economy…I can't advise on those.'

'Not your problem, my people are looking at those. Your job is to spend four or five days in each factory assessing their production capability – volume, range, flexibility, management efficiency, state of training, industrial relations, ok? Start Lagos, then Nairobi and finally Jo'burg. After that, take a couple of days in Cape Town, we'll put you in a decent hotel and you can relax in the sun, write your reports and email them back; after that, back to dear old blighty.' Only a Hungarian-Czech would refer to England as 'blighty' but Stefan was proud of his colloquial English.

'It'll kill me,' I protested, 'I can't stand heat.'

'Gradely lad,' said Stefan in his thickest mid-European, 'nice change for you from frizzling cold and raining with piss. I'll put you through to Margot and you can sort out visas and tickets. Don't forget jabs.'

Stefan was confronting me with a challenge: solve the case by the end of January because February is a write-off – why did that feel familiar?

After Margot had done with me, I phoned Bill Jones's practice and made an appointment for tetanus, yellow jack, malaria and the rest.

I booted the computer and searched online for AGROW's website. I thought they could be a dot org bogus educational charity. AGROW.org wasn't it but I found AGROW_soc.org. uk. The website was amateurish, straight off the word processor, Courier font, black on white, poor stuff compared with Chris's designs. The pages for 'AGM and Gathering' (*'Gathering?' Get them!*) were still online. I downloaded everything in case the AGROW webmaster woke up and updated the site. I spotted something – lunch was at 1.00 pm and the meeting closed at 5.00; no dinner. That confirmed what Finley had said. But Caroline had stated that it was to be the AGROW AGM and *dinner*. Martyn was planning to dine at Skipton and stay overnight. What was he up to? Planning to get so ratted at lunch that he wouldn't be fit to drive home for a fragrant evening with Caroline? Or part of the lure to get both Chris and Caroline at Fellbeck that evening? Or neither?

I went back to the AGROW website. The Group Mission Statement said that AGROW was committed to a global campaign to banish the dominant Western world view by expelling materialist reductionist science, medicine and economics in favour of revolutionary change towards a society founded on spiritual values derived from ancient wisdom revealed by enlightened Gnostic philosophy (*so there!*). It didn't state whether the revolution was to be violent. I expected it to be more a matter of thoughtful letters to *The Guardian* than AK47s in Westminster Abbey. Caroline's verdict on AGROW seemed not far off the mark. Then I remembered Enderby's rent-a-crowd at Ditchfield Sceptics, and wondered how harmless it really was.

I moved on to the pages announcing the AGM. Registration would be followed by twenty minutes of meditation, led by the Chair, after which they proposed to get down to business – first, adoption of the annual accounts presented by Mr S. Waters, followed by the election of officers. Next on the agenda: consideration of a major project for a permanent AGROW centre for activist training (that sounded a bit ominous), study groups, seminars and the like. Discussion would be led by special financial adviser, Mr. Alexander Scott McIver (*McIver!*). I could imagine my ex—partner holding forth on capital, liquidity and fund raising whilst pencilling in his fee.

After cleansing their minds of materialistic matters with the aid of coffee and biscuits, the meeting would move to presentations of a more spirited nature. Dr Pascal Threnadie de Morzine would open with a paper on "A Strong Shamanic Revival in the Western United States". This was to be followed by drinks and lunch (please click the appropriate box for special dietary requirements: vegan, vegetarian, fisharian, eggarian…) I wondered how Finley and his catering packs of tomato soup and cotton wool bread rolls had coped with the gastro challenge. Afterwards there was to be Martyn Enderby on *Towards a Post-Materialistic Economy* followed by Mr S. Waters on *Sacrificial Rituals in Ancient Religion*. Finally, as the climax of the day, the Group would adjourn to the sound stage studio (*aka* basement coal cellar) for *Recital by Wi Cho-Cho Chang of 7th Century (BCE) Dissonant Jomonic Heterophony.* Proceedings would close with meditation.

The website confirmed names I had spotted in the hotel register: Ms Amelia Partington, Hon. Sec. and Martyn Enderby, Chair, together with Threnadie de Morzine, staying overnight but S Waters was not and neither was Alexander Scott McIver.

I attended at Tom's office promptly, 'Before we start on our review of the evidence, how's the main man framing?'

'If you mean Chris,' Tom said, 'not well at all. He's oscillating between overwhelming grief and blaming himself for letting Caroline go off with Mrs Watts. We're not going to get anything useful until he comes out of shock.'

'Would it help if I visited him? Not as an investigator, just as a friend. I'm good at listening when I have to.'

Tom assumed a wry expression. *(Doesn't see me in the comforter role?*) 'It's a possibility. But a prison visiting room doesn't lend itself to a counselling session. Leave it for now. I'll let you know when he starts to settle.'

It was time for practicalities, 'I'm going to be busy part of next week on a job for APC,' I told Tom. 'After that, February's a write-off because Stefan's sending me to Africa. I expect to have the case wrapped up before then.'

'Isn't it solved already?' Tom asked, 'and no, they haven't found the murder weapons and no, there are no forensic results yet.'

'It would save time later if we ask now if Kent prefers "over" or "sunnyside up".' I meant for facial decoration purposes.

Tom looked blank, I did not hasten to explain. 'How do the missing weapons help the defence case?' He wanted to know.

'It doesn't help either side yet,' I conceded, 'when will we get the forensics findings?' Tom didn't commit himself.

'What about summarising progress to date?' I suggested,

employing the executive tone brought on by five minutes-worth of Stefan. Before Tom could object, I bounded on, 'The police theory is that Chris took Caroline from Preston to Fellbeck. She went willingly because Chris said he had an appointment connected with his website business. She was alive and well on arrival at Fellbeck, unless forensics have found blood in Chris's car. Caroline got out of the car voluntarily, she wasn't dragged out because that would have left marks, probably on her arms and there weren't any. The police claim they quarrelled violently whether outside or inside the house. He struck her on the back of the head with something large, round and heavy rendering her unconscious. He dumped her on the sitting room hearthrug and cut her throat with something like a slaughter man's blade. He must have brought both weapons with him, the murder was pre-meditated, not a crime of passion.

If they claim that Chris fabricated the Benson document as an alibi, he must have done so at least three months earlier because I've had it since the beginning of September. Gloria's evidence that she picked up two calls in Chris's absence supports the existence of a person calling himself "Benson".'

'Not really, the police can say that those two calls were not from Benson, who doesn't exist, but from Chris himself, pretending to be Benson.'

'Chris's affair with Caroline started at the end of March and Benson first contacted him in April. So, within a month of the affair starting, Chris was inventing this Benson character as an alibi for murdering the woman he had just fallen in love with?'

Tom wasn't having that, 'We don't know what the forensic evidence is.'

'Unless it's pretty startling, Kent's bum is well out the window with his "crime of passion" scenario. They'll have to get honest and prove motive, means and opportunity, like the rest of us.' Tom didn't think it was quite as simple as that. I bumbled on anyway, 'At the latest, he started planning the murder in

August. Is that how he spent the summer holiday? I know he was bored and unhappy because he was missing Caroline, he said so. Was he so cross with Caroline for allowing Martyn to take her off for what he thought was a second honeymoon that he decided to cut her throat? After she came back they made up their lovers' tiff. Nevertheless he stuck to his plan to murder her, is that their case?'

Tom objected, 'The prosecution don't have to prove that Chris fabricated the Benson document. Suppose there's nothing sinister about Benson. He's a harmless eccentric who approached Chris to build him a website. Having received the manuscript at the end of July, Chris thought he could use it to get Caroline to Fellbeck. It had to be an evening when Martyn was away so that Caroline could come with him. Once Chris knew that Martyn was going to be away at his AGM, all he had to do was invent an appointment with Benson. The other phone calls were genuine.'

'Surely they have to do better than that to get a verdict. Caroline sat on my sofa, the night she was murdered and told me that Martyn's "second honeymoon" was no such thing. It was a concentrated book writing session. When she got back, she and Chris had a riotous reunion in the heather.'

I was starting to suspect that I'd gone on too long. Tom confirmed it, 'Ken,' he said, 'there's something in what you say. There are problems with the prosecution case, I can work that out too and our counsel will give them a hard time in court (*so bugger off and leave it to the professionals...*) but that won't get us the verdict.'

I wasn't going without a final shot, 'If Benson is real but harmless why don't the police get out there and find him? With their resources it shouldn't be difficult because he won't be using a pseudonym. All Kent needs is an innocent although half-baked Benson in the witness box and his job's a good 'un. But they'll fail, Benson isn't his real name because he's a member of the murder gang. He was plotting to get Chris to Fellbeck

142

with Caroline. If we're right it'll use up police overtime and hamstring Kent's investigation.'

Tom was losing patience. 'To begin with, DCI Kent hasn't been informed about the Benson document yet. And what's the defence's alternative? Chris was the victim of a complicated conspiracy: a portable power generator, a computer in the closet, recorded aircraft noises and at least two murderers, Benson and Mrs Watts and probably a third murderer behind the door. What we have to remember, Ken, is that this is a jury trial in a courtroom. The police have a dead girl and a bloodstained lover. Their case is that he did it – whether he did it in a moment of madness or planned it in advance won't concern the jury too much. As things stand, if you offered me fifty-fifty on a not guilty verdict, I'd bite your hand off.'

'Don't do it,' I advised, 'I'll get you better odds before I've done.'

Tom wanted to know what lines I was working on. 'For a start, the front door key. The police found it on the mat on the inside. They assumed that Chris had locked the door from the outside on leaving and posted it through the letterbox. How did Chris get a key in the first place? The murderers needed access at the rear to connect the power supply. You've seen how easy that would be. When Chris went for the police, the gang loaded the kit into their transport, locked the front door from the inside, wiped the key and dropped it on the mat, restored the padlock to the back door and shot off. When I return the key they lent us I'm planning a chat with the agents.'

Belatedly, Tom had something positive to offer, 'These cases often arise out of a love triangle. Lovers don't kill their mistresses as a rule. Lovers kill husbands – like the Thompson and Bywaters case – or husbands kill cheating wives. This case is different.'

'You mean because the police have already charged their man?'

'And Enderby has an alibi.'

'Which the cops accepted at face value. Caroline told me all about Martyn's alibi three hours before she was murdered. I don't believe it.'

'Be careful,' Tom warned, 'it's a delicate area and whatever you do, don't talk to Enderby – harassing the grieving husband is bad news.'

'I've no intention of talking to Martyn Enderby; you can have him. I've serious doubts about him as a murderer. He's a spiritual pacifist and feminist vegetarian. The murderer smashed Caroline's skull and then ripped her throat open with a butcher's knife – how vegetarian is that?'

'Hitler was a teetotal vegetarian,' Tom said, deftly dismounting Hardy from his high horse.

I persisted, 'Martyn can't be Benson – wrong height, wrong voice and Caroline would have seen through his disguise instantly.'

'So why bother looking into his alibi?'

I got up, 'Because there's something odd about his arrangements. It's a potential crack in the carapace and probing may produce a spin-off.' I left Tom to unscramble that and got out before he vetoed the plan.

20

I packed my overnight bag and set out. On the drive to Skipton I started to wonder whether I had been a bit previous with Tom, rejecting Martyn as the murderer before I'd told him about Ditchfield Sceptics.

It was a November day almost exactly a year ago. McIver had phoned, did I fancy an evening's entertainment of a philosophical nature? 'See Ken, I'm involved with the Ditchfield branch of Sceptics in the Tavern, we're holding a meeting on Tuesday at 7.30 in the upstairs room at the Duke.'

'Sceptics in an upper room, is this a new religion? Plotting to destroy the fabric of society as we know it?' McIver assured me that the intention was the opposite – to engage in a constructive examination of alternative philosophies that might, if unchallenged, prove to be no' offy beneficial. McIver had laid on a lecture by Mr Martyn Enderby, a leading New World theorist, entitled *Out of Character: The Mystery of Human Motivation*. Out of loyalty to our 30-year partnership, I agreed to attend. At least, I'd be well placed for remedial medication.

Martyn Enderby looked like a smooth operator. He was in his mid-forties tall, slim and handsome, in a way which I found effeminate (*Neither slim nor handsome, you Hardy?*). McIver introduced his guest, telling us that our speaker had taken a degree in philosophy at Oxford, going on to carve out a career as thinker, author, lecturer ('and activist', Enderby interposed in a low voice). McIver's spectacles flashed dangerously – never a good idea to interrupt Scotty in full flow – but without resorting to the sgian-dubh tucked into his sock he opted to ignore

Enderby's intervention and applied the chairman's classic put-down, '... so without further ado...'

Enderby rose to his full six foot one greeted by polite applause from the first dozen rows and wild whoops around me at the rear. Their hero flashed a white-toothed smile at his disciples and posed while the welcome subsided; in black blazer, chinos and cravat he was not my idea of a dangerous activist. Nor was he a crazed wreck crouched in his attic composing a stream of vituperative pamphlets excoriating Einstein, denigrating Darwin and flagellating Freud. I had selected a seat on the back row where the company was dodgy but the exit adjacent. It didn't take Enderby long to open his box of tricks – "good" news was signalled by a smile, the contemptible reductionist views of the scientific establishment with a curled lordly lip and mentions of his own flimsy philosophy by a portentous expression and a slow nodding of the head to convey massive significance. He began, 'Out of character – how often do we hear that expression when neighbours, friends, family members react to some shocking event. Out of character... meaning that once again, science *has no explanation*,' (an inclusive twinkle, delighted titters and a ripple of applause from the rear). I was reminded of a headline in one of our great national Sunday newspapers reporting the "discovery" of a statue of Elvis on Mars – *Science has no explanation* it announced in 28-font bold.

Meanwhile Enderby had lowered his voice confidentially, as he developed his first subject: 'The so-called mystery of human motivation,' he was saying, 'was no problem for the sages of ancient religions possessed as they were of deep spiritual insights to human consciousness. He went from there into a long discussion of Reincarnation. I had heard the story before – children born to a life of misery imposed by a disastrous karma carried over from a wicked ancestor. But Enderby introduced "new evidence" which "proved the deep truth of reincarnation"

(Nod, nod). He was talking about how, if a birthmark on a child resembled one on a deceased person, it meant that characteristics better consigned to the grave would reappear in the living. Personally, I'm the proud possessor of a birthmark on my neck suggestive of a hangman's noose. In one of her consoling moments the wife had dismissed it as the outcome of a fumbled breech birth. (*Born back to front and wrong side out ever since you, Hardy*). But my little school friends were of the Enderby persuasion. I was the reincarnate of a murderer, whose crime I was doomed to repeat. Who was to be my victim? In view of fantasies featuring the delectable Mrs Enderby sitting onstage, it had to be Martyn.

Enderby had moved on to the modern theory of Multiple Personality Disorder which he denounced as a pathetic secular alternative to reincarnation. He triggered amusement on remarking that a school of American psychiatry had notched up a record 27 different personalities residing in one body (*$1000 per personality?*). I joined in an open-minded grin.

Finally, he launched into Spirit Possession – a seriously recognised "fact" discovered by the ancient Sumerians – and seriously gruesome too. Modern research, by an alternative school of psychiatrists, Enderby revealed, *proved* that over 70% of people had experienced the attachment of a spirit entity. Noting that Mrs E's cardigan had slipped attractively, I was wondering about getting attached to the spirit of Casanova.

That pleasing line of thought was shattered as Enderby exploded into his grand finale. It wasn't clear how he got there but the previous hour had been a sweetly reasonable softening up for the real stuff. '… what my movement offers,' he was telling the hall, 'is none other than a spiritual revolution; the conquest of materialism; the victory of a completely new world-view; re-dedication of the West; total dominance of the feminine principle; the elimination of deadly drug-dependent medicine by faith-based care. AGROW will transform our hospitals from

147

soulless disease factories to temples of holistic healing. We will overthrow sterile secular science in favour of life-based wisdom exemplified by the ancient philosophers of the orient' and more and more. It was rousing stuff, and none more roused than the speaker himself. I glanced at his wife who had crossed her legs defensively (*nice ones*) and was looking out over the heads of the audience; it looked suspiciously like distancing. Enderby's peroration roared to its revolutionary conclusion. 'My movement, "Action Group for the Re-spiritualisation of the West" demands action,' he declaimed, 'a spiritual call to arms. We utterly condemn this morally bankrupt society to oblivion.' Foaming at the mouth seemed imminent as he shrieked his final demand: 'Action to convert the West to a New World agenda of love and peace. We act now or perish.'

Enderby sat to a shell-shocked silence. Relieved that it was all over, an idiot woke up and clapped once, then stopped. It was enough. The supporters club snapped out of its dream of bowler-hatted bankers hanging like bunches of grapes from the lamp posts of the Mall. They were on their feet, clapping furiously, chanting 'Aggro, Aggro' (clap, clap, clap). The girl groupies in front of me, lacking male shoulders, climbed on their seats and began whooping and waving their arms in the air for the (absent) TV cameras. They afforded cover for my escape. On my way to safety, I put in a parting glance at Mrs E. She was applying a word to her husband's ear prior to leaving the stage. She did not look right suited.

I slipped downstairs where, cocooned amongst the civilised and peaceable drunks in the public bar, I was meditating on the concept of a third pint when I found McIver handing it to me. 'Do you have to entertain that sort of hooligan?'

'We're sceptics, Ken. Know the enemy, learn to recognise those that would destroy intelligent thought and kick us back into the Dark Ages: disease, starvation, superstition, mass murther and single entry book keeping...'

Before Scotty could finish, the Darling Leader appeared on the staircase attended by acolytes. Two steps from the foot of the stairs he paused in his pomp to survey the peasantry below. In his lightweight trench coat, its near-bridal whiteness setting off his lightly tanned features, he posed then swept out, looking neither to left nor right and attended by a cloud of virgins stringing their lyres and prophesying miracles.

'...Forbye, in this case, there is another reason,' McIver concluded. Failing sex, it must be money. I did not enquire further.

Now, twelve months on, I still struggled to cast Martyn as a wife-killer – not the lurking behind the door with club-hammer and butcher's knife sort.

It was a few minutes before seven when I put the Merc in the visitors' car park at the rear of the Ram's Head. I walked to reception where a different girl checked me in. I asked if Finley was around, he wasn't.

'Do you have a night manager?' I asked. The girl said Mr Ratcliffe, who came on at eight. 'Where would I find him?' He had an office in the basement.

I saw that room 31 wasn't their finest but there was a window overlooking the car park and across the passage was the fire exit, the usual locking bar type. I unpacked my bag and descended to savour the Ram's Head cuisine – almost defrosted gammon steak with chips, peas and Yorkshire bitter. After that I walked out by the front door. The reception desk was unpersonned.

I walked round the side of the hotel and found a door at the bottom of stone steps underneath the fire escape. It was unlocked and opened into the basement passage with a door marked "Night Manager" opposite– nicely secluded with private egress to the exterior. Ratcliffe was in his office; I introduced myself as 'Room 31' and wondered if I could have a word. The football on his TV was a European match, Milan had scored in the first half. Now, with fifteen minutes remaining they were still leading 1 –

0 and passing the ball around amongst themselves. 'Looks like game over,' I said.

'Don't know why I bother, might as well blow the whistle soon as the first goal goes in.' Ratcliffe was bald and officially retired – my guess was that he was doing the job for cash in hand and nowt said. I took his spare chair.

'Fairly quiet in the evenings, this place?'

Ratcliffe was gloomy about the prospects, 'Quiet side of dead, this time of year.'

I dug a tenner out of my pocket and kept it folded in my hand. He spotted it, no flies on the night manager. 'Mr Ratcliffe,' I began, 'you had a group in the hotel last Tuesday for an all-day event. Some of them stayed over on Tuesday night. Called themselves AGROW; you remember them?'

'Yes and no. I got no aggro out them, if that's what you're getting at.'

'What I'm interested in is any unusual comings and goings. Were there any movements late on?' Ratcliffe took another look at my hand with the sticking out corner of banknote, perhaps calculating whether it was worth inventing a tale...?

He decided against, 'No. Bear in mind all the guests have a front door key. I don't spend the night sitting on reception watching the door. I have duties elsewhere in the building' (*like watching football*).

'So persons could easily come in and out at any time unnoticed?'

Ratcliffe shoved his chair back, 'Hang on, who are you?'

I reckoned that this was the moment when I might get something useful or else the door. 'Ken Hardy's the name,' I said, handing him my card – the "paralegal consultant" one. 'I'm acting in connection with a legal matter, a murder case to be precise.' That raised his interest. 'What I'm going to ask you is strictly your business. If we can deal with it now – well and good. If not, we may be forced to call you as a witness. That would be a serious inconvenience because the case is likely to go on for four weeks. Shall we go on?'

'That depends', Ratcliffe said, retreating in averagely good order. What I wanted to know was his nightly routine. After I had doubled his money, I got what I was looking for, amounting to a short row of marbles. He claimed to carry out checks of the premises, desultory, I didn't doubt, inside and outside. I concluded that it depended on Ratcliffe's private activities, what was on television and the state of his sleep deficit. Anyone slinking into the hotel, dishevelled and bloody, would be dead unlucky to run into the night manager.

That was all I was getting out of him, so I opened my fist and put the two tenners, not as crisp as formerly, on his desk. Without comment, he unlocked the drawer in his desk and slipped the notes into a small cashbox. At that moment, on the stroke of injury time, the Milan goalkeeper mishandled a high cross and dropped the ball at the feet of the Dutch centre forward: 1 – 1. Ratcliffe sat staring at the screen with his mouth open to watch the replay, presenting me with a free view of the contents of his drawer.

'Bloody hell!' said Ratcliffe, 'extra time'. He closed the drawer and locked it. I asked if he minded my staying on to see the result. 'Nay lad,' he invited, 'help yersen.' It was all in vain as far as the Dutch were concerned because Milan scored from a professionally faked penalty in the first period and that was that. I thanked the night manager, then asked if he knew the name of the chambermaid who would be dealing with the third floor rooms. 'Our Norah', he said, 'she's the only one on till Christmas.'

Back in my room, I wrote a few notes on the interview. I left out my suspicions about the white packets that Ratcliffe had carelessly exposed when he opened his drawer. They could be painkillers for his bad leg.

At 10.30, I opened the curtains at the window overlooking

the car park. The view covered the whole area including the way in from the back lane. I stepped out into the corridor, quietly released the catch and opened the fire door an inch or two. It was a heavy, regulation door and there was no wind to speak of. I took the lift to the ground floor, went out, unobserved, through the front door and walked round to the car park. I got my briefcase out of the car and slammed the door shut. To complete the exercise I tramped up the fire escape steps and in through the fire door. I closed the door leaving a two-inch gap as before.

I awoke, as normal these days, at three a.m., visited the *en suite* then looked out into the corridor. The fire escape door was ajar, exactly as I had left it four hours earlier. Ratcliffe's patrols had failed to detect that the fire door was open. I preferred the alternative explanation – he'd been too busy running his own small businesses to bother. I reset the bar and went back to bed.

In the morning, I found our Norah bustling in and out of 34. She didn't mind a quick word about last Tuesday night in 31. Norah was in no doubt as to events. 'I knew straight off by t'stain on t'bottom sheet,' she said. That was not all, 17 had not been slept in – turned the bed back and rumpled the bottom sheet a bit but she hadn't slept in it. 'You can always tell,' said our Norah and boosted the Ratcliffe takings by another ten pounds on the spot. Room 17 had been occupied by Amelia Partington, AGROW secretary.

I made light of my findings on Enderby's cast iron alibi. 'It's a bit odd, but if he had made a night of it for the purpose of shagging his General Secretary, so what? How seriously spiritual is that?'

Tom had an alternative theory, 'Or Enderby was worn out by the stresses of the AGROW AGM, stayed in his room all evening and then had a disturbed night with erotic nightmares.'

'A lively lot – you have to say that for AGROW.' I made for the door. 'Tom, do you think BT could trace Benson's calls? After the reception desk closes down you can dial straight through to the various departments – the numbers are listed in the book. Benson's calls were all between 4.30 and 5.30.'

'Dates?' Tom asked.

'That's the snag: between 21st April and 31st July and then between 8th September and 23rd November. There's not much chance of Chris remembering them all. He had one on the first day after the summer holidays, that's a firm date – 9th September. You can add the first Thursday in May – he might not remember that one but I do. It was Benson's first call. Chris told me about it.'

'I'll check with Chris, first.'

'Good, tell him you've got a genius on the case.' At least, I'd found Tom a source of recreational drugs.

21

I left Tom and climbed the stairs just in time to be caught by the wife's phone call. 'What's this about you not retiring?' I reminded her about the terms of Stefan's takeover.

'It's a two year contract until they finally take over next September.'

I had misunderstood, Doreen persisted, 'I know about that. How come you're a private detective all of a sudden?' (*Just you wait, our Paula*).

'Nothing exciting', I said, 'ferreting out bits of information for Tom.'

'I've heard different', Doreen said, 'Tom's well chuffed with what you're doing.' I claimed a paltry contribution towards promoting justice in Ditchfield. 'If that's your programme, you're never going to be out of a job, are you?' Having cornered me, the wife put the knife in – a familiar technique which I have never learnt to counter. 'You'll want to know how things are going on the Costa del Sol.' Telling the truth seemed unattractive, 'I won't waste time on the phone telling you,' she said, 'miscarriages of justice can wait over the holidays, and the works will be shut, so book yourself a flight to Malaga before it's too late. I've made a lot of new friends over here so you won't be stuck for company – better than traipsing from one pub to another in the wet.'

I tried a sacrificial gambit, 'Why don't you come here, aren't you underestimating the festive opportunities in Ditchfield?' Perhaps it was a line fault but the reply sounded rude. I had no more pieces on the board so I resigned, 'I'll see what's available and ring you back. Ten days maximum.'

'It'll do you good', the wife threatened.

I phoned Helmsley and Jordan at Braxtonby for an appointment. 'I'll be returning the key that they kindly lent to Mr. Harrison.'

Then I phoned Ed Willis at the works and asked him when Stefan's load of wonder material was expected. 'Monday morning,' said Ed.

'Suppose we discuss a test schedule on Monday – over coffee?'

Iberia offered me a seat to Malaga at an ungodly hour on December 22nd and a return flight on January 3rd. Screaming kids all the way out and hangovers back. No wonder the death rate is higher during the holidays.

I booted the computer and opened the AGROW website to find out about joining; it was simple enough. I typed out a reference strongly supporting the application of Mr. K. Hardy for full membership of the group for the signature of A. Scott McIver CA. I printed out an application form, filled it in and phoned McIver. 'Something I'd like to have a word about, Scott,' I told him, 'you'll want to invite me for coffee.' I started up the Merc and drove out to his place.

It was a memorable occasion. "Old men forget…" true enough, if Henry V meant the wedding anniversary but they don't forget everything. I was remembering the evening in 1968 when I sat with McIver in the public bar of the Rat and Parrot. We were colleagues at the time at a traditional Ditchfield engineering company that was steadily descending towards oblivion. McIver had his business plan ready for founding Ditchfield Packaging – with forecasts on the back of a fag packet.

The plot involved taking over Bertoni Ltd, a local plastics manufacturer. 'They owe CMI the thick end of £80,000 for raw material and time expires next Wednesday.'

'How do you know?'

McIver grinned, 'I am a Scotchman, Kenneth, and therefore I know everything. CMI's credit controller is frae Dundee.'

It was a choice between awaiting the inevitable or taking a chance with McIver. We started up Ditchfield Packaging Ltd amidst the wreckage of the Bertoni crash. We had a tough three years pulling the firm together followed by a tough twenty-five years making it grow.

Done himself all right, had McIver. His place was beyond Ditchfield's green belt, city by-pass and other inconveniences. It verged on the baronial. I counted the upstairs windows and was unclear why he needed five bedrooms for one McIver, unless he was co-habiting with three housekeepers and a piper.

He greeted me from behind a tactical smokescreen, led me on what seemed to be a long tramp to the kitchen, switched on the kettle, favoured me with a wolfish grin and asked me to name my business.

There was no point in beating about the bush with McIver so I asked, 'What's your connection with AGROW?'

I got the affronted Presbyterian glare, 'Behave yoursel' Kenneth.'

'You're simply advising them on the capital project for building a training centre? At a place called Fellbeck – small beer, for you, isn't it?'

He agreed, 'But one thing leads to another, ken.' I asked, in confidence, what he reckoned the project was worth. 'Thick end of half a million – you cannae expect to change the world on the cheap.'

'And you're talking ten percent?' No answer, which could mean more.

'See, Ken, they're a glaikit flock of feckless intellectuals *but* they've connections to prominent people with serious money.' I was surprised that serious money was interested in backing Enderby's spiritual terrorism. McIver put me right.

'There exists a minority in that category. They've inherited their fathers' assets and their mothers' brains. What's your interest?' I said that I found their philosophy made a change. I believed I had something to offer of the hard-nosed business variety; I counted on him to support my application. 'I ken there's mair to it than that, Ken,' he said, 'but I'll no' enquire.' That was as veiled as McIver's rebukes generally got.

I handed him the letter of introduction, 'One day I'll show you how to write one of these,' he signed it nevertheless, 'watch yoursel' with that Amelia Partington.' Did McIver know about the Ram's Head bed sheets – in principle?

At his front door, 'What do you think AGROW is really about Scott?'

'You heard Enderby at Ditchfield Sceptics last November.'

'They plan to restore the reign of Philosopher Kings.'

'Which never existed,' said McIver and closed the door.

After thirty years, how much did I really know about McIver?

I drove into town. The ironmonger recognised what I wanted. He produced a suitable lock with three keys; I asked if he had the same with four. He looked at the keys. 'Cut you an extra one? Come back after 1.30.'

Jason showed me his list of plant hire companies that had lent out small generator kits between the relevant dates. Opposite three of them, he had pencilled in the names of their customers with phone numbers, there were no "Bensons". I asked about the others. 'They don't disclose clients' names.'

'Fair play,' I said, 'neither would I in their position. Leave them with me, meantime would you like to research the customers you have identified? If they're bona fide, they'll probably turn out to be tradesmen or small builders. All you can do at this stage is to ask them whether the generator was for their own use or did they hire it on behalf of someone called Benson.' Jason made a photostat copy of his list for me.

I photographed the Fellbeck front door key, measured it, took a rubbing and went to collect my padlock.

Braxtonby was where Charles Dawson had joined Attwood's Strolling Players. It had changed beyond recognition since the 1860s to become what estate agents like to describe as a 'thriving market town'. Its sudden growth was explained by a finger post showing the way to "The Old Railway Station". When the man from ICI axed the railway Braxtonby had already lost its rural virginity and become a dormitory for Manchester executives. Having deduced the social history of Braxtonby, I completed my victory by spotting the front door of Helmsley and Jordan, Solicitors and Estate Agents in the main street.

The building was old and over-heated. This was just as well for the girl on the reception desk who was wearing as little as possible above the waist. It was a disappointment when she looked up because when the mass of brown hair fell back, her face looked squashed, top to bottom. It was small, with a low forehead and slitty eyes with black eyebrows forming a straight line above her nose. Her breasts were magnificent, in spite of which, she looked cross.

'Yeah?' asked reception.

'Hardy, here to see Mr. Green.' I saw from a sheet of notepaper on her desk that the firm had three partners: Green was not listed. Unless they had an over-manning crisis, they were substantial for country solicitors.

'Have a seat', the receptionist invited, 'Mr. Green won't be long.' I beat a retreat and sat. Before long, Green appeared ushering out a pair of potentials. The man was a smart late-thirties with his even smarter early-thirties partner who, nice backside notwithstanding, was not getting enough. They looked like four-bed, two-bath, detached exec with large garden and double garage prospects. Green saw them off with ceremony and turned to me.

'Mr. Hardy? About Fellbeck isn't it?' I agreed and suggested that we speak somewhere private. Green took me through to his office. My idea had been to milk Helmsley and Jordan for information on Fellbeck by pretending an interest, I rejected that approach. It would make a change from telling lies.

'This isn't about buying the property', I told him and handed my card across his desk. 'Mr. Harrison is grateful for the loan of the key,' I laid it on his desk, 'actually it's about the murder.'

Green was disappointed that I wasn't a buyer but keen to learn more about the 'shocking' event, 'The actress who was raped and murdered?'

'The victim was a teacher and no lovemaking was involved.' He shrugged and said it was local gossip. I went on to confirm that Harrison and Potts were the defence solicitors in the case. I was present in a paralegal capacity on their behalf.

'Which aspects interest you in particular?' Green asked, recovering from his twin disappointments – no sale, no sex.

'My information is that the Fellbeck property is owned by a family trust and you act as agents on their behalf. Your firm has done this for a long time.'

'Since the nineteen-sixties.'

'We've identified an issue concerning security at the crime scene. Could you tell me how many keys you hold for the front door?' I thought he might shy at that one. I was all ready to advise him on an egg-sucking basis about withholding information in a murder investigation; I didn't have to.

'Three, including this one,' Green got up, went to a wall cabinet, unlocked it and placed two more keys on the desk. They all looked old.

'The police didn't take one in the course of their SOC investigations? Apart from the loan of one to Mr. Harrison, you've had just the set of three all along?' Green claimed they'd had very little contact with the police so far other than confirming that they were the agents for the property. 'You've never had more than these three keys? You didn't once have four?'

Green stiffened his back, 'not in my time, Mr. Hardy, not since 1982.'

'What about the back door?' I asked, 'it's fitted with a lock, which looks original but the door isn't locked and there's no sign of a key. Do you have the keys for the back door as well?' Green was not comfortable about this; he admitted that they held no keys for the back door lock. I pressed on, 'The back door is secured by a padlock which isn't at all satisfactory.'

Green opened his mouth as if he was about to intervene on the lines of "what's that to you?" He had a lot of teeth but they weren't in good nick. I kept talking hoping that it would encourage Green to close his mouth, 'The defence has an interest in the security of the site. The police have completed their SOC investigation. They're off the premises but we haven't yet seen the laboratory report. The defence will want an independent forensic examination and it's likely that the police will want a second look themselves. You can appreciate that neither side would welcome the evidence being disturbed by intruders.'

Green sat looking at me for several seconds, then, 'In my time, and I can go further back if necessary,' he said, 'there has been only one key to the back door, which was kept on site, for reasons of local convenience (*hanging on a string through the letterbox?*). After that key went missing, the padlock arrangement was fitted.' He went back to his cabinet and came back with three padlock keys. I asked whether Helmsley and Jordan had fitted the padlock. 'The owner of South Lea, the farm on the other side of the Preston Road, did it for us. That was Mr. Lewis, who we've known for many years since he bought South Lea.' He paused and leaned forward confidentially, 'in the country we tend to look out for one another and these matters are sometimes dealt with on an informal basis.'

I assured him that I was in sympathy with gobbin-like business procedures (*no wonder there had been trouble with squatters*). 'The thing is, with that padlock,' I said, 'you don't need a key to get the door open. The fixing screws are all exposed so an intruder can open the door by removing four woodscrews.' I produced my own superior padlock assembly and put it on Green's desk. 'I wonder whether you would consider having this fitted instead? I think this is the simplest way to improve security.' I demonstrated the advantage of having the fixing screws hidden beneath the hasp in the closed position. I put on a winning smile, 'in the spirit of rural informality, Mr. Green, I'd be happy to fit it for you. It's no problem for me, I am local, I can do it this weekend and get my assistant to drop in the old padlock on Monday. Then I think we can all rest easy about security. The alternative is to have the back door altered to take a modern lock which would be expensive. But I can arrange it if you prefer.'

'You'll need to take one of the new keys?' Green asked.

'No, you keep the set of three, the padlock self locks.' I demonstrated, 'I'll keep the padlock open until it's fitted to the door, then all I have to do is snap it shut. That will restore full control of the property to you – with our compliments.' He accepted promptly before I passed him an invoice for seven quid plus labour. I opened up the lock and then handed him the three keys. I got up; there was an air of friendly relaxation, not a bad lad for an estate agent. Hopefully there was more to come so I offered cheering news.

'I understand that a charity organization is interested in buying Fellbeck. A friend of mine is a member – AGROW, they call themselves. I spelled out the acronym for him. I'm told they have plans to convert the house to an educational centre. It sounds serious.'

'Really?' (Mentally calculating his commission on £250K?) 'I take it they've already viewed the place?'

'We've had one interested party who borrowed the key over a weekend – said he wanted his surveyor to have a look. The name AGROW was not mentioned. I've heard no more since April so I thought the idea had died. Most likely that was a different enquiry altogether.' I was betting that it wasn't.

'I'll keep you updated on AGROW's project,' I promised and left.

22

I drove to Coldedge to ensure a mobile signal then stopped and phoned Niall from the car. 'South Lea at Coldedge, on the opposite side of the Preston Road from Fellbeck. Built shortly after Ezra Dawson's Fellbeck. Can we check on a chap there called Lewis? He was the farmer there within the last ten years. He may have sold up and retired. If so, is it possible to find out who the owner is now? I'm sure Jason could do it.'

I phoned Pam to see if Tom was back from visiting Chris. He was, she put me through. He didn't sound cheerful.

'Well I've got all sorts of nice things to tell you,' I said, 'but as it's Friday, you'll have to meet me in the Duke at five, else you won't find out.'

For a successful young lawyer entering a pub on a Friday afternoon, Tom did not look happy. He dropped his flank forward physicals into a chair whilst I fetched him a drink. 'How's Chris?' His expression remained pessimistic. 'Be careful with that face on', I advised, 'if the wind changes…'

'I'll risk it. Cheers'. Even the first healing draught of the weekend did not appear to help matters, 'Chris asked about pleading guilty to get it over.'

'Guilty? Not insane is he?'

'The psychiatrist has been having a go at him and he says that he's not psychotic, or psychopathic or schizophrenic or any of the other "ics" which might cause him to murder his girlfriend.'

'I could have told you that for half the price.'

'The diagnosis is that he's depressed.'

'Brilliant! How bad is it? Is he on suicide watch or Prozac?'

'I had a word with the Governor. He says they're aware of the situation but he prefers to rely on informal precautions – checking more often.'

I asked whether Chris had come up with any new information. 'Could he put dates to any of Benson's phone calls?'

'Not exact dates but he was able to bracket dates for some of the calls'. Tom got out his notebook. 'He's got 5th to 7th May – that was the first Benson call early in the summer term.'

'That's right, and it was definitely Thursday 6th May.'

Then several from early June until late July, he can't recall dates. The one he's sure of was the first day of the autumn term, 9th September. Finally, he thinks 16th November, when Benson phoned him to confirm the meeting at Fellbeck. It's something to work with so I'll see if BT can help us. What are all these nice things you've got to tell me?'

'It'll cost you.' Tom drained his pint, picked up my empty and hulked off to the bar. He was not in the mood to be interested in suspicions or wild speculations so I decided to stick to the facts. 'I've been talking to Helmsley and Jordan – a Mr. Green.'

'What did a Mr Green provide?'

'More on the front door key issue', I told him. 'As we know, Chris left Fellbeck to phone the police. He closed the front door but couldn't lock it because there was no key, so he left it like that. When the police brought him back, the front door was locked and the key was inside on the mat.

I checked with Green and he showed me two keys in his locked cabinet plus the key I'd just returned. He says there have always been three keys, since 1982. They all look the same – original Victorians. Where did the key on the doormat come from?'

Tom brightened up marginally, 'Go on.'

'I asked Green whether anyone had viewed the property recently. He said "yes, back in April", but he'd written it off as a non-starter. I said that it was a slow burner, not a write-off. Then he said the interested party borrowed a key for a couple of days, saying that they wanted their surveyor to have a look. That would have given them time to take a moulding so they could have a copy made. If the key the police have is a recent copy then someone has some explaining to do.'

'Interesting, if I can see the police key, I should be able to tell?'

'If it's a copy – straightaway – unless it had been aged chemically. In that case, a simple metallurgical analysis would settle the issue.'

'But if it matches the originals we're no further forward.'

'Except, where did Chris get his hands on a previously unknown key?'

'Did Green give you the name of the man that borrowed the key in April?'

'No, and I didn't ask him.'

Tom was disappointed, 'Why not, Ken? If the man that borrowed the key matches our description of Benson...'

'Tom, he won't, no point in me rushing it. If the key on the doormat is an original that means someone had key number four all along.'

'I could push DCI Kent for an analysis done on the key they've got.'

'Yes, but save it. There's no point in warning Kent what we're up to. Why not hang about until I can get more evidence? Let's see if I can track down the locksmith that made a copy. If I can, that'll settle it.'

I needn't have worried. Tom's fertile imagination had already dredged up another objection. 'Having a copy made wouldn't prove a connection with the murder. Suppose it was a genuine enquiry. They wanted to get colleagues to look at the place, get a surveyor in, and so on. To save the bother of traipsing off to H&J each time, they had a copy made up. Now they've dropped the idea of buying the place, didn't want to own up, so they posted their copy key through the letter box and walked away. All they are responsible for is causing the manufacture of an unauthorised copy and using it to enter the property without the knowledge of the owners. It lay there on the mat until Chris found it while he was doing a recce for the murder. You've already shown that he didn't need a key to get inside Fellbeck.'

'Just a screwdriver. It's a bloody good job,' I said, 'that you're not running the prosecution, otherwise Chris would be looking at brochures for prisons offering luxury life sentences. I've had Jason putting in hours at the library trying to identify all the Bensons within a thirty mile radius and then phoning round to ask who they were murdering on the evening of 23rd November. So far he's made no progress.'

Tom was not surprised, 'You need far more resources than that to track down a suspect.' He finished his drink and left.

On Saturday morning, I drove out to Fellbeck as promised and fitted the new padlock. Back at the flat, there was a message on the answer phone – the lovely Virginia wished to help me with aspects of the case. Would I like to join them for supper, say 7.30? The idea of a mystical encounter with Virginia was irresistible. An evening of roses and wine had to be healthier than the Frog and Toad.

'Ken, I'm way behind,' said Virginia when I arrived, 'would you mind awfully popping the gangsters round to my sister's; it's only five minutes by car.'

The kids came tumbling downstairs in their pyjamas carrying bags for the morning. It looked like a rehearsed routine. They were Aislin and Seren, seven and five respectively and seriously evil. They were on first name terms with their parents and extended that courtesy to me. I got directions from their mother, made sure they were strapped into the back seat and set off. The gangsters were in high spirits, they much preferred auntie Georgie's house they said, being equipped with cousins, two of whom were *boys,* though it had to be admitted that (uncle) Dave was not a patch on (dad) Niall as a story-teller. 'Niall does all the voices,' Aislin said. After that they started up a chant:

Naughty Jeanie went to TEEEOWN
Someone pulled her panties DEEEOWN!

The next two lines broke up into wild giggles after which they started again from the top. I heard two encores and then deliberately turned left instead of right at the next T-junction. Cries of 'No, no Ken, it's the wrong way.' I pulled up, transferred Aislin to the front seat (wails from Seren) and appointed her navigator. Two minutes later the job was done and dusted.

I joined Niall before the sitting room fire for the sipping of Gs & Ts. 'Is Tom remustering as a manic depressive do you think? After work I met him in the Duke. He sat there with a Friday face on, drinking my beer and thinking up arguments in favour of the prosecution. After that he legged it.'

'Take no notice,' said Niall, 'he's always like that part way into a case. It's the legal temperament; he'll be all over you next week.'

The lovely Virginia floated in looking ethereal in a long, loose dress in earth shades of pink and brown too subtle to risk comment. I noticed her 1960's style of walking: hips leading and swinging her arms outward as if offering to embrace all and sundry (*I'd like to build the world a home and lock the buggers in*). I made an appreciative noise. 'Indian cotton,' said Virginia, swishing the skirts about, 'do you like it?' I liked what was in it but failed to mention that. Virginia produced tagliatelle, with wild mushrooms (*hallucinogenic?*), Mediterranean vegetables, no chips.

After dinner, Virginia showed me the holistic way to load the dishwasher whilst Niall investigated the possibility that he had won the Lottery. 'Niall thinks that with the right combination of telepathy and distant viewing he ought to be able to predict the results,' his wife said.

'I didn't know he was telepathic.'

'He isn't, but I am.' I wondered why she couldn't be telepathic on Niall's behalf. 'Because that's not what telepathy's about.' Which explained everything.

After pouring the remains of the white paint stripper into my wine glass, Virginia produced a map of Northern England and spread it out. 'I've been researching your crime scene, Ken. Why was Caroline Enderby murdered at Fellbeck and what was the motive?'

I was more interested in Virginia's opinion, but I gave her mine for starters. 'It's a deserted Victorian mansion with a forbidding atmosphere in a remote location. The topography of the valley blocks mobile signals. That meant that Chris had to drive to Coldedge to contact the police leaving time for the murderers to escape. As to motive: I don't know.'

'Not bad', said Virginia, 'as a cognitive approach.' I could see that "cognitive" implied idiotic. 'The clue is the ambience; look at the map.'

She had drawn a pencil line, starting from Lancaster in a south-easterly direction. 'There you are: Gallows Hill, near Lancaster, to Fellbeck and finishing at Pendle Hill. What does that say?' Surprisingly, I didn't know.

Virginia enlightened me, 'Fellbeck is on a ley line'.

'What's a ley line when it's at home?' Virginia explained that it was an alignment running through ancient sacred sites believed to have special energy and cosmic power. The more intersections you have on a point the greater the energy – Glastonbury Tor's one of the best known.'

'So you mean if a place is on a ley line it's an excuse to go there to partake of booze, class A drugs, unprotected sex, heavy rock and murder?'

'No one is saying we have to accept it, Ken.' Niall spoke up loyally, 'Virginia's trying to throw some light on the world view of the perpetrators.'

I apologised and had just enough sense to ask Virginia to explain what the significance might be of the points forming the Fellbeck ley line. 'You've heard of the Pendle witches, Ken?' I had of course, they were locals.

'There's a reference in the Benson document isn't there?' I asked Niall, 'the leader of the strolling players devised a drama about them.'

'Good,' Virginia said, 'we know that the activities of the witches centred on Pendle, they were tried at Lancaster and hanged on Gallows Hill – there.'

'What about Fellbeck, then?'

'I don't know yet,' Virginia admitted, 'the general theory is that place names ending in "ley", or "lea" which is just a corruption, indicate ley lines. That would explain South Lea across the road. And "fell" in Fellbeck implies evil. I think that Fellbeck might have been the original site of Malkin Tower, where the Pendle witches held their covens. No one knows where the Tower was or what it looked like.'

'Not a witch yourself?' in candlelight, she could pass as one darkly.

'Of course she is', said Niall, ' – a white witch.'

'There's a reinforcing factor here,' Virginia said, she drew a second line passing southwest from Leyburn in Yorkshire, bisecting the gap between Fellbeck and South Lea to Leyland. If that is a second ley line it's really powerful.' I suspected that the same trick could be done with red telephone boxes. I said nowt about that.

Back at the flat, I restored myself with baked beans on toast and bottled beer. I'd had my fill of paranormal connections and gleaned nothing in the way of facts. What had my evening with the psychic Madame Potts really been about?

23

On Monday morning, I put my head in at Niall's office door. He was cleaning his glasses, which meant that he detected my presence as a talking blur. 'It was good of Virginia to go to all that trouble', I said.

'It gave her a chance to express herself in the kitchen – Tibetan psychedelic herbs. If you'd known what was in the soup you wouldn't have touched it.'

'The soup was magic. I meant all the trouble she went to over ley lines.'

Niall expressed reservations about swallowing ley lines along with hallucinogenic mushrooms. He put a final polish on his glasses and inspected me at short range. 'Whether you believe in ley lines or not, do they constitute a motive for murder?'

I changed the subject, 'You haven't forgotten about Lewis?'

'It was a simple matter of checking the local estate agents to find who handled the sale.' He handed over a sheet of paper inscribed with scribbles.

I passed it back. 'Did you ever think of taking up medicine?'

Niall deciphered for me, 'Lewis was the owner of South Lea from 1962. We're not interested in the previous owner? No? Good. Lewis retired when his wife died. He sold up and went to live in North Wales. He died there a year later.'

'Who bought South Lea?'

'Mr F. H. Meyer, completion was in September 1998'

I thanked him and went back to the flat. I put the kettle on for coffee and got out my Preston phone directory. I was betting that it was out of date; I was in luck: F. H. Meyer, 42 Walpole Gardens, Longacre Crescent. If that was him, he wasn't short of a bob – an apartment on the 4th floor of Walpole Gardens, in the fashionable part of Preston *(If there is such a thing)*. I dialled the Preston number. It rang.

'What?' It could have been a rough-tough woman executive or the cleaner.

'I'd like to speak to Mr Meyer.'

'Oo?' I said I understood Mr Meyer lived at Apartment 42.

'He doesn't live 'ere.'

'You mean he's moved away? Do you know when?'

''Ang on, I'll see.' Receding shuffling sounds as the slippered lady went to seek information. After a short pause, I heard her returning, ''E used to live 'ere, but 'e's gone.' The phone went down with a bang. I made coffee and phoned Niall's secretary, 'When he's free, would you ask Mr Potts if I could borrow Jason for the afternoon, say from two o'clock onwards?'

It was time to set up the tests on Stefan's super new material. At the works, Ed was ready for me. 'The main claim is that you can reduce film thickness by fifteen to twenty percent and end up with a cost saving.'

'So we'll make representative samples, send them to the lab and see whether their claims stand up?'

Ed agreed, 'I'll make space on the schedule to start on Wednesday morning, all done by the weekend.'

I went into town and bought a set of Ordnance Survey maps covering the area of Virginia's ley lines. They were bigger scale and more reliable than the tourist map that she had used. I opened out the dining room table, laid out the maps to join up correctly and taped them together. I hadn't been able to get the Ordnance sheet for Leyburn; instead, I estimated the bearing from Leyland from a road map and drew the line on that angle. It passed between Fellbeck and South Lea. The line from Gallows Hill to Pendle summit missed Fellbeck by a furlong and crossed the Leyland to Leyburn line in the field between Fellbeck and the modern Preston road. I didn't know what accuracy the mystics worked to but I guessed it was near enough.

Virginia rang, (*so she really is telepathic?*) 'I need to connect with Fellbeck to interpret it properly. Would you take me there?'

'Would tomorrow do? I need to organize a key.' I didn't, but why tell the lawyers? We agreed 9.15, hot from the school run.

'Fancy a drive in the country?' I asked Jason. At Braxtonby Jason parked outside Helmsley and Jordan. I handed him the old padlock. 'Give this to the receptionist. Tell her it's from me for Mr. Green.' He was back in a couple of minutes and we drove to Preston.

Walpole Gardens was an executive-style development – big lawn in front, no gardens. I got Jason to park fifty yards short of the site entrance and handed him a copy of the photo of Caroline that I had borrowed from Chris's flat. 'I want to find out whether there was any truth in the school rumour about Meyer and Caroline Enderby,' I told him. 'I already know that Meyer lived in one of the top floor apartments here until March last year. We'll concentrate on Walpole Gardens and ask people if they recognise the woman in the photo.'

'What's the story?' Jason wanted to know.

'People may recognise the photo from the newspaper reports of the murder,' I said, 'say that we're part of the legal team looking for information in connection with a murder case. Then show them the picture and ask if they recall seeing this woman arriving or leaving the building at any time up to last March. If you get one that sounds convincing, try for more details – date, time, anything of interest. Don't press them too hard – they might imagine themselves on television and get their imaginations into overdrive. I'll do the top two floors, you start on the ground and we'll meet back at the car.'

At the main entrance, there was the usual security

arrangement with rows of buttons labelled with the occupants' names. We could try bluff.

Jason had a better idea. 'There's a service road leading round to the back, to the car park. There'll be back doors where people put out their rubbish bins to be emptied. I bet someone will have left one unlocked. It's always happening up our street.' He was right, we were in.

There was no point trying 42 on the top floor, 41 and 44 did not answer my ring – out earning their six-figure salaries. 43 panicked and shut the door on me. 45 was a pleasant middle-aged woman who would like to help, "that was a dreadful business, wasn't it?" but they had only just moved in. The third floor was no help either.

I went back to the car and waited for Jason. I expected him to take longer because the lower level flats were smaller – eight on each floor. I also thought that the owners would be younger and more up Jason's street. After fifteen minutes, I began to fear that I had dropped him into the clutches of a desperate housewife. A couple of minutes later he came back only slightly dishevelled. He had a couple of possibles – not good enough.

We were starting to rethink when a trim figure in blazer and school mini-skirt walked past. Her navy beret was perched rakishly on top of blonde curls – a senior girl on her way home from school. Without a word, Jason got out of the car and followed her along the pavement clutching the photo. He caught up with her at the entrance to the development and they stood in serious conversation, the girl was looking at the picture and nodding. After five minutes, Jason came back looking pleased.

'You're not in love again?'

The boy sleuth ignored that, he was full of other information I did not need. 'Her name's Briony,' he confided, 'she's in her final year in the sixth and she's planning to do Human Biology and French at Nottingham.' (*An international career in the sex industry?*) 'We're going to meet next year when we're both at Uni.' (*A bilingual stripper with legal adviser as partner*). Finally, Jason jolted me out of my geriatric fantasies. 'Briony recognised the photo. She says that a woman just like Mrs. Enderby was a visitor at Walpole Gardens but she hasn't seen her for over a year. She used to park her car round the back and sometimes it was still there in the morning.' Briony lives at 34 and she could see the car from her bedroom window, it was blue.'

'Brilliant! Just what we need.' We drove back in triumph.

'No chance today, or tomorrow I'm afraid,' said Tom's dragon.

'It can wait, it's only a breakthrough,' I told Pam, 'tell him I was asking.'

I wrote my report and then settled down to a disgusting Monday evening with Chris's Jack the Ripper library. The phone rang, 'Miss Deedes here from the reference library,' it said. We arranged to meet in a discreet wine bar (*as opposed to Julio's indiscreet one*) at 6.15 on Wednesday.

Tuesday morning began with a breathlessly excited weather forecaster. 'Clearing skies have resulted in *struggling* temperatures with a widespread frost and icy patches on untreated …(breath) *Roads!*' It was comforting to know that temperatures were putting up a fight on our behalf. Whilst I took a simple breakfast, morning television interviewed an American Third Division celebrity anxious to tell us how much she "*lerved her familee*". Fearing cue for a song, I switched off.

Virginia welcomed me, looking delectable. She took me into the dining room where she had a map of England spread out on the dining room table. 'Look at that,' she instructed, 'while I put my coat on'. There were now three ley lines instead of two. Virginia had drawn a new and much longer line from Lindisfarne in Northumberland, crossing the other two near the point she had assumed Fellbeck to be and ending near Weymouth in Dorset. She came back in her coat and boots, 'Well?'

'This new line from Lindisfarne, that's Holy Island, isn't it? What's at the other end? Weymouth?'

'Ken! Not Weymouth,' said Virginia. She put a slender finger on the point. 'Cerne Abbas, it's a village, too small to be on this map.'

'What about it?'

I was expected to know, 'The Cerne Abbas giant, carved on the hillside.'

'You mean the naked man with a big club and willy to match?' Virginia gave me a look. I pressed on, 'I thought it wasn't genuine, an eighteenth century student prank organised to annoy the bishop.' She admitted that was a theory concocted by sceptical materialists *(like me)*. Virginia preferred the alternative: it really had been carved three thousand years earlier as part of a Bronze Age fertility rite. She admitted that the Hell Fire club may have tidied it up a bit, 'And that's all there is to know about the sceptic version.' When she looked like that I wasn't going to argue.

24

The clear skies had persisted so far, so had the frost, which was sparkling in the sun as we drove out of town. It was that rare sort of morning which threatened to make December popular in North East Lancs. I did not expect it to last, but with the lovely Virginia strapped in alongside, why knock it? She asked me to repeat what I'd told Niall about my coffee shop dream and Jenny Finch. I took her literally and told her nothing else.

When I turned onto the muddy track leading to Fellbeck, Virginia stopped talking. I thought she was worried. I took a sideways glance; she was looking straight ahead, deep breaths, eyes wide open. I pulled up facing the front door. Virginia asked me to check that it was locked, it was. I stood back for a moment looking up at the massive stonework with the 'ED' carving above the porch. In the bright sunlight the house was sparkling with frost and doing its best to look innocent, 'Who are you trying to kid?'

I walked Virginia along the side of the house. The water slipped silently alongside as before; what did it take to make it chatter or lap against the banks like a proper beck? At the back door I released the new padlock and put it in my pocket. She followed me into the scullery and to the door leading into the main part of the house. I opened the scullery door and held it open for her. It was a plainer version of the doors in the residential part of the house nonetheless, it was solid. In spite of the sunshine outside, the passage was gloomy – the only light came from the entrance hall at the far end. The fanlight over the front door was glazed with a sunburst pattern in Victorian stained glass allowing some light to burst through. I got out my torch and switched it on. Virginia said, 'We don't need that. Caroline's body was found – where?'

'The sitting room, it's the second door on the right.' I followed her up the passage, her heels clicking confidently on the oak floorboards. (*Has she been here before?*) She was wearing a white skirt with pleats which flickered interestingly below the hem of her camel coat. We turned into the sitting room. The sunlight streamed through the big windows illuminating the tatty furniture, faded red curtains and the grimy wallpaper.

I spoke quietly, as if something was listening. 'Caroline was found here, lying in front of the fireplace. There was a brass fender here with bloodstains and hand prints that were probably Chris's, forensic have got that. Virginia was standing in front of the hearth, gazing up at the ceiling. I was about to ask her about the carving on the bosses when a sharp tapping sound came from above, seven or eight taps and then nothing. I felt the hairs go up all down my back. 'Frost melting on the roof...?' I whispered hopefully, 'water dripping between the slates onto the attic floor?'

'No it isn't that. Ken, come here, feel the draught.'

I stretched out my hand towards the fireplace, 'there's cold air coming down the chimney. You'd expect that in winter.'

'No, feel here, she was pointing down to where Caroline's body had lain. 'Can't you feel the cold draught coming up from the floor?' This was Borley Rectory stuff. I put my hand down level with her ankle. I took my glove off, I wasn't certain; Virginia was. If there was a cold draught it was going straight up her skirt. 'This is where Jenny Finch was murdered as well.'

'I've only seen the newspaper report from sixty years ago – not very detailed. It could have been the room next door.'

Virginia shook her head. 'It was here, but that doesn't matter.' She was looking up at the wall above the fireplace.

I remembered the picture that hung there when I spoke to

Ostrick. I fancied I could make out a faint memory of it on the wall. 'Could all this date back to the founder, Ezra Dawson? Ezra died in 1891 but I met an old shepherd in the village whose great grandfather worked here as a young man – Ezra was a right nasty piece of work, Dick said.'

She was looking up at the wall as though the picture was still there. 'Yes, he still is.'

'Dick Barber said that when Ezra's wife was taken with consumption he wouldn't have the doctor and the talk in the village was that Ezra had suffocated her with a pillow.'

Virginia was still looking at the "picture", 'Mmm'. She didn't explain.

I asked if I could show her something in the room next door. I took her through the connecting door.

'According to Chris's statement, this was the murderers' escape route,' I said, 'I think it may have been a dining room, being between the sitting room and the kitchens, but it's big enough for a billiard room.'

Virginia looked about her, 'Ezra used it for meetings. I've a strong sense of that – a dozen or more people.'

I pointed to the floorboards on the inside of the door, 'what do you make of these spots on the floor?'

Virginia crouched to look: a slim figure, small breasts, neatly booted feet peeping from under her skirts, dark hair veiling her face. *(Stop looking at her)*. 'Candle wax: red and green; nothing to do with the murder, candle wax doesn't hold messages – red and green suggests a children's Christmas party.' I put out a hand to help her up. She took it and stood close smiling into my face, 'Sorry, Kenneth, nothing there'.

We returned to the sitting room. Virginia said, 'Ken, this is what I want to do. Dreadful things have happened here: three murders at least. They're not important, *(they are to me)* but I feel a presence. I need to be alone; otherwise it won't reveal itself.'

'I'm not leaving you in this place.'

Virginia smiled in a motherly way; making me feel like a seven year-old. 'Yes, Ken, I'm a sensitive, a trained medium. Give me half an hour, I want you to go back and sit in the car – don't move. On your way out, put the padlock back on the door and lock it.'

I could hardly believe that, 'But you'll be locked in!'

Another smile, *(one step at a time, children)*, 'For safety. If an intruder were to interrupt, it could go horribly wrong. Sit in the car. When I've finished, I'll wave to you from the window.' I protested, but we did it her way or not at all.

I dallied, 'What if you don't come to the window?'

'If there's no sign after forty minutes, come in. You may find me in a trance state, if so, don't do anything. Whatever you do, don't try to bring me out of it. Just sit with me until I wake up naturally.' She smiled at me, 'don't look so worried Kenneth, go away.'

I did as I was told, when Virginia looked like that it was hard not to. Selfishly, I was glad to be out of that place. I got into the car. What if there was an emergency? The mobile would be no use – no signal. I sat for an age staring at the window of the murder room; thirty five minutes by my watch, then the faded curtain swung back and she waved. I walked round to the rear of the building and unlocked the back door. Virginia was waiting inside, white-faced.

'What's up? You look as if you've seen a ghost!'

She took a step over the threshold and stood there swaying. I caught her, put my arms round her and helped her down the steps. 'Hold me and rub my back', said Virginia. She pressed against me, 'nice,' she said. It was nice – too nice – I was hard pressed to conceal the effect on my lower region. She must have noticed but she didn't pull away. I asked how she got on. 'Interesting, shall we go?'

The back door was standing wide open. I stepped up to close it – and froze – heavy, thumping footsteps walking away up the hallway, slow, one …two…three… It had followed her to the scullery door. This time it wasn't PC Dunn collecting evidence. Before I could move, Virginia was past me to the scullery door, wrenching it open, 'Stay there Ken,' she hissed at me and disappeared up the passage. I wasn't staying anywhere, I followed her.

This time there was extra light coming in from the open door behind us. All it showed was that the passage was empty. I caught up with Virginia standing transfixed in the sitting room. 'Shit!' she whispered, 'I thought he was going to materialise.' I was bloody glad "he" hadn't.

She was shivering, so was I. I locked up quickly, took her back to the car, started the engine and turned up the heater, 'Are you all right?'

She gave me a peaky smile and shivered violently, 'No but I'm getting there. The cold outside is nothing. It's the cold inside. I've lost a lot of energy; it sucks it out of you.'

I asked what the antidote was. 'Coffee, black, very hot, lots of sugar – and a warm place to rest.' I put my foot down. There was no suitable stopping place on the Ditchfield road. I headed for the flat. Virginia closed her eyes and seemed to fall asleep. When I pulled up she woke with a soft moan and asked where we were. 'My place, come in, don't argue'. She didn't argue, but I took her by the arm anyway and got her indoors and up the stairs. Luckily there was no one about. I took her into the sitting room and sat her in one of the fireside armchairs. The central heating was off so I plugged in the big convector heater. 'Sit still', I said and went to the kitchen, switched the central heating on, turned it up and started the coffee – Arabica double strength.

When I came back, she was sitting where I'd left her with her ankles neatly together, pale and interesting. 'Here we are,' I said, 'official Lazarus formula, recommended for corpses of all types.'

She took a couple of sips, 'Ken, you're very keen to solve this. Were you in love with Caroline?'

'No more than the rest of Ditchfield.' I fetched the photo that I'd rescued from the flat.

Virginia gave the picture a glance and handed it back, '*She* was in love'.

'She was in love to the end. Caroline sat here on my sofa and told me on the evening she was murdered. And you can get off, sharp,' I told the cat, which had curled up on Virginia's lap while my back was turned.

'No', Virginia protested, 'he's what I need. He's drawing out the evil.'

'He's evil enough already.' Virginia sipped more coffee which she said was 'lovely and just right'.

'No rush,' I said, 'tell me when you're ready.'

'You're being very masterful,' she said with a knowing smile, 'am I quite safe?' I let that one go. Having absorbed his ration of evil, the cat stalked off to the kitchen. I went to get Virginia a refill. When I came back, she had taken her coat off and was showing a touch of colour.

'You're looking better.'

'Would you turn the heater off now? It's making the air dry.' I did that. 'We've found Malkin Tower,' Virginia said, 'I'm sure. That agrees with the ley lines, three of them, very powerful.'

'You mean where the Pendle witches met? But that was two hundred years before Ezra built Fellbeck.'

'We don't know what Malkin Tower was like. It may have been a shepherd's hut or a peasant's hovel. But it could have been a substantial building; one of the witches is known to have owned property. Anyway, whatever evil went on in Ezra's time wasn't the beginning. Think of the name – "Fellbeck".'

'Doesn't that just mean the beck coming from the fells?'

'It doesn't rise in the fells. It comes down from the moorland – short of the high fells country. There's another meaning in Anglo-Saxon: unlucky, evil.'

'It's just a beck, what was evil about it?' She was confirming what I already felt. I wanted to know why.

Virginia gave me a dainty shrug, 'Could be anything, a colony of monks massacred by a Viking raiding party like at Lindisfarne.'

I was getting impatient, 'We're back to the Dark Ages now. How is this to help with Chris Berry's defence case?'

Virginia smiled indulgently, 'It doesn't, Ken, I'm sorry, it doesn't help at all and it never will.'

'I was hoping it might help to get inside the minds of the murderer.'

Virginia shot that down, 'No, the house was used for the murder for practical reasons: it's empty and isolated. It suited the purpose, nothing supernatural. But I'm sure there's a presence; you felt it too, didn't you?'

'I felt it just now with you, but not with Tom. I wouldn't like to spend a night there on my own', I admitted.

'Don't. People have gone out of their minds that way.' (*I might be willing to risk it as a twosome*). 'There's nothing there, it's confusing you.'

I promised not to attempt a night vigil. Virginia got back to the point. 'Forget Fellbeck, you won't find the murderer there. Look for Benson.'

I had a last try, 'Chris stated that when Benson let them in, the house felt warm, almost inviting. There was a log fire in the sitting room but that would have taken forever just to warm up that room, never mind the entrance hall as well. Could the warmth have been paranormal?'

Virginia was recovering, she tackled me with conviction, 'There's nothing supernatural about Caroline's murder, Ken. It was human and nasty.'

'All right, I have a witch of whatever variety in my sitting room telling me that Fellbeck is a seriously spiritual location defined by ley lines. The house is haunted by a spiritual presence which may be evil and which narrowly failed to materialise.'

'If it had appeared, I could have discovered what it was about. In these cases there's often a message. But it would be unimportant as far as you're concerned, Ken, because it would have nothing to do with Caroline's murder.'

I supposed that was a result of sorts. 'In your capacity as official *claire voyant* to the defence team, where should I be looking?'

'The usual boring old thing – love, sex, jealousy, revenge – Chris wasn't Caroline's only lover after she married Martyn. Is there an ex out of his mind with jealousy? *(Meyer?)* Or was something terribly wrong with Chris?'

'As a cynical old sceptic, I should be pleased, but you've rather killed off the romance,' I complained.

'Sorry Ken, there's nothing romantic or paranormal about this murder.' Suddenly Virginia was deathly pale again. Talking seemed to have exhausted her. She quickly finished her coffee and stood up. I found myself coming over protective *(Protective? Not like you, Hardy)*.

I said, 'do you want to pop downstairs and see Niall?' She didn't. 'Good, I'll take you home.'

She looked up at me with a sad smile, 'I'd rather you took me to bed.' She had to be kidding, what would the lovely Virginia want in bed with Hardy?

'Certainly, so would I.' I picked up her coat and held it for her to slip into. Then I drove her home and waited at the gate while she opened her door.

On the way back, I thought of something: Virginia had mentioned jealous ex-lovers, did that exclude a multi-cuckolded husband? Why had the witch got me to take her to Fellbeck?

Was she trying to simply put me off the place by scaring me rigid? Had the lovely Virginia taken *me* for a ride that morning and overdone it just a touch?

25

Pam Fisher phoned, 'I gave Mr. Harrison your message, he can give you five at five to five.' Nothing if not precise, Tom's dragon.

Prompt before five, I told Tom what we had discovered at Walpole Gardens. 'I reckon this is hard evidence. If it's correct, Meyer's up to his neck in motive, means and opportunity. He's suspect number one.'

T. Harrison refused to be excited, 'We need confirmation. I wouldn't like to depend on Briony's evidence in court.' I saw what he meant, also saw the way a Ditchfield jury might see it. 'When do you plan to see Meyer?'

'It'll have to be next week now. Remember I've a job to do for Stefan? I'll try for Monday.'

'Well, let's see if we can rattle his cage a bit. But Ken, *(always a "but" with lawyers)* don't go over the top.'

I offered Jason's services for the rest of the week. 'He's been trying to locate the source of Benson's hired generator to run the lights at Fellbeck. Can you keep him busy until I've finished for Stefan?'

'Where is Jason now?'

'Niall grabbed him, said he's got a job for him.'

'Right monkey,' said the senior partner and reached for his phone. *(Was there tension in the partnership over this case?)* Diplomatic-like, I bowed out. I had reasons of my own now for wanting Jason to be with Tom rather than Niall.

By the end of Wednesday afternoon we had a machine making samples from Stefan's wonder material. I left them to get on with it and drove back to the flat for a wash and change before setting off on my date with the librarian.

Miss Deedes was sitting gauntly at a table for two, sipping Americano. I ordered similar and sat down to enjoy the volleys of bangs and crashes from the Italian coffee machine. I produced a printout of the Benson text.

'This what I want to know about,' I began. To my considerable relief, Miss Deedes grabbed the document and set about scanning the pages at a phenomenal rate. That done, she proceeded to tear me off a strip. 'You said, Mr. Hardy that you want to look into the background of the Jenny Finch murder in 1934, with particular reference to Nathaniel Ostrick. Now you've produced what looks like a biographical fragment dealing with Charles Dawson, a Victorian theatre manager, who *might* have murdered an actress forty years earlier.' She passed the document back, 'I can't help you...'

I began to express disappointment, but the archivist had not quite finished '... unless you are prepared to be more open. You're not an author, are you? Are you a journalist looking to dig up something sensational about the murder of Caroline Enderby?'

It was my turn to come the frosty, 'Not parajournalist, but paralegal, here's my card. This concerns the defence team in the Enderby murder case and I can't risk any of it leaking into the Ditchfield gossip machine.'

For a moment I thought Miss Deedes was going to issue an invitation to "step outside". I was not looking forward to her left jab. Instead, she laughed, 'If we've finished insulting one another, Mr. Hardy, shall we leave it there, or get down to business?'

I got down to business. I explained the significance of the Benson document. 'I can't show you the original because it's an exhibit for the trial. The original looks old – hand written on old fashioned legal paper, yellow round the edges, and the handwriting style looks Victorian. If the actual age of the document is important we can have that confirmed professionally. I'm interested in what can be extracted philologically. When I came to you at first, it was about the Fellbeck murder in 1934. There are clear similarities between the two cases which cause me to wonder whether there was a copycat element in the Enderby murder. The killer in the earlier case was the farmer, Nathaniel Ostrick. It has been suggested that he was related to the Dawsons. If you come across any information on that it could be useful, if only to avoid wasting time on a false lead.'

Miss Deedes explained that she could not undertake this as part of her library duties, so would have to charge for her services, at the eye-watering rate of, 'I'm afraid, Mr. Hardy, seven pounds per hour.'

I beat her up to eight pounds fifty, 'I shall need an invoice from you for services rendered so I can recover expences. You'll want to declare the income for tax purposes. Could you phone me with a brief progress report, say 6th January? My name's Ken.'

'I'm relieved you turned out to be a businessman,' said Emmeline.

The trials in the works finished, I wrote up my report for Stefan and emailed it, copy to Ed; job done. I was relieved to get back to the investigation – my end of January deadline was beginning to loom.

On Monday morning I rang Gloria at St Cuthbert's. I asked about the chances of contacting Meyer. 'Ring me again between 11.15 and midday', she suggested, 'he should be free then. I'll put you through to his office.'

'Will he be teaching for the rest of the day?'

'Almost, he's only got one period free.' I phoned the school again at 11.25 and got straight through.

'Meyer. Yes?'

A charmer, but Chris had warned me. I explained that I was assisting Harrison and Potts with the defence brief for the Berry murder case.

'What do you mean by "assisting"?'

'I mean gathering information in a paralegal capacity. You knew both the accused and the victim. Berry was working in your department so you are clearly a source for the background to the case.'

'Why should I talk to you?'

'That's your decision, Mr. Meyer. If you're not willing to talk on an informal basis you're likely to be called as a witness. I thought you would prefer to avoid a court appearance. The trial is expected to last four weeks.' (*Never threaten the customer, it might work*).

'I'll give you ten minutes. Four o'clock in my office,' he instructed. He made it sound as though I was reporting for six of the best. 'If you're more than five minutes late I won't wait.' Now he sounded like a cut-price airline. I accepted and rang off.

Progress, I thought. Since I knew where he'd be all afternoon I could safely have a sniff round South Lea in his absence. In case Meyer nipped home during the lunch hour, I left it until one o'clock before I set out.

South Lea was on the "new" Preston Road from Coldedge. The country was a little less rugged at this end of the valley; there was a modern bridge over the beck, wider than that on the Braxtonby road. Away to my right was the dark mass of Fellbeck, John Bolton's sheep spread over the big home field, no one about. I turned left onto the farm track leading to South Lea and drove beside the beck, bare trees to the left, hedge-topped bank on the right – almost a copy of the approach to Fellbeck, but shorter and much better kept. I pulled up at the front door and got out.

From where I stood, it was obvious what Edward Dawson meant in his 1890 letter to Charles. Cousin Ludwig had built his house to rival Fellbeck. The front elevation looked like a cut price version of Ezra's house. The windows were the same design but only three quarters the size. The stone porch had cylindrical pillars assembled from four foot sections: no expensive fluting or artistic taper. The triangular pediment was plain fronted, no carving. The effect was flat-pack Palladian. I needed to make sure that the house was empty. I didn't want to be caught snooping by Meyer's cleaner. The bell pull was the same wrought iron affair, except that this version had been oiled and it worked smoothly, the bell clanged inside the house. I prepared to put on my fake fertiliser sales act. No one came.

I set off to walk along the beck side of the house. Whereas the side elevation at Fellbeck featured ten windows at ground level, here there were six – nice try, Ludwig. The yard at the rear was of similar size but the barns were in much better condition. They were all locked, promising something of value inside. The top half of the door of one was swung open and pegged back. Inside was a lightweight trailer for towing behind a vehicle and a useful-looking hand cart with fat pneumatic tyres. There were no animals: no whinnying horse, no dog.

I walked back down the other side. The windows were all neatly curtained, a bit sad, really. Had Meyer bought South Lea as a love nest for Caroline only for her to walk out and take up with one of his own staff three months later? I got into the car and drove back to Ditchfield.

Gloria was bustling around her prep room, she pointed to Meyer's office door and told me to give it a knock. Meyer's temper matched his appearance – grizzly – a big man, big head, starting to lose hair, late forties I guessed. He was a solid job – bone and muscle, no fat, powerful. He could have passed for a Boer farmer; it was easy to pick up the traces of the clipped Afrikaaner accent. His face was lined and looked resentful. He was not welcoming but why should he be?

'Hardy?' he said, 'take a seat, what do you want?' I opened up on similar lines to our phone conversation. Meyer brushed it aside, 'I know all that, get to the point.'

I asked what Meyer made of Chris Berry? 'As a teacher, you mean? Conscientious, keen on his work – so far.'

'He wasn't your first choice, was he?'

'No. An offer was made to my first choice which was declined. I wanted to keep the post open and re-advertise but I was outvoted on the selection committee and they offered the post to Berry.'

'So the relationship didn't start off on the best footing. How did he shape up in practice?'

'Quite effective but influenced by fashionable theory picked up at University. Prone to spending too much time on the hopeless cases.'

'Isn't there an obligation to at least try?'

That did the trick. Meyer snorted and launched into a denunciation of "child-centered education" and its pernicious conseqences. Privately I agreed but I thought that the longer he ran on the more he would loosen up, so I sat back, looked interested and let him get on with it. He concluded, 'In this country, we're told that children will *refuse* to learn science unless we make it fun for them. The parents don't encourage them to work, education is provided free as a human right so learning is expected to be effortless. On leaving school their children will be offered university places or jobs as a continuation of the painless process. The mothers chauffeur them to school and pick them up afterwards or else they stay at home and play video games.'

'Surely,' I baited the bear a bit further, 'the school run is safer …?'

Meyer leant forward across his desk and confronted me, 'In Ifrica, Mr Hardy, young children walk two or three miles to school, often barefoot through the forest. Schooling is a privilege. Their parents know that and they pay for it. The children know it too and they arrive keen to learn.'

'Have you taught there, Mr Meyer?'

'Yis I hiv, (*when he was worked up it brought the accent on*) six years in northern South Ifrica, close to the border with Zimbabwe, dangerous sometimes. Our school was constructed from breezeblocks with an earth floor and tin roof – built with pride by the parents.'

'A mission school?' It was, he confirmed – run by the Brookheath Christian Brothers. Like the locals, he was proud of it. I wondered why he had given up in favour of decadent Ditchfield – that could wait.

'Mr Meyer, were you aware that something was going on between Berry and Mrs Enderby?'

'There are always whispers in a mixed school, especially with an attractive, outgoing woman like Mrs Enderby. I don't take them seriously.'

'Does the name "Benson" mean anything to you? C. Benson, possibly?'

Meyer seemed genuinely puzzled, 'I don't think we've got a Benson in the school, why do you ask?'

I passed over that. 'What about outside school?'

'No.'

'How about Charles Dawson?' Meyer hesitated this time and then came back saying unless I meant the boy in 5BS – no.

'Have the police contacted you since the murder?'

'A pair of constables called the following evening. Apart from Bolton at Sunnyside, I'm the only neighbour.'

'In that case I don't need to waste your time on the details', I said, trying to sound relaxed, 'I assume they just wanted to know whether you were at home.'

'That's right', Meyer confirmed, 'I was out at the relevant times.'

'Have you anyone to vouch for you that evening?'

'Yes.'

'Could I ask who it was and for what part of the evening?'

Meyer's jaw tightened. He stared aggressively, then, 'I've already told the police about that Mr Hardy. I assume they'll advise the defence in due course.'

I got a whiff of a cover-up but I wasn't about to get any further. 'How would you describe your contacts with Mrs Enderby?'

That did not improve the atmosphere either, 'What do you mean?'

'I understand that you helped her with her Drama teaching – setting up the new drama studio and scenery and effects for her productions.'

'I did help her in those areas when she first came.'

'So you weren't especially friendly? I mean in a social sense.' Meyer was emphatic – there was nothing between them on a social or personal level. 'Just one more question, Mr Meyer, do you know the husband, Martyn Enderby?'

'Enderby? Never met the man.'

I tried a long shot, 'Mr Meyer, do you keep sheep?'

There was a pause then, 'On a small scale, why?'

Why had that unsettled him? I turned up the heat with raised eyebrows and a knowing smile, 'Just simple curiosity, Mr Meyer.'

It was obvious that he didn't believe me. Did he deduce an interest in his throat-cutting expertise? I got up, offered thanks for his time and left. I wasn't sorry when the door closed. I mouthed 'thanks' through the prep room door, gave Gloria a wink, and left.

Back at the flat, Directory Enquiries gave me the number for the Brookheath Christian Brothers. Brother Vincent answered the phone – gently. I explained that I was acting for the defence team in a criminal prosecution – a murder. Brother Vincent was not put out, he ministered to sinners: violence and death were right up his cloister, 'What is it you want to know, Mr Hardy?'

'I'm trying to trace Mr Hans Meyer, a science teacher. He was working in a school at Ditchfield in Lancashire until the 1980s, probably, then he left to teach in one of your schools in South Africa. Would you be able to confirm?'

Brother Vincent was briskly on the ball. 'I should be able to,' he said, 'I don't remember Hans Meyer myself, but if you hold the line, I'll check our records. It'll take me a few moments, he should be on our card index.' There was a diminishing slap-slap of sandals on a cold stone floor. I waited for a couple of minutes. Then the sound of returning sandals and a triumphant Brother Vincent came back on the line. 'Well done, Mr Hardy, your information was exactly right (*how Christian to give me the credit!*). I found his card; Mr Meyer replied to our advertisement in the *Times Educational Supplement* in March 1987. He came for interview and accepted our offer of a post commencing in September the same year. From the record, it seems we were impressed by him.'

'And what happened after that?'

Brother Vincent sounded crestfallen, 'I'm sorry, Mr Hardy, that's all the information we have. After that Mr Meyer would have been passed on to Johannesburg. They're the only ones who can help you.'

'As it happens,' I said, 'I expect to be in Johannesburg on business for a short time at the end of February.'

'Splendid!' Brother Vincent rejoiced and came across with the address. 'I'll write and warn them to expect you. I'm sure they'll do what they can.'

I met Tom in the Duke, 'how did it go with friend Meyer?' I gave him a quick summary. Tom seemed disappointed by the lack of blood.

'You mean confront him with his affair with Caroline? Not over the top you said, remember? I was a bit more subtle than that. If I'd gone for his gizzard today, I'd have been out on my ear and that would have been the finish until you got him into court. There's more to be got from Meyer. He claims to have given an alibi to the police but refuses to give details.'

I told Tom about Brother Vincent. 'Why do we need to know about Meyer in Africa?' Tom wanted to know.

'Because Gloria, the lab technician, knew Meyer before he went to teach there. She said that when he came back he had changed for the worse. Why did he leave as a reasonable human being and come back a brute? I want to know what's behind this Mr Angry act of his. It won't cost anything because I'm visiting Jo'burg for Stefan in February.'

Tom showed rare signs of enthusiasm, 'Meyer's a serious suspect, isn't he? He lives a mile downstream of Fellbeck. My guess is that his alibi won't stand up, which is why he wouldn't disclose to you . If he had an affair with Caroline and she ditched him he's got motive in spades. He might well have violent tendancies. You're right, Ken, he could have done it.'

It was my turn with the cold water, 'But not on his own. He's not Benson – wrong build altogether, slight but unmistakeable Afrikaans accent. Caroline and Chris would both have recognised him the moment he opened the door at Fellbeck. But he fits the bill for the killer behind the sitting room door. He's a powerful bugger, could have finished off Caroline before she could utter a squeak and he knows how to use a knife. We've still got Benson and Mrs Watts to account for before we can stick it on Meyer. That's why I asked him about Benson.'

Tom saw what I was thinking, 'We can demonstrate a motive for Meyer, but how did he recruit the other two? Why should Benson and Watts want Caroline dead? What's next on the programme?'

I didn't answer any of that, 'Could you ask Chris if he minds us having a look at his emails? I don't think he'll object. There won't be anything personal because Caroline only contacted him on her mobile. They never emailed or wrote letters. I need his account name and the password...'

'Wait a minute,' Tom interrupted, 'you're not talking about hacking someone's email account are you?'

I was indignant, 'The very idea! Sooner or later the police will be all over Chris's email records. We might as well know if there's anything there they might use. It's the same as when you wanted possession of his PC before he was charged. I'd ask Chris myself, except you weren't keen on me seeing him in his present state of mind.'

Tom wasn't keen to go into that, 'What about following up on Meyer?'

'Let him stew over the holiday. He realises things are looking shaky.'

'I'm surprised that you've been so quick to write off Martyn Enderby.'

'Who said I had? My problem is that I can't see him as the murderer. Anyway, you said not to approach him until after the funeral.' Tom moved on to tell me about the deplorable state of English rugby.

26

The following morning there was an email from Amelia Partington, the General Secretary of AGROW. She approved my membership application and quoted my personal password for the Members Only section of the website. I used it to open up the list of officials. I already knew about Enderby (chair) and Partington (sec) but I also found Sam Waters (treasurer). As treasurer, Waters might have been the one to borrow the Fellbeck key last April. Dr Pascal Threnadie de Morzine (without portfolio) made up the team on the Steering Group. Scott McIver was mentioned as special project advisor. Contact details for all the Steering Group members – except McIver – were included, together with photographs and brief biographies. Right, we're in! I wrote a cheque for posting to Sam Waters.

There was also a General Committee which included all the Steering Group plus half a dozen other names. I deduced that serious business *(murders?)* was handled by the Steering Group while the General Committee dealt with issues like the cost of biscuits for meetings. Where business realities are concerned I'm a committed Parkinsonian – the ideal number of members on the board is one, failing that, three.

I dialled Amelia's daytime number. The receptionist at West Midshires Education Authority identified Ms Partington as Senior Adminstrative Advisor in FCC (Faith, Culture and Community) Department and put me through to her office.

'Kenneth Hardy? Amelia here, welcome to AGROW! What can I do to help?' It was intimidating, but I fought back. I claimed to be inspired by the Mission Statement and was looking forward to reading the study materials – that was what they called the collection of papers on the website.

I continued, 'There is something that I'm anxious to discuss with you and I don't think it would be appropriate to attempt it on the phone.' She totally understood, could I indicate general context? 'Sponsorship, I'm searching for an inspiring cause and I think I *may* have found it.'

'It's a busy time of year, Mr Hardy. *(But not too busy to pick my pocket?)* Would after hours tomorrow suit – say a quarter to five?'

'Perfect.'

After this exercise in deception, Wooster might have mopped the brow and summoned Jeeves with the coffee. I made my own and then started on the mass of strange ideas on the AGROW website. There were several dozen thoughtful offerings to be found. According to a leading cosmologist the entire universe was under the control of Human Consciousness. He didn't explain how the universe got along for 14,000,000,000 years before we evolved to help out. A distinguished physicist explained that no subatomic reaction could proceed without a Conscious Being on hand to collapse the wave function – whatever that meant. There was an economist who wanted the government to pay a "Citizen's Wage" to everyone (in return for…?). No need to worry about death, a surgeon wrote, because "Near Death Experiences" *proved* that the departed *(including the wife's mother?)* would be waiting at the end of the tunnel to welcome us to a new and fulfilling existence. I read Pascal Threnadie's piece on the "Shamanic Revival in America" and how the newly graduated witch-doctors from Northwestern Forest U were carrying out feats of spiritual healing. No patients were "cured" or got better, they were all "healed". Martyn Enderby had co-authored with a female feminist a paper on "Towards the Sexless Society" thereby accelerating the primacy of the female principle and abolishing competition and hence warfare in favour of sharing between persons and nations.

I was disappointed – rather. AGROW looked like a big tent for those whose conventional careers had landed in a lay-by so had wandered off into the mystic wilds hoping to regain attention. It struck me as silly but harmless – exactly the way Caroline had described it. I couldn't find anything that suggested Action, until I hit on an exception. Sam Waters had spoken at the AGM on "Sacrificial Rituals in Ancient Religion" the full text was here for paid-up members with strong stomachs. I had expected a paper on goats and cockerels, but Human Sacrifice was what interested Sam. He analysed peat burials and post-hole interments where human remains were found in the foundations of buildings. He spoke warmly of Aztec priests who ripped the hearts from ten thousand live victims a day on top of a pyramid thereby creating colourful rivers of blood. He mentioned suttee with Indian widows jumping onto their husbands' funeral pyres. I tried to imagine the wife leaping onto mine but only got as far as her heaping on more logs. The audience joined Sam in deploring the intervention of the brutal (British) imperialists who had suppressed this spiritual activity. That was more like it!

I consulted Sam's details. He lived at Rawcliffe, a village near Harrogate. His daily commute was to Bingley where he lectured at West Riding Technical University, in turn, no distance from Skipton. It explained why he skipped the Ram's Head experience after the AGM.

Next day, I drove to the West Midshire offices and was offered a seat in reception. After a few minutes, a power dressed figure in a dark blue suit with a fitted jacket and pencil skirt came tapping down the corridor. This was Amelia Partington, a shapely five foot four, curled blonde hair and a short-span administrative smile. Her office heels raised her by another four inches and enhanced her posture to make the most of her not inconsiderable bust and bum. I put her in her early forties and built to keep one warm in bed.

Amelia proposed that we adjourn to a small wine bar that she knew of. The place was modern and character-free, artfully designed to wow Local Authority bureaucrats. We sat side by side on a long leather seat, behind an MDF-topped table. I ordered dry white for Partington and South African Merlot for me. I went fulsome on how impressed I was by the AGROW study materials on the website. It all "chimed" (*good that, Hardy*) with the evolution of world-view in my own consciousness. Amelia smiled encouragingly as I went on to express my admiration for the Fellbeck project and asked to know more.

'How much do you know already?'

'Only what's on the website.'

'Martyn Enderby launched the concept at a Steering Committee meeting; he's chair and principal driving force. That was in May, so the project is well forward. Provisional costings are complete (*thanks to McIver?*); main concern at this stage is fund-raising – key to driving negotiations forward for completion by mid-June next year followed by restoration work and alterations to make building fit for purpose by end November 2001.'

I got down to business, 'I am considering a support donation on condition that the funds are ring-fenced to the Fellbeck project. I mean not dissipated to general expenditure.' I went on to explain that I was engaged in selling the company of which I was part owner. 'The price is agreed, in the eight figure range (*wow!*) but final settlement won't take place before July.' (*September, but never mind the odd couple of months*). 'I don't see a problem there, if AGROW exchange contracts in June of next year...'

'June 21st is target,' said Partington, discarding doubts and definite articles in a oner.

'Assuming four to six weeks before completion, my funds

will be available on time. I'm talking big five figures here.' The tone of the conversation changed abruptly; so much so that Amelia's warm and be-ringed hand slipped under the table and onto my knee. 'However, I would need a private talk with Mr Enderby before committing myself. Can you arrange?'

Amelia crossed her legs, demonstrating a well shaped calf, 'Of course, but not immediately', she warned, 'he's travelling a great deal; speaking engagements – getting the message across,' she smiled, I smiled back (*more faces than the Town Hall clock you, Hardy*), 'and you know about his bereavement?'

'Dreadful, yes, I was thinking after the funeral? I'm around in January but on business in Africa until end February.'

'Shall we make first week in March target for your meeting?'

I allowed Partington to order a return round and to move her leg into contact with mine thereby causing brief speculation on making Amelia target. Meanwhile she chatted in a relaxed way about Martyn and his creativity, 'He's the man to watch. He's about to change the western world-view.'

I wanted to know more about the AGROW leadership, 'I see the Steering Committee is a compact group, that's excellent. Your role is to look after the nuts and bolts – the essential professional? I hope the mystic membership appreciates your input.' Nothing beats blatant flattery.

Amelia flashed me a smile, 'I sometimes wonder,' a touch wistfully.

'What about Pascal Threnadie?' I asked, 'what does he do?'

Amelia's smile changed to something on the wry side, 'Don't forget the "de Morzine", he's very keen on that.'

'So he's what? The intellectual, the theorist the philosopher?'

'Something like that.' I spotted a clear absence of warmth. (*Found yourself a fault line here Hardy?*)

I saw her to her small Citroen in the staff car park and thanked her for seeing me at short notice. Instead of the cool hand on meeting, there was a quick hug with a subtle forward thrust below the waist – work in progress for Amelia? I recalled McIver's warning about "watching yon Partington". It wasn't my celebrity looks that stimulated Amelia; it was my cheque book. I drove home to a disturbed night, pestered by a dream of Partington performing in the lady administrator position.

27

The following morning as I was heading out, Tom blocked the way – old habits of a flank forward. 'I decided to order a second post-mortem,' he said, 'I know the pathologist. He'll call me on Friday morning.'

'Anything in particular?'

'Two things', Tom said. 'The police haven't found either of the murder weapons, so it's unlikely they will now. We only have the injuries to go on, so we need a second opinion on what caused them. The other thing is defensive injuries. The police pathologist didn't find any. If Nick confirms, it doesn't help the prosecution's violent quarrel and crime of passion scenario.'

'Good. Also if Chris didn't have a door key to Fellbeck, how could he have got Caroline inside without using force at some stage? If he smashed her skull outside the house, how did he get the body inside without leaving traces?'

'Forensic should settle that one', Tom said, 'let's meet at two tomorrow.'

I walked to the library and searched their directories for locksmiths in the Harrogate area and west as far as Bingley. There were dozens of them in the yellow pages, all keen to fit locks to your new patio, upgrade your door locks or restore your security after a break-in. I was looking for an old-fashioned craftsman who could replicate a Victorian key from a cast. I found half a dozen possibles. I booted the PC and printed copies of Enderby's and Waters' photos from the AGROW website. They were small but recognisable.

Jason came up, looking worried, 'Mr Harrison has asked me

to have a look at Mr Meyer. I don't know where to start with him being South African.' I told him the little I knew – enough to give him a start.

I eliminated the modern locksmiths on the phone. The "possibles" called for a personal visit. When shown the photo of the Fellbeck key most of them backed off. 'Not in that line for years', they said. Some of them knew "an old chap". That way, I collected three old chaps who were not in yellow pages. At the second attempt, I struck lucky. It was a tiny, rundown shop in backstreet Yeadon. The hand painted board over the door said "Hindley, Locksmith". There was no one at the counter, but when I shouted, a stout mucky-looking sixty year-old came through from the back, puffing and wiping oily hands on an oily brown apron. 'Now then!' he shouted; loudly, because of being a Yorkshireman, but also because he was deaf and too obstinate *(like the rest of them)* to wear a hearing aid.

I put the photograph and my drawing on the counter, 'Do you recognise that key?'

'Yer what?' Mr Hindley glared at the evidence then looked hard at me, 'What about it?'

'Do you recall making a copy of it, last April earliest?'

'What do you want to know for?'

I produced my card, which Hindley examined, leaving a large oily thumbprint. 'It's to do with a murder, at a farmhouse in the fells district.'

'Fells? *Lancashire?*' *(That explained everything for Hindley).*

'We think someone connected with the case obtained a key last April and had a copy made. Can you suggest who might have made it?'

'Yes', said Hindley, 'it were me and it weren't last April it was sometime in t' summer. I were asked for a copy to be made from a moulding – cash. Not the sort of key you get asked for every day.' I asked if the customer had left the moulding with him. 'He did, else how could I have copied it?' I asked how many keys he'd supplied. 'Just the one.'

He didn't remember much else, 'it were months back, think on.' Being cash down, he hadn't kept a record. I showed him the photos of Enderby and Waters. 'Nowt like either of them.' Could he describe the man? 'Working lad, young, skinny-like, blue top and jeans. Thought it was daft him having his pixie up on a warm day, still, that's t' style i'n't it?'

'Pixie?'

'Pixie 'ood like little lasses wore in t'winter.'

'Do you recall anything about the way he spoke?' Hindley shook his head; his visitor had not said a right lot to notice.

Unless he was a master of disguise, the man Hindley had seen had not opened the door at Fellbeck. I recalled the lad who delivered the Benson document at St Cuthbert's. 'Did he collect?'

'Aye, same lad and paid – new fivers.' (*Benson's style all right*)

'The name wasn't Benson, was it?'

'Might have been. Might have been Smith, Jones, or owt like that; no names, no pack drill.'

'Thanks for your help Mr Hindley, keep the card,' I said, 'and if anything else comes up, could you phone me straightaway? This is a serious matter, you understand.'

The shop man reared up at that – a touchy, standard issue tyke. As a locksmith of fifty years standing, he didn't need me to tell him about his obligations (*which didn't include keeping proper business records*). I drove back to Ditchfield. It matched the way Benson had done business with Chris – the same lad delivering and collecting. But we hadn't found him either.

It was time to find out about Sam Waters. I phoned Green at H & J. 'I've some interesting news, Mr Green. You remember the person who borrowed a key to survey Fellbeck last April? Was it a Mr S Waters?' Green consulted his record and confirmed

– Sam was our man. 'Waters is an officer of the AGROW group that I mentioned the other day, and they are seriously interested in the property. You should be hearing from them early in the New Year,' *(brighten up his Christmas)*.

I reported progress to Tom. 'The murderers made themselves a copy of the front door key. That means that the key that the police found on the doormat has to be a copy – and brand new.'

Also, with my new padlock on the back door, the murder gang was locked out of Fellbeck.

Next morning, I handed the car keys to Jason. 'I'm interested to know how the murderers made their getaway,' I told him. 'I reckon it would have taken three of them ten to fifteen minutes to get out to the Braxtonby road once Chris was off the premises. Chris drove all the way to Coldedge before he phoned the police at 9.28. That probably means he was out of the house about 9.20. By the time the police picked him up and reached the bridge on the Braxtonby road, it would have been, say, 9.50, giving the gang thirty minutes to get clear. It could have gone wrong. Suppose there had been a police patrol on hand when Chris phoned from Coldedge? That could have caused them to arrive at Fellbeck at least ten minutes earlier. Ultimate disaster: suppose Chris had met a police patrol on the road and succeeded in flashing them down?'

Jason objected, 'It was a foggy night and with oncoming headlights in his eyes he might not recognise the police car until it was too late.'

'I know, but the gang would have had it on their minds. It would make them nervous. If they rushed the job, they could slip up and leave evidence behind. We are not dealing with professional criminals.'

Jason said, 'They could have got out the back way, across the field to the Preston road, but what about tracks across the field?'

'Remember when we walked down with Alison?' A slightly glazed expression came over the Apollo-like features. I had doubts concerning Jason's memory of that expedition, so I hastened to remind the lad. 'The track from the farmyard gate to the Preston road is well churned up by trucks and tractors.' Jason smartly vetoed that theory, 'Yes, but if the gang was using a van, its tracks would show up on top of the trucks and tractors because its tyres were much narrower.'

I wasn't for placing too much confidence in the constabulary as eagle-eyed Indian trackers but there was an alternative. 'They parked the van out of the way and shifted their equipment on a hand cart with low pressure pneumatic tyres (*I know of one*). They could have hauled that over the grass, leaving no tracks to speak of.'

'It's getting a bit complicated,' Jason said, 'and there's at least one padlocked gate to get through.'

'That's why I've given you the car keys. Alison said that the delivery drivers know where to find the key for the road gate. I expect that they're hidden under a handy boulder or in a crevice in the wall. See if you can find it, if so, the murder gang could – and no cheating, no asking Alison.'

'Would it be all right if I dropped in and said "hi" to Alison?'

He probably would anyway, 'If that's all it is, ten minutes maximum,' I said, 'Don't say anything about keys, just you were passing. Phone in from Sunnyside in case I need the car. Think on, we can't contact you while you're down by the beck.' I suspected there'd be things on the programme apart from "hi" so I decided to make the best of it, 'Ask if she's noticed any police activity at Fellbeck. And no sex,' I warned, 'today's boggart day. Any child conceived on a Friday will be possessed of the devil. It'll grow up to be a monster and murder you for your money.'

Jason was intrigued, 'I've never heard that before.' *(Neither had I.)*

207

He was about to set off when, 'Ask if anyone at Sunnyside noticed police activity in the home field after the murder.'

'Like looking at tyre tracks?'

'I mean like a pack of hungry wolves on the trail.' I was kicking myself for not thinking of that when we visited at first. 'Stop off at the Preston Road gate first. See if you can find the key, then walk across to the yard gate and check there. When you're crossing the field, follow the tyre tracks and see if there are any narrow enough for a 30 hundredweight van, After you've done all that, you can take ten minutes off for a *brief* word with Alison. Got all that?'

Jason repeated his instructions, I confirmed, he shot off. At least it would give them something useful to talk about.

28

Stefan phoned. 'I've seen your report, Ken. How would you summarise?' That meant he had not read it but if he liked my back of a fag packet version he would glance at the Executive Summary.

'The material runs on your existing plant and makes a stronger film. On most products you can take advantage by reducing the film thickness and consequently the cost.' Stefan asked where the snag was. 'It's incompatible with conventional material. A small amount of cross-contamination results in scrap film weaker than wet toilet paper. And you wouldn't be able to recycle the factory waste for the same reason.'

'So it's a no-no?' Stefan asked.

'No, it's a way you might get an advantage over the competition. APC's production is not all on one site.'

'Gotcha!' said Stefan, (*a Sun reader?*), 'sort out products best suited to Wonderthene and dedicate a site to those? It's worth thinking about. We'll talk about the Africa project in January.' He rang off, I went to the shops.

When I got back, Jason had left a recorded message. Moments later the phone rang. It was Jason, live. I said, 'Back here quick sharp and no more wifing it wealthily at Sunnyside.'

Jason had found both padlock keys in twenty minutes, including walking from one gate to the other. He had not noticed van or cart tracks across the field, 'Just tractor and HGV tyres, all fresh. The morning after the murder, Mr Bolton and Alison went down to see what the police were doing – there was nothing going on at the back of the house and they haven't noticed anything since.'

'Good,' I moved on, 'Mr Harrison needs at least one more witness at Walpole Gardens besides young Briony. I think we ought to set about it differently. Knocking on doors didn't get us far, did it?'

Jason agreed, 'I could try at a weekend?'

'No, people don't like having their "great weekends" interrupted except by Jehovah's Witnesses. Why not try a leaflet?' We sat at the kitchen table and sketched it out. Underneath a big scan of Caroline's photo – "Have you seen this woman?" Then go on to say this is Caroline Enderby, found murdered at a farmhouse outside Coldedge on 23rd November *(Bloody hell, nearly a month ago)*. To assist with the legal investigation, we would like to hear from anyone who recalls seeing her arriving at or leaving Walpole Gardens. If you can assist please phone this number in strict confidence asking for Mr Hardy.'

Jason went off to deploy his IT skills and was soon back with a proof. I took it to Pam who made a couple of changes "for legal reasons". 'Print off three dozen, get yourself into the flats somehow short of housebreaking and put a leaflet in each door.' Jason pointed out that there was no need to get inside because there were individual mailboxes at the front of the building – American style. 'Report when you get back.'

I went down to Tom's office at two o'clock. 'Post mortem first,' he said, 'it's straightforward.' Tom's man had not differed much from the police pathologist. 'He finds that the initial injury was inflicted at the upper rear of the skull. The shape of the depressed fracture indicates a hard object with a spherical surface of about five inches diameter.'

'Meaning only one surface had to be spherical', I interrupted, 'the rest of the object could be any shape.'

'There was one blow, which would have rendered the victim unconscious immediately and would probably have caused death within thirty minutes to an hour if untreated. Bleeding would not have been heavy.'

'Going on to the knife,' Tom continued, 'the same story as the police report. It had a sharp, heavy blade, similar to that used by a slaughterman. A single cut round the throat severing all tissues down to the bone. If executed whilst the victim was still alive there would have been heavy external bleeding. According to Chris's evidence, her throat was cut within two or three minutes of the first attack – possibly even less.'

'So where are we now?'

'No defensive injuries, as before. That confirms that Caroline was taken by surprise.'

I had a thought, 'at the moment of impact on the back of the head, would there have been a blood spray? I'm sure I remember that from a newspaper report on another case.'

'Soon see', said Tom and picked up the phone. 'Nick? Tom Harrison. We're looking at your post mortem report. My colleague wonders whether there would be a spray of blood at the moment of impact from the blunt instrument.' The pathologist talked for a few moments.

'He says it's likely, but not certain. If there was, the spray could have travelled up to six feet. We'd be looking for minute blood spots probably not visible but showing up under forensic testing.'

'Something else,' I said. 'When Caroline left my flat that evening she was wearing a silk scarf with a Paisley pattern. It wasn't included with the list of clothing in the police pathologist's report, was that an oversight?'

There was another short delay before the pathologist answered – there was no scarf. I said, 'That leaves us with three missing items: a round-headed club, the knife and the scarf, all removed from the crime scene. Have forensic found any spots?'

'No they haven't,' Tom said, 'but there weren't any on Chris's clothing either, which weakens the prosecution case.'

'And supports our theory of a third murderer behind the door. He hit Caroline from behind as Mrs Watts closed the door. He caught Caroline as she fell and carried her to the fireplace. He laid her down on the hearthrug and finished her off by cutting her throat.'

Tom agreed. 'She was taken by surprise, so there was almost no sound...'

'And there were other distractions: the aircraft noise, Chris starting up Benson's PC, Benson going to "reassure the ladies", then the power was shut down and the lights went out. In the circumstances we can't be sure of the exact sequence. Having closed the door, Watts blocked it with the chair whilst her chum did his butchery and then the pair of them were off through the door leading to the dining room, locking it behind them and through the kitchen to join Benson in the scullery. As soon as Chris leaves to fetch the police they lock the front door and drop the key on the mat, lift the computer and audio equipment from the closet and load them into the transport, unlock the internal doors, screw the padlock back onto the back door and leave. I reckon that with a bit of organisation they're out of the house in ten minutes and clean away up the Braxtonby road in fifteen – easy.'

'Suppose it went wrong?' the Devil's Advocate wanted to know, 'If the police arrived too soon they'd have been trapped.'

'They knew that Chris couldn't get a mobile signal without driving up the hill to Coldedge. I think the time interval between Chris leaving the house and the police bringing him back was at least half an hour – loads of time. They could even have gone out the back way.' I told Tom about Jason's expedition to find the keys for the two farm gates. 'I doubt if the police paid much attention to the back of the property. That's the cunning bit about locking the front door, dropping the key on the mat and leaving a sitting room window unlatched. From that time on, the crime scene was from the front door to the sitting room.

Our two PCs, Cartwright and Tace, had that worked out before forensic arrived.'

'Possibly,' Tom said. He produced two wads of paper and gave one to me. 'The forensic report', he said, 'Have a read later and let me know if you spot any omissions or other problems.'

'You've read it', I said, 'what have you spotted?'

'Most of it is as we'd expect and it's not particularly helpful to either side: there are unidentified fingerprints all over the place, going back years, probably; but nothing conflicting with Chris's statement.'

I broke in there, '…The table and the bentwood chair are still in the computer closet, but they've been wiped and so has the front door key that the police found on the mat. Why? The folding chair that Chris says was used for blocking the door has gone, taken by the gang. It's consistent with an intention to discredit Chris.'

'It could be.'

'I've told you about Hindley, locksmith of Yeadon. That episode has got "Benson" written all over it – using a young lad as his messenger, cash up front in new fivers. Helmsley and Jordan's man confirms that a Mr Waters borrowed a key back in April for an inspection of Fellbeck and Sam Waters is the treasurer of the AGROW group.'

Tom was hopeful, 'You think Sam Waters and Benson are the same?'

I got up, 'I'll have a look at Sam and then we'll know.'

'Hang on,' said Tom, 'I got the password from Chris for his email account at the school.' He handed me a sheet of paper with the magic formula.

'How is he? Last time we spoke you were afraid he was suicidal.'

'He's calmed down; he seems detached, floating. It happens with some prisoners on remand, it's a limbo. They switch off until the trial. We're going to have another go at getting bail next month.'

I went upstairs and picked up my phone. There was a recorded message that sounded like a reply to Jason's circular. I left that and rang Gloria. 'On 23rd November, the evening of the murder, do you remember whether Chris was in the Prep Room when you left?'

'Yes, he was, we had a joke about Meyer playing Santa at the staff Christmas party.'

Gloria had a thought, 'hang on, Ken, I need to check something'. She was back in seconds, 'I left early that night. It would have been half-past four, normally it's after five.' I asked if she was sure. 'Certain, I've checked the wall chart for last month. We're going to Tenerife for Christmas. I discovered my anti-tetanus jab was out of date and went for a booster. Does that mess something up?'

'Not to worry', I said, 'as long as we know.' I returned the recorded message and got Herbert Stewart. We agreed that I should call at eleven on Monday morning.

I booted the PC and opened the St Cuthbert's website. I got into Chris's email account and opened his inbox, so far, straightforward. I took a quick look through Chris's messages and found nothing of interest – now for Meyer.

I guessed that all the email accounts ran on the same username, which was "stcuthb". Each account would have its own password; Chris's was "sciberry12". Easy, Meyer is head of science so he has to be "scimeyer1". That failed so I tried "scimeyer01" and that didn't work either. Surely, he doesn't have a different format altogether?

Jason looked in, 'Any replies to the leaflet from Walpole Villas?'

'Yes, one. I'm going to see him Monday morning.' Before he had time to offer I added, 'No need for you, he doesn't have a daughter fair.'

Jason caught sight of my monitor. 'Trying to get into something?'

'You know nothing about this', I said, 'I'm trying to hack Meyer's web mail account at St Cuthbert's. I'll be in there ere set of sun.'

'Lovely,' said Jason and sat down at the keyboard without being asked, 'haven't a war dialler, have you?'

'Whatever that is when it's at home. No.'

'Never mind, you've been assuming that the passwords are ordered according to seniority,' said the hacker. 'Suppose it's chronological order. Suppose the school IT wizard allocated numbers in the order that the teachers applied for a web mail account. Who in science would have the most need for a personal mailbox?'

'Try Gloria'. Jason typed "scigloria01" into the password box and tried to enter. That was rejected but "scidavis01" worked, disclosing yards of messages ordering pens, paper and poisonous chemicals. 'I'm worried about you,' I told Jason, 'you seemed such a nice lad at first.'

'We know that Mr Berry is the most recent member of staff. He's "12" and Gloria Davis is "01" so I can simply count down. Meyer duly turned up at "08". His inbox was not overpopulated. I took over the chair from Jason and ran down the list. They were all education-like messages, except one, dated 10th June from Menderby@AGROW_soc.org.uk. It read:

> *Dear Hans,*
>
> *Thanks for mailing the document you discovered. It throws considerable light both on the history of the Fellbeck property and another matter. It will be key to forwarding our project.*

Love and peace.
Martyn

'What's he talking about?'

'I'll tell you when you're older. Meantime, one of your ex-teachers has told me at least one whopping porky.' I wrote a note for Tom, saying: 'Another breakthrough. Anticipate crawling drunk at Duke 18.30 be early if you wish coherent account.' I folded it, passed it to Jason and asked him to hand it to Pam, 'Mr Hardy's compliments and could she ensure that Mr Harrison sees this before close of play?'

29

I beat Tom into the lounge bar of the Duke by ten minutes. The pint waiting for him was hardly flat at all. He passed no comment but sat expectantly waiting to be dished the dirt.

'There was nothing in Chris's inbox of interest to us or the police.' I passed him my printout of Enderby's email, 'This popped out of the woodwork.'

It must have been obvious that I had ignored Tom's injunction against hacking. He did not refer to this. Instead he read the email and handed it back. 'You think Meyer came across a document whilst refurbishing South Lea? It might be nothing more than farm accounts. Enderby only gives a hint as to content, but you're assuming it was the Benson document.'

'Whatever the document was, it means that Meyer's holding back on something. He told me that he'd never met Enderby. Now we know that wasn't true. What other skeletons has he got? On Monday, I'm off to see a second witness at Walpole Gardens who claims to have seen Caroline there. If the second witness confirms Bryony Cooper's evidence, Meyer has lied about his involvement with Caroline. We'll be left with nothing but his alibi to crack.'

I got a grunt for that stroke of genius. In the hope of fortifying him against the next development, I bought Tom a second pint. 'Bad news is we can't prove what time Chris left school on the night of the murder. Gloria chose that evening to go off early for a vaccination.'

'I've decided to chance it on a bit of independent forensic',

Tom said, 'confined to blood spray between the sitting room door and the fireplace.'

'What about the front door key in police possession? Could he get a sight of it?'

'Nothing to see. There are no fingerprints, it's been wiped.'

'That doesn't matter,' I said, 'is it another original key that Green claims to know nothing about, or is it the copy that Hindley made? He only needs to look at it. You see the implications?'

Tom saw all right, 'I'll see what we can do.'

'Will you ask about the fire remains?'

Tom was not keen on that idea, 'What are you hoping to find out? By the time they get to look at them, those ashes will be six weeks old.'

'As long as they haven't been disturbed, quite a lot. It could be vital.' I went on, 'police forensic haven't mentioned ashes, so we can assume they haven't touched them. They didn't look to me as if they'd been disturbed. Now, Chris could have left school any time after 4.30 that afternoon because Gloria had left early. Suppose he drove to Fellbeck, let himself in and lighted a fire in the sitting room. He arrived at my place at 5.45. So the very latest he could have put a match to the fire was 5.20. Think back to your Boy Scout days. You build a log fire, you light it and leave it to burn itself out. Unless someone comes and stirs it up, the ends of the logs don't burn away. That's exactly what the remains looked like when we saw them.'

'Good,' said the Leading Defence Lawyer, 'are you going to get to the point, or am I forced to buy you a beer?'

'No. This brief is costing too much already. According to Chris, Caroline was murdered at about 8.40, which agrees with the pathology report. After he broke into the room, he spotted her body by the light of the fire, at say 8.45. When the police brought him back, the flames were out but the ashes were still hot, PC Cartwright remarked on it. That would have been about ten

218

o'clock. I don't believe that fire could have lasted for over four and a half hours untended. Forensic should be able to estimate how big the original fire was, carry out a couple of tests, and come up with a start time. I'll be surprised if the fire was lit before seven o'clock. Chris and Caroline were at their teachers' meeting from 6.30 until 8.00. The murder gang lit the fire.'

The shock of that suggestion caused Tom to forget his liquid obligations. He started to leave, 'It's a good thing you're taking a break in Spain.'

On Sunday, I broke whichever Commandment was relevant and drove to Rawcliffe in search of Sam Waters. Having tracked down Sam's modest bungalow, I found it locked, barred and generally deserted. Battling manfully through the fumes of industrial-scale Yorkshire pudding production, I enquired from the lady next door.

'You won't get that Sam Waters for a fortnit or three weeks happen,' she said, 'he's on his 'olidays. Greece as normal.' I should have thought of that. What else for a leading intellectual of West Yorkshire Technical University but extended meditation in the Elysian fields of Homer, Plato and Aristotle? Bet he's half ratted on vintage Ouzo at this moment.

On Monday, I set about the Stewarts. They were an emaciated pair, finding it hard to make a do on their pension. The flat was cold and musty-smelling 'Are you paying for information?' he asked. I said not but he told me anyway. Their flat was on the ground floor, second door along from the lift. They claimed three sightings. Two of them were around the middle of the day. Under torture, they agreed to between eleven in the morning and two in the afternoon. 'It was summer, like,' Herbert said. They could not remember dates, but the times were open to interpretation as an innocent conference during school holidays, perhaps about a stage set rather than a *sex fest*.

'What about the other occasion?'

'Eight o'clock in the morning,' Mrs Stewart put in, 'winter, I remember it was dark. I was bringing in the milk when this young woman came out of the lift. She didn't look at me but shot off, seemed flustered.' Again, no date but with Bryony's sightings I ought to be able to rattle Meyer at the right moment. I thanked the Stewarts and disgorged a tenner towards the milk bill.

I phoned Tom and told him the latest on Walpole Gardens. There were no double back somersaults, 'Another nice lead Ken, but we need something more solid. I wouldn't be happy about putting Bryony Cooper or the Stewarts in the box unsupported.'

He was right, so I admitted it. 'I think there's more to be got out of Walpole Gardens,' I told him. Tom reminded me that Sam Waters was heading my list. 'Unless you want me to cancel the Costa, fly to Athens and tackle Sam on the steps of the Acropolis there's nothing I can do until he gets back from his winter break. And just imagine your mother-in-law's reaction.'

Tom made no verbal response to that advice but a powerful shudder said it all. I tried to reassure, 'It could work out for the best. If I can get Meyer up there as top murder suspect that still leaves us short of contenders for the Benson and Watts duo. Sam is pencilled in as a possible Benson and the best way to get at him is break down Meyer's position first.'

'I can help there, Ken,' said Tom. 'Meyer has a sister, unmarried, staff biochemist in Accrington hospital. Jason has just found out.'

'Tell him to hold his horses, will you?' I implored, 'if Ms Meyer gets a whiff, she'll be tipping Hansie off, sharp.' Tom agreed.

'That's why, when I talked to him, he clammed up about his alibi. If it's his sister, he doesn't want her involved. I want to catch the bugger cold, one to one. Meyer's weakness is his short fuse.' *(Not like you, Hardy)*.

We exchanged season's greetings.

★

I was packed ready for purgatory, Spanish-style. It loomed upon me that it was my last chance of a potable pint *this year*. I took action. Safely installed in a corner of the Duke's bar (no involvement in improbable festive rounds), I lurked like Fagin and reviewed the situation. Without actually breaking any pots, I reckoned that progress was creditable. I had one firm suspect and more leads than Battersea Dogs Home. Perhaps taking a break at this point was not such a bad idea; ten days suspension of intelligent thought might trigger a brainwave.

30

Having ingested an airport breakfast, the flight to Malaga was less gruesome than feared. The ankle-biters and their keepers had evidently gone on ahead. I took a second breakfast, a coffee, a doze and then...

At Malaga arrivals I was ambushed by a squat figure. 'Kenneth, why do you have to look so bloody English?' demanded the wife, 'and where have you been? The rest came through ages ago.' (*Also, Merry Christmas*). I pushed the airport trolley along after her. It was hell-bent on going crabwise. The reason was obvious to a distinguished engineer: one of the wheel swivels had seized up at 45 degrees to the intended direction of travel. No time to fettle it; I let it steer into the wall, picked up my bags and trudged after the wife. Neuro scientists have discovered that the older you get, the faster time passes, but did they try ten days amongst the expats? Nevertheless, I survived.

*

The space provided for visiting at Ditchfield Prison was mainly grey with metal chairs and tables arranged in two long lines. I was shown in through the visitors' entrance at one end and invited to sit at a square formica-topped table. My mood as I waited for Chris was stoical. So was his when he arrived; he sat facing me with both hands palms down on the table. I inspected him; he examined something beyond my right shoulder.

He was pale and a bit drawn, I guessed from broken sleep, but otherwise better than I expected. He might even have put on a bit of weight. Eventually we made eye contact; I grinned at him and he looked away. I skipped the 'how are you?' and 'how are they treating you?' and got down to business.

'Chris,' I began, 'I don't expect we've got long, shall we get on with it?' The room was filling, chairs were scraping on the stone floor, conversations of the "hey up our kid, yerrate?" kind were starting up. There was little danger of being overheard. Three warders stood with their backs to the wall, spaced out along the length of the room, eyes on the crowd. All the same, the atmosphere was more relaxed than I'd expected.

I continued, 'Is there anything I can do on the outside, any messages – parents?' That got a headshake. 'Already visited?' Nod. 'Anyone you'd like to see?' No. 'Anyone you'd like me to see?' No answer.

'The teachers' meeting that you and Caroline went to, who hosted it?'

No answer. I shoved my chair back and made to get up, 'Look Chris, if you can't be bothered, I've got other things to do.'

'Mrs Adcock, so what?'

I should have realised: the caring approach got me nowhere. I brisked up the tone, 'Three months back I asked how you were getting on with Meyer.'

'Where's this getting us?'

'Nowhere if you don't frame. You likened it to an armed truce. Did Meyer's attitude change after that?'

'No, so what?'

It was brass tacks time. I gave Chris a quick survey of his predicament. 'Look, the police have charged you with murder based on their crime of passion scenario. They claim that you and Caroline had a violent row which culminated in her death at Fellbeck. Bloody rubbish, no evidence, we know that, I'm on the way to proving it. Big but: as things stand, it won't stop the judge and jury lapping it up and the media will love it.'

'I've already made a statement...'

'Which you are sticking to – no changes, no second thoughts?' He was sticking with it. 'Good. So we're building a defence based on your account. Short of pleading "guilty but..." there's no other option. What do *you* think is the weakness in your story?'

For the first time Chris was looking me in the face, 'The prosecution case is a pack of lies but it's simple. Mine is the truth but it's complicated.'

I considered kissing him, but postponed that idea for fear of upsetting the warders. 'Your statement involves a gang of three murderers, including one woman. So why would all those people want Caroline dead? That's my main problem. I need to find Benson.'

I was getting to the crisis point. If I could get Chris to stick with it we might get something. The danger was that he would collapse and go back to his cell. Not being a trained counsellor and as time was limited I could think of nothing better than to push on.

'Let's go back to that day in March.' He knew which day I meant. 'It kicked off with a row between you and Meyer. What was that about?'

I needed to get him to talk. My question was relevant enough and it was a diversion from dragging out memories of Caroline. He relaxed a bit.

'To begin with, it was a professional disagreement. Meyer walked into my class at the start of a lesson. I was trying, by means of a little discussion with the kids to introduce the idea of temperature. I don't suppose Meyer liked what he heard. It would have been more his style to write "PV=RT" on the board and then dive into thermodynamics.'

'With 3C? Not really?'

'I'm exaggerating,' Chris admitted, 'Meyer told me to carry on, which was impossible because he was creating a diversion by walking round the class flicking through their exercise books. Finally he picked up Yvette Pearson's book, marched to my table and stabbed at two homework items and asked in a loud voice why Yvette's last two projects had not been marked. I told him there was a reason and I would explain later. Meyer walked out, shouting that he wasn't interested in excuses.'

'I bet the class loved that. Did you take it up with him?'

'Later that morning I went to his office, told him that Yvette was copying other children's work after I had marked it and putting her so-called homework in late. I showed him the evidence. Meyer refused to listen, I accused him of unprofessional conduct by tearing me off a strip in front of my own class and it ended in a shouting match.'

'Nothing in that really,' I said, 'typical boss versus subordinate punch-up. Happens all the time in badly run factories everywhere.' Chris agreed.

'The following morning, which was a Saturday, you turned up at my place at coffee time and said you were in love. Was there a connection?'

'Sort of,' Chris said, 'to keep out of Meyer's way until he calmed down I took my sandwiches to the staffroom in the main building instead of going in the prep room as usual. Caroline appeared and sat next to me. It was the first time we'd spoken since the day I got the job.'

'You told her about your run-in with Meyer. What did she say to that?'

'She said "join the club, he's been falling out with everyone this term, cock up on the reindeer front suspected". After that she asked a favour. She had an after-school play rehearsal and was short of a prompter.'

'So like a gent, you agreed?'

'She finished at half past five. Caroline asked if I fancied a run out to the sticks, "the best country in England, all the way up to Carlisle." I would have settled for slag heaps and derelict pit-heads if she was there so I accepted.'

'Did you meet anyone else on the way out? Anything odd strike you?'

'That time in the afternoon the place was empty apart from cleaners. But Caroline wanted us to leave separately. She said to stick around out of the way until I saw her drive out. "Give me five minutes start then drive through the gates and turn left towards Preston." She'd catch me up three miles out of town at the Fox and Goose layby.'

'Conspiracy for two,' I said, 'if a woman sets a trap, walk into it. Go on.'

'I waited by the main doors until I saw Caroline leave then I walked out to the car park, opened up the Ford and threw my bag of marking into the boot. Getting into the car, I happened to glance up at the Science block. There was a figure standing at the top floor laboratory windows looking out. The sun was shining through the glass behind him and dazzling me. I couldn't make out a face. It was a tall, bulky figure, I was pretty sure it was Meyer. What was Meyer doing in the Chemistry lab at that time on a Friday? Out of school at four o'clock on the dot was Meyer's style. To be polite, I raised a hand – the figure stood rigid. It could have been the cleaner's husband or a maintenance man or anyone. I got into the car intending to sit there for five minutes as Caroline had instructed. Suddenly I didn't want to sit with the watching figure staring at my back. I drove out of the car park.'

'Let's have a break,' I suggested. I'd expected that Chris would find it a strain to talk about Caroline but as he got into the story he seemed to relax. The warders did not seem in a rush the throw the rest of us out; a nice quiet job for them, I guessed, as long as we sat talking quietly. There was a drinks machine against the wall, 'I'll get us a couple of coffees?'

I came back with the drinks. Chris said, 'This is about Meyer...?'

'Could be, he's in the frame. That top floor lab has got windows all round, hasn't it? Supposing it *was* Meyer watching from the window. He saw Caroline leave and turn right into town. Then you drove out and turned left. Not your normal direction is it? Usually you would have turned right towards town. If he stayed where he was, two minutes later, Caroline would have appeared from the town direction and carried on in pursuit. What was she driving?'

'Martyn's big black 4x4.' *(Couldn't miss that, could he?)*

'Where was Martyn?'

'Off the radar, in Poland at a conference at Bydgoszcz University – *Love and Peace in International Politics*.'

A warder came and tapped Chris on the shoulder. 'Coming,' he leant forward and murmured, 'Thanks for looking after the PC.'

'What was that Berry?'

'See you again, Chris,' I said loudly, 'soon…all right?'

'All right.'

I came out of HMP Ditchfield, dazzled by the January morning. I reported the conversation to Tom, 'I'm sure Chris doesn't know anything about Caroline's affair with Meyer. He assumes that Meyer's hostility is down to the run-in they had in March. I don't believe it. I think Meyer guessed from the start that Chris was her new lover. I suspect that Meyer tipped Martyn off.'

'Do you think Meyer was doing a bit of stalking?' Tom asked. It does happen with cast-off lovers. It has been known to end in murder.'

That gave me a bit of a shiver, 'We know that there was contact between Enderby and Meyer. If it was innocent, why did he bother to deny it?'

'Tipping the husband off is also the sort of thing a discarded lover might do,' Tom said, 'I've a date for the funeral: 26th January, it's a Wednesday, 11.30 at the cathedral.'

'Cathedral job followed by a boiled ham do?' Tom was light on details except that Canon Jeffreys was preaching and the interment was at her parish church.

'Will the police will be there, lurking in the back row, checking on the mourners?' I asked, 'what about the defence?'

'I'll look in for the service,' Tom said, 'you?'

Meyer's reactions could be interesting, but I wanted to keep my head down as far as Enderby was concerned. 'I'll let you know. I'm off to see Sam Waters', I reminded Tom. 'If he's a possible Benson, we have three murderers lined up, Sam at the front door, Meyer's sister as the welcoming Mrs Watts and Hansie with a club waiting behind the door.'

'Don't Zulu knobkerries have a round end?' Tom asked, 'we're looking for something rounded to match the skull injury.' The case against Meyer was hardening all the time. I was optimistic as I drove over the border.

31

Sam Waters was a bachelor. That was clear as soon as he opened his front door releasing the aroma from inside the bungalow – burnt fat, unwashed socks, stale fag smoke and the dank smell that comes off unserviced males. Sam was mid-forties, round and bald with a reedy, high-pitched voice, a strong Cockney accent and a crumpled drip-dry shirt. He was seriously challenged on stature, five foot three, I reckoned. None of that squared with Chris's description of Benson. Shit!

He asked me in and proceeded to make "coffee" with instant de-caff and dried milk. 'To wot do I owe…?' asked Sam.

I didn't prevaricate, 'I've recently joined AGROW and I'm particularly interested in the Fellbeck project. I believe you're one of the leading figures, Mr. Waters?' Sam liked the sound of that. He swelled up like Mr. Toad, adding a bit of extra tension on his waistband and we got down to first names.

'Yeah,' Sam admitted, 'suppose I am, reelly.' He grinned, exhibiting bad teeth in a toad-shaped mouth, 'I was one of the executive committee that surveyed the place. That was what, April last year?'

'Seems an odd choice for what the Committee has in mind. It's been unoccupied for years. The locals seem to think it's practically derelict.'

'Yeah, well that's what they fink,' Sam said, 'once you've had a proper butcher's, you see it's in better shape than you might expect. Work on the roof needed, no question, but that's to be expected.' I asked about the wiring, heating system, boiler and so on. Sam admitted that all those needed replacing.

'Someone's had a go at the ground floor circuit, which is fair to middling. The rest are rubbish.' *(Exactly what I found).*

'Big money, isn't it?'

Sam agreed, 'But that's work in progress and if anyone can raise that kind of cash, Martyn Enderby can.' He lowered his voice and confided, 'You know, Martyn said to me once, "People think England's a big country, Sam, but the real decisions are made within a small group and I know most of them". I reckon he does, too.'

'What's the house like inside; do you see it as a potential training centre?'

Sam squeaked enthusiastically, 'Brilliant! There's this massive space *(He means the dining room?)* it's practically a ready-made lecture theatre – perfect proportions for acoustics. It's my speshulty see, I lecture on Acoustics of Buildings. There's something else as well, something you can't buy.'

'Go on'.

'Ambionce! When we went to survey the place, Martyn spotted it right away; he could feel it. When we've done the inspection he says that he wants to stay behind for a solitary vigil, and to leave him to it. I seen him next day and he's inspired; never had a spiritual experience like it.'

'I read the paper that you gave at the AGM,' I said, '*Sacrificial Rituals in Ancient Religion* is that a speciality of yours too?'

'Nah,' Sam said modestly, 'not reelly. Martyn asked me to write it. It's not original research; it's a survey of the literature.' I claimed to be interested in the section about sacrificial burials. 'Funny you should say that,' said Sam, 'it's pretty speculative, I thought of leaving it out but Martyn was keen – insisted on it.'

I'd had enough of Sam's de-caff and his armchair. It was lumpy and smelt of cat pee. I got up, said I must be off and thanked Sam for the chat, 'You've given me a lot to think about on the Fellbeck project.' For once, that was true. Sam put on an ear-to-ear grin and led me to the front door. I admired the battered patch of winter grass and the untidy rose border. 'You keep that nice and neat Sam, have you got land at the back as well?' He took me to see. It was bigger than the patch at the front and dominated by a garage, big enough for a couple of Transits, murderers for the use of. 'Don't tell me you just keep a lawnmower in there?'

Sam squeaked with pleasure, ''Ave a look at this,' he invited and opened the doors disclosing a mud spattered red van – F reg – to one side and a long low shape covered by a dust sheet on the other. Sam whipped away the cover like a stage magician. It was a Jaguar SS sports, *circa* 1938 in glossy British Racing Green, 'Six cylinder overhead camshaft… how about that, then?'

Nothing else would do but to walk round the beast, cooing reverentially, and begging to sit in the driver's seat. Fair play – it was very pretty. 'Bet you don't go to work in this, Sam?'

'Not often,' he admitted, 'and then only in summer.'

'If I were forty years younger I could cause some damage with a tart trap like this.' Sam giggled and blushed – tart traps and their contents were not Sam's scene. At the back of the garage, there was a workshop with a bench, a small lathe, vertical mill, grinder and drill. 'Make your own parts?'

'No option 'ave I? They're hard to get these days and when you can source them they cost an arm and a leg. So I make 'em: nuffink else for it.'

I cast a last lingering look at the SS, Sam closed up the garage and we walked back to the house. 'Good Christmas?'

'Yeah, just back from Greece.'

'Brushing up the philosophy for AGROW?'

'Nah,' Sam tittered, 'leave that to Martyn, Pascal and that lot. It's where I go this time of year. Never snows, normally.'

It was all I needed to know. I thanked Sam again for his time, to say nothing of the decaff. Sam waved me off with his Mr Toad grin and I felt significantly rotten.

As the car warmed up the guilt dissipated. The essence of cat pee had migrated from Sam's armchair to my suit. I was critical of Sam's housekeeping standards until I had a nasty thought. *(How do you know your place doesn't smell similar, Hardy?)* Remember the Zone, HMP Ditchfield? After a while smells just fade into the background. Fighting off panic, I returned to the flat, took a shower, got the vacuum cleaner out, hoovered the carpets, swept the kitchen, disinfected the bog, dusted the furniture, changed the bedding, started up the washing machine, sprayed all round with essence of lavender, did the same to the car seat and took my suit to the dry cleaners. The cat legged it, he hates the hoover.

I put together a summary of the visit. I was confident that Sam could have made the moulding for the Fellbeck key. He could easily have plugged in temporary power and the rest at the murder scene. As a lone bachelor, he probably had no alibi for the evening of the murder. There was no petrol generator in his workshop but he could have hired one and delivered it to Fellbeck in his van. In that case there ought to be a paper trail. He might have borrowed off obliging friends up the pub but he struck me as a solitary toad. He wasn't Benson but he was devoted to Enderby.

There was no evidence of a connection with Meyer; I needed a way of winkling that out of him but without making waves at AGROW. That was the problem – the more questions I asked the thinner my cover got – it was starting to hamper me all round.

I typed out notes to myself and gave a copy to Pam for Tom's files. 'Tell Mr. Harrison it's pretty speculative at the moment.'

I phoned the Accrington hospital switchboard. The operator was not cooperative at first but after I'd told her it was a family matter of a legal nature she put me through to the lab. A reluctant sounding Dr Meyer answered the phone herself. I assured her that I would only be taking up five minutes of her time, and offered to put her through to the legal secretary at Harrison and Potts who would confirm my *bona fides*. That seemed good enough.

Prompt at seven, I parked outside her bungalow and walked up to the front door, no steps – gentle ramps instead, which seemed strange.

There was a security system like the one on Tom's building. I pressed the buzzer, spoke the words and put my visiting card through the letter box. There were faint scuffling noises from within before the door opened and all became clear. Dr Josephine Meyer was a cripple. She wore leg irons strapped outside her trousers and supported herself on a pair of crutches. I supposed she was in her early forties and still blonde although her face was drawn with constant pain. She was used to people being taken aback at first sight. 'It isn't polio, Mr. Hardy, if that's what you're thinking, but a virulent form of arthritis. I can't help myself, but if I can identify the pathogen – that's my research project – I may be able to prevent other people contracting it.'

'Which is more than the mystics and faith healers can do,' I said.

She did not want to hang around, 'You said five minutes, Mr. Hardy. My sitting room is designed around my disability, so you wouldn't find it comfortable. Shall we deal with your query here?'

I got on with it, starting by explaining my position. 'I spoke to your brother at the end of last term. I asked him a routine question, namely, where was he on the evening of 23rd November, and could anyone vouch for him? He said that he was with someone else that evening. Then he refused to say any more.'

'That's easy, Mr. Hardy. Hans and I exchange visits, roughly on a monthly basis. On 23rd November it was his turn to come to me. He arrived at about seven. We had a meal, sat and talked, played Scrabble, I won 3-0 and Hans went home around 10.30. He's inclined to be protective, that's why he didn't want to involve me.' She smiled fleetingly, a nice smile.

I said, 'Is it usual for you to wipe the floor with Hans?'

She actually laughed this time, 'At scrabble? No it isn't, he had his mind on something else, something at school I expect. He's dreadfully conscientious.' A family trait, I reckoned.

On the way back, the brainwave that had kept me waiting for a fortnight arrived. Inspiration struck during a second solitary pint at the Duke. If Josephine Meyer was not lying, and it would be natural if she was, Hansie's alibi was rock solid. What remained was his relationship with Caroline and hence a powerful motive for her murder. There was no point in grubbing for more evidence from the residents at Walpole Gardens. Who else might be around the Gardens at eight in the morning? The postman.

I rose early, drove to Preston and was by the Walpole Gardens entrance at 7.30. At ten minutes past eight the postman arrived, sorted a large bundle of letters into the individual post boxes at the entrance and turned to leave. I waylaid him bearing a copy of Jason's leaflet.

The postman admired Caroline's photo. He confirmed having seen her leaving the Gardens in a blue car, 'Two or three times but not for over a year – September before last?' *(Meaning September '98)* He was in a position to know because Walpole Gardens had been part of his regular walk for the last three years. In the interests of English Justice he gave me his name, rank and number and hoped not to be bothered further.

Tom was suited for once. Postmen are more convincing than teenagers or pensioners, was the lawyerly view. Then he asked me not to pursue Meyer further, 'For the moment'. Shortly afterwards I found out why.

Tracking down Mrs Adcock was a matter of ringing round the schools in the Preston area. I hit the right one at the third attempt and suggested to the girl on the switchboard that I ring Mrs A at lunchtime. 'She wouldn't like that. She doesn't like being disturbed during her breaks. Hot on breaks is Mrs Adcock.' She recommended phoning the Music department at two.

A lad answered, 'Hold on, Mrs. Adcock'll be with you in a minute,' he put down the receiver with a thump. It was clear what was going on – 4B boys were in full cry, enjoying their brand new baritone voices.

God is drawig 'is sword
We are barching with the Lord

They were also a touch adenoidal after their Christmas colds...

Crooks ad braggards bay 'ave their little day
Wee will dever bow the dee...

Warned 4B. So there! The chorus roared to its finale with crashing chords on the pianoforte. Better, I thought, than whining into a mike about hard-hearted totty.

Mrs Adcock picked up the phone, 'Yes? What's to do? I'm teaching.' She sounded middle-aged, militant and musical.

I gave her a rapid ID followed by, 'I'm told that you host a teachers' discussion group and your last meeting was on the evening of Tuesday 23rd November. Caroline Enderby was there with Chris Berry, both from St Cuthbert's, Ditchfield?'

'That's right Mr. Hardy and after that they left and he murdered her.'

'That's for the Court to decide. I'm researching for the defence team.'

Mrs Adcock was sceptical, 'Defence? You mean he's got one?'

'Certainly, and there's a strong suspicion of a miscarriage of justice, that's why I wanted a quick word.'

'Oooh! I see – just a minute.' Mrs Adcock rattled out instructions to 4B on using the interruption profitably, and if

I hear a peep out of you lot!' Mrs. Adcock did not sound like a devotee of Child Centred Education; in her book, I guessed, children's "needs" centred on shutting up and getting on with it.

'Right Mr. Hardy…,' suddenly she was keen to engage with this here: sex, blood, murder…Wacko!

I kept it brief. They had arrived for the meeting just on six thirty, Mrs Adcock confirmed, 'We broke up at 8.00 pm. That's the usual; I never let it go over an hour and a half.'

'Did you notice anything about Caroline and Chris? Were there signs of tension between them?'

That got a short laugh, 'Depends what you mean by tension. If you mean the effort of keeping their hands off one another, certainly.'

'How long had they been coming to these meetings?'

'Caroline had been coming for three or four years, very regular, she was. Chris Berry? That would have been his second. That's right; he came with her to the summer meeting last June, and then this one. Before that she always came on her own.' Mrs Adcock confirmed. (*She never came with Meyer*).

I asked whether the meetings ran on a regular schedule. 'More or less: one each term. It's the last thing we do before finishing – fix the date for the next one.'

'Apart from the group members, would anyone else know? I mean, do you circularise the dates around schools – anything like that?' Mrs Adcock said not, but there was nothing confidential about the arrangements, 'if one of the group wants to bring another teacher along, that's fine; we're not a terrorist cell.' I wasn't so sure about that as I left Mavis Adcock and 4B to *Clang, Clang, Clang on the Anvil*.

Next morning, I headed into Niall's office, 'Do you mind if I have a look at something on Chris's PC?'

He didn't. I went through to archives and booted Chris's machine. On my mind were Chris's last words at the end of my prison visit – "thanks for looking after the PC" – he'd said it in front of the warder. Unless he thought the man would take it for a reference to Chris's non-existent pussy-cat, why had he taken the risk? Was there something that he particularly didn't want the plods to see? I sat down, resolved to plough through everything on the hard drive again until I found it.

After an hour, I gave up and shut down. I couldn't find anything that looked suspicious. As I crept out through his office, Niall and his client were laughing about something. No tears, what's the matter with him? I skulked back to my own territory.

32

'About the sitting room fire,' Tom said, 'I rang NCF – that's Northern Criminal Forensics, an independent lab – they're prepared to have a go.'

'Meantime,' he said, 'I've been slogging away at the backroom stuff. Bank accounts, credit cards, unpaid bills, basically there's nothing there that helps either side. Caroline had about a fiver in her account, no savings and an ongoing credit card debt. Nothing catastrophic, she used to let it build up and then clear it on payday.'

'Sounds pretty responsible for a modern girl. Chris?'

'Also clean as a whistle,' Tom said, 'small balance in his current account, separate savings account with ten thousand stashed away.'

'Saving up to get re-married,' I suggested.

'There's something else...' Tom put on an expression that I interpreted as 'let's get it over with,' unusual for a criminal law solicitor, well hardened to death sentences with costs. He went on, 'We've briefed a barrister. The bail hearing is coming up at the end of the month at the Crown Court. We need a barrister for that.'

'Would I have heard of him?'

'No, and it's a "her", Gillian McFadzean.' I was surprised at a female barrister wanting to defend a case of a murdered girlfriend. 'Not how it works, Ken, Gillian's looking to make her mark. By the time she's finished, it'll be high profile. She's out to win – aiming for silk.'

'What's she like?'

'Feminist from Glasgow, dislikes men, father was a drunk, probably beat up her mother every Saturday, *but* – she hates the polis even more. She's insisted on hiring a professional Criminal Defence Investigator.'

'And she already has one lined up?'

Tom was uncomfortable, she had. 'He's called Briggs and he's ex-DCI, Halifax CID – he resigned to set up his own agency. He has contacts, knows police procedure back to front. Fell out with the Board over cutting corners, didn't get his promotion and walked. She's worked with him several times already, claims he's red hot.'

'I bet,' I said, 'sharp as shit and twice as nasty. Got a right pair haven't you – a man-hating barrister from Pollokshaws and ex-CID chip-carrying Hardhouse Briggs of 'Ull, Ell and 'Alifax, and they've both got it in for the polis. Tom, is the objective to win the case or sell the scenario for a crime series on TV?' That was where I succeeded in going too far: never lose your temper in a business dispute, but in a family disagreement make a point of it. I was modestly satisfied with my efforts.

Tom was revving up to cling to his professional dignity. 'Look Ken, I'm sorry about this, you've done us proud, and I think you could have got us there.' He shrugged, 'you see how it is?'

I got up, 'I see all right. I've got the bag; Briggs gets the benefit of my labours on a plate plus the kudos if his boss pulls off a verdict.' I made it to the door without tripping over the carpet.

'Where are you going?'

'Heathrow – I've got personal business up town and it seems a good time to see to it. After that, I'm off to Africa on Stefan's behalf. If anyone asks I'll be back at the end of February.' I left, closing the door behind me with some precision and much dignity.

I walked on to the nether end of the building and found Niall packing up his writs and wills for the day. 'I expect you know what's going off in the Berry case?' he did; he suggested I sit down. 'I wondered if you could do something for me? Caroline's funeral is on the 26th. I intended to go, but I can't now – I'm off to Africa for a month. I'm interested to know how Meyer behaves – it could be revealing, bearing in mind that he's the cast-off lover and his cast iron alibi's on the brittle side. I'll print off an image from the school website for identification.'

Niall reached for his diary, 'You want me to go?'

'No, Tom'll be there for the professionals. I'm looking for spiritual sensitivity and deep perception, could you ask the lovely Virginia?'

'On what pretext?'

'Whatever's suitable – as a friend of Caroline's? Virginia will think of something: like they were bosom pals when stripping around the Barbary Coast.' Her husband did not find that humorous. 'Sorry, I'm a bit upset.'

Niall asked about demeanour, 'Is she to weep buckets?'

'No, stay brave, perhaps the odd sniffle, but I need to know who does turn the tap on and whether it's genuine. Virginia will know in a flash.' Niall thought that was likely. 'And she'll look ravishing in the outfit that you'll be buying for the occasion.' Potts did not dispute that either. 'Give the bill to Harrison – expences essential to the investigation. It'll be best if she finds herself a secluded spot with a good view – and well away from Briggs.'

'Why avoid Briggs?'

'Because he'll fancy her something rotten and a refusal might offend.'

'Ken, why are you interested in this?' Niall sounded concerned, 'you're dropping the case… aren't you?'

I wanted Niall to be in no doubt, 'The case has dropped me,

I'm not even demoted to the substitutes bench – *I'm out, the bag.*'

'…and you've business in Africa so why bother?'

'To ensure that my work on Hans Meyer doesn't go to waste. I don't like being lied to *(try that on for hypocrisy, Hardy)* and as the discarded lover with a violent disposition, Meyer's four lengths clear in the suspects stakes.'

'You're quite sore about this?'

'Why not? But mainly it's for Chris, who's a mate. If Virginia experiences a flash of *claire voyance* I'll make sure it gets to the right people. I haven't met Briggs of 'Alifax but if he's strong on spiritual sensitivity and deep perception I'll be amazed.'

Having made myself a brew and thought about it, I cooled off. If Meyer was the guilty party, it would be routine for ex-DCI Briggs to crack his alibi and stitch him up. But if Meyer's alibi really was sound as a pound my original suspicion remained: that Caroline's murder really *was* down to a deluded group of intellectuals presided over by Martyn Enderby, betrayed husband and New Age philosopher. Perhaps the master detective could extract the truth from Enderby and his AGROW pals with sensitive interrogation on the lines of, "… and who did you sleep with on the night you murdered your wife, Mr Enderby?" in which case, fair play to the lad. For my money, the way to penetrate the AGROW circle was undercover treachery, laced with bare faced flattery and false offers of funds. I recalled with confidence the advice of Bertrand Russell, "to explain the course of Western Philosophy look no further than the cash flow". Not quite what he said, but that's what he meant. So, to penetrate AGROW, promise cash and see what shakes loose.

Notwithstanding my Drama Queen exit from Tom's office I was not leaving on the first flight out; there were things to be done. One of them turned up that same evening.

'Emmeline Deedes here, Mr. Hardy, we have some

information for you.' I arranged to call at eight the following evening.

I sat down to pound out a brief for Briggs. Next morning I took it along to Tom's office. The main man for the defence was looking wary so I was short and to the point. I dropped the brief, over which I'd laboured into the night, on his desk. 'This puts the lad in possession of all facts available to me with my compliments. There is a proviso: it's for his eyes only and he does not mention my name to *anyone* in connection with this case. I don't expect him to have a problem with that as it will enable him to claim the credit. He needs to crack Hans Meyer's alibi and it's game over. By all means give him my phone number. I'll be back from Africa some time in March. I expect him to have the case done and dusted before then.'

Moving quickly on, I phoned Stefan's secretary, revealed my travel plans and promised to keep my mobile switched on. 'Hold on to my documents. I'll come out to Watford to see Mr. Kovacs and pick them up then.'

Vaccinations? Hell's bells and bugger! I phoned Bill Jones's surgery for a promise of prompt perforations. I wasn't the only one to suffer. Next on my calling list, the cattery, 'He's due his cat flu booster next month,' they said.

'Excellent. Blunt needle, in hard, that'll wipe the grin off his whiskers.'

'*Mr. Hardy!*'

I phoned Gloria at Cuthbert's, 'Can you remember whether Meyer had a management meeting or anything else that would have kept him back after school last March; probably the Friday before the Easter break?' Gloria asked if it was important.

'It could be.'

'Right, he's teaching I'll nip into his office now.' Two minutes later Gloria was back, 'Sorry, filing cabinet's locked there might be a chance later.' I told her my travel plans and threatened to ring her again when I got back.

I phoned Green at H&J and asked if he knew the name of the last tenant at Fellbeck. 'Before my time,' Green said, 'but I'll find out.'

33

The Deedes home was a substantial end-of-terrace three bed in a quiet street. It reminded me of my student digs in South Harrow: early-twenties Percy Bilton finest and bloody freezing. Emmeline let me in, 'Shall we go into the kitchen, it's warmer,' she suggested.

She arranged her charts on the table, 'We've got two families here, the Dawsons and the Ostricks. Let's start with the Dawsons; history of the Dawsons of Fellbeck begins with Ezra Dawson born 1814, died 1891.' She ran through the main points, 'Ezra married Lizzie Jarvis and they had three sons: Charles, the actor, came first. Lizzie was pregnant when she married Ezra.'

'We know that Ezra and Charles didn't get on. Did Ezra think he wasn't the real father, and that's why he resented Charles?'

'Whatever the reason, Charles disappeared from home when he was about 14. He never went back. There were two younger brothers: Walter the lawyer and Edward. Walter's grandson, Jarvis, runs the Dawson family trust which owns Fellbeck and the remaining land.'

Emmeline went on, 'that leaves Edward. He ran the farm after his father died and stuck at it until his own death in 1931'.

'Is that where Nathaniel Ostrick fits in?'

'Yes, Ezra had a sister, Mary Dawson, who married Vlad Ostrog in 1853. Vlad was probably a Russian immigrant – he bought the South Lea property and farmed there. He *may* have been the brother of Michael Ostrog. Does that name ring a bell?'

'One of the police suspects in the Ripper case?'

'Good. Michael was a bad lot, but he was just a petty thief and nothing to do with the Ripper murders. Vlad's wife, Mary, née Dawson died in 1854, giving birth to Ludwig. Ludwig grew up and took over South Lea when his father died in 1885. Ludwig changed the family name from Ostrog to Ostrick presumably to sound more English.'

I interrupted, 'Why didn't he go for something posh: Osborne or something?'

Emmeline gave me a glare, 'Obviously to retain continuity with his business contacts. Shall we go on?' I collapsed. 'Ludwig married Rose Adams and they had a son called Nathaniel, born in 1891.'

'Before or after his Uncle Charles Dawson died?'

'After,' said Emmeline, 'the following month, do you mind if I finish? Nathaniel lived at South Lea working on the farm with his father. After war broke out in 1914 he volunteered, was sent to France and was wounded in 1915. It was then discovered that he spoke fluent Russian and he was transferred to Intelligence as an interpreter. During that time he must have been attracted to the theatre because he didn't return to South Lea but stayed in London and emerged after the war as a professional actor under the name Vernon Adams.' Emmeline brought proceedings rapidly to an end, 'Ludwig died in 1919, Edward Dawson bought the house and land and amalgamated them with the Fellbeck estate. Meanwhile Vernon met an actress called Jenny Finch and their affair turned serious. Edward died in 1931. Probably because of family pressure, Vernon left the stage and returned as Nathaniel Ostrick to manage the farm. Nathaniel lived there until he murdered Jenny Finch in 1934, no one knows why and then hanged himself.' I knew exactly why – Jenny told me.

'That's the story,' Emmeline folded her charts and passed them to me.

'Thanks,' I said, 'that's brilliant; you've put the whole thing in context for me. Have you had a chance to look at the Benson document?'

'Not my field,' Emmeline said, 'but I've got a resident expert.' She left the kitchen and came back a few moments later shepherding a smaller person of about forty five with brown hair and eyes, attractive and plumply animated. 'This is my sister, Aethelflaed,' she announced. They stood side by side looking at me, one gauntly serious the other with a cheery smile. As sisters, they couldn't have been more different.

I must have looked blank, 'Everyone calls me Ethel,' said the plump one.

'They do not call me Emm,' the gaunt one warned. 'Father was a keen Anglo-Saxonist, our brother's called Edmund.'

Emmeline anticipated the incoming question, 'But mother was French and as I'm the eldest she claimed the privilege of naming me.' (*Mais enfin, maman 'as l'affaire wiz a small fat Anglais, et voila! Ethel!*). 'Ethel is a historical novelist', said Emmeline, and left us.

Aethelflaed sat in her sister's place and produced the printout of the Benson document. 'I don't publish under my own name, of course. I do all my own research and I have written about the Ripper period.'

'Have I read any of your books?'

Ethel grinned, a touch ruefully, 'Doubt it, I write from the feminine angle.' (*Oh God! A creative feminist*).

'Who do you think wrote the document?'

'The author was not a professional historian and the text isn't quite right for 1891. I would put it between the wars,' said Ethel. 'He had a good knowledge of the Victorian theatre. Also he knew something about social conditions in the East End of London at that time. Nathaniel Ostrick aka Vernon Adams ticks the boxes as the author. It's a partial biography of Charles Dawson, the Victorian actor who was Nathaniel's great uncle. I think Nathaniel wrote it during his time at Fellbeck. How does that fit your murder investigation?'

I gave Ethel a quick summary, ending, 'The defendant, Chris Berry, claims that a man calling himself "Benson" used the document to lure him to Fellbeck, which is remote and standing empty, at a time when Caroline would be with him. Chris never met "Benson" until the night of the murder. Now he's been forced to expose himself, if we can identify him, we'll crack the case.'

Ethel viewed me with large brown eyes, 'Oh god, a man with imagination.'

'You don't think that the author was one of the murderers?'

'No, that would make the document modern, probably 1960s which it certainly isn't. Unless you can think of a better candidate, it's Nathaniel for me,' said Ethel. *(Me too: he hanged himself in 1934 and I met him in 1992)*.

I said, 'Two similar murders of actresses have taken place at Fellbeck. Also, although the document is obscure, Charles Dawson late of Fellbeck, *may* have murdered an actress in a similar manner in 1891. Suppose that the murderer in Caroline's case has some sort of connection with Fellbeck or the Dawson family?'

'Or imagines he has,' Ethel said.

I said, 'Could Charles Dawson have been Jack? If not, was his actress the Ripper's last victim?'

Ethel wrinkled her nose, 'No evidence for that', she pronounced.

I said, 'Have we got a serial killing spanning a hundred years? Suppose Charles killed Florence, then Jenny was killed by a Dawson descendant and Caroline was murdered in the same room as Jenny Finch. We've run out of Dawson men.'

Ethel corrected me, 'Jarvis, the trust chairman is still around.'

'He's too old and he lives abroad. Was Caroline murdered

by someone who thinks he's a reincarnation of Nathaniel? According to the theory they don't have to be related.'

Ethel laughed and torpedoed reincarnation, 'If god wanted us to believe in reincarnation he would never have given us DNA.'

'All right, reincarnation is rubbish. But I've heard Martyn Enderby lecturing and he's a reincarnation enthusiast.'

'I agree that Caroline was murdered by some deluded person,' said Aethelflaed, 'If her husband really believes in reincarnation, he's deluded.'

I decided to leave it there, 'Ethel, I'm off to London and after that to Africa on business. I won't be back until the beginning of March. Could you look in on Caroline's funeral for me? There are three people I'd like you to spy out: Martyn Enderby, Hans Meyer and Virginia Potts. I'll email photos. 'I'm interested in how they conduct themselves and how they interact. See if you can spot our deluded person.'

Aethelflaed laughed and accused me of watching too many TV detective dramas, 'and if I'm asked?'

'Just say Caroline was your friend. She helped you with your research for a new theatrical novel. Her name will figure in the acknowledgements.'

34

As a mind clearing exercise, I phoned Wilkinson's mass murder HQ. The main man picked up the phone. The cries of doomed and dying animals provided background music. 'Pete,' I said, 'I'm off to London and then Africa at the weekend. I fancy a drink first, are you on?'

Wilkinson was prompt and positive, 'Why not? She'll be watching *Midsommer Murders*. I'll give it a miss – too much blood for me. And think on, get a taxi.' That was fair warning.

★

The bubbly blonde receptionist from the public library was getting down to business. Somehow her silky white nightdress had slipped up over her thighs. She moaned softly and wriggled. I eased towards the gate of heavenly bliss. Then her mobile phone started tweeting. I swore, reached, grabbed, killed it and woke up. A bloody dream! It was not the receptionist's mobile, it was mine. I'd forgotten to cancel the alarm.

I crawled out of bed, dragged my sick headache to the kitchen, gulped down a pint of warm water with four aspirins and went to fumble with the shower taps. As six-pint hangovers went, it was no worse than I deserved. I shaved, (*God what a face!*), hunted in the fridge, drank the orange juice, fried the eggs and bacon and got them down with hunks of bread and butter and a quart of strong tea. The morning had begun disappointingly but there wasn't that much of a hurry; the 12.30 express from Preston would do me.

I rang down and asked for Jason, checked my paperwork and finished packing. I assessed my Ripper collection and crammed the one with the best index and bibliography into my coat pocket. One should always have something sensational to read on the train. When Jason came up I asked how he was getting on with Caroline's genealogy. 'I'm stuck at the moment on her maternal grandmother, but otherwise it's been a straightforward search.'

'Don't bother any further,' I said. Jason asked if there was anything else, 'Something I could look at while you're away?'

'I'll call you before I fly out.' We ambushed the cat and pushed him into his carrying basket. He didn't like it, fought, spat and then swore all the way to the cattery. On arrival, he stopped swearing, alighted from the basket, stuck his tail in the air and rubbed round the kennel maid's legs. *(Rat!)*

I managed a doze on the train. It was no distance from Euston to Achraj's place but in my fragile state I took a taxi. Achraj Singh appeared at reception and greeted me. His establishment was a small 3-star in a quiet street behind Woburn Place. I found it twenty years ago and used it ever after. I could have gone up market when the business grew but never bothered. Achraj ran an orderly house frequented by Punjabi business gentlemen. They did not come in drunk or sit up half the night playing heavy rock on the other side of the wall.

'Welcome, Mr Hardy. Business?'

'Of a sort,' I admitted.

'There, and I am thinking you had retired.'

'No more than you, Achraj.' That was the end of the personal enquiries.

There was time to phone the University of Southeast London. I enquired for Dr Pascal Threnadie. 'Oo?' I repeated the name. 'Nah, no one here called that. Wass he do then?' I ventured a guess around Asian Philosophy. 'You mean Dr Pascal Threnadie de Morzine. Why didn't you say so?' I was put through to the relevant secretary and made an appointment. I did some more reading, dozed, took a Rogan Josh with water on the side at the local Indian and ended up with an early night.

Next morning I phoned Green at Braxtonby. He had a partial answer, 'The last tenancy agreement expired in 1978 – before my time. There's been nothing since.' I asked whether Helmsley and Jordan would have acted for the tenant. 'Unlikely, we were acting for the landlord. Do you want to know who handled it?' I said no rush because I was going abroad for a month.

I arrived on time for my meeting with Dr Pascal Threnadie de Morzine and sat impatiently outside his office whilst the clock crawled on for half an hour past the time of my appointment. It put me in the right frame of mind to review my tactics, which were simple enough. My intention was to needle the doctor into an indiscretion. Specifically I wanted to know whether Pascal was a possible member of the murder gang or whether to write him off. After that, there was nothing to do other than gaze at his notice board displaying information about his "ground-breaking" course on *The Post-materialist Society*, a schedule of forthcoming lectures, a list of overdue essays with a threat of possible penalties for further procrastination.

Eventually the door opened and an administrative-looking person came out mopping his brow. I seized the moment and went in. Pascal made no response as I entered, except to cantilever an emaciated arm across the desk with an ascetic hand on the end of it, 'Mistair 'Ardee?' I took it cautiously. It was cold and communicated nothing. I let go before something broke.

The office was cluttered. Threnadie's desktop was mainly taken up by his computer system – tower, monitor, printer and all. A plaster bust of Gandhi occupied a small table to my right. On the wall behind the desk was a big map of Asia. To one side hung a framed text with Aryan decoration: *We look forward to the past. The future is behind us.*

The learned doctor's appearance was appropriate to his position as Senior Lecturer in Eastern Philosophy. He was bald on top with a grey-brown ponytail at the back. His face was thin and sallow featuring a pair of downward sloping eyebrows giving a melancholy effect and suggesting a critical view of the follies of the *canaille*. I was confident of my inclusion with that class. His complexion was waxy, set off by surprising large and very yellow incisors. His person was skeletal suggesting a work-in-progress hunger strike. His grey suit hung about him in a satisfactorily ascetic fashion; his tie-less shirt was artfully open at the top exposing a scrawny throat that a plucked chicken might be proud of and a hollow chest. Deep suffering was etched everywhere. His appearance fitted his voice and accent which featured the lofty contempt of the Parisian left bank intellectual although his country of origin was open to speculation. He didn't suggest that I sit down, so I shifted a stack of papers from the only available chair onto the floor and sat.

I opened the bowling, 'Good *afternoon*, Doctor de Morzine,' a testing delivery since our appointment had been for 11.30 am and it was now five minutes past midday. It flew unregarded to the wicket keeper.

'I have recently become a member of AGROW,' I continued, 'I see from your website that you sit on the Steering Committee, so I want to ask you a couple of questions. Your replies may affect my future decisions.'

A substantial sneer began to bloom, 'what sot of decisions?'

'Financial'. That settled the sneer and clarified Pascal's position on materialism. I suspected that his lectures on *The Post-materialist Society* advocated generous transfers of wealth from the toiling *canaille* to the pockets of intellectuals of a certain kind. 'I read your AGM paper on shamanism – primitive isn't it?'

Pascal came in pretty sharp on that, 'primiteeve?'

'I understand that shamanism involves every animal, plant, tree and rock having its own spirit, or consciousness if you prefer. According to the Anthropic Principle, which I find is *key* to AGROW thinking, *(Good stroke that, Hardy – lifted off their website)* the entire universe is under the control of human consciousness. How does that work if your human consciousness is outvoted by a block vote of sceptical Saharan sand flies supported by progressive pebbles on Brighton beach? It sounds as though you're at odds with your colleagues.'

Pascal regarded this with supreme contempt. He spluttered something about 'ancient wisdom'.

I interrupted (rudely), 'Ancient rubbish – "looking forward to the past".' I indicated the text on his wall. 'Face facts,' I advised, 'my concern is the Fellbeck project. It demands a large investment. In view of the limited resources of AGROW that can only be provided by investors who need to be convinced on the feasibility of the project. You propose to devote the Fellbeck centre to residential courses on Shamanism. You seem to imagine that you can cover the investment besides raising funds for future development by promoting the primitive practices of stone age witch doctors whose purpose was to terrify and rule the rest of the tribe by black magic?'

My research was paying off. Pascal Threnadie de Morzine could not believe what he was hearing. He tried to break in but he was so mad that he couldn't get his words lined up beyond the fact he was not accustomed to being insulted by an ignoramus.

I continued, 'I recently heard a lecture by your leader, Martyn Enderby. AGROW is in business to achieve a spiritual revolution. He was passionately clear on that. Ever heard of a revolution that succeeded whilst going backwards in two different directions? You're on a loser. Forget it.'

I commiserated, 'Sorry Pascal but this is not a wander through the glades of academe. This is about money. I've got it, you need it. I'm a business man; businessmen talk like this. I'm talking about the Fellbeck project. As a member of the Steering committee you're committed to *driving* the movement forward. I see progressive philosophy going on at AGROW, *(lies!)* however I will not invest in an organisation with split objectives. As a worker in the state education sector, Dr de Morzine, you're familiar with the theory that money grows on trees. It doesn't; the Fellbeck project is a business enterprise. What place is there for your shamanic studies?'

''Oo are you to ask?' Pascal wanted to know.

'I've told you, I'm a potential investor currently the largest of those offering to finance the project. Without my contribution, it won't happen. I'm in a position to offer a six-figure investment as my good friend and colleague Alexander Scott McIver will confirm.' (*Lying bugger, Hardy, the wife would kill you*). 'What financial projections can you show me showing the return on shamanic courses at Fellbeck?'

'Zey are in preparation.'

'I look forward to seeing them. Why do you think that Fellbeck is essential to the group's needs? You've seen the survey report of our mutual friend, Mr Sam Waters. I can show you modern buildings in the area at half the price, requiring no restoration and minimal conversion work. What's the attraction of an isolated 19th century mansion in a state of decay?'

'Ambionce,' said Threnadie, 'eet 'as the spiritual presonce. You cannot instil certaine philosopheek values in an environment of glass and concrette.' (*He meant like the building we were sitting in where he was receiving a fat salary for doing just that*).

'The locals say Fellbeck's haunted, if that's what you mean. Not a lady in white on the back stairs – they mean an evil spirit. You don't think that could be a deterrent to your students?'

'*Au contraire*,' Pascal insisted.

'Why do you think there's a supernatural presence there? You all inspected the place last April, did you see anything?'

'No.'

'Hear anything? Any unexplained noises?'

'Yes, many sings.'

'Old buildings do that, especially if the roof is falling in. What else?'

'The 'istory of the pless. Dids of a certain teep have occurred. M'sieu Enderby kept an overnight vigil for dip meditation. *(And shagging Virginia).* He said it was the most inspiring of his life.' It was the same tale that Sam had come up with but given Pascal's personality problems, it had taken longer.

'Sign on for an AGROW residential course and be scared shitless? I should get on with those projections if I were you,' I advised, 'but my opinion is that courses on shamanism are a bad idea.'

I got up. 'Doctor de Morzine, I must have figures from you no later than April 1st. Ms Partington will confirm that this is *key* to driving the project forward. A draft course prospectus and a curriculum should accompany the projections.' I placed one of my cards on his blotter – not the one referring to Harrison & Potts.

Pascal dismissed Amelia's opinion, 'Matters of academic policy are not the concern of Ms Partington. She 'as ze 'abit of exceeding 'er brif.'

I got the impression that her briefs had something to do with it.

'Is that *all*?' He was impatient for his lunchtime cold water. This was the moment when eagerness for closure might provoke an indiscretion. I sat down again, 'There is another question I need to ask'. I gestured towards the bust alongside him, 'I see you are an admirer of Gandhi?'

Threnadie did not bother to suppress a new sneer, '*évidemment!*' I don't understand the French reputation for suave diplomacy. In my experience, they tend to err on the abrupt side of bloody rude. (*Unlike you, Hardy*).

255

'The Mahatma advocated non-violence. In your opinion are "deeds of a certain type" *ever* justified?'

'Of cos not, violence is never justified.' I stared hard at him and tried to look as though I was there for the afternoon, '... Except where there is an overwhelming spiritual reason. *Comprenez*?'

I rose and walked to the door. 'I look forward to your projections Doctor de Morzine. I emphasise that these are *key* to my investment decision. I don't suppose Martyn would be pleased were my money to go to a rival organisation. I strongly recommend that this discussion remains confidential until the issues in question are resolved. April 1st? Projection? Supporting documents? I look forward to them.'

There was a toilet two doors down from Threnadie's where I indulged in a celebratory pee. I had not behaved as badly as that for some time. He wasn't Benson – not with that accent – but if he could rake up a good enough spiritual pretext he might have taken part in the murder of Caroline. Was he the philosopher who touched her up in the kitchen? Had she then kicked him in the balls? Was he the killer waiting behind the sitting room door? The next move was to get Briggs in there with his ex-CID mac.

I set off down the corridor which extended to the corner of the building and made a left turn. Approaching the corner and out of sight from the next section of corridor, I heard a voice raised in irritation. 'I am telling you, this essay is of moderate kalitay, *extremement* moderate, you are fortunate to be awarded a Bay meenus...' It was Threnadie de Morzine. Short of the corner, I stopped to listen.

Pascal was interrupted by the voice of a distressed damsel, 'But I don't understand, last term I got A's for everything.'

'*Oui, last term,*' Pascal was unsympathetic, 'this term sings are different.'

'I even got an A+ once'. Sob, 'and after what I did...'

Threnadie cut her off at the stocking-tops, 'Zat is enough!

We will tok about zis in my offeece.' Footsteps started coming towards me. I set off and met the unhappy couple at the corner. The damsel was a plain girl of 18 or 19 with shapeless legs, frizzy blonde hair, a plump face and thick spectacles.

'But Pascal…'

'*Doctor* Threnadie de Morzine to you, Miss Smithson.' That kid hadn't got an A+ as an essayist. As we passed, I caught Pascal's eye, gave him a wink and got a pop-eyed glare in reply. It was nothing new – even in my day lecturers of a certaine teep were known for trying it on with female freshers.

Miss Smithson trailed disconsolately after her tutor, her upper arm decorated with a red bruise, her twofold plan – get a first and get a man – in shreds. Cruel to women, are we Pascal? Including Amelia? Now there's a thought.

35

I wasn't anticipating a great weekend but there was no way out. If I'd spent more than a couple of hours in London without seeing our Matthew there would have been nuclear missiles incoming from Malaga. The problem was that we don't get on. In spite of trying, something always goes wrong. I went to see him playing centre half for his primary school. He wasn't that bad but he kept checking his tackles at the last moment. I said to him at half time that if he didn't go through with them he wouldn't win the ball and being timid was the best way to get hurt. In the second half he shut his eyes, threw himself bravely into his first tackle and broke his ankle. Thanks, Dad! He didn't bother with football after that.

I met Matthew at lunchtime in a gastro pub. I ordered at the bar and we sat down. 'Why are you two splitting up?' I supposed that he meant his parents.

'Why do you think that, Matthew?'

'Mam's living full time in Malaga and you're in Ditchfield.' I reminded him that I'd only just got back from spending Christmas together in Spain. Also, I had a job in Ditchfield until September. 'Yeah, but what then? You hate Spanish beer, you hate the climate and you're superior to all expats…'

After that, he wanted to know about "this case". He must have heard it from his sister. I briefed him on such bare details as I thought he could handle. 'Not got very far have you?'

I told him that I'd only got far enough to have the prosecution case thrown out. 'Why are you going on then? If this Chris is going to get away with it, why not leave it to the lawyers?' The ruthless logic of the unemployable young – I said I thought I owed it to Caroline to find her killer. 'Come off it, Dad, she's dead. A bit late for a banner with a strange device isn't it?'

'No, it isn't. She's entitled to justice. And there's Chris, suppose we get him off but the plods never get the real killer, he's going to have fingers pointed at him for the rest of his life.' I got up, 'Come on, Matt, you can show me this rat hole you're living in. Your Mother will need to know.'

'Whatever,' Matthew took me there. As we climbed the narrow staircase, 'if you notice a funny smell, it's the corpse I'm keeping in the broom cupboard.'

There was a funny smell all right, 'What is your Mother going to say when I tell her you've taken up necrophilia?'

'It's not a career choice, just a life style like racing pigeons.'

The flat was minute, which was a good thing in one way because it was obviously too small for me to sleep there. It was cleaner than I expected. The corpse-like smell was standard issue for a multi-occupied tenement building – rising damp, dry rot, burnt cooking fat and drains – not much Matt could do about that except complain and get thrown out. I spent some of the afternoon trying to find answers to the questions I was expecting from the wife like how was he making a living? As far as I could make out the answer involved a combination of state benefits and undeclared income as a freelance writer. 'TV scripts, film stuff, commercials,' Matt explained airily. My guess was that not a right lot got written and what was had a tendency not to be paid for. I didn't ask about the libretto for the smash-hit musical just over the horizon. He was not planning a star role, 'Thanks for passing on your singing genes, Dad.'

I was relieved to find that he had a plan for the evening until I heard the details. He'd got tickets for a new play, 'It's going to be big. It's in a small theatre where they put on try-outs for the Royal Court. It got a great crit in the *Guardian*.' He was right about small – just as well because apart from us, the audience numbered

23, I counted. The synopsis in the photocopied programme notes explained that it was about a revolutionary cell in an unspecified city in a post-Blairite Neo-Fascist state. The director was a veteran of Agitprop and the Cold War and out of respect for the demise of both enterprises, he took his curtain call in deep black making a meaningful contrast with his cast who took theirs in nothing. The leading actress was a middle aged dyke which put a bit of a damper on her uninventive sex scene. There were acres of swear words, none of them new and plenty of far-left slogans which weren't new either. I sat through it. At the end, Matthew stood, whooped and clapped loudly enough to cover for the rest of us. We went for something to eat and Matthew explained all the vital points that I'd missed. 'The trouble with you, Father is that you're a typical northern working class Tory.' I wanted to know why that was worse than a Metro benefits supported Trot. This was not made clear.

Afterwards I got a taxi. Matthew said he was walking back and I said he wasn't. It was starting to rain so I won. The taxi couldn't get up the street to Matthew's place, due to a Fascist parked at right angles across the road with his bonnet up. Our taxi stopped at the corner. Matthew took hold of the door handle to disembark then said, 'look Dad, I've got a meeting with a television producer tomorrow afternoon (Sunday?)...'

It was the most sensible contribution he'd made all day, 'Right Matt and you'll need the morning to prepare. Why don't I look in again on the way back from Cape Town – tell you what went on?' We both knew I wouldn't so we shook hands. Matthew baled out, shouted, 'Take care, Dad,' stuck his hands in his anorak pockets and shambled off up the street, an awkward figure, big enough to look after himself, but vulnerable. There was a sudden need to swallow hard. Sons either turn out like you, which is frightening, or totally different making communication impossible. The taxi took off towards Achraj's place. I made a resolution for my next existence – girls only.

Girls are easier, assuming you get them on the pill soon enough and they sometimes grow up to become useful creatures, even affectionate; but boys! I was confident that Achraj would agree, I knew my Dad would if I'd thought to ask.

I phoned Stefan's office on Monday morning, '11.15 on Friday, half an hour for a quick update,' the great man instructed.

Next I phoned Jason. He'd solved the problem of Caroline's maternal great grandmother. Her great grandfather had met and married her in South Africa. 'Mr. Potts reckons she was a mission child, perhaps an orphan, parents unknown.'

'And she was a native?'

'She must have been,' Jason said, 'does that make a difference?'

'It could account for Caroline's hybrid vigour, otherwise irrelevant. Anyway that's enough of that.' Jason wanted to know if I'd come up with any other research for him. 'I'm off the case now, Jason. Ex-DCI Briggs has taken over. If he hasn't cracked it, by the time I get back he might be glad of a lift; meantime, report back to Mr. Harrison.'

That left me with four days to fill in London. Easy – I contacted our London rep and we set out on a farewell tour of my major London customers. On Friday morning, I paraded early for my briefing with the CEO. He was on schedule as usual. I was in his office at 11.17 and out again half an hour later. I gave him his final verbal warning, 'I don't know anything about Africa.'

Stefan took no notice, 'You know how to run a factory, that's what I need. Email your reports and phone me when you get back to Ditchfield. And don't wander off in the bush on your own.'

The reception area downstairs had gone quiet for lunch. I grinned at the girl on the desk, found a seat in the farthest corner and rang Virginia. 'How enlightening was the funeral?'

'Meyer was there with colleagues from St Cuthbert's. He looked quite upset, more so than the others.' (*Remorse or bereavement?*) 'The cathedral's a difficult place for picking up vibrations, it's got the spirituality of an indoor swimming pool.' I settled for a quick assessment: did he do it or not? Virginia said that was unfair, was I pressing her? I denied it. Virginia greeted that with, 'What a shame,' then recovered, 'the teachers were sitting in one of the centre pews. Meyer was at the end, slightly apart from the others, suggesting a desire to distance. I need eye contact for an aural reading which was impossible because I was behind him in a side pew and I could only get a general impression. I picked up undertones suggestive of involvement and severely damaged aura.' It was the mystic equivalent of a "definite maybe".

I asked about the other players. 'The school choir sang nicely – High Church litanies – kyries – you know.' (*I didn't*). 'Two of Caroline's pupils read the lessons. The Canon preached, as you'd expect from the Chairman of the Governors, he didn't say much.'

I thought I knew the sort of thing – "terrible loss to the school, inspired, caring teacher, great love for her art and for the children, missed terribly by her colleagues. In her memory, and (with deep sincerity) contribute generously to the cathedral roof restoration fund". 'Very good Ken.'

'What about Enderby?'

'He spoke the eulogy. 'He's a brilliant man and an excellent speaker, he was intensely moving at times.'

'Was that down to technique?' Virginia was firmly for sincerity. 'Did he refer to their personal relationship – were there any hints about tensions in the marriage?'

'The opposite – he was lyrical about their love story. He did mention Caroline being a free spirit.'

'Isn't that PC for "tart"?' Virginia's response to that was cool. I pressed on, 'bearing in mind that he had a wagon load of motives for killing his unfaithful spouse, wasn't the eulogy just an upper class snow job?'

Virginia was vehement, 'No, he's not responsible for Caroline's murder. His aura denies it *totally*.'

No messing with dispassionate analysis; interesting, I thought. So organise a boarding party. 'Virginia, I agree. To be honest, I suspected Martyn Enderby at first, simply because he's straight out of the detective's handbook: motive, means, opportunity – three boxes, three ticks, and he's the wronged husband – guilty. *But* he's deeply spiritual and committed to non-violence. The manner of Caroline's death was obscene. It's inconceivable that Martyn Enderby could have condoned it, let alone carried it out.' I was modestly satisfied with that as a working class snow job.

So was Virginia, she laughed, a touch wildly I thought. She put on a cooing tone, 'I hope that's not all we agree on, is it Ken?' (*Bitch!*) Nothing daunted, I misunderstood. I was anxious to get the right message passed back to Martyn so I laid it on. 'Martyn isn't a suspect, he's a victim. It's unfortunate that circumstances didn't allow you to get a deep reading on Meyer. There are some strong leads on him. However it's academic now as far as I'm concerned. It's up to Briggs, now. He's the right man to build a textbook case against Meyer, meanwhile I'm off to Africa.'

I expected her to close down the discussion. She had a statement from me of Enderby's innocence but that wasn't enough for the lovely Virginia. 'Ken, don't rely too much on Mr. Briggs. I was able to manage a snapshot reading. He's spiritually dead and devoid of integrity. He's completely unsuited to this case.' I thought that was a bit hard on Briggsie bearing in mind the crosses he had to bear in life: Halifax FC and Yorkshire bitter for a start. I had an idea what was behind her adverse assessment: she looked at him, he noticed, he started undressing her.

'The case couldn't be more simple,' she was telling me, 'it's classic Spirit Possession.'

I was confused. After our visit to Fellbeck she had diagnosed Caroline's murder as "the usual boring old thing – love, sex, jealousy, revenge". I mentioned this.

There was an answer, *(surprise!)* 'You're misunderstanding, Ken. Not everyone who has motive rushes off and commits murder. But a demoniac is much more likely to. Motive *and* possession are the fatal combination.'

'How do you get possessed?'

'You have to be *vulnerable*, a damaged aura is fatal.' She made it sound like catching a cold: if you're run down you succumb. I asked if it was a fair analogy. Virginia was under-impressed, 'Ken, you have a genius for reductionist banalities.' I accepted that as a mystic "Yes".

Nothing else would do but her loveable, materialistic, secular and stupid friend had to say it, 'In that case, you don't mean it still could be Enderby?'

Virginia clouted that delivery into the gasworks. 'No Ken! That's exactly what it can't mean. The aura of an SP subject is unmistakably damaged. Martyn Enderby's is spiritually perfect. It radiates strength, love and peace.'

'Who could it be then? Me, for example?' I was remembering my foggy experience at Fellbeck, muddy shoes, hangman's birthmark, and the coffee shop business. 'What about my aura?'

Virginia giggled, 'Ken, your aural sickness is about something else altogether – deprivation.' She giggled again for emphasis and then dropped her voice a tone or two, 'If you're worried Ken, there are techniques. When you get back invite me up for coffee… just an hour…we could do some healing.'

That did it. I'd had enough of being prick-teased by the lovely Virginia. I promised to think about all she had told me, thanked her politely for her professional advice and shut down the connection.

I hate mobiles for long conversations – anything more extended than "I'm on the train". I stumbled out with one ear white and the other red.

It hadn't been a waste of time. At least I knew what the lovely Virginia was about and if she passed on any of my passionate exoneration of the bereaved to the incomparable Martyn and his AGROW gang it should thicken up my cover. If not, san fairy ann.

I set off to walk to the station. A march into town down Watford's red brick and tile terraces could only be an aid to dip meditation. Perhaps a spiritually dead, integrity-free detective really was what this case needed. I hoped so. Briggs could snaffle the credit. All I wanted was for Chris to get his life back. On the other hand, if Briggsie's subtleties failed was I prepared to accept Virginia's offer? In return for my coffee would she outshine the library receptionist? More likely it would be, "No, no, Kenneth you misunderstand, unhand me you secular brute, or I shall scream!" *(Blast and bugger!)* But help was at hand for, round the next corner, if not a mirage, was a pub. There is one potable ale in North London. They had it.

It took a pint and a half of Directors' bitter to restore rational thought. The SP theory would get me nowhere. The only person who could have murdered Caroline single-handed was Chris. That was the police case and we'd picked the bones out of it two months ago. If it wasn't Chris, you had to accept his statement: murder gang, technical complications, improbabilities and all. Some supernatural power, I thought, to organise that lot – a bit more complex than thumping noises in the passage. Had *The Presence* clocked on early to light the sitting room fire?

36

Back at the hotel, I left it until seven and then phoned the Deedes establishment. Aethelflaed answered. I asked how she got on, what was her impression of Martyn Enderby?

'Complex – what he said in his role of bereaved husband was unexceptional and unexceptionable and beautifully delivered, it has to be said. But then he drifted into a spiritualist sales talk and Caroline's devotion to supporting his life's work.'

'Devotion? That's good,' I said, 'The November before last I heard him lecture to Ditchfield Sceptics. She was there on the platform trying not to look as bored as I felt. Then, when he got to his rousing peroration and went clean over the top – whoop, whoop, scream, scream from his rent-a-crowd students – Caroline made her excuses.'

'That's not what I was getting at. When he started in about the "great work" I found him quite unnerving; I kept picking up flashes of something manic in his voice.'

'Do you think he might be a schizoid?

'I don't know, Ken,' said Ethel, 'I'm not a psychiatrist. I do know someone, but he wouldn't give an opinion without meeting the subject. My impression is that they switch suddenly from being detached and unreachable into voluble and excitable and then back again. Martyn fits the frantic part but I can't imagine him ever as silent and withdrawn. '

'What about Meyer, did you spot him?'

'Very controlled, impossible to detect much at a distance. I think he was genuinely upset but too tough to show it.'

'Or was it remorse?'

'Equally possible.'

'And the lovely Virginia Potts?'

'I had a good view of Virginia. She's got a massive crush on Enderby. Never took her eyes off him. He knows it, he shot a couple of glances her way with a "what do you think of that?" look.'

'How would you sum her up?'

'Nice hat, no knickers.' (*Ethel!*) She asked if there was anything else.

'Yes, I don't know whether this is strictly for you or Emmeline.' She promised they'd sort that out between them. 'It's speculative I'm afraid, but Emmeline worked out Charles Dawson's family tree, and you've analysed the Benson document. I'm interested in tracking some of the people he was involved with and their descendants.' I gave her a list, 'I realise you won't be able to trace them all – changes of name and that sort of thing. Florence Roper, the girl Dawson *might* have murdered, should be top of the list. According to Benson, her real mother seems to have farmed her out to her married sister Martha Roper and Florence took her stepmother's name.'

'That was common, even with respectable people. If they found themselves over-supplied with kids they lashed them around a bit,' Ethel said.

'Don't spend too much time on it,' I said.'

'What about Martyn Enderby?' Ethel asked, 'there might be something there.'

'Yes please. Also, you might like to have a look at his personal website. Give you an idea of the sort of people he mucks in with.' I gave her the URL.

★

On Monday morning, not too early, I phoned Claudia's office. I got a pretty sharp, 'yes, who is this?' American idiom delivered with an Est'ry accent. I explained my mission. She agreed, said she would meet me in a certain wine bar at 6pm for half an hour maximum. I promised to be punctual.

When Claudia arrived, she spotted the only possible "KH" and walked over to my table. She was not as I had expected. The way Chris pronounced her name, "Clowdia" had led me to expect something Teutonic. I anticipated an *Amtssitzglamorblondeschein fraulein* – two metres tall in stilletos, mass of blonde hair, figure like…well never mind, polished legs up to 'ere, a cruel skirt, black leather sharp-waisted jacket, predatory pout and hard, damned hard.

'Mr. Hardy?' Claudia's Issex accent had softened. The shove-off voice I'd heard was for time-wasters – plenty of those in the merchandising business no doubt. I stood up, she took my hand briefly, sat, and I went to the bar to order. From there I could spy out the land. She was wearing a navy trouser suit under a cheap suede three-quarter length winter coat lined with imitation lambs' wool and flat shoes. Her hair was blonde but it was tightly bunned at the back of her head and covered with a navy blue woolly hat – winter in EC3. Her handbag was for keeping things in – lots of things – it confirmed that her elopement with her smart-arsed boss had not worked out. She was ringless, her hands were nice enough but her manicure was practical, def'nal DIY as they might say in Issex.

She opted for a dry white, so I got myself a red wine. I had feared American milky coffee – approved beverage for an Americanised industry. Doesn't even wake you up, just makes you pee. Claudia sipped, 'Nice', she said, 'it's been one of those Mondays'. She smiled briefly, which softened the lines that were starting around her mouth – no make-up hardly any lipstick. I offered to get straight down to business, after all, she had specified not more than half an hour. 'It's all right, no hurry.' Perhaps she was glad to relax, talk and let the rush hour subside before leaving for an evening with telly and cat.

I tried to make it relaxing. She knew about Chris's predicament. An internet "friend" had informed her, "Hi Claud heard your ex is banged up for murder, narrow squeak eh? Ha-ha!" I asked if the police had contacted her and she said 'no'. (*Why bother when they have all the evidence they need?*) I asked if she would like to know what had really happened and how I got involved. I was ready for her to shy away from that, but she said that she would like to hear because it didn't fit the Chris she had known. I told her the tale cutting a lot of corners and ended up by saying that it was hard to believe that he was capable of a crime like that: the cold-blooded planning involved in getting Caroline to the deserted farmhouse and the horrendous way she was killed. 'If they'd had a flaming lovers' row and he'd given her a shove and she'd fallen over and hit her head on something hard…that would be different.'

'I don't believe it,' Claudia said, 'I still wouldn't if it was the "giving her a shove" version.'

'I wanted to see you because you knew the man better than anyone. When you were together, did he ever show signs of violence – towards you or anyone else? Had he a violent temper?'

'No,' said Claudia, 'if Chris had a fault as a partner, it was the exact opposite. Sometimes I used to tell him not to treat me like cut glass. "I won't break", I said. (*Another woman had said that too*). He was that sort of man. He wasn't effeminate, no way, he was just… gentle.' I wondered whether that had been the problem but I knew it would be complicated so I left it.

'What was he like emotionally?'

Claudia looked me straight in the eye, 'intense, very intense, it worried me sometimes. I used to wonder if I was up to it.' Could she think of an example? 'It's difficult to remember anything specific,' she said, 'more of a feeling.'

'The break-up, was it do with the demands of the job? You were going through testing times at work, all sorts of things taking off, opportunities, let-downs, late nights, meetings, hours on the phone, go, go, go. You were coming home shattered. Chris was working long hours as well. His job was tiring because of the concentration needed but not emotionally demanding like yours? Often you came back to an empty flat. Was that how it was?'

'It sounds like a good excuse,' Claudia said, 'that was part of it.'

I'd done enough. We chatted for a few minutes. Claudia said that she'd be happy to help any way she could. 'That's up to the lawyers,' I said, 'I don't think there'd be any question of you appearing as a witness. They might like a statement. Would it be ok if I ask them?'

'Yes,' she finished her drink and stood up, 'You know I mentioned about Chris being intense? One night, just before we got married, he said if I were to have an affair with another man; he'd kill me and then himself. I just laughed.'

'You were dead right,' I said, 'it's the sort of daft thing young men say when they're insecure.' I watched her walk away, no bounce, I hoped she hadn't far to go. I'd come expecting a flash tart with an eye to the main chance and found a sad girl with her life drifting away up a one-way street.

37

The heat at Lagos was wicked; it hit you as soon as you stepped out of the aircraft. It was like being beaten round the head with a hot frying pan. The locals took no notice, they ran about shouting to one another. The taxi was even hotter with bum-burning seats until we got moving which was a slight relief. The air conditioning wasn't doing much but the driver missed out the city centre and the traffic jams in favour of the pretty way through the shanty towns. He let me crack open a window at my own risk. Finally, the hotel was equipped with a system that worked.

That was the pattern for the trip: quick dashes between air-conditioned factories – you can't make polythene film in a temperature of 120 degrees, it blocks itself silly – and hotel swimming pools. The factories at Lagos and Nairobi were working five days a week which meant a fresh start every Monday, tons of scrap and damn-all useful production before midday. The ex-pat supervisors were legless every weekend, the workers were willing but badly trained. The Jo'burg factory worked 24/7, just like ours at Ditchfield, consequently their efficiency was the best of the three but only on paper because the shop floor atmosphere was hostile. I didn't look for the reasons: they were nothing to do with me. My reports to Stefan told it as seen and my overall verdict on all three was "forget it".

Before leaving on the holiday leg to Cape Town, I phoned the Brookheath Christian Brothers at Jo'burg and explained who I was. I was passed on to Brother Endymion, 'by all means call in,' he said in a Paul Robeson bass, 'if you know this town I needn't warn you to take a taxi from the hotel.'

The Brothers were housed in a collection of small offices in part of a disused warehouse in a run down industrial area. Brother Endymion was an impressive figure. He addressed me in the formal style of a man speaking his second language. I wondered whether his origins were Zulu, however his desktop did not feature a knobkerrie, an assegai or other equipment for dealing with sceptical agnostics. Instead, the polished pine surface supported a large leather-bound copy of the Catholic Vulgate and not much else. I was reassured until I reflected that it would take one clout with the heavy volume and from Endymion's point of view, "job's a good 'un". He reinforced the point with a hand-crushing welcome. His face shone, not from the heat as mine did, but from health, hygiene and moral certainty; if anything, his saintly smile added to my apprehension.

'As you've no doubt realised, Mr Hardy, we are a teaching order with several mission schools. We run the administration from here.' He leaned forward and lowered his voice an octave, 'now Mr Hardy, how may I help you?'

His massive mitt curled around the heavy bible ready for action, 'Has...' I quavered, 'has Brother Vincent told you about my interest in Hans Meyer?'

Endymion purred like Shere Khan, 'He has, tell me more Mr Hardy.'

I recounted what little I knew about Hans Meyer up to 1987 when he moved to South Africa. 'Six years later, in 1993 he rejoined St Cuthbert's and was appointed Head of the Science Faculty – a senior management post. Members of staff (*one member of staff*) have told me that he returned a changed man – cold, withdrawn, unfriendly and authoritarian.' Endymion nodded and that was all he said. I pressed on, 'after a promotion, people often feel the need to distance themselves from colleagues but I'm told this amounted to a personality change perhaps caused by something that happened whilst Meyer was out here. Unfortunately he refuses to talk.'

'I take it you're not acting for Meyer himself?'

Endymion would have done all right with the Inquisition. 'No, can you bear to listen while I tell you about the case we *are* defending?' A life devoted to contemplating eternity was proof against impatience; I went on to summarise the circumstances of Caroline's murder. Endymion wanted more, 'you haven't told me what any of this has to do with Hans Meyer.'

'The police have charged Berry but have no motive to pin on him. There are two persons who had motives. One is the wronged husband, the other is Meyer. In spite of his denial, I have been able to show that Meyer conducted a secretive affair with Caroline Enderby for up to two years. I suspect that she was the one who ended it. Her affair with Chris Berry began three months later in March, last year. I think Meyer realised immediately what was going on. Not only had he been ditched but his successor was a junior member of his own staff. We know that he was persistently hostile to Berry from then to the time of the murder. Other members of staff noticed and commented on it. There were professional differences between Berry and his boss, but nothing serous enough to explain Meyer's attitude; it was almost paranoid.'

'You mean like Captain Queeg and his ball bearings?'

I got to the point, 'The defence only have to show that the prosecution case is not beyond reasonable doubt. But the verdict will be delivered by a jury whose thinking is likely to be emotional – give us a beautiful victim, a blood-boltered lover, which is about all the police have and we'll give you a murderer.'

Brother Endymion put his size fifteen hands flat on the desk top, leaned forward and said, 'Earthly justice is like that, Mr Hardy.'

I refused to be comforted, 'I can't sit back and let an injustice happen.'

'You've explained how Hans Meyer might have a motive as the rejected lover. But few Christians resort to murder for that reason; why would he?'

'I think Meyer's change of personality is significant. I've interviewed him; he struck me as embittered, there was something not right in the man's eyes, there was nothing Christian there that I could see. (*How would you know, Hardy?*) If you can cast any light, I think you should tell me.'

'You're correct up to a point,' said Endymion, 'I met Meyer when he came out here and afterwards. At our final meeting I didn't like the look of the man any more than you and that's why I sent him home,' he smiled half apologetically, 'I thought the change might be a cure.'

'Between your meetings with Hans Meyer what happened?'

Endymion sat back, serious faced, 'I need to know what your position is. I can't disclose personal information without good reason. Brother Vincent at HQ says that you are not a lawyer, but you're acting in a paralegal capacity.'

I put my passport and my card down on his desk. 'I realise that isn't proof of my status, but if you phone this number in England, you'll get the legal firm of Harrison and Potts. Ask for Mr Harrison, who is the senior partner and he'll be able to confirm what I've just told you.' It was risky, what if Tom said that I was off the case? But I couldn't think of anything else.

Endymion picked up the phone and began prodding in numbers. After a pause, someone answered. 'Good morning, I am Brother Endymion of the Brookheath Christian Brothers phoning from Johannesburg, could I speak with Mr Harrison?' I prepared for disaster. Endymion's call continued, 'in court all day?' Nasty moment, if they put him on to Niall...? 'That's unfortunate, perhaps ... I see, you are Mr Harrison's legal secretary?' He was speaking to Pam. 'I'd like to ask you something ma'am,' he had switched on his best *Jungle Book* purr. The bugger was charming her pants off... 'Mr Harrison is the defence solicitor in the case of *Crown versus Christopher Berry*. Yes? I have Mr Kenneth Hardy in my office. He tells me that he's a member of the defence team in a paralegal capacity. Can you confirm ... Thank you Mrs Fisher we are most grateful. God bless you.'

Endymion put the phone down, 'I'm sorry to have doubted you Mr Hardy, what would you like to know?'

'Everything you've got time for?'

Brother Endymion made time. Meyer had come out to Johannesburg in 1987 when he was 32. He was sent up north to teach at a mission school near the border with Zimbabwe – a difficult area – where he got excellent reports from the Principal there. Three years later, he married a fellow teacher at the school: Anna Heitings. They were clearly very happy and in '92, Anna announced that she was pregnant. Shortly afterwards Anna got special leave for a couple of days to visit her parents who were farmers about 50 km from the school. While she was there, the farm was raided. Anna and both her parents were murdered. 'I won't burden you with the details,' promised Endymion, 'but it was a nasty business, even for that type of crime. You see, in remote areas like that, not everyone is behind Mandela's Truth and Reconciliation programme. Some want revenge and there is a lot of history,' said Endymion, 'I don't suppose these attacks get much coverage in the West.'

I asked what the outcome had been. 'The murderers were never found, they rarely are,' said Endymion, 'the police had almost nothing to go on and the locals were too frightened to talk.'

'What about Hans Meyer?'

Endymion sighed, 'that's the other part of the tragedy. Meyer took it very hard, as you would expect, but his grief turned to something darker and he became embittered, not just against

275

the murderers but against black people generally. If it had been a simple question of bereavement, I would have fixed him up with an exchange posting to get him away but it wasn't, so I offered him compassionate leave. "Take a year off and go back to England," I said, "then see how you feel". He asked to sleep on it and the following morning, he gave me his resignation. I haven't seen or heard of him since.'

'I was hoping to take a trip to the school where Meyer worked and see for myself.'

Brother Endymion was against the idea. 'You'd be wasting your time. It'll take you two days to get to the place, and the same coming back – one plane, one train and a long, very hot and uncomfortable bus ride. The Principal retired three years ago, the teachers who knew the couple will have moved on. We rarely let teachers remain in place for more than five years – we're like the army. All you'll get there now is rumour; the hard facts are what I've just given you.'

'What about the local police?'

'They may think that you're looking for ways to put the blame on them because the victims were white. They could even turn hostile.'

I thanked him for his advice and took it. Cape Town was different. I sat around in cafes and did some thinking about the information that Brother Endymion had supplied. I wandered on the waterfront, found a few pubs and talked to the locals. I typed up my final report and emailed it to Stefan. That took three days but since Stefan was paying, I might as well take the whole week. I phoned Green at Braxtonby and reminded him who I was.

'I'm in Cape Town; I've been on business here. Have you heard any more from AGROW?' Green said not. I had encouraging news, 'I've spoken to them and things are going forward. They need to contact the owners about the proposed change of use. I believe the chairman of the trust lives on Malta.'

'Mr Jarvis Dawson, he went out there five years ago'.

'It's been suggested that I break my return journey at Valetta *(It hadn't)*. I wouldn't need much of Mr Dawson's time. I'll have to change my flight and hotel arrangements, so I need a quick decision, today if possible.' Green said he would do his best. I promised to phone again at 4 pm Braxtonby time.

38

I checked in at the Valetta hotel, phoned the taxi firm that Jarvis Dawson had suggested and booked a driver for the following morning. Jarvis was white on top, light brown elsewhere and slim for a City lawyer. He invited me into the sitting room. It had big French windows and a view across the Med towards Sicily. The maid brought coffee and I tried to soften Jarvis up a bit by telling him enough of my private business to encourage confidence. It wasn't a total success.

'You're telling me that you're not in fact a private investigator, Mr Hardy? The impression I got from Green was that you are acting for the defence.'

I gave him my best "honest Ken Hardy – straightforward Lancashire businessman" look, 'No. The young man who has been charged with this murder is a friend of mine, and I also met the victim, his girlfriend on two or three occasions. The defence solicitor is my son-in-law. I offered to help out on a temporary basis – free of charge of course. In January, the defence was in a position to appoint a professional investigator, an ex-CID officer.'

'So what prompted this visit?'

'A couple of things, one is that I'd like to get your permission to run an experiment at Fellbeck. The defence case rests on Chris Berry's statement of what happened there. The police don't believe it's feasible; I want to establish whether it is.'

'Not like these televised re-enactments that look like street theatre?'

'No, strictly private and no drama; I need to borrow a key

from Green to get into the house and he'll want to clear that with you.'

Jarvis sat for a moment, 'I can trust you not to set the place on fire?' I agreed – the house and contents guaranteed not to be hurt or inconvenienced. 'I'll phone Green in the morning. I'll be interested to hear how your experiment turns out.'

'Do you know anything about the AGROW group who are interested in Fellbeck?' He didn't, so I went on to tell him. 'They're a mystical focus group and they want to convert the house to use as a Spiritual Education Centre. The value of the property to them depends largely on its history and spiritual associations.' Dawson's eyebrows shot up. 'Apart from two nasty murders, they think that the place has a spiritual presence.'

Dawson grinned and shook his head, 'Sounds eccentric to me,' he said, 'I haven't lived there since 1941. My father had his legal business in the City; we lived on Richmond Hill. In 1940, when I was ten, the blitz started and Daddy packed us all off to Fellbeck for safety. We stayed there until the summer of '41 when Hitler invaded Russia and we thought the blitz was over.'

'Did you like Fellbeck?'

'Hated it – cold, wet, isolated, no one to play with – but haunted? I never lost any sleep! We were glad to get back to Richmond. The War Office took over Fellbeck for the duration.'

I recounted Dick's story about the Italians at Fellbeck. 'They refused to stay at Fellbeck because it was haunted and begged to be allowed to sleep on the farms where they were working.'

Dawson laughed, 'Was that their story? Spent the rest of the war in the hay with the land girls is more like it.' The man was beginning to open up, 'that summer I passed the Common Entrance. I was packed off to Somerset to boarding school, the rest of the family carried on at Richmond. Three years later a German V-1 flying bomb landed on the house – Mummy and the girls were all killed. My father was working at the office when it happened.' After the war, Jarvis had qualified, gone into partnership with his father and eventually taken over the firm and the trust. He had never married – a lonely life doggedly making money.

Suddenly, 'Stay to lunch? If you want a potted history of Fellbeck and the dreadful Dawsons I'll tell you what I can.'

Two large gins, half of a bottle of claret and a couple of brandies later, I asked, 'does the name Benson mean anything?'

Jarvis blinked, 'I don't think so, Ken – explain.' I summarised the Benson document and its bearing on the case. 'Do you know who wrote it?'

'I can't prove it but my money would be on Nathaniel Ostrick – some time after he came back to run the farm at Fellbeck.' I asked if he'd ever met Nathaniel. 'No, we never visited. When he murdered Jenny Finch, three years later, I was just four, remember.' I asked where Benson might have got hold of the document. 'Unless he found it lying around the house, I couldn't say.'

Jarvis got out of his leather armchair, 'this is the nicest part of the day come for a walk round the garden.'

39

The engine note dropped, we were starting the descent into Manchester. The fat chap in front of me took his seat back out of my lap. I put my book down and had a stroke of genius. The more I thought about it the better it seemed.

Caroline was not murdered at Fellbeck, but at South Lea – Meyer's place. When Chris left the house to get help, the body was transferred to Fellbeck and dumped in the sitting room for the police to find. The rubber tyred handcart I'd seen in Meyer's shed was perfect for the job. Darkness, mist, Chris's shocked state and the superficial similarity of the two houses would do the rest. It solved several problems at a stroke – no need for a temporary power supply, no equipment to remove before the police arrived, an easy explanation for the house feeling warm – it wasn't deserted Fellbeck it was Hans Meyer's house next door at South Lea.

Supposing that Josephine had agreed to provide the alibi, her brother could have been the killer behind the door – motive, means, physique, the lot. There was an alternative. Suppose Meyer had made his house available for the murder gang. Meantime he was taking a pasting from his sister at Scrabble and building himself a cast iron alibi.

The following morning I got the car out and headed for Preston. From there, I took the Harrogate road as far as the right turn signed "Coldedge"; clearly marked and unlikely to be missed. The road took me past the small sign on the right for South Lea farm, crossed the bridge over the beck and climbed to the left up to the top of the ridge where, a mile outside Coldedge village, it joined the "old" Braxtonby road. Most importantly, the roads met at a sharp angle. In his statement, Chris had described his shocked state as, "driving like a zombie". With fog on the road, chaos in his mind, he would barely register the minor Braxtonby road cutting in from the left as he plunged on through the dark, desperate to raise the alarm.

Still less, on the return journey, confined in the back of the fast moving police 4x4 he never noticed the change of route as the car carried straight on through the foggy night towards the real Fellbeck instead of bearing slightly left to South Lea.

It all fitted. I was taken by surprise by the reflex left turn back down the hill to Fellbeck. In order to get the Mercedes round I had to back up and take a second shunt. That explained why John Bolton's delivery drivers preferred to drop off at his Preston Road gate. Fancy trying to get an artic loaded with animal feed round that corner!

I crossed the bridge at Fellbeck then up the other side of the valley past Sunnyside and on to Braxtonby. I stopped off outside Helmsley and Jordan's office. I was in luck – Green was in the office and he had checked on who had acted for the last Fellbeck tenant. 'It was Jefferson Whalley at Ditchfield. Of course he's long since retired and passed on.'

'The lease expired in 1980?'

Green said, 'No, it still had years to run. The tenant died.'

I said, 'I've got a meeting with the main man of the AGROW group early next month. I'll be asking him how things are progressing with the Fellbeck project. If you like, I'll let you know what he says.' Green said he certainly would like. No harm, I thought, in keeping a rod in pickle at H & J.

I carried on to join the main Preston to Harrogate Road. The signpost at the junction pointed back to Braxtonby – no mention of Coldedge. I drove back to the flat and checked in with Stefan's office. The great man was away, 'no problem Mr Hardy, I'll let him know you're back. He'll be in touch.'

Everything I'd seen on my morning expedition had been favourable. The email message in Meyer's inbox wasn't specific but clearly a document of considerable interest had changed hands. My money was on the Benson document. Both men had motives for the crime and the Benson story had triggered the plot in the mind of one of them.

I needed to get inside the house at South Lea but I knew that Meyer had bought the place for refurbishment so it could have been simple enough back in November to clear the sitting room to resemble its Fellbeck counterpart. Did Meyer know where the key was kept for the farm gate? He must do.

I was right suited. The question was when to close the trap on Hans Meyer. Not yet, I thought. The more information, the more cut and dried the accusation, the better the chance of shaking an admission out of the suspect. Next job was find out what Briggs had discovered. I picked up the phone.

When I called at the Garibaldi the pub was busy for a midweek evening. The man I wanted to see was propping up the bar. 'How was New Zealand?' I asked.

'Hard work, not like your safari. You've given up the detective business then?' I admitted it. 'Waste of time, sticks out a mile it was lover-boy that did it. Schoolteacher – just shows what they get up to,' added Wilkinson gloomily.

'Can you get me a slaughterman's knife, Pete?' I asked, 'not new, one that's been used, older the better.'

'It'll cost you.' I bought him a pint. 'I bet that's on expences too.' He should know after drinking his way round Auckland.

I showed him a photo of the carving on the fireplace at Fellbeck. 'What do you think that is?'

Pete glanced at the carving on the boss. 'Where's this from?' I told him. 'Not a coat of arms, is it?'

'Bearing in mind where it comes from I wondered whether it might be mystical, superstition of some sort. What do you reckon?'

'Don't know, mind if I show it to Father Riley?'

'Mention it at confession regarding your latest murder then he won't tell anyone.'

That got a hard look from Wilkinson. 'What's got into you Hardy?'

I decided that the very funny joke I'd heard in the public bar of the Duke could wait. It was about the Pope.

40

I picked a bad day. Ex-Detective Chief Inspector Briggs's expression matched his surroundings. His grim appearance was enhanced by a physical aspect ratio approaching unity. He had a big square face and shiny black hair well glued to his skull. His upper lip was obscured by a dense black moustache, trimmed short like fur. He offered a square hand. His handshake was hard, not a bit funny, which perhaps had contributed to his departure from CID.

'Hardy', I said, 'Ken Hardy.'

'Reginald Briggs.' I had never met a live "Reginald" before. When I was a six year-old there were two of them on the wireless: distinguished cinema organists. I had deduced that "Reginald" was not a first name but a title awarded to top organists. Briggs was not a "Reginald". For a start, his fingers, short, stubby and generously nicotined, did not look good for much more than half an octave. He would also have had trouble reaching the pedals.

In a bid to lighten the atmosphere, I asked if he had Benson behind bars. I knew he hadn't because Wilkinson would have said.

'No,' said Briggs, ''ave you?' Evidently he thought that constituted a draw.

'Come in t' office,' he said, 'I'll get t' lass to brew us a coffee.' Coffee in Halifax sounded like a threat. "T' lass", when she arrived was about 28, a slimmer version of her employer but no nymph. Briggs addressed her as "Kath" and introduced me as "Mr Hardy". She gave me a quick grin. I was wrong about the coffee. Organist or not, this Reginald was not to be underestimated.

His office walls were panelled floor to ceiling in darkened mahogany, an unsuitable choice since the exhausted photons of natural light that struggled through the grimy sash window provided no more than a sinister gloom by way of illumination. There was a heavy dark brown desk for Briggs to rest his belly on and a big dark brown table for laying out evidence (*or suspects*). The woolly dark brown carpet could be relied on to conceal bloodstains. I looked round the office walls for the Perspex panels decorated with pictures of victims, preferably gruesome, and photos of suspects annotated with cryptic comments and connected by arrows drawn in thick black chinagraph pencil. But the walls were bare; clearly Briggs had no time for the methods of television crime squad detectives – another reason why his career had stalled.

'Just back from Africa? Like it?'

'Too hot and too dry.' Briggs nodded sadly, I'd done well, he remarked, to stay out of the sun. Outside, through the mucky glass, I saw that the rain was now stair-rodding onto the grey slated roofs of downtown Halifax. Had I been anywhere except the West Riding, I could have felt at home.

Briggsie took a slurp at his coffee and leaned back in his swivel chair, recklessly I thought. He stroked the fur on his upper lip, clasped his hands behind his head, adopted a threatening scowl and said, 'I'm right glad you've taken the trouble to come over, Ken. (*He looked anything but "right glad"*). It's an unusual case and you've given us a *bit* of a start. (*Thanks, Reg!*). We haven't identified the Benson character yet, but I *suspect* that he's the key.'

This was good news, no messing around with original thinking but was the "we" merely royal or did Briggs head up a sizeable squad of sleuths? I moved to clarify the position, 'As you know Reginald, I'm off the job with effect from your appointment. As far as Harrison's concerned the purpose of today's visit is to make sure you've got all the background you need.'

'Right,' he said, 'I intend to go through the whole case to see where we stand. I'll indicate what progress has been made while you've been sitting under a sunshade and you tell me if you've had further thoughts.'

That seemed fair to me. 'Before we get into the detail, how strong is the defence case? Do you accept Chris's statement?'

'On the face of it, it's improbably complicated,' began the master detective, '…then I went through your notes on the police case and I agree that the prosecution doesn't look right clever either. They claim that Berry was acting alone. So how did he manage it? This Caroline strikes me as a capable girl but there's no indication that she tried to resist. Two murder weapons and neither of them found, that's two items of bad news for the prosecution.'

'Three,' I said and reminded him of the missing scarf.

Briggs went on to shred the clouds of optimism, 'Before long, CID will realise that this isn't a walk-over after all. Then they'll be digging like demented badgers and it's possible they'll drop on summat in injury time to swing the jury their way. I want to stop this trial before it starts, once you're in court you can forget about justice – it's a game of chance.'

We were agreed on that. 'You've looked at the SOC?'

'I have. Grisly.' *(In the same league as Briggsie's office?)*

'Enderby's AGROW group reckon there's a supernatural presence. Did any spirits materialise?'

'They did not,' said Briggs, 'else I would have detained them for questioning.'

I asked about ghostly footsteps, 'If you heard anything like that,' I advised, 'remember the roof in that place is shaky. A temperature change or the wind catching the ridge could cause the joints to shift in sequence. A wave running from end to end of the structure could cause just such an illusion.'

I saw that Briggs was impressed, 'Is that the engineering explanation?'

'It's a hypothesis awaiting experimental proof.'

'I'll tell you summat,' said the master detective, 'the building has been standing empty for years, mucky as a Manchester cellar'oyle, various persons including unidentified intruders marching in and out delivering hairs, fibres, fingerprints, second-hand condoms. It would take two years to sort out that lot. You might have hit something with the ash in the grate. Who lit that fire?'

I said, 'do you know if the police have run a reconstruction?' Briggs said that they hadn't, 'as far as they're concerned there's nowt to reconstruct.'

'Is there anything to stop me doing one? I've spoken to the chairman of the owners' trust and he raised no objection.'

'You can check with Tom Harrison. He'd warn the police who would then leak it to the media. You'd have TV cameras, reporters running wild, paparazzi – bear in mind when the police run that sort of stunt they've got resources to control access, we haven't. If we tried it'd be a shambles and all the publicity would be adverse.'

I said, 'This won't be a full scale re-enactment, just tests of a few points with no more than three of us. Why not come along to see fair play? I'll tell Tom after and he can do as he likes. He can't sack me twice.'

'You'll need a front door key.' Briggs opened one of his desk drawers and slapped a mint version of the Fellbeck key down on his blotter. 'No need to bother Green,' he said, 'I called on yon Hindley lad, he'd kept the template. I mentioned the matter of his business records so he offered me an extra copy for nowt. Take it.'

'What about Meyer?'

'He's admitted to an affair, more or less between the dates you suggested. I asked why she'd broken it off. He claimed that *he* had ended the affair. She wasn't committed enough to go through with it so he showed her the door. He's still sore, that was plain.'

'It was a mistake to buy that place as a love nest for Caroline. He was out to rival the Enderby property which was what she wanted to escape from. What else?'

Briggs said, 'I asked him whether he tipped off Martyn Enderby about his wife and Chris Berry, he denied it. I said, 'You knew what was going off between her and Berry didn't you?' I then asked him the nature of the document that he'd given to Enderby? That shook him. He claimed it was a deed defining the boundaries between the Fellbeck and South Lea estates back in the 1880s. He happened on it in the loft at South Lea.'

'What about his alibi for the night of the murder?'

'We won't crack it in a hurry, our Kath's on the job.' said Briggs.

'Isn't it a fact that a too-perfect alibi is grounds for suspicion?'

Briggs waved that aside as Wimseycal and made a decisive proposal. 'Fancy a pint?'

'No. I could force down a couple, though.'

Briggs took me round the corner to the Gamecock, saying that he found it homely. I saw why: the saloon bar was a throw-back to the Rat and Parrot in its glory days. The dark brown beams were set at a height calculated to hit me at eyebrow level and miss Briggs by a margin. The pub was empty save a couple of derelicts on the bench handy to the bar. I realised that they were snouts from Briggsie's stable when he bought them a pint each. We had sandwiches made with Yorkshire brown bread with Yorkshire butter, Yorkshire ham and Yorkshire pickled onions on the side. Privation struck when they were fresh out of Yorkshire mustard. We made do with English.

I asked how he got on with tracing Benson's telephone calls.

'Not right well. It's surprising how many calls that school gets after hours.'

I said encouragingly, 'at least we know that the calls existed because Gloria picked up two of them.'

'Unless Berry faked the lot.'

I went up to the bar to get the pints we came for. The snouts stuck their noses up like expectant whippets; they were unlucky, I was not paying for Briggsie's information. Briggs turned to the life-and-death matter of Rugby League football and the imported Australian stars who were too pansy to play in freezing mud so it was turned into a summer game for family picnics.

Back in the office and fortified with Kath's tea we got round to Martyn Enderby's alibi. Briggs had followed up my enquiries at the Ram's Head. 'You were right about Ratcliffe, the night manager: he had a nice business going.'

'Past tense?'

Briggs grinned an evil grin, 'Past tense. I also got a list of his regulars.'

'He keeps records?' I found that hard to credit.

'Does he heck? Skipton's a small place. He was at school with half of them. Any road, I put mysen round and finally struck lucky. One lad admitted that he'd paid a late call on the evening in question.'

'Social call was it, not commercial?'

'That's what Billy Nuttall claimed (*under torture?*). I agreed to believe him. Anyway, at around midnight, he finished his business with Ratcliffe and came out of the door beneath the fire escape steps. He spotted the lights of a vehicle coming up the lane and about to enter the visitors' car park. Being of a nervous disposition (*and not because of what he'd got up his jumper*), Billy ducked back down the basement steps out of sight. The vehicle parked up and its headlights flashed, off, on, off, like a signal to someone inside. The driver got out, closed the door without slamming it and walked quietly to the fire escape. Billy watched as he climbed the steps to the first floor landing. The man pulled the fire door open and stepped inside; the door then closed and barred behind him. He was lit up for a couple of seconds by the light in the hotel corridor so Billy got a quick look at him. He described him as...' Briggs consulted his notebook, 'posh looking, fairly tall and thin and smiling "to his self like he was up to summat."'

'He must have been posh for Billy to classify him on a fleeting look.'

'I don't know about that,' said Briggsie, 'it's the first thing they notice – smell money a mile off. Also Billy says the car was a black 4x4.'

'So we might have Martyn Enderby coming back to the Ram's Head at midnight, creeping up the fire escape to be greeted by Amelia Partington who had been waiting by the window in his room. Thanks to Norah Ratcliffe, we know what happened after that. Do we know what time he went out?'

'No. The last sighting I got from any of the staff was 6.30pm. Enderby was in the residents' lounge talking to a chap with a grey ponytail and a foreign accent and a smart woman of about forty in a business suit.'

'The woman sounds like Amelia Partington, secretary of AGROW and the man is Dr Pascal Threnadie de Morzine,' I said, 'he gave one of the lectures at the AGM.' I told Briggs about my chat with Pascal, with observations on his sex life.

'Nowt in that,' Briggs said, 'it's what intellectuals do instead of work. Still, if he's a sex-rat and cruel to Miss Smithson, there might be opportunities. Next time I'm up t' smoke I'll get round to him. On t' road back I'll fit in a word with yon Partington. *(Should I warn him?)* But top priority in my book is Enderby. Got the full set, hasn't he – motive, means and opportunity?'

'Have you spoken to him?'

'I paid a brief call and asked routine questions about his

movements on the evening of the murder. He pretended to tell me the truth and I pretended to believe him.'

'You didn't confront him with the evidence?

'No point in showing our hand at this stage.'

I said, 'Having met Enderby do you rate him capable of this?'

Briggs opened his safe, took out a large brown envelope and invited me to take a butcher's. Inside were half a dozen large glossy photos of Caroline's corpse at the Scene of Crime. I spread them out on the desktop then sat and stared. After perhaps two minutes, Briggs said, 'Seen enough?' I nodded. He put the prints back in their envelope. I went to his toilet and washed my face.

'Now then,' said Briggs when I returned.

'I needed to see those,' I told him, 'I was beginning to think that Chris was being a bit of a wimp. Reading a pathologist's report is one thing, but seeing what they did is another. And they are just photographs. He came on Caroline's body in a strange, dark place with nothing but the light of a dying fire. How do you set about forgetting something like that?'

Briggs made no comment. 'Question: is that Enderby's style?'

'I don't know. I've heard it said that anyone is capable of murder; but that? I've never met him, but after hearing Enderby lecture on his love and peace agenda. I can't see it. Could it be murder by proxy – suppose he paid to have her killed?'

Reginald disposed of that idea, 'Never is that a contract killing. This here,' poking a stubby finger, 'is the work of a man in a frenzy; it's personal.'

We were getting no further on with this conversation and I had a point to clear up. 'What about Sam Waters? He's a write-off as Benson for four reasons…'

'What's the fourth?'

'Breath.'

Briggs grinned, 'Knocks you flat doesn't it? I checked with Chris Berry, he says Benson was not halitosic when they met at Fellbeck. So why are we interested?'

'He's the only one in the AGROW inner circle that could do the technical bit – set up the generator, sound effects and so on.'

'He's got an alibi,' said Briggs, 'he was at a meeting of the Harrogate branch of the Classic Sports Car Club at 7.30 the evening of the murder – I checked with the secretary. What's more, Sam was the star. He gave a talk about upper cylinder wear on pre-war Jaguars. The secretary said 20 members attended (*seated well back from the podium?*).'

Back in civilisation, I ran into Tom. 'How did it go with Reggie Briggs?'

'I've filled one or two gaps for him. He's away like a big hairy hound, I've handed him a winning position.'

41

How had the murder gang created the aircraft noise? That was what bothered me about my reconstruction in spite of my confident noises to Tom back in December. I'd been able to show that AGROW had hired an amplifier and loudspeakers for Wi Cho-Cho Chang and kept the kit overnight.

I phoned Amelia Partington. 'Ken! *Good morning*! Long time no hear!' At least one AGROW executive knew how to greet a potential donor. I explained that I had been researching in Africa. With a single bound, she reached the wrong conclusion, 'Ken! Fascinating! You must write us a report for the website.' I said that she could rely on that. *Agricultural Film Manufacture in sub-Saharan Africa,* I thought. How spiritual is that?

'Amelia, the AGM at the Ram's Head; you had a musician booked, but he had to cry off.'

Partington knew who I was after – 'Wi Cho-Cho Chang'.

'I'm helping to organise an event,' I said, lying effortlessly, 'a small affair for a group of like-minded people…' I had some job on to avoid giving Amelia their names and addresses there and then as potential AGROW recruits, 'possibly, but these people are interested in the evolution of European music. I think he could provide illustrations for an upcoming seminar… that is if he's fit. I could mention AGROW to them after.'

She found the number, 'you'll probably get his wife, Audrey Bryant – she handles bookings for him.'

I phoned the Bryant number, which was in the Hull telephone district. I explained my mission, no detail apart from the proposed location – Halifax. I imagined Briggs enthusing over atonal chant as an aid to interrogation. Mrs Bryant wondered where I had heard of Wi Cho-Cho Chang. 'I'm a member of a society called AGROW,' (*my first reliable statement of the morning*). 'Mr Bryant was engaged by them for their Annual Gathering at Skipton last November but unfortunately he had to withdraw.'

'Yes, that was unfortunate, it's never happened before. Two days before, he started a sore throat and the next day he'd lost his voice completely.' I asked whether Chang normally went with his own audio kit to the venue, which Mme Chang confirmed, then said that AGROW had preferred to supply their own. They were planning to carry on afterwards. (*Spiritual karaoke?*) She then moved seamlessly to demand a deposit. I explained the tentative nature of my enquiry and left Reginald's address so she could send a leaflet.

I walked along the High Street to consult young – well, middle aged – Mr Geraint Wragby, son of the late Lance. I told him I wanted to create a deafening noise like a low flying jet aircraft inside a small space, (*think broom cupboards*), without a mains power supply. 'Battery operated CD player,' he advised. I asked if it was available ex-stock?

'I can get you one in about three days for £42 plus VAT remote control included.' I asked if he knew where to obtain a CD to produce the desired sound. It was Geraint's day for knowing everything, Lance would have been proud. He gave me the phone number of a Manchester company specialising in theatrical sound effects.

I now had two possibilities. The kit hired by AGROW for Wi Cho-Cho Chang would be more powerful, but might be too much for the dodgy wiring, besides being cumbersome to transport and install, and, more importantly, for effecting a quick getaway. From that point of view, I preferred Geraint Wragby's battery operated player but would it produce enough noise? Suck it and see.

42

'Hello Mr Hardy,' said Gloria, 'how was Africa?' I sat on the nearest Prep Room stool, 'Hot and dry; how was Ditchfield?'

'Dry and freezing. It's been the driest February for 50 years. Anything exciting happen? Lions wandering about, crocodiles?' I said no lions, they were all living it up in Kruger National Park and I was in the wrong place for crocs. 'I wouldn't know,' Gloria lamented, 'never been to Africa have I?' She dropped her voice a couple of decibels, 'did anything turn up about...?'

She had caught me out there, 'I never mentioned that. Did I?'

'No,' Gloria said, 'not directly.'

'On the understanding that it stays between us two, something did happen and it might explain why he was a changed man when he came back. He got married. She was expecting a baby and then she died in distressing circumstances. He tried to carry on, it didn't work so he came back.'

Gloria said nothing for several seconds, then, 'I shouldn't have asked.'

'If he'd been more open, wouldn't people would have understood?'

Gloria seemed to agree, 'His choice, so it'll stay that way.' The Prep Room phone rang and she picked it up. There was a bit of telephone gabble from the other end, then 'no, you've got the wrong department, Mr Henderson's in Maths. You won't get him now, try in the morning.'

'Anxious parent?'

'Internal,' said Gloria, 'PE department, they think Henderson's gone home with the wrong pair of trainers.'

'You can phone round the school on the inside line after hours?'

'Internal calls work that way all the time,' said Gloria, 'External calls are different. During the day they come in through the switchboard. When the switchboard goes on night service external callers dial a number according to the department they want.'

'What went wrong just then?'

'PE dialled 03, which is Science, instead of 04 for Maths.'

So was Benson a member of staff, or someone with access to the internal phones after hours? It explained why Briggs couldn't trace the calls.

I reached reception on my way out. There was a large notice board on the adjacent wall which you could miss unless you went right up to the desk. It was headed "Evening Courses" and it listed the courses on offer at the school with times and locations – garden shrubs, finger painting, astronomy. All about embedding the school in the Local Community and raising a bit of extra cash. Classes ran from seven until nine in the evening, except one: *Tai Chi – Thursdays at five o'clock, Music Room, with Virginia Potts (Mrs)*. It was almost five but Betty was still in plump possession of the reception desk. 'It's about the facilities for extramural courses,' I said.

'Assistant Bursar you want for that, love. See if she's in?' "Love" agreed.

Mrs Welford emerged, misunderstood in a flash and handed me a photostat list of the courses currently available.

'I don't want to attend a course, I want to *run* one.' Mrs Welford did not seem pleased with the prospect of my valuable custom, but she undertook to answer my questions.

I explained that I was a member of an academic society – AGROW – no doubt she had heard of them, fortunately she hadn't. We were thinking of offering an evening course in *Modern Shamanism* for up to twenty students, I said. Mrs

297

Welford did not seem bothered about the course content, she was a practical lady. 'Would it be a series of lectures?' she asked, 'what sort of facility have you in mind.'

'More in the nature of a workshop,' I said, 'there will be practical activities involved. My colleague attended the Tai Chi course last year in the music room. She thinks that would be ideal. Mrs Welford marched me to the music room and unlocked the door. It was an open space, with chairs stacked along one wall and a piano. 'You can't use the piano, it's kept locked' Mrs Welford said, demonstrating severely, 'and any electrical equipment you intend to use must be submitted in advance to Site Management for safety testing and approval.' Did that apply to a battery-operated CD player? It did not. There was a door at the back of the room. 'What's through here?' I asked and had the door open before Mrs Welford could intervene. It was the teacher's room with a desk; on the desk: a telephone.

'I'll give you an application form,' the Assistant Bursar threatened, 'fill it in and submit it to me.' I had everything I needed.

I drove back to the flat and phoned Halifax. I got Kath. 'He's out on another job,' she said, 'he's planning to visit next Friday morning to see Mr Harrison. I'll ask him to give you a knock when they'd finished.'

43

If Chris was feeling any more positive it wasn't obvious. He sat as before, hands flat on the top of the table. 'While I've been away,' I began, 'you've had a chat with Reggie Briggs?' Chris nodded. I tried to sound encouraging, 'good man to have in your corner.'

Chris wasn't convinced, 'Think so?'

'Bloody sure so,' I said. 'I don't know if anyone's told you but Briggs is an ex-DCI. He ran CID at Halifax before he went independent.'

'Why didn't he stay in the police?'

'He saw a business opportunity. Since he put his brass plate up, defence lawyers have been fighting to get through his doorhole. We got him on your case because McFadzean gave him his first big break as a Private Investigator, so she gets preference.'

'So it's old pals?'

I wasn't standing for that, 'Briggs is a professional, Chris, he knows police procedure inside out and he knows their weaknesses.'

'Hasn't got far with tracing Benson's phone calls, has he?'

'I know it's asking a lot for you to remember actual dates, but can you remember what days of the week they were on?'

Chris looked past me, 'Briggs asked... I've tried... it won't come.'

'That's all right, it was a long shot. I'll tell you what I found in Africa.'

I climbed the stairs to my flat and phoned Briggsie, 'I've just been to visit Chris Berry. When you saw him what did you make of his mental state?'

'Negative, on the verge of depression I'd say.' Was he told that Berry was on suicide watch from December to the end of January? 'No,' said Reginald, 'I should have been.'

'I think he's on a downer again. I've told Tom and suggested he get your opinion.' I went on, 'I've made a bit of progress on the Benson phone calls. I asked Gloria Davis if she could recognise any pattern in the calls – she's not going to remember any actual dates now. Gloria thinks that the two calls she picked up when Berry was out were on Thursdays – only a feeling, mind.'

'Well I've got news for both on you,' said Briggs, 'we've a definite trace on the November call. It was from the public telephone box in Coldedge High Street, at 5.20pm and was terminated at 5.23 on Tuesday 9th November, *Tuesday,*' he added to rub it in.'

I decided to be brave, 'So on 9th November, Benson asked Chris to meet him at Fellbeck in two weeks time. Written instructions for finding the place would be in the post. That's the vital call, isn't it?'

Briggsie was not turning back somersaults. 'It doesn't get us any further forrard. There was a call to the school. We can't prove it was from Benson, only that there was a call around that date and time. We haven't got Benson's note with directions for Fellbeck. Chris says he read it and binned it.'

Reginald was right of course. I said, 'I've got one or two things to discuss. Kath says you're coming over to see Tom.'

'I can spare a few minutes, say 10.30 in your office?'

My arrival on his doorstep was a surprise to Sam Waters, 'Sorry to just drop in Sam. I tried to catch you at college.' Sam was not upset, he invited me in. I steered clear of the aromatic armchair and took a hard wooden seat instead 'better for my sciatica.' I felt safer there – cats go for comfort.

'To wot do I owe…?' Sam enquired.

'Is it right you've had a visit from Reggie Briggs?'

Sam hadn't enjoyed the experience, 'Visit, you call it? More like interrogation, where were you on the night of…?'

'Take no notice, Sam' I advised, 'you have to make allowances for Reg, he's ex-Halifax CID. Twenty years of feeling collars takes you that way.'

Sam arranged a shaky grin, 'Well I don't know…'

I did not want any of this getting back to AGROW, 'Sam,' I implored, 'forget it. You told him where you were that evening and named what, twenty witnesses? End of subject, now, that wasn't why I came.'

Sam was still wary, 'Go on.'

'Can you let me have another look at your workshop set-up?' Sam's guard came down with a clatter, 'yeah, what is it you want to know?' He took the key from its hook whilst I took Sam into my confidence. 'In September the sale of my old company will be complete and from then on my time's my own. I'll need something to keep me busy. I'm thinking of a set-up like yours.'

We went out by the back door, Sam opened the garage. I was able to show proper reverence to his shrouded SS Jaguar, 'that's what I call built'.

Its owner gave me his toad-like grin, 'Ennit just', he said whipping off the veil. It was like Cleopatra emerging from her eight yards of Axminster. '1938, 102 horsepower.'

The Jaguar was parked over the open maintenance pit. 'I take it she's off the road for the winter?'

'S'right,' Sam said, 'it's when I get the maintenance done.' I asked whether it concerned upper cylinder wear this year. 'No, nothing major – new pins and bushes for the universal – waiting for them back from hardening.'

'Must get a bit parky in here,' I said. Sam said he'd a paraffin heater. I looked around for the usual sort of outside lavatory heater – hardly adequate for Fellbeck, I thought.

'No,' said Sam, 'it's an industrial hot air blower, warms this place up in a tick.' Nothing else would do but to demonstrate. He was right, once ignited the brute built up a steady roar and the warm air came blasting out. It was portable. It would fit into his van.

I went on to inspect Sam's workshop, getting enthusiastic about his array of tools – all neat and tidy. 'What I have in mind,' I told Sam, 'is a 1928 12/50 Alvis I've got my eye on – complete restoration.'

Sam was anxious about the welfare of the vintage treasure. 'Sounds great!' he said, 'are you, like, well… qualified?'

'I was in management for a good few years', I admitted, 'I'll have some skills to brush up.'

Sam was all solicitude, 'if you need any help Ken, don't hesitate.' We went back to the house and spoke about the delights of the vintage motorcar. When I judged that Sam's defences were sufficiently lulled I began to make parting noises. With Sam's hand on his front door knob I said, 'Sam, you know the survey that you and the other AGROW members did at the Fellbeck place? Was anyone else there apart from the committee members – I mean did they have a surveyor?'

Sam was pleased to shoot that down, 'Why would they need a surveyor with my degree in building construction? Nothing a surveyor could tell them that I couldn't – for free.'

'And the survey was spiritual as well as structural?'

Sam nodded, 'S'right,' he said, 'another reason for keeping it in-house.'

I persisted, 'was anyone from outside involved on the spiritual side?'

Sam was beginning to look wary again. I tried to reassure him, 'Look, I'll tell you in confidence, Sam.' The wary look faded, it struck me that Sam's devotion to Martyn Enderby was green-edged. Sam was aware of his own gopher-class status, excluded from the Enderby magic circle. Now and then it bugged. I charged on, 'Martyn needs to raise half a million for the Fellbeck project and it isn't as easy as he'd hoped – even with his top level contacts.'

Sam was on the inside track for once – what had that done for his confidence? 'Yeah, I guessed that much. The rich don't get that way by chucking it about, do they?'

'In strict confidence here, (nod, nod), this is my position: I can cover Enderby for twenty five percent, no problem, but the project has to be right.'

Sam greeted that news with a bad-tooth whistle; in the confined space of his entrance hall, I wished he hadn't. 'He'll bite your hand off.'

I swallowed and went on, 'Last month I called in on the other member of the steering group, Pascal Threnadie de Morzine. What's your take on Pascal?'

'Pain in the arse,' said Sam bravely, 'but he's needed because he's big in the academic world.'

'Maybe, but he worries me. His ideas on the project don't line up. See, I'm ready to come on board for Martyn's Spirituality Centre but not the de Morzine plan for a Residential College of Shamanism with Pascal as Principal. It's a licence to lose money.' It sounded that way to Sam as well, he nodded. I continued, (*if you're telling the tale make it big*), 'A month ago, I was all ready to start writing cheques but now… I mean no one is going to invest in a project with split objectives. Would you?' Sam was clear that he wouldn't.

'Sam, when the steering group went to survey Fellbeck was there anyone else present besides you, Enderby and Pascal de Morzine?'

'Yeah,' said Sam, 'in a sort of advisory capacity, there was. She's a medium, a sensitive she calls herself. Officially, she's not a member but she's a big mate of Martyn's. She was definite on there being a spirit presence in the place. She gave Martyn the idea for his overnight vigil.'

'I might know this person,' I told Sam, 'was it Virginia Potts?' It was. 'Was she the only outsider?'

'Yes,' Sam said, 'her car wasn't available for some reason, so I picked her up on my way over.'

'How did she seem at Fellbeck?'

'A bit over-excited, if you ask me. At the end she asked to be left alone in one of the rooms for twenty minutes. She came out white as a sheet and said she was convinced. I thought she was going to faint.'

'Then?'

'That was it. Martyn asked me to take Pascal to Preston – right out of my way. He had bugger-all to say for himself. Like he thought Virginia had stolen his thunder and he wasn't best pleased. She stayed behind with Enderby.' (*Talk about leaving a rabbit in charge of a lettuce*).

'Sam,' I said, 'you've saved the ship, mate. Not a word about this, but if that Virginia reckons there's a spirit presence at Fellbeck, it's good enough for my money.' (*And if "that Virginia" is behind the Fellbeck project, I was right not to trust her or Niall*). I left Sam alone with his glory.

44

Wilkinson phoned me from his office at closing time. I hardly recognised him. 'Is that you, Peter? What's to do? Are you all right?' He sounded as if he was stricken by something virulent. He was.

'Ken, that photo, I showed it to Father Riley. I thought he was going to excommunicate me.'

I said, 'What are you on about? It's just a photograph of a carving.'

'That's what you think. I gave it to Father Riley and said a friend of mine had taken it and did Father know what it was about?' He took one look and shot off with it. I followed him to the church office, he got me inside, shut the door and locked it behind him. He took another quick look then ripped the photo up, threw the bits on the back of the fire, crossed himself and stood watching it burn. He never said a word but I could see his lips moving.

Then he started on me. Who had taken this and why? Where? How had I got hold of it? I said it was just a picture of a carving in an old house. Riley said that it was about evil and just touching it and having it in my possession could put my immortal soul at risk unless I got urgent help.'

'What did that involve?'

'Six Hail Marys for a start. A whole lot more to follow that I didn't understand because it was Latin. I've been shaky on and off all day.'

'Did you ask him why he was upset?'

'I did,' Pete said, 'but he wouldn't discuss it, just said to dismiss it from my thoughts, pray for forgiveness, keep on with the Hail Marys and see him again in seven days. Had I got any more copies or shown them to anyone else? '

'Did you tell him that you didn't take the picture and you weren't there when I took it?'

'Eventually, when I got the chance. Then he calmed down a bit and made me swear never to go near the place. I said I only had the one print. He said to tell you and advise you to seek guidance.'

'Pete,' I said 'if I'd realised it was going to cause all this bother with the church I would never have shown it to you. He must realise it's not your fault.'

Wilkinson was magnanimous. 'It's all right,' he said, 'I've done as he told me. It's on your conscience now. It'd be best though, for a bit anyway...'

'I know, I'll keep out of the Gari until this business is done with.'

I phoned the Deedes organisation, they had information for me. The sisters faced me across their kitchen table which was well littered with papers. They had been working on the leads I left with them.

'Florence Roper first,' Emmeline began, 'nothing. Either Roper was not her real surname or she was born outside London.'

'What about Enderby?'

'Straightforward enough,' said Emmeline, 'his grandfather was Heathcote Enderby, a fashionable painter who made a fortune from his society portraits. When Heathcote's first wife died leaving him without issue he married a local farmer's daughter much younger than himself. Edith promptly presented him with a son: Nathan Enderby, born in 1936.'

'Odd choice of name.'

Emmeline carried on, 'So young Nathan grew up to inherit. At Oxford, he took up with a brilliant English Lit student of advanced views and slipshod habits. Probably Nathan's father realised what was afoot and issued an ultimatum. The young couple were married in time for Martyn's arrival.'

Ethel was there with the bad news, 'When Martyn was eleven his father went out and shot himself in the barn at Heywood – profound depression brought on by his drug habit. Martyn was boarding at prep school at the time.'

'And we don't know what effect his father's death had on the boy.'

I got out a copy of the photograph which had nearly got Wilkinson excommunicated. 'What do you make of that?'

'Did you take it?'

'Yes. It's a carved boss on the fireplace at Fellbeck. I told her about the lively reception it got from Fr. Riley.

'I'm not surprised,' said Ethel, 'the symbol in the centre of the boss is a lily flower. The images round the outer circle are *fleurs de lys*, and the Roman numerals in between, are D C L X V I or 666.'

'Why would that upset Riley?'

'666 is the number of the beast – Satan's trademark. Fr Riley suspected your friend of cavorting with Satanists at moonlit covens and murdering babies at the crossroads – not acceptable fun for good Catholics.'

'So Caroline's body was found lying in front of a fireplace carved with Satan's stigma. What should I deduce from that?'

'You're the detective, Kenneth. Unless the carving's new it must go back a hundred years to Ezra. It's probably not significant.'

45

Jason was mystified, 'Why have we come through Preston?'

'Wait and see. Take the turn at the sign for the Preston to Coldedge road.' I got Jason to pull up at the foot of the hill just short of the South Bridge. We got out and walked to the bridge for a look. 'Now, on our right, the track to Meyer's farm at South Lea is similar to the one at Fellbeck except it's in better condition.'

Jason said, 'Just now, we turned right off the Preston to Harrogate road. The best way to Fellbeck from Preston is to take the next right turn, signed for Braxtonby. You don't get a Coldedge sign on that road until Braxtonby.'

'I know. Supposing with a bit of camouflage South Lea could pass for Fellbeck in the dark. From the front, the two houses are very much alike. Chris had never been to either place. All the gang had to do was to word the directions so he took the wrong road, and set up a dummy Fellbeck sign here. I think Caroline Enderby could have been murdered at South Lea. While Chris Berry went to get the police all they had to do was transfer the body to Fellbeck and clear off. Think on, when the cops took Chris Berry to Fellbeck, he was in a state of shock crammed in the back of the police vehicle. It was pitch dark and foggy. He wouldn't have had a clue where he was going.'

I gave Jason his orders, 'I want to time the journey on foot from South Lea to Fellbeck and back here. We need to know how long it would take to transport Caroline's body from South Lea to Fellbeck on a handcart, then bring it back here, empty. Don't run but don't loiter around composing sonnets and picking daisies.'

While he did that, I leaned over the stone parapet watching the water flow under the bridge. There was hardly enough current for a decent game of Pooh sticks. "Driest winter for 50 years", Gloria had said. That explained why the water level had dropped to no more than eighteen inches. 'You can see the bottom,' I said, 'no proper rain for weeks.'

Jason joined me. He was quiet for a moment, which made a change, then suddenly, 'Don't move Ken, stay where you are.' Then he was down on the bank tearing off his shoes and socks and rolling up his trousers. I pointed out that the water would be freezing. Jason started to wade into midstream. It made him gasp a bit but he stuck it. He stood below me almost to his knees in water, 'Can't you see?'

There was something shiny on the bed of the stream. Jason asked if there would be fingerprints. 'That depends, try to pick it up by one end.' He did that and held it up so I could see. It was a knife, a big one with a wooden handle. *The* knife? Dropped there by the murderer?

'Jason, I think you've found the knife the police were hunting for. Wrap it up in your hanky and come back here. Careful, those stones on the bottom look slippery.' Too late, he put one foot into a hole and fell flat on his face with an impressive splash. He righted himself, still hanging on to the prize and I helped him back on the bank. I picked up his shoes and socks. 'Right Jason, car – passenger's side – quick-sharp and we'll get you up to Sunnyside. Let's see what Alison can do in the way of first aid.'

He was lucky; Alison was in one of the barns, doing something with pigs. In no time she had his wet trousers off.

'Now,' I said to Alison, 'can you keep him warm for an hour? I've got an appointment at South Lea. After that I'll come and take him home. He's had a bit of a shock, keep him quiet and no excitement, just hot tea.'

I put the knife in a clean polythene bag and drove back

to South Bridge, then along the farm track to the house. The forecourt was still empty. I turned the car round, parked up and switched off.

Ten minutes later, Meyer drove up and parked alongside then turned and gave me a hard stare. I got out feeling a bit shaky around the knees. I was face-to-face in an isolated spot and he was a big lad twenty years younger, two stones heavier and armed with a short fuse.

'Do you mind if I come in for a moment, Mr Meyer? I'd like a word.'

He came a few paces towards me and stopped, 'What about?'

'Reginald Briggs asked me to check a couple of points with you. Also, we may have found the murder weapon.'

Meyer turned a pair of hot brown eyes on mine, 'What's it to do with me?'

'It was in the beck a couple of yards this side of the bridge and less than halfway from the bank on your side. I had a colleague with me and we spotted it from the bridge. It was only visible because the water's so low.'

Meyer turned away, walked to his front door and unlocked it. 'You'd better come in.'

I followed Meyer into the house and along the hall passage. I was looking for resemblances to Fellbeck, although because Meyer was refurbishing there could have been all kinds of changes since November. The staircase was to the right of the entrance – first box ticked. The second was a negative: there was no sign of a door into a closet like the one where Chris had sat at Benson's computer. Further down the passage was a pair of solid oak doors facing one another. The main passage was shorter but there was a door facing from the far end which corresponded to the scullery door at Fellbeck. Meyer opened the first door on the left. If my theory was correct this was the room where Caroline really had been murdered. It looked the same size: two windows on the front of the house looking out on the courtyard and three facing the beck. There was a stone fireplace, devoid of demonic carvings and smaller than its rival at Fellbeck. That explained the small brass fender. The gang had planted it at Fellbeck complete with Berry's prints in blood.

Meyer had a desk facing down the room and behind that, in the corner was a door leading to the next room – again, like Fellbeck.

Meyer dumped his briefcase on the desk. 'We can talk here.' He gestured an invitation to a nearby chair and sat at the desk. 'Now, this so-called murder weapon...'

'I haven't got it with me,' I said, 'it's on its way to forensic.' *(Lying bugger, Hardy, it's in a polybag in your glove pocket).* It's a plain blade, quite heavy, about ten inches long with a wooden handle. I noticed clear signs of recent sharpening.'

He looked hard at me, 'According to the press reports, the murder weapon was a slaughterman's knife. Your description sounds like a large kitchen knife,'

'I wouldn't rely on the press. In this case their information was second-hand. The police pathologist didn't rule out other types of knife.'

'Why didn't the police find it?'

'I'll ask them. Perhaps they only searched upstream from the house to the Braxtonby road bridge because they assumed that was the murderer's escape route.'

Meyer was dismissive. 'This knife has nothing to do with the murder. Most likely it was there for a completely unconnected reason.'

I got up, 'Mind if we look at something else?' I took him back into the passage and up to the entrance. 'When you bought this house, was there a closet set into the wall here?'

'No', said Meyer, 'and I don't think there ever was one.' I followed him back down the passage but this time he turned right into a space a similar size to his sitting room *cum* study.

It was empty, Meyer pointed to the right hand corner. 'You can see where the staircase is. There might have been a closet there once but that wall's solid.' He demonstrated with his large fist. 'I haven't got to this room yet, I have some alterations in mind, at the moment it's exactly as Lewis left it – seen enough?' I had.

As we crossed the passage on the way back to the sitting room I glanced to my left. The wall above the front door was solid – no fanlight as at Fellbeck. Instead, daylight came into the hall from a vertical window immediately to the left of the door – narrow, like an arrow slit. Another blow – my alternative scene of crime theory was looking shaky.

Back in Meyer's sitting room, there was another matter I wanted to clear up: the document that Meyer sent to Martyn Enderby. It was on the tip of my tongue to ask how he had known of Enderby's interest in Fellbeck, when I felt an interesting vibration in my groin area – the mobile in my trouser pocket. I fished it out, apologised and took the call. It was Alison Bolton, 'No rush picking Jason up, Mr Hardy,' I betted there wasn't, 'his clothes are taking a while to dry out and he's staying for supper with us.'

I agreed, 'It wouldn't do to take him home wet, what would his mother say?' Alison indicated that Mrs Goode was not the only female likely to have views on that subject. We closed the call.

That put the tin hat on it. My theory depended on there being no mobile signal at the murder scene. Therefore the scene of crime could not have been South Lea; I was back with Fellbeck.

Meyer intervened, 'I think you should tell me what this has all been about.' Jason was not going to complain at the delay while he took supper off Farmer Bolton and advanced his cause with the fair Alison. I sat down and told him.

'When I came to see you in December you didn't feel able to be open with me on some points. Especially the nature of your past relationship with Caroline Enderby and the alibi which you said you had given to the police but refused to disclose to me. That caused the defence to involve Mr Briggs.'

Meyer conceded, 'I didn't know who I was dealing with at that time, so the best policy was to say as little as possible.'

'What I can tell you is that he's been able to resolve both matters.'

I made "get up and go" movements and caught sight of a chess set laid out on a side table. He noticed my interest, 'do you play?'

'I'm years out of practice.'

Meyer walked me to his front door, 'By the way,' I said, 'in case you're wondering about your non-existent broom cupboard...'

'It did seem a bit odd, the way you were looking around.'

'When relations were at a low level,' I told him, 'the question was raised of whether certain events took place here, rather than at Fellbeck...' He was looking at me in total disbelief. 'DCI Briggs has been able to settle that: Caroline was murdered at Fellbeck and you were not involved. You won't be needed as a defence witness.'

I handed him my card, 'why not ring me sometime? Drop in after school one evening and I'll try to give you a game – rustle up a bit of supper afterwards.' (*Two lonely old codgers*)

This has turned out more pleasantly than I expected, Ken,' he said. I agreed.

I got back into the car and tested my mobile – a perfectly good signal. I drove round to Sunnyside. Regardless of what I'd just told him, Hans wasn't entirely out of the woods; that depended on his alibi. Meantime I was not going to press him about his relations with Enderby. Martyn was the bigger fish and I didn't want him warned off.

Jason had finished filling his face when I arrived and his clothes were pronounced wearable. While he dressed, I had a word with John Bolton. 'Do you remember the last tenant at Fellbeck? He gave up there twenty years back.'

'He didn't have much option,' said John, 'he killed himself.' (*Not another murder at Fellbeck?*). I asked if he meant suicide. 'What it amounted to, but it wasn't on a purpose. Silly devil tried to drive his tractor across the slope in the home field, picked the steepest part up near the Braxtonby road. Tractor tipped over and broke his neck. That caused a right to-do. Post-mortem and that, and he'd left no will, lawyer was in and out for weeks, furniture, sheep and farm equipment had to be sold to pay the debts.'

I asked who the solicitor was, John couldn't recall the name. 'It wasn't a man from Ditchfield was it – Whalley?'

'That was him, fancy name – Jefferson Whalley – definite.' I went one further and asked if he remembered the name of the tenant. Bolton put on a scowl suggestive of fierce concentration, 'I remember his face,' he said.

Jason reappeared, fully dressed and the young couple started on what threatened to be a lengthy farewell. I was having none of that and got Jason in the driving seat sharp. He was showing off his three-point turn in front of the farmhouse when John Bolton appeared. 'Andrew was his name,' he said, 'Andrew Masham. He made a right good job of mashing himself and all – accidental death.'

Jason was none the worse for his heroics at the beck. 'What are you doing the evening of Friday 17th March?' Jason said nothing important. 'Good, because I'm planning an experiment at Fellbeck and I need an assistant. I want to establish whether Chris Berry's statement is feasible. Are you on?' He was.

'Now this is important to the defence case so I don't want dissension breaking out in the ranks. You know that I'm officially off the case and everything's been handed over to Reginald Briggs. The defence team will get the results when I'm ready and not before. We'll be working outside office hours and I don't want any mention made to Mr Potts either because he would be obliged to pass it on to Mr Harrison. Briggs knows about it and I hope he'll be able to act as witness. I've also cleared it with the owners. If you're still not happy about all that just say so.' Jason was happy. What was more, he offered to do the job unpaid.

'We'll see,' I said, 'I'll leave you my spare car keys. Pick up the Merc after the office closes on Friday 17th and meet me at Fellbeck. I'll be there before you.'

'What time?'

'Fellbeck front door at half-past eight, sharp. I want to do the tests after dark to make it realistic. Bear in mind there's no mobile signal at Fellbeck; you won't be able to contact me so make sure you're on time.'

46

The heavy hand of the ex-law sounded on my front door. Reg Briggs had not forgotten how to stage an official entrance. I asked about his morning. 'Checking the evidence; you have it to do with these cases on the off chance the suits have missed something. They haven't, there was nowt to miss.'

'What about Caroline's mobile?'

'She had two – very organised, the lass. She reserved one for Berry and used the other for everything else: work, social, domestic and hubby.'

'Caroline and Martyn went off to the Bahamas at the end of July. She came back alone. He set out for a lecture tour in Australia, she rang Chris, and they had a grand horizontal reunion until the new term started. So we expect a gap in both mobile records while Caroline was abroad.'

Briggsie was not up for a tutorial, 'Owt else, guv?'

I updated him on Sam's role in the AGROW survey of Fellbeck. I added, 'Threnadie de Morzine was also of the party. I think Pascal's a loose cannon and so does Sam. That could be a fault line in the group.'

'Alright Ken, let's stick a wedge in and see if we can crack it. I'll get round to him,' he promised and checked his watch.

To save time I decided to keep Virginia's involvement with AGROW's Fellbeck survey to myself. 'When do you plan to set about Enderby?' Briggsie said he had no plans. 'Meyer's slipped down the league so isn't Martyn the chief suspect? What's changed?'

Reginald was conciliatory, 'Nothing, McFadge fancies her

chance of breaking him down in the witness box. She wants to hit him with the goings-on at the Ram's Head – see what shakes loose.'

'My reconstruction at Fellbeck – we need it to test Chris Berry's statement. Otherwise the prosecution can claim that our interpretation of the crime scene is a fantasy.' Briggs was ok with that.

I went on, 'Could you get the defence forensic to do an extra check? As far as I can make out, the police team concentrated on the immediate murder location: sitting room, front door, hall, and the closet. We need to interpret the forensic evidence in terms of Chris's statement...'

The master detective was getting fidgety, 'Come on, spit it out Ken.'

'... The murderers were in a hurry to get out and they might have left fingerprints, especially on or inside the fuse box or around the back door.'

Briggs said, 'Leave it with me, I'll let you know – that all?'

'One thing,' I produced the knife that Jason had almost given his life to retrieve and told him the story.

Briggs slipped the evidence into his briefcase. 'We might just have got something here. I'll give it to Nick: see if it's a feasible murder weapon.'

The master detective was leaving, 'Ken, thanks for that, it's great having your input,' was what he said. His expression said otherwise.

He paused at my door for the final put-down, 'I could tell (*superhuman intuition?*) you weren't right happy with Meyer's alibi. I got Kath to do a quick 'ousetwouse. She cracked it: Josephine's neighbour says he spotted her brother's car parked outside around 7.30. He asked Hans to come out and give him a hand reversing his caravan up his drive – which he did. *QED.*' (*Bugger!*)

After Briggsie had kissed goodbye I phoned Amelia

317

Partington, 'Remember when we met in December we spoke about finance for the Fellbeck project. If he's interested it's time I talked to Martyn.'

'There's certainly interest,' Amelia reassured me, 'say next week is target?'

I set about hiring a Transit van and a petrol generator.

★

The master detective was morose on the phone even for a wet Monday in Halifax. 'You were right about Caroline's mobiles,' he began. Never mind the rain, enough reason to be morose if I'd spotted something that he hadn't. 'It's looking like she was with Martyn for three weeks.'

'That's what Caroline and Chris said, at different times – three weeks in the Caribbean.'

'She came back about 15th August and started using her general purpose mobile again. Here's the "but", she didn't phone Berry on her adultery mobile until 29th August; she was back for two weeks before she contacted him.'

'Who *did* she speak to?'

'Kath's onto that,' Briggs said. 'Apart from routine contacts like the village baker, Kath identified Major Wilson: her brother. Kath phoned him and he confirmed. He was posted at short notice from overseas to the Army command course at Aldershot. He fitted in four days with his sister from 16th August before it kicked off, so nothing in that: they hadn't seen each other for going on two years. You see the problem?'

I did, it stuck out a mile, 'After Wilson went back to Aldershot on the 19th that leaves ten days unaccounted for until she contacted Berry. If she was seeing someone else in the blank period and Chris found out, the prosecution have got their murder motive on a plate.'

'What's the innocent explanation then?' Briggs wanted to know.

'She was taking a break, giving herself space, take your pick. The Bahamas had been a disaster, she came back convinced that her marriage was over – that's what Caroline told me the evening she was murdered. But rather than dive straight into bed with Chris, she took time to make sure that he was *the one*, not a straw man she'd clutched at. She made that mistake with Meyer. Now she's grown up and so has her love affair. We have to fill in the missing days and show that far from sleeping around she was acting responsibly.'

'How much more would the jury prefer a standby lover or six?' Briggs put the phone down leaving a whiff of foreboding. If there was a shred of evidence to be had from the mobile records the cops would be there with knobs on. Enough sensation for one day; I set out for Ditchfield Public Library.

My visit kicked off with a disappointment. The bubbly receptionist had got her to a nunnery in Records department. Her replacement was an older lady, '1980?' She said, 'We'll have that on microfilm.' She sent me to bother Emmeline who got me started and left me to it. After scrabbling and scrolling around I found the report of the inquest on Andrew Masham, Grand Prix tractor driver, broken neck, death instantaneous, verdict: death by misadventure, followed by remarks by the coroner on safety training in the farming industry. At least someone had enjoyed himself. The postscript interested me: "Mrs Pat Masham was last seen some two weeks prior to Andrew's accident. Efforts to trace her have so far failed leading to the possibility that she has gone abroad." Had someone else found life at Fellbeck unappealing or had there been yet another murder and suicide event there?

There was a genteel message on my phone when I got back. Martyn Enderby would be *tahbly* pleased. I phoned. We made a date for 'tomorrow at 10.00': coffee, no lunch, fund-raising on the cheap – very high class.

47

Enderby's place gave an impression of money in decline. The long track up to the house was rutted, overgrown and hadn't been cleared for ages; the long grass brushed loudly against the bottom of the car. At the front of the house was a courtyard with stables on the left. They were closed up, bar one, where the half door stood open enabling an interested brown horse to observe my arrival. As a tradesman, I drove round and rang the backdoor bell.

The owner let me in, his appearance hadn't changed since my sighting at Ditchfield Sceptics – double breasted dark blue blazer with anodised buttons, striped shirt, club tie, immaculate chinos and polished black shoes with laces. Close up, he looked in his mid forties, slim, five-eleven, face verging on pretty with high cheekbones, slight hollows beneath, tapering to a pointed chin – not strong, the sort women like – a gentleman pacifist. 'Kin, good to see, doo come in,' Enderby addressed me in the accent that lost the Empire. I had the advantage in that I already knew him as the mystic terrorist of eighteen months ago. He didn't recognise the sceptic stalker on the back row, or the spy in the public bar. He extended a long, artistic hand unsuited to contact sports (*like wife slaughter?*). There was something about his eyes that I didn't fancy, they alternated between evasive and intense.

Martyn led me up the hall, family portraits to right and left, Victorian to 1940s, from small-farming Enderbys to 'Heathcote Enderby, my grandfather,' Martyn stopped in front of the 1920s gentleman, 'he painted all the top society people.' (*And founded the family fortune*). We paused by a post-war couple, 'my parents'. His mother had been looker once now careworn. Dad was a mess; his country gent jacket hung about him two sizes too big, he'd anticipated the Sixties and paid the price. 'My father was a poet, ultra modern, not tahbly commercial,' said his son. I didn't mention the fatal accident.

Martyn took me into the study, leaving the door open. It was a large bright room with light panelling and a view down the drive. The wall facing his desk held the Enderby library. A few classics: Plato, Aristotle, Descartes, Grey's *Anatomy*, Charles Darwin's *On the Origin of Species* – all useful sources of quotes for rubbishing. The majority were new: New Age alternative philosophy, alternative medicine, alternative science, alternative universes and alternative religions all in their bright alternative dust jackets. Enderby observed my interest in *Switching off the Cancer Gene*; he took it down from the shelf. 'I've just reviewed this – brilliant, (*the book or the review?*) he proves the connection with meat eating. His subjects were Chinese cancer sufferers he switched the gene off and then on again by changing their diets.' His eyes lit up, 'it makes one wonder whether one should go *all the way*.' I took that to mean from vegetarianism to veganism. 'I write a lot of reviews – *New Statesman, Guardian, Discovery*.' (*OK bomb aimer, stand by for name-dropping*).

The wall behind the prophet's desk was a pictorial progress through the right people. I recognised a failed US Presidential candidate, a millionaire folk/soul singer who was not to be moved out of cowboy boots and ragged jeans and the potty laird who campaigned to have the Scottish Highlands repopulated by Afghan Mujahideen. Gamely they had all pasted on smiles and grasped Martyn's hand for the camera. Surplus Royalty was there – keen competitors at living off the land. Others formed a *tour d'horizon* of Enderby's rise to fame in the mystic mayhem business: Martyn delivering a keynote address, Martyn in the USA acknowledging a standing ovation from West Coast matrons (whoop, whoop, yell, yell), Martyn back in the UK leading a conference toast – plastic coffee cup held high. An aged philosopher of love stood confused in a crumpled mac, an earnest group on the lawn of a baronial hall were spellbound as a younger Martyn expounded his spiritual philosophy. *(To a materialist cynic, it all missed the mark by a margin wide enough to make a circling seagull blush).*

Pride of place went to a large picture of another sort: 'The Cockatrice,' Enderby explained, 'a mythical beast.'

'Very colourful,' I said. It looked as if it had been painted by numbers.

'Ears,' said Enderby upper-classily, 'another time I'll bring you up to speed on the mythology behind it.'

I was more interested in his pair of bronze candlesticks. The lower part resembled a famous Stone Age statuette: a crudely carved, massively pregnant, impressively ugly female. One of the pair held a red candle about a foot long; the other was green *(Spots on the Fellbeck floor?).*

'Your candlesticks are interesting,' I said, 'what's the story?'

'I'm sure you recognise the Venus of Harmstadt?' Martyn said. He was sure I didn't. 'An Upper Paleolithic religious figure, carved in soap stone about 15,000 BCE. You get the message?' his face lit up, 'it inspires our philosophy at AGROW – *proves* that religion was born out of feminism.' I suggested Mother Earth. '*Right,* Kin!' Good stroke that – I was on board. 'After that, in the west at least, it was downhill *all the way*: modern man, sun worship, violence, conflict, war, materialism. Fortunately, the Tao of the East took a different turn, until the British arrived.' It was news to me that Asian history was violence free until our ancestors turned up. *(It's all our fault, thank* God!*).*

What occupied my thoughts was the shape of the statuette's stomach. Grasp by the candlestick end, an easy swing at the back of the victim's head using the bulging stomach as the striker – what had you got? A circular depressed fracture, immediate unconsciousness, murder weapon number one. 'Awful,' I said.

'Doo sit down,' I took the seat on the suppliant's side of the prophet's desk. Set into the wall behind him was a small safe, the door half open. 'I'll get coffee. Decaff for you? Actually at this time of day I usually take herbal tea.'

'Rahlly?' I was getting the lingo (*"rahlly?" covers a range from mild interest to contempt*). 'Count me in, Martyn.' He got up and walked out leaving the safe open but almost closing the study door behind him and exposing a red devil mask hanging on the inside: horns, teeth, goat's beard, the lot. I moved to the door and listened. Martyn was making a phone call in the kitchen. All right to poke around his study so long as I didn't listen to his phone conversation. I took down the mask and tried it on. Once I had the eye holes aligned it gave the instant anonymity that I remembered from children's Halloween parties. Masked, you could do and say things that you wouldn't dare barefaced. *(Like smashing the wife's skull)* I replaced the mask on its hook got out my camera and took a couple of shots.

Martyn was in full flow on the kitchen phone, time for a peek in the safe. It was small and contained a stack of files and papers in brown envelopes, not the object I hoped for. I went back to the door. The kettle had come to the boil, Martyn's conversation had not. I took one of the bronze figures, placed a standard size paperback behind it for scaling and took a couple of camera shots. I was right about the size and weight: a quick swing and curtains – the blackout variety.

Martyn came back bearing his organic brew. I was in the act of replacing the book. 'You must read that,' he said, 'take it with you. The author graduated in physics then went off to the Amazon basin to become a shaman.'

I examined the front cover, '*Crow Cosmogony* by Roland Freelife, he doesn't mean the "Membury Three"?'

Enderby did not do jokes, 'Nee-oh Kin, he refers to the Crow Indians, a North American tribe. It's an essay in pre-materialist sahnce, brilliant.'

'I see-ah,' (*brush up your diphthongs Kin, start using them nye-ee*), 'and the mask there, behind the door – is that shamanic?'

'Good try, Kin,' (*one does so adore being patronised*). 'It's reproduction English seventeenth century.'

'Time of the Pendle witch trials?'

'I see you're *aware* of local history.' I sipped politely at the herbal dishwater. Enderby launched into his lecture on Western capitalism: globalisation, secularism, commercialism, colonialism and of course, money, which he rejected (*but needed in spades*). It called for a philosophical body-swerve, but he was well practised.

'You see, Kin, we are in business to create an entirely new world-view, away from meaningless materialist sahnce and towards life, joy, spirituality and the enhancement of human consciousness. We totally reject the proposition that evolution is driven by chance environmental change. It has been *proved* that the universe is controlled by human consciousness, in fact the cosmos *is conscious itself*, every planet, every star, every tree, every rock. You're aware of the *hard mind-body problem*? It has baffled every philosopher from the ancient Greeks. Now it's solved, definitively solved. I've solved it – here!' He strode to the bookcase and returned with another brightly jacketed volume, self-published and printed in Latvia. The fixed gleam in the eye was back, I thought it was time to cool him off before he got ideas with a bronze candlestick.

'Martyn, it's inspiring to hear you,' I told him, 'that's why I'm here to talk investment.' That did the trick, nothing like the mention of money to focus a mystic. 'You're not the only ones in the field. One way it's good, the media are giving these ideas more than a passing nod – BBC, Channel 4, but what distinguishes AGROW from the crowd? What about the "A" here? What sort of action are you talking?' (*A bomb at the Cavendish? A machine gun attack at the Royal Society*).

'We aim to bring on our revolution by spiritual means.'

'If that fails?'

'Failing which, ultimately nothing is ruled out.' This was more upfront than Pascal, but it was the sad old story in the end: love, pacifism, as long as it works. *(But if it comes to hey lads hey! – Rousseau's out, Robespierre's in – guillotine time ladies, a basketful of heads, get knitting, no bother).*

'Martyn, it's hard to say how inspired I feel to hear you take that line' (*he's mad*). 'But I have to say this… has AGROW really got the *steel* for a revolutionary movement?'

Enderby rose to that. 'Kin, I say it again. First and foremost we are a spiritual movement but if it means achieving our objectives by other means, then unhesitatingly we say *YES!*' Enderby's palm smote the desktop. For a marginally effeminate man it was an odd gesture – comic but not vulgar.

I rose to give Enderby a quick high five before the moment died, '*YES!*'

'I'm beginning to understand Fellbeck,' *(Not half!)* I told him, 'you want to create an Education Centre, but not just that – a training camp for spiritual terrorists.'

Martyn smirked, 'Spiritual terrorists, I like that.'

I moved to the practical, 'But Fellbeck – the building – not the easiest is it? Of course you've taken financial advice? I had speech with Sam Waters, he agreed my ballpark figure of four to five hundred k – start to finish. Sound engineer, Sam, I go along with that.'

'Ears,' Enderby was wary all of a sudden.

'You held a personal vigil there, a Road to Damascus moment? How did that convince you that it had to be Fellbeck?'

'I was already aware of the property and its aura.'

'You mean it's supposed to be haunted?'

Enderby was dismissive, 'not haunted in the populist sense, we leave that to SPR and the paranormal scientists. Fellbeck has a spiritual presence.'

'You believe the place has its own consciousness?' He did, emphatically.

'*I was guided:* it was ordained that the day we surveyed Fellbeck fell on the feast of Walpurgis'. That meant bugger-all to me, but I was about to receive instruction from a Premier League fantasist. I sat like a back shelf nodding dog whilst Enderby took the trip. 'It begins with an 8th Century English saint called Walpurga. She was the first woman recruited by Boniface to drive his mission forward; you see how the connection with feminism comes in here? Over the centuries Walpurgis Night spread Europe-wide – except in England, (*savages!*) – crudely, as a witches' festival.'

I stopped the nodding dog routine. 'It was life-changing?'

Martyn Enderby held me with the glittering eye, 'the presence spoke to me, implanting the power to create an entire new culture.' (*Wow!*). For a moment, I feared he was going to speak in tongues but sensing my limitations he continued in what his class imagined to be English (before "Istry" arrived), 'Ears, Kin, ears. You see, I am essentially inspirational, creative…' his expression became deeply veridical *(but not quite vertical)* as he inclined his head towards his raised palm, his expression slipped into what Caroline had described as his medieval saint pose, eyes cast upward in adoration – self-adoration mainly. I was losing the battle not to laugh, I fumbled for my handkerchief, then just in time I recalled that this man was not a spiritual stand-up comedian. He had butchered Caroline and left her lover clutching the can.

'And Walpurgis Night comes round again?'

The gaze travelled down from the infinite and fixed on me. I sat rabbit-like in the headlights. 'Last year I received the call, the inspiration, the empowerment. This year I move on to the celebration, the consecration, the dedication.' He didn't get a high five this time because I was feeling slightly sick. I had realised what he intended to celebrate.

The glare of inspiration moderated. Enderby had recalled the purpose of the meeting. He got out the offertory plate, 'Kin, perhaps we could have a brief word about...funding?' A fleeting smile – diffident? Was it heckerslike diffident, he was on the grab. It was time for me to put the money, or at least the illusion of money where the con was. Then, loudly, the front door bell rang.

Martyn looked at his watch, 'oh dee-ah, nixt appointment.' He stood and I followed him to the front door (*a front door visitor*). No longer diffident, the inspirational leader was back, busy, businesslike, impeccably connected to the *very best people*. 'This will be Sir Ed'ard Fen'orth,' (*"ws" silent as in 'anchor*), 'I think he's on for ten k, Kin,' he confided. His voice dropped to a conspirator's whisper, 'lunch should clinch it'. He opened the front door to a tweedy person, 'Sir Ed'ard! Beee-ang on time!' They clutched one another as they shook hands. 'Now, here's the programme: a quick stirrup cup, then the Black Eagle on the Harrogate road, new fish restaurant: French chef, French wines, French waiters, spoken of for a Michelin star next yah.' Then he remembered to get shot of me, 'Kin, this has been most rewarding, (*it had, but not for him*) we *must* do it again – sooon. *Get you up to speed*' (*Writing a cheque? No chance*). He was back with the knight, 'Ed'ard, you really must cast an eye over the new hunter – *value* your opinion.'

I responded to my erstwhile host in my best industrial, 'Loook forward to that Martyn, thanks for th' tea.' I nodded to the tweedy knight and lurched off. Enderby muttered something to his knightly guest. I thought I caught the word "builder". For Sir Ed'ard: ten thousand gets a slap-up lunch, (*fish and stingy fries with thin wine and insolent waiters*). For Kin: one hundred thousand gets a teabag herbal. (*Shut up you,*

Hardy, you've had a simply super morning, he got nowt and you copped the lot.)

Having left by the wrong door, I had to carry on lurching round to the back to fetch the car. I drove back gently around the manor. As I emerged into the front yard a young lad came out of the stable – small, thin, wearing grubby jeans (unfashionably distressed with horse-shit appliquée) tucked into muddy boots and grey polo-neck sweater out at the elbows. I stopped and rolled down the window, 'yer rate?'

The boy stopped, he came over and stuck his carroty head in at the window, 'Now then?'

'Mr Enderby's bought himself a new hunter? Asked me if I'd take a look.' I wanted to get him into the stable, away from the house windows. I got out and we walked across. The lad's name was Jeff Sullivan. I guessed his age at 16 or 17, but being undersized, jockey build, he could easily have been older. Jeff said he worked mainly at the livery stables up the road, but he put in a few hours at Heywood – paid better than livery – 'The usual – stable work, grooming, exercise the mare – the odd errand.'

'To Ditchfield?'

That line of questioning fell at the first fence, 'Ditchfield? You're joking. One bus a day, Ditchfield.' (*How many to Yeadon?*) Jeff was saying no more, even for the fiver that nestled in my fist.

'If he asks, tell Mr Enderby I liked the look of her 'quarters' (*I hadn't been near the creature*). Jeff grinned. I made to turn away then stopped, 'This murder, strange business, wasn't it?'

'Not really,' said Jeff.

'What's the crack? Who did it?'

'Not the one they've collared for it.'

'Who then?'

'Himself – no danger – obvious.'

'Why obvious?'

Jeff explained patiently, 'Married going on six years. Coupla years, OK. Then not getting enough, she's at it, putting it about. He's had enough even if she hasn't. Chop!'

Gobbin grapevine, unbeatable here, useless in court. The fiver disappeared quick sharp into Jeff's back pocket.

48

'Kenny-boy!' it was Stefan roaring down the phone. He had read my African report. 'More oil in your lamp than my whole team of fucking experts!' A compliment: he wanted something. I made modest noises and waited for the blow. 'None of the operations you looked at are feasible, different reasons, all killers. So listen…' here it came, 'this time I'm on target – SME operation outside Cape Town. Serious.' He wanted me to fly to Heathrow, meet him at Watford and then go on to Cape Town.

'How long this time, Stefan?'

'Why?' I explained that I was shortly required at Ditchfield in connection with a murder trial. 'You have murdered who?' From a Cold War East European it was not necessarily a joke.

I said, 'No one you know – I'm a witness.' I told him the trial would be opening in mid-April at Ditchfield Crown Court.

'No problem Kenny, I want an in-depth appraisal, ten days maximum, plenty time. You like it, I take it from there.'

I was off the case, so why not take the money? I agreed.

I phoned Briggs and briefed him about my Cape Town job.

'Ten days? 'Appen we'll make a do on us own,' said the master detective.

'You said you'd have a word with Pascal de Morzine next time…'

Reginald resented my implication, he interrupted, 'Correct! And I did. I saw your friend Pascal and I don't reckon him as Benson because of his comic accent. But he gave me an alibi for Enderby and himself. He states that after the meeting they talked in the bar with Amelia Partington. Sam Waters was not present; he doesn't know what time Sam left. At 6.30 the men left in Enderby's 4x4 and drove to Keswick where they visited a retired academic that Pascal had known in Paris. They had a long talk and returned to the Ram's Head at 10 pm. Pascal then turned in. He claims that his friend, Dr Pickett, was pretty frail when they visited in November. He died suddenly in January this year. I sent our Kath up to Keswick to confirm the story. Apparently Pickett was independent minded and insisted on fending for himself. Around New Year one of the neighbours, not having noticed any signs of life went round to check and found the old lad apparently on his last legs. She called an ambulance and he died in the hospital – double pneumonia.'

'You didn't have chance for a word with Amelia Partington?' I knew he hadn't. 'Why not get Kath to drop in for a chat between ladies?'

'To what end?' Briggs wanted to know.

'Amelia was in the Ram's Head lounge with Enderby and Pascal de Morzine until 6.30pm. You've got a sighting from the staff and that agrees with that. What happened after that? When did she see them next? If she clams up, Kath could drop a few hints about Enderby's bed sheet and the unused condition of Amelia's bed. She'd prefer not to have that talked about in court?'

'Worth thinking about,' said Briggs, 'might be interesting to know why she dislikes Pascal an' all.' I took that for a guarded 'Yes'.

There was time to tidy up the loose ends. I looked in on Pam, 'Could you mention to Mr Harrison? If he wants me for a witness in court shouldn't he do something about a statement? I'm off to Africa again.'

A minute before five I tapped on Niall's office door and looked in: empty, desk top clear, nothing on the hat stand. I came back one door and walked into his secretary's office. Dawn was pounding the keyboard. As I walked in, she glanced up at the clock and went on typing. Rushing to get a document completed before 5.30, she didn't want interruptions. Good.

'Dawn,' I said, 'sorry,' (type, type, type) 'is Mr Potts about?'

'You've missed him, Mr Hardy, it's Thursday, (type, type, type) he's generally off at five sharp, Thursdays.'

'I need to print something off Berry's PC for Mr Briggs, urgent. Is the archive room locked?' Hardly missing a beat on the keyboard, Dawn opened her top drawer and handed up a key (type, type, type). I went back to Niall's office, let myself into the archives and switched on the lights. I reckoned that if the Masham file was there it would be in the oldest rack against the far wall. It was. I lifted the folder out of the rack, pulled out a pile of papers and took them to the table. On top was a hand written note from Andrew Masham to Jefferson Whalley, dated January 1978. It confirmed that he had read and signed the lease, but it also mentioned something else.

Dear Mr Whalley

I've signed the papers and enclose herewith. Also I came across the enclosed manuscript in a cupboard at Fellbeck. It means nothing to me but I thought it might be of historical interest so I think you had better have it.

Yours
    Andrew Masham

I ran through the other papers, they were all legal stuff, 20 years out of date. There was no sign of the manuscript, which *could* have been the Benson document. That made two possible Benson documents: the document Meyer handed to Enderby and this one – presumably found by Niall.

Masham's signed lease document had a length of black legal tape attached to the corner. Had a fourth Fellbeck key once been on the other end of that? No way of telling. I switched on Niall's photocopier and made a copy of Masham's letter. Then I restored everything, locked up and went back to Dawn's office (type, type, type) and popped the storeroom key back into Dawn's drawer.

I waved the photocopy in her direction, 'thanks Dawn, all done…'night!'

''Night Mr Hardy,' (type, type, type).

Supposing the document Meyer had sent to Enderby really was about nothing more than boundaries. I reckoned I knew where "Benson" got his manuscript and, I was willing to bet, a Fellbeck door key.

I drove to St Cuthbert's and parked in a far corner overhung with laurels. At five minutes past six a group of a dozen or so assorted ladies emerged through the swing doors, chatted briefly and dispersed. Five minutes later a lone figure followed: slim with long black hair wearing a beige shower proof and carrying a thin folder. Virginia walked to the car park got into her yellow Fiat 500 and drove off with never a glance in my direction. Tai Chi was over for another week.

I sat on in the car park. According to John Bolton, Mrs Masham's disappearance followed by her husband's fatal accident had landed the ageing Jefferson Whalley with a load of work. At the finish, did the solicitor file everything, including Masham's spare key, and with a sigh of relief leave it for Niall to discover years later? How did the document and the previously unknown Fellbeck key come into the possession of the murder gang unless Niall himself was one of them?

I remembered what Niall had said at the start: "Find Benson and you've cracked the case". Had I found him? Had Niall made the "Benson" phone calls from the back office while Virginia was teaching an after-school Tai Chi group on

Thursdays. Chris and Gloria both *think* that most of Benson's phone calls happened on a Thursday. The only call Briggs had traced was the final one from a public phone box which was *not* on a Thursday.

Conclusion: a two pint problem. I took it to my usual temple of healing and installed myself in the quiet corner. The lovely Virginia claims that the police have already got Caroline's murderer under lock and key. She explains that Chris committed the crime while possessed of a malignant spirit.

According to Sam, she sold the idea of a spirit presence to Martyn Enderby when AGROW were surveying the house for a training centre and sealed the contract on the Fellbeck hearthrug? (*You would think that Hardy*).

Caroline was getting in the way of Martyn's ambition and Virginia's lust: enough to mark her down for death? Who devised the plot to lure the lovers to Fellbeck using the Benson document? The creative Martyn was a strong competitor but had he the bottle to carry it through? No facts: just a load of speculation. I moved on to a third pint.

49

Early on Friday I collected a white Transit from the van hire and loaded a small petrol generator from the plant hire. My first call was at Braxtonby to borrow one of the Fellbeck keys, which I didn't need, but it put me onside.

At Fellbeck, it took half an hour to connect up the power supply and install everything. I started the petrol generator, and tested the lights. I crossed fingers and booted the PC for maximum load on the aged circuit. I waited until the desk top display came up then inserted my CD with the copy of Chris's Benson website; everything worked as it should. I hid the CD player away at the back of the closet and tried the jet engine sound effect. On maximum volume, it wasn't as loud as I'd hoped but Benson may have had a more powerful version. I did a quick soft shoe walk down the passage and threw the switch on the fuse box – lights out, under 10 seconds. Chris reacted to the power failure, felt his way in total darkness to the sitting room door and found it jammed, forced the door and found the body. The murderers were well away through the dining room door, locking it behind them; no sweat, and loaded the generator into their transport.

I fetched logs and kindling from the shed. NCF had calculated the weight of fuel from the ash residue – I used the same amount. I would light the sitting room fire at 5.30. If Chris was the murderer, he must have left Fellbeck no later than 5.25 in order to collect Caroline from my flat at 5.45. It remained for Jason to arrive and act out the routine and for Briggsie to stand as umpire.

I decided to see what was in the attic. I climbed the open steps, lifted the trap door, switched on my torch and flashed it around. The space under the roof was clogged and littered with the lumber of a century. The trap door was close to the front gable so there was only one way to go. I was looking for a place where Andrew Masham might have hidden his wife's body.

Against the rear gable end, I found a steel chest, six feet long and four foot square, the size of an old-fashioned press. Dumped on top of the chest was a Victorian cast iron office safe. The undisturbed coating of dust said that no one had been there for years, perhaps twenty years. The key was in the lock, I turned it and the door creaked open – nothing inside.

I wanted to see what was inside the steel chest, but the safe sitting on top must weigh more than a hundredweight. It was awkward in the confined space but I got my hands under one end and managed to drag it to the end of the chest. The difficult part was to lift it down without putting my back out and sending the safe through the ceiling; I was on a bad errand. I turned to the chest – padlocked and no key. I needed proper equipment; the chest had not been opened for over twenty years; it could wait a bit longer.

I went downstairs, waited until 5.30, then lit the fire in the sitting room, locked up, drove into Coldedge village and parked outside the pub. Vic was behind the bar, polishing glasses. I ordered a pint and asked after Dick, the retired shepherd. 'You're a bit late,' said the landlord, 'we buried the old lad in February – end of an era really.' I drank to that and asked Vic about the last tenant at Fellbeck. 'Masham, you mean, the chap killed in a tractor accident? That was just after I took this place, I remember him.'

'I've heard that he and Mrs Masham didn't get on latterly. She walked out two weeks before the accident. Did she ever turn up?'

Vic said, 'Nay, not that there was owt to come back for.

Masham's assets were put up for sale, just about covered the burial and the bank overdraft, I reckon.' I had an uneasy feeling that Masham's wife had never left. I drove back to Fellbeck to await Jason.

Kath arrived first, 'I couldn't get you on the mobile. Uncle's apologies, he won't be back till late. Can I help instead?'

Jason was prompt at 8.25 and we ran our reconstruction. It worked.

★

On Monday, Kath took me through to her uncle's office. Briggsie was wedged at his desk hidden behind *The Yorkshire Post* which he lowered and regarded me with disapproval. 'Off on your travels again?'

I dumped a polythene bottle containing 2.27 litres of brown water in his desk. 'There you are Reginald, half a gallon of beck water for analysis. What did forensic make of the knife?'

'Nowt,' said the master detective, 'signs of sharpening, but it would never have been sharp enough. It's an ordinary kitchen knife, poor quality imported steel and too light for the job even if you could get an edge on it. It's an unwanted complication. Forget it.'

'Fingerprints on the fuse box?'

'Wiped clean; the whole backdoor area.'

I said, 'Key, fuse box, backdoor, wiped – why? To destroy evidence.'

Briggsie regarded me smugly, 'The fuse box had been wiped on the outside', he said, 'they've found unidentified prints inside. It's a matter of elimination.' He made it sound as if it had all been his idea.

'We know Sam was inside the fuse box last April. He tested the circuits as part of his survey. We'd expect to find his prints.'

'Who else?'

'Everyone else who was on that AGROW survey party: Enderby, Pascal Threnadie de Morzine and Virginia Potts.'

'Why would any of that lot want to mess with fuses?' He had a point.

'How did it go on Friday?' He meant my reconstruction at Fellbeck.

'Never touched the sides, pity you couldn't make it, everything worked.' I got out my report with timings listed and put it on his blotter. 'Pick bones out of that then, Kath can confirm. I made up the fire according to NCF's estimate and lit it at 5.30. By half past eight it was out and dead cold. Jason had to use his torch to find the dummy I'd made up to represent the body. The latest Berry could have lit the fire on 23rd November was 5.25 because he arrived at my flat at 5.45. The fire must have been lit between seven and 7.30, because it was still burning when Chris found the body, and the embers were hot when the police came on the scene at ten. That means the murderers lit the fire.'

'What about the getaway?'

'Chris phoned the police from Coldedge at 9.28 meaning he left the house at 9.20, give or take. By the time the police picked him up and got into Fellbeck, it must have been going on ten o'clock.'

'Did Jason hear the generator?'

'Yes, the sort of noise you might expect round a working farm. Kath doesn't think that Caroline or Chris would have thought it suspicious. When they got inside Mrs Watts explained everything by saying they were on temporary lighting while the builders were in.'

Briggs gave the fur a relaxing massage whilst he read my report. 'I reckon that'll do. I'll pass it on to McFadge and it's up to her how she uses it in court. Where can she contact you in Cape Town?'

'Pam will have the details.' I put a photo of Enderby's

candlestick statuette on his desk, 'how do you fancy that as the first murder weapon?'

Briggs sized it up, 'it's a possible, more likely than that knife of yours.'

(*Knife of mine!*) I fought back, 'What about Amelia? Why didn't she use the bed in her room?'

All in vain, 'Quite interesting is this,' said Briggsie, 'I got our Kath to look into it, hang on a minute.' He picked up the phone and summoned his niece. 'Tell Mr Hardy what you got from Partington,' he invited.

'She was reluctant at first,' said Kath, 'Finally I got her to loosen up and she admitted to friction between herself and de Morzine arising from the previous AGM, in November 1998. What it amounted to was that he had made unwelcome approaches.'

I wasn't letting her away with that, 'Come on Kath, Amelia's no shrinking violet, there was more to it than "unwelcome approaches". Tell me what you told your uncle. I can take it; in fact I'm older that he is.' (Uncle Reginald was keen to confirm this statement).

There was certainly more to it. Last year, De Morzine had sweet-talked his way into her hotel room before Amelia cottoned on to his intentions. When she told him in no uncertain terms that there was nothing doing, he got physical and according to Amelia she counted herself lucky to get away without being raped. 'It was a right nasty experience,' said Kath, 'I think it was a relief for her to talk to another woman after bottling it up for so long.'

'Bearing in mind what Caroline told me about his behaviour in her kitchen and my observations of the doctor at work on a female student do you agree that Pascal de Morzine is a nasty as far as women are concerned?'

Kath did agree – with emphasis. 'Regarding the Enderby/ de Morzine alibi,' she continued, 'Amelia confirms that the men left together at 6.30 after the conversation in the bar. Left on her own, she had dinner at the Ram's Head – which we've confirmed – before going to her room and locking herself away for the night. She was not looking for a return match with Pascal. As to the unslept-in bed, Amelia claims to be a paid-up insomniac. She prepared for bed early, never a good idea if you're a bad sleeper. She was about to drop off sitting up in bed with a book when about 10.30 she heard a persistent soft tapping at her door, followed by someone trying the handle. After a couple of minutes, Pascal, assuming that it was him, gave up and went away. That put paid to thoughts of a proper sleep so she got up and snoozed in the chair for the rest of the night.'

'Always said they were a lively lot at AGROW,' I said, 'who spent an exciting hour or more in Martyn's bed?' I had a good idea, but no evidence.

Kath went back to her perch at the reception desk. I changed the subject, 'There's something else. It came to mind when I ran the reconstruction. The computer would be no problem nor would the sound effects, all they had to do was plug in and out again, but how did the AGROW gang manage the generator in and out?'

Briggs claimed to have thought of that but did not come up with an answer, 'Did one of them hire it, who from and in what name? The lad Jason has tried, so has Kath and we've got nowhere. Who delivered it to Fellbeck after dark, wired it into the fusebox and tested it? Then after the murder, removed it off site before the police arrived?'

'The only member of the committee with the technical ability is Sam Waters.'

'Who was lecturing at Harrogate fifty miles away at 7.30,' said Briggs.

'Right, but if the generator was available close to Fellbeck, preferably sitting on a lightweight trailer, Sam could have escaped from the AGM as soon as he'd finished delivering his paper, hitched the trailer onto his van and delivered it to Fellbeck. Bear in mind it would be dark by five and the Boltons would be closing down for the night. All little Sam had to do was unhitch the trailer outside the back door, remove four woodscrews (loosened in advance), run a cable from the generator to the fuse box and connect it to the only serviceable circuit. After that, a quick test and bugger off *ventre a terre* to Harrogate.'

The master detective was unconvinced, 'So Enderby didn't let on to Sam exactly what the generator was for? Or happen he hinted at some sort of mystic session: getting the resident spirit to materialise or some other daft thing he might have convinced the lad to do the job and he might have managed between it dropping dark and his deadline at Harrogate. But, think on, what happens when Sam realises that he's an accessory to murder?'

I said, 'Either he goes straight to the police and confesses all – which is no use to the murder gang – or he denies all knowledge.'

'Forget it,' was Reginald's advice, 'under gentle pressure, *(laid out on his office table?)* Sam Waters would have cracked long since.'

Briggsie was right, but he had another candidate, 'Meyer? Him with the cast iron alibi? He had time before he reported for Scrabble at seven.'

It was my turn to cast a damper, 'I've just come from the plant hire in Ditchfield. I hired a generator from them for my reconstruction. When I returned it this morning I chatted up the manager and asked if, in the past, they'd lent something similar to a Mr Meyer. With a bit of persuasion he got the register out. They had, in October '98 – eleven months before the murder. Meyer had just bought South Lea. He probably needed temporary lighting at some stage when he started doing the place up. There's been nothing since.'

That got a healthy sniff from the master detective, 'Unless he changed his supplier. I'll get Kath to check again under the name "Meyer" this time. Reginald's tone was not enthusiastic. 'What about the getaway?'

'Easy,' I claimed, 'they could have had the trailer hitched to Enderby's 4x4 in advance. All they had to do then was disconnect the wires from the fuse box and replace the woodscrews in the back door. Then they would drive round to the front where they would load the PC and the other bits and bats before locking the front door and dropping the key through the letter box. They could have been off site by the time Chris had finished his 999 call at Coldedge. Jason and I did it in ten minutes.'

50

Pam said, 'A message from Mr Harrison: the police are pressing for Chris Berry's PC. Have we finished with it? The prosecution want to check it.'

'There's nothing there of interest,' I said, 'so they might as well have it. There's a complete record backed up on the partnership server. The police have Chris's laptop. Can we swap?' Pam thought it would not be that simple.

★

Two weeks later the flat door needed a shove to get it open against the heap of mail. Cape Town had gone well but had taken longer than expected. Stefan had joined me as planned then insisted on checking everything again. I had barely a week in hand before the trial. I tramped downstairs to see Pam, 'any messages?'

Pam said there was only one that seemed important, 'you're to ring DC Gormley, the minute you get back. Here's the number.'

'It has come to Police notice,' said Gormley, 'that you made unauthorised entrance to the scene of crime at Fellbeck.' I did not like the sound of that. Gormley elaborated saying that on 30th November, he feared that I was responsible for interfering with material evidence at the site, which as I no doubt knew, was a serious matter. I reminded him that the scene of crime was released to Mr Harrison on the 30th. I had accompanied the defence lawyer to Fellbeck on that day with PC Dunn from Coldedge in attendance. The conversation then flagged.

'What's to do, DC Gormley? Not another piece of missing evidence? I mentioned Caroline's Paisley scarf, to say nothing of two murder weapons.

'There's no call to be like that, Mr Hardy.' We closed the discussion.

(You're a bully, Hardy, especially when jet-lagged). I phoned Briggsie and outlined my chat with Gormley. 'You'll hear no more about that,' said Reginald.

'How's the case going?'

'Nobbut moderate.'

I demanded clarification, 'by "moderate" you mean "average" in correct English or are you speaking Yorkshire?'

He said, 'Correct Yorkshire – "rotten".'

'New police evidence?'

'You could say that. I'm over to Ditchfield tomorrow, case conference in Harrison's office from midday – likely to go on all afternoon, happen we could have a chat after.'

The lad sounded worried so I raised the ante, 'Bring your toothbrush and your striped pyjamas and stop over. I'll take you to a proper pub, we can have a bar supper and an in-depth pint.'

I sorted the unwanted mail into a neat stack ready for the shredder and started on my final report for Stefan. I got two thirds of it done then went to catch up lost sleep with *Jack the Ripper: the Real Case*. Then, with a jolt, I realised that all three Ripper books were a month overdue at Ditchfield Library. After that, overnight flight or not, it was a fight to get any sleep at all.

We got the corner table at the Gari. Reginald opened with one piece of news. 'Finally, we've got a squint at the front door key that the police recovered at the SOC,' he announced, 'it's not a copy, it looks the same age as the three that Green has in his office. Any road, it's no great significance.'

'Unless it *had* turned out to be the Hindley copy. That would have scuppered the prosecution in one.'

My betting was that it came off the tag attached to Andrew Masham's letter, along with the original Benson manuscript. Thence Niall to Virginia, Virginia to Enderby, but there was only one way to prove it and that was from the inside so I said nothing about that. 'What are the cops sticking their brush up about now?'

Briggs turned his mouth down at the corners, 'They reckon they've got new evidence. That knife for a start, their forensics don't agree it's too light to be the murder weapon. After Berry murdered Caroline, he had time to nip down the field to the South Bridge and drop the knife in the water before going to phone for the police.'

'They'd better check their own records. After we found the knife, I told Meyer. I knew he'd got an alibi but I thought it was worth a try. Meyer said the police searched the beck from the South Bridge some distance downstream after the murder and found nothing. So it could only have been dropped off the bridge sometime later. It wasn't Berry.'

I ordered twelve ounce rump steaks, chips and peas twice and two more pints. I asked what else had come up.

'They've named Berry's ex-wife, Claudia, and Caroline's parents as witnesses.'

'I talked to Claudia in January, she didn't say anything damaging. I don't know about Caroline's parents, Tom didn't want me to approach them.

'CID have been trying to reconstruct what went on during the gap between Caroline returning from the West Indies and contacting Berry on 29th August. How much of that time were you around?'

'I hardly saw Chris after school broke up. He was deciphering the document for the Benson website, typing it up and designing the website. He went off down South for a few days. When he came back I was in the States seeing our kid. I wasn't back until August 31st when Chris was away playing

345

Heathcliffe to Caroline's Jane Eyre: romping round the moors and behaving badly in the purple heather.'

'Cathy,' said Briggsie, 'Heathcliffe and Cathy. Jane Eyre was pals with Mr Rochester.' He would know of course: it all happened in Yorkshire. The steaks arrived so I covered my confusion by demanding extra chips. 'When next did you see Chris Berry?'

'8th September, the day before term started at St Cuthbert's. I passed him on the stairs. Briggs wondered how he looked. 'Walking wounded,' I said, 'or limping. On the Friday, he dropped in after work and stayed to supper.'

'Cooked by you? By,' said Briggs, 'to be young with a cast iron stomach.'

I asked what he thought the police would make of the case. 'A weakness of the prosecution case,' pronounced the master detective with his mouth full, 'has been the lack of motive (*he's noticed!*). Now they've seized on Caroline going missing for two weeks. Suppose Berry sussed that she'd been AWOL all that time before summoning him to make up four legs in bed. Later, when he got back to reality it started to bug and the more he thought about it the more he resented it. Then when she started getting serious about a permanent relationship...'

'But they're guessing,' I interrupted, 'I'm the only one that knows about Caroline wanting to make it permanent. She told me three hours before she was killed. She was worried about telling Chris.'

'But that's just your submission,' Briggs said, 'no corroboration.'

In a move to lighten Reginald's mood I told him, 'There's a ginger stable lad at Heywood, part-time, called Jeff Sullivan. He trousered a fiver of mine in return for his opinion that the case was cut and dried. Said Enderby did it, on account of her extra murals.'

'You didn't get a receipt?'

'I asked if he'd done errands to Ditchfield. He turned that idea down flat – one bus a day to Ditchfield. Even more difficult for the key business with Hindley, in which case…'

Reginald was not enthusiastic, 'The description you got from the school receptionist could fit any number of lads. As for Hindley, he's short sighted with his glasses on and half blind without.' He launched an unprovoked assault on his apple dumpling.

I wasn't for giving up, 'The school receptionist's description doesn't rule him out. Same applies to Hindley's evidence.'

'Kath can find out if he's got a driving licence, if not he's out. But if he has, I'll have a chat with the lad.' I shuddered.

'What's the other bad news?'

'Their remaining witness runs a gay wine bar in Ditchfield.'

'Julio? A bit of light relief. What's he going to say? Caroline was in his bar with a male person? Probably turn out to be her tax accountant. They surely can't be hoping to build up a motive for murder based on gossip in a wine bar? Just supposing Berry found out that she was up to something, why concoct a complicated plot guaranteed to land him on a murder charge? Why didn't he give her a black eye there and then and walk out? What sort of reason for murder is that?'

Briggsie blew that out of the water before it got off the ground, 'Kenneth,' he said, 'I've done a lot of murders (*Doesn't he mean investigated a lot of murders?*) and it's hard to find a rational motive amongst the lot of them.' He gave the facial fur a bit of a work over. 'See, in Berry's case, there is previous –his marriage. She walked out on him, didn't she?'

'And jumped into bed with her boss and now she regrets it. All Claudia said to me was that Chris was on the intense side as a lover but physically gentle. What about the main man? How's he making out, is he up for it?'

'Chris Berry,' said Reginald, 'is not framing right well. In fact, McFadzean (it was the first time he'd given his barrister

347

her right name) is in two minds about putting him in the box. Three quarters of the time he's hardly with us and it's a fight to get anything out of him, other times he's over-excited and won't shut up.'

'If she doesn't put Berry up she's throwing in the towel, isn't she? Wouldn't the jury take it for an admission?'

'Even Marshall Hall never pulled that one off,' Briggs admitted, 'but if she does put him up and he breaks down it'll be worse.'

'That all the bad news?'

'I think they've got something off his PC.'

I objected, 'but I went through everything and backed it up onto the firm's server. I took another copy and loaded it on my machine, there's nothing there. I told Tom before he released to the other side.'

'I know, Ken. But if Chris saved something, then deleted it, one of their experts could have recovered it. Anyway we don't know how bad it is until they come across with the text.'

'What odds are you offering on the verdict?'

Reginald consulted his moustache, 'Six to four shot,' he said. It seemed a long time ago that we'd talked about getting the trial stopped.

We put the peg in and I rang for the taxi.

Next day Pam rang and asked me to go and see Tom. Apart from chance encounters in the corridor it would be our first meeting since he handed me the bag. 'Ken, we're going to need you for the defence,' he said, 'I want to sort out a witness statement with you.' I asked what evidence they wanted to cover. 'Character reference for Berry, that's what it amounts to. There's also the matter of your conversation with Caroline. Ms McFadjean has been fully briefed on what was said. In court, restrict yourself to answering her questions, don't elaborate, that's important. The same applies to prosecution questions, only more so.'

'What about my findings at Fellbeck, the reconstruction exercise? You're not going to pass that up, surely?'

Tom shuffled his bottom and dealt a conciliatory hand, 'No, of course not – don't get this wrong, Ken – but while you were in Cape Town we decided that the best tactic was for Northern Criminal Forensics to re-run all your observations and take them into the witness box rather than you.'

'What did they conclude?'

'They confirmed your findings.'

'But being professionals, the evidence will sound more convincing coming from them?'

'We don't want your position with the jury weakened by you being attacked in court over evidence that was collected... well, a bit informally.'

'Too right it was,' I said, 'let's get on with this statement then.' After that I took the lad for a pint. By now, it was plain that keeping my undercover sleuthing activities away from the court was essential should I be forced into desperate measures. I said nothing about that.

51

The case, when it opened in Ditchfield Crown Court was less exciting than I had anticipated. The press were magnificently restrained: *Lancashire Ripper Trial Opens – Horror at Haunted Farmhouse*. Days followed of sitting out time in the witness room while the prosecution had their innings. It was like being in quarantine and about as much fun. *War and Peace* took a hammering.

The witnesses were split between two rooms like rival football teams. Enderby was called for the prosecution and we never met. That was lucky.

At the end of the first week, Hans Meyer came in the evening for a game of chess. I asked whether he'd attended any of the court proceedings. 'I managed to get in for a couple of hours on the second day,' he said.

I asked what impression he'd gained. 'Hard to say, based on one session,' Hans admitted, 'the defence counsel spent most of the time laying into the prosecution's forensic evidence.'

'Some of it is shaky,' I said.

'I gathered that, she seemed sound to me, but she was very aggressive. I thought the younger of the two policemen was going to break down. He might well have done if the Judge hadn't stopped her.'

'What was the problem with the police evidence?'

'The fire in the living room – both the police constables said there was no fire burning in the grate when they arrived. They went further and said that the ashes were cold indicating there had been no fire in the grate that evening. '

'They both said that?'

'Yes.'

'I'm not surprised McFadzean got worked up. Either they're lying or Chris Berry is. It's a vital piece of evidence. What next?'

'She laid into the police forensics expert concerning the ash left in the grate. He confirmed that there was no warmth in the ashes when they tested them, but then admitted that was the following day.'

'What then?'

'McFadzean promised that the defence would show that if left to itself, the fire would have been reduced to embers within two and a half hours, meaning that if the fire was still burning when Caroline was murdered it could not have been lit by Berry.'

'This is what she's built her reputation on – attacking police evidence.'

'Don't you think it's risky?' Hans asked, 'don't judges get wise to that?' He advanced a pawn, unmasking his bishop on my king, 'check'. I could see the "check" but wondered about McFadge's tactic. Hans brought up a knight and put my king in "check" again. I moved my king out of "check".

'I got the feeling that the Judge was getting restive and so were some of the jury.'

'Perhaps resentment at a bossy woman bullying a young policeman.' I looked again at the position on the chessboard. Hans had blundered; he'd exposed his queen to my bishop. I swooped and grabbed the white queen. My opponent smiled sadly and moved his knight. 'Checkmate, Ken'. (*Bugger!*)

'Did you speak to any of Caroline's family at the funeral? Hans said he hadn't approached her parents, 'But I did have a brief word with her brother – nothing personal, I just said what a fine teacher she was and how good with the kids.'

I asked how Chris looked in court. 'Not good, I'm afraid: white faced, fidgety, looks as if he's lost at least 5 kilos.'

We met at the coffee shop where her sister had held our original *rendez vous*. Aethelflaed came bouncing in and asked for Fino on ice. I said it was good of her to give up her afternoon in favour of a hard seat in the gallery. 'Not at all, it's a prime source of material. I often go when there's something good on,' (*murder, robbery with violence, rape?*). '

The "something good" was McFadzean cross-examining Martyn Enderby. 'McFadzean started gently, commiserating with him on his loss of a beautiful wife. Then she moved on to the marriage. What did he mean exactly by describing Caroline as a "free spirit"? Would it be accurate to describe their marriage as an open relationship?'

'Enderby agreed up to a point, "My vocation demands a good deal of travel whilst Caroline was committed to her teaching career. So we spent a certain amount of time apart."

"McF: But you don't mean "open" in a sexual sense?

ME: Nee-oh.

McF: Let me take you back to last summer, Mr Enderby. You had arranged a holiday with your wife in the Bahamas?

ME: Ears.

McF: Were you aware at that time that Mrs Enderby had been having an affair with the accused since the previous April?

ME: No.

McF: How would you describe your relationship during the holiday?

ME: Idyllic.

McF: A second honeymoon?

ME: Absolutely."

'McFadzean went on to ask him about their "second honeymoon". Enderby explained why, although he had booked the villa for four weeks, Mrs Enderby cut her stay short and returned home alone. He claimed that was the plan because he was working on a new book. After that he set off on a lecture tour to Australia.'

I said, 'That's what Caroline told me. Did she ask about their relationship after Enderby came back?'

'She did,' Ethel confirmed, 'that was when he turned the tap on – "always treasure the memory of those weeks... Caroline brutally taken".

After the break for mopping up the witness, McFadzean was back on witness's claim that he was unaware of Caroline's affair from April to November.'

'Did he stick to that?'

'Not exactly, he said that at a "serious talk" that Caroline instigated on Sunday 21st November, she had admitted to a "bit of a fling" with Mr Berry. During their holiday, she began to have serious doubts about that relationship... McFadzean stopped him there and asked whether the purpose of Caroline's phone call to Chris Berry on 29th August had been to end the affair. Enderby claimed that had been his wife's intention but when they met, the affair flared up again only to die down again until by 21st November she had resolved to end it permanently. "In fact, on that evening she talked for the first time about interrupting her teaching career to start a family."'

I said, 'Enderby's talking about his marriage like something out of *Barsetshire Towers*. Were the court going along with him?'

'At that point yes,' said Ethel, 'but then the defence got into his behaviour on the night of the murder. It began with why he had booked in for the night at the Ram's Head, half an hour's drive from home, when the AGM was scheduled to close at 6pm.'

'That's simple,' I said, 'it was to ensure that Caroline went with Chris to Fellbeck.'

Ethel said, 'His explanation was that the original plan had been to hold a dinner after the AGM, after which he would not want to drive home. This was cancelled due to insufficient numbers. However, he had neglected to cancel his room booking. Certain colleagues (specifically Dr Pascal Threnadie de Morzine and Amelia Partington, the AGROW secretary) were staying overnight. He and de Morzine spent the evening visiting a dying friend. Meantime, McFadzean suggested, Mrs Enderby would be alone at home having ended her affair with the accused. Enderby claimed that she intended to leave the matter of breaking off their relationship until after her teachers' meeting. Consequently he did not expect her home until ten. After their "mercy dash" to Keswick he dropped de Morzine at the hotel and drove home to find the house empty. He waited for over an hour, then, finding Caroline's mobile was switched off he gave up in despair and drove back to the hotel for the night.'

'Nice work,' I said, 'in one bound our hero deals with his clandestine midnight return to the hotel, via the fire escape like a murderer in preference to the front door like a gent. At the same time he provides Chris Berry with a cracking motive for his crime of passion. Was that the end of that?'

'No,' said Ethel, 'more like the end of the beginning...'

"McF: Rather an odd decision in the circumstances. You spent the night in your hotel room?

ME: Yes

McF: Alone?

ME: Of course.

McF: I see. How do you explain the stains found on your bed sheet by the chambermaid the following morning? (gasps in the public gallery)

ME: I suggest that they were left behind by the previous occupants and the hotel had omitted to change the sheets afterwards.

McF: Surely this was a serious omission. But you did not mention it to the chambermaid or complain to the management when you left?

ME: No. I had other things on my mind.

McF: Mr Enderby, you have told the court that on 21st

November, a reconciliation took place between you and Mrs Enderby. She admitted to an affair with Christopher Berry, and promised to end it irrevocably on the evening of Tuesday 23rd. She went further and committed herself to becoming a devoted wife and mother. You maintain that was an accurate account?

ME: Yes, of course.

McF: And yet, on this night of all nights in your marriage, the forensic evidence shows that you neglected to make love to her. Why?"

Objection. Sustained, followed by a warning from the judge.

"McF: But then you didn't make love to her on the following night of 22nd November either. Rather cool for a passionate reconciliation, wasn't it?"

'Objection. Sustained, followed by what sounded like a final warning.'

'But,' I said, 'she'd made her point. The jury must have reached their own conclusions?'

'Of course,' said Ethel, 'sailing close to the wind is part of the job description for a defence barrister. After that, Sir Arnold Gaulby QC for the CPS was up requesting permission to re-examine. That went on for over half an hour, the marriage according to Saint Martyn, its tragic end and the love that could never die. By the time Gaulby finished Enderby had been in tears twice, it was hankies all round, jury for the use of, sobs from the public gallery and the Judge looking pink round the gills. Quite brilliant.'

'He's Welsh, you see.'

'Yes,' said Ethel, 'but next week the defence get their innings. They've got enough evidence to shred the police's "crime of passion" story. Stand by for fireworks.' If only.

At the end of the first week, the remaining witnesses were released for the weekend and warned not to discuss the case and to clock in on Monday morning on pain of the thumbscrew and rack. It seemed a pretty poor reward for performing our civic duty.

Briggsie met me at the back door and shoved an envelope into my pocket. 'This here's a copy of the late evidence they claim to have got from Berry's PC,' he said, 'it looks like they've held it over till next week on a purpose. Their IT witness will be last up – sink the defence before they kick off.' (*Briggs was a ruthless bugger when it came to mixing metaphors*). 'It looks as if our side will be in there batting by Monday afternoon. You'll be next in after Berry so you'd best know about this.'

'But I don't know?'

'Exactly.'

'Do you believe they've only just found it?'

'Have they buggery, it's a routine check on a suspect's computer – search for and restore deleted docs. They've known about this since Harrison came clean and handed them Berry's PC to play with. I wouldn't have bothered, they thought Berry's laptop was all there was.'

'Can the defence complain? I mean about concealing evidence until now?' Briggs was not optimistic – that would have been to betray his origins.

I walked back to York Terrace, through what used to be the Barbary Coast. I broke the journey at what once had been the Rat and Parrot. 'I hear,' said McIver, 'that you're in trouble with the law.' When I got back to the flat I sat down and opened the envelope. It was plain text and read like a diary entry.

Thursday 12th August. Depressed. Woke at three this morning and lay there until eight imagining Martyn working on Caroline with imaginative sex. Got to find something to do. Can't do any more on Benson's website. I've found some images of Victorian East End slums: drunks, worn-out women, ragged children. You can almost smell the drains. Four more days to get through before Caroline comes back.

Friday 20th August. Still nothing from Caroline. Finally got some sleep. Decided to get some exercise. Bought a guide to moorland walks, found a three-hour route as a starter and ended up with pie and a half at the local in a place called Brookford. Walked back to the car reckoned that straight on through the village would put me on the Ditchfield road. Two minutes later I realised – white gates with the name "Heywood Place" painted in bold – the Enderby property. Before I always arrived from opposite direction. I stopped. Why? It's stupid. Caroline's 5000 miles away. Or … she's back, it's over. I had to know.

Set off up the lane slowly. Hedges overgrown all along. Can't see house until you get past the left turn at top. Nervous as hell. Spying or stalking? No way out – no room to turn round – have to carry on and U-turn in front of the house. Near the bend. Down to a crawl, just as well. Sit-up-and-beg bike came belting round the corner, braked hard, skidded, old woman jumped off just before the bike hit my front bumper and fell on its side. Stack of envelopes scattered all over.

Old lady said 'Sorry dear, hope there's no damage.' I picked up her bike straightened handlebars and put chain back on. Otherwise ok.

Pretty neat dismount she did.

She said husband was cavalry. Used to ride to hounds. Gutsy old bird.

Said no one in at house, just been there with a circular.

I said they're still on holiday?

No. Mrs Enderby *came back*. Organised children's races last Saturday.

Visitor staying, he picked her up from the fete afterwards. *(He!!)* Seemed fond of one another. Then hopped on bike and away. I got back in car and sat. I've been dumped. That stupid row we had. She's away with someone else. *Bitch. Lying Fucking Bitch.* Stopped off at Tesco for bottle of scotch. I'll see her in a week. *Just You Wait Slag*.

Sunday 29ᵗʰ August. It's over. Caroline phoned. 'Chris, I'm back. Please come? Seven o'clock? Can't wait. I love you. Bring your walking gear.'

I'm not saying a word – I don't want to know. OK so suppose it is just a fling. Live it. Live it till it dies.

It wasn't hard to see what the prosecution would make of it. They had a row before she left. He expected to hear from her as soon as she got back on the 16th August. There was nothing. Time dragged on, what was she up to? Then the chance discovery – she had a man staying. When he finally heard from her on the 29th suspicions had already taken root. If he had gone and had it out with her there and then it would have been different. But he didn't, he said nothing, just let it ride. So the suspicions festered until... It was rubbish of course, anyone who knew the couple would know, but the jury didn't and neither did the judge. I knew what happened when Chris turned up that evening for their reunion – he told me a week later. But that was hearsay. The trial was underway it was up to his legal team now.

During the Monday lunch break I got a word with Reginald. 'I've looked at the text they claim to have recovered off the PC.'

'It's genuine,' said Briggs, 'I've found the cyclist lady that crashed into Chris Berry. Her name's Phyllis Calvert, widow of the parish. I asked her about the man she saw with Caroline at the fete. She saw them from a distance walking away towards the gate. All she got was a back view.'

'What about Calvert's view of their relationship?'

'They were walking with their arms round each other.'

'You mean like brother and sister?'

'Happen, he didn't have his hand up her knickers,' said Briggs squalidly, 'so brother and sister could be right.'

'Are we sure that's all there is in the deleted file? They haven't just disclosed what suited them?'

'That's to be seen,' said Briggs.

I went back to my perch in the witness room.

Chris was in the box for a long time. I was called at 10.15 on the Wednesday – just in time to miss my tea break. I marched into the witness box, took up the book and swore to be good. I had the words memorised. Instead of reading the prompt I shouted them out whilst running a quick scan of the public gallery. I wanted to know if Enderby was present; he was not. After his ordeal on the stand, Chris was looking the perfect loser: slumped in his seat, haggard, bog-eyed and pale grey. Judge Slagdon-Pryce also looked unhappy. He was perspiring, fidgety, and when he took his spectacles off to wipe them his eyes were red and the pupils dilated. I reckoned he was on a downer. I then looked away sharp because Mrs McFadzean needed my attention for checking my ID.

Then, 'Mr Hardy, how long have you known the accused, Christopher Berry?'

"KH: Since September 1998.

McF: Which was seven months before his relationship with Caroline Enderby began?

KH: I believe so."

Over the next ten minutes I was encouraged to tell the court that Christopher Berry behaved throughout as a kind, caring and thoroughly decent young man who showed no sign of aggressive or violent tendencies towards women, children or even my cat. As far as I could tell, neither the judge nor the jury took the least bit of notice. They wanted something more lively. When Mrs McFadzean went on to probe my relationship with Caroline Enderby (Mrs), interest broke out all round.

"McF: How would you describe it (my relationship)?

KH: Friendly.

Judge Slagdon-Pryce: Witness, Counsel for the Defence has asked you a question. I do not find your off-hand style of answering appropriate. Explain what you mean by "friendly" (and dish us the dirt, rat)."

Tom had briefed me that Slagdon-Pryce was a Court of Appeal judge, big wig, red robes and no gavel. He must be addressed as "My Lord" all the way, although the professionals rendered it as "Mlud". I was having none of that, if he wanted his medieval title he was getting it – in full.

"KH: My Lord, what I meant by "friendly", My Lord, was that the "relationship" (*raised fingers indicating double quotes, alternatively a pair of rabbits*) was restricted to passing on the stairs. She would be hurrying up or down to meet or leave the accused. There would be a short but friendly conversation of the "hello, how are you" sort. We were on first name terms. Over several months, these encounters became more extended but remained superficial."

Slagdon was looking impatient. I beat him to the draw and kept talking, (*You wanted details matey, enjoy!*) "This was how things stood until the evening of 23rd November when, approximately three and a half hours before her death and the accused being at the time absent, Mrs Enderby entered my flat and a more extensive exchange took place, My Lord."

Judging by his expression, Tom, sitting behind McF was not pleased with his witness. He was not in a position to say so. Slagdon-Pryce was not over the moon either, because he told Mrs McFadzean to get on with it and not waste the Court's time (*and whose bloody fault is that, then?*).

"McF: If your Lordship pleases. Mr Hardy, you are saying that the only meaningful conversation you had with Mrs Enderby was on the evening of November 23rd.

KH: Yes.

McF: Could you tell the Court what transpired?

KH: (With a sideways glance at His Lordship) In detail?

McF: In the essential details."

The jury sat up like a double row of meerkats, the judge seemed to be slipping into a coma. I explained the circumstances: she was waiting for Chris, she wanted to know how I thought Chris would feel about an immediate move to a permanent relationship.

"McF: Did she give a reason for asking?

KH: She said that Chris had stopped talking about it. I asked whether she meant that he was cooling off and she said that she was not talking about affection or sex. I understood her to mean the long-term future of the relationship.

McF: Was that all?

KH: No, we discussed it at some length but that was the meat of it. She said that at the start they had agreed to give it twelve months, which would mean until April this year before deciding.

McF: But now she wanted to bring that deadline forward?

KH: Mrs Enderby said that her marriage had collapsed since the summer holiday and she did not want to continue any longer.

McF: Did you offer an opinion?

KH: Yes, I said in that case, get on with it.

McF: Immediately?

KH: Yes."

McFadzean wrapped up the interview. She hadn't asked any details about the state of Caroline's marriage, in particular that she was scared. I thought I knew why: it wouldn't help the defence to make a half-baked accusation without evidence to back it up.

Prosecuting Counsel rose to cross-question. It was not the lean and hungry Gaulby QC, but his junior, a wisp of a lad just seventeen stone and barely out of nappies. His name was Davis Briscoe. He appeared to be breathing hard from the effort of getting up, or perhaps impatience to get into the fray. He looked pretty pleased with himself and his accent was to match.

"Davis Briscoe: Mr Hardy, you have given an account of your conversation with Mrs Enderby on the evening of... (consults brief, breaks into a sweat) 23rd November last year.

KH: Yes.

DB: You tell the court that your contacts with Mrs Enderby had been brief and superficial hitherto.

KH: Yes.

DB: Then you claim that on this particular evening, Caroline Enderby took you into her confidence regarding her complex relationships with her devoted husband (murmurs of approbation from the public gallery) and the accused and went so far as to ask how she might resolve it. Why did she do that?

KH: I don't know.

Judge Slagdon-Pryce: (emerging from his coma) Mr Hardy, I have already warned you about giving flippant answers to Counsel's questions.

KH: I'm sorry, My Lord. It appeared to me that Counsel was inviting me to speculate, My Lord. Mrs Enderby had indicated that she believed her marriage to be at an end.

Judge: Answer the question.

KH: My Lord, my understanding is that what I think Mrs Enderby thought is not evidence. (Hurrying on before His Lordship had me locked up), what I can offer, and this is mere speculation on my part, My Lord, (a tiny nod from McF and a scowl from Tom) is that Mrs Enderby knew that I was on friendly terms with the accused and hoped that he might have disclosed his feelings to me regarding a permanent relationship.

DB: And had he?

KH: The last time we discussed his private affairs was on the evening of 10th September. He had returned on 8th September from spending a week with Caroline Enderby (mild sensation). I asked how it had gone (titter from the gallery). He described himself as "so much in love it's ridiculous" (more titters, cry of "Silence in Court"). He did not go from there to discuss a permanent relationship as opposed to a passionate love affair.

DB: What was discussed on that date?

KH: As far as I remember, his part-time website business and in particular the document delivered to him by a Mr Benson at the end of the summer term. He left it with me to read. I looked at it later that evening. It was difficult to decipher, I gave up after the first couple of pages and put it in my filing cabinet.

DB: Locked?

KH: Yes, locked. It stayed locked in there until I realised that it could have a bearing on this case. I then gave it to Mr Harrison. (Sir Arnold Gaulby scribbled a note, which he folded and passed to his junior. Judging by the leader's expression it said "stick to the fucking point"). Fatty Briscoe begged his Lordship's pardon, read it, turned the colour of tinned salmon, mopped his brow and continued.

DB: Mr Hardy, I take it that this conversation, which you claim to have had with Caroline Enderby, was interrupted by the arrival of the accused.

KH: Yes.

DB: Quite. How would you describe the situation between Mrs Enderby and yourself when the accused arrived?

KH: Friendly (I could see by the look on the Judge that I wasn't getting away with that). She had explained her concerns. It sounded to me like the routine insecurity of people in a love affair. I had suggested that Berry had not pressed her because of their prior agreement. His divorce had gone through, he was aware that she was in a much more difficult situation. She should not mistake his restraint for fading commitment.

DB: And during this intimate conversation, while you were sitting…how?

KH: *(Why haven't I spotted what he's up to? Is the cat about to shop me for perjury?)* Side by side on my settee.

DB: (Suppressed excitement) Side by side, with this exceptionally attractive woman and you claim that no physical contact occurred?

KH: No.

DB: You admit there was contact?

KH: Of an insignificant nature.

DB (Perspiring) Describe it.

KH: At the finish Caroline Enderby gave my hand a quick

squeeze, got up and said, Thanks Ken, I've been a silly moo, I'll tell him tonight. (Cries of "oh" and laughter in court).

DB: (Rallying bravely) That was the scene when the accused entered?

KH: No. I heard Berry coming up the stairs. I expected him to knock on my door but I heard him set off up the second flight towards his own flat thinking to find Caroline there so I went to my front door and called him back. He was carrying a pile of exercise books for marking which he said he would dump and then come back down. I returned to my kitchen. Caroline was putting on her coat and scarf.

DB: When Mr Berry joined her what form of greeting was exchanged?

KH: They kissed, and then left to go to their meeting.

DB: Mr Hardy, you have been married for over 35 years?

KH: Yes.

DB: But you and your wife are now separated?

KH: No.

DB: You sold the matrimonial home in August 1998 and since then you have lived in a flat in Ditchfield. Your wife bought a house near Malaga in Spain where she is now resident. Does that constitute living together?

McF: Objection.

Judge: Overruled. Answer the question." (*Slagdon determined to get his kicks one way or another*).

I explained that Doreen had been anxious to move out to support her widowed sister and that I was under contract to APC Plc, the purchasers of my company, until September 2000 to train their staff, meet certain guarantees and see the takeover through to completion. My living arrangements during that time were temporary. I continued...

"KH: If it has anything to do with the case, I went out to Malaga in December so that my wife and I could spend two weeks together over Christmas and New Year. I don't call that separation.

DB: Nonetheless, during the period in question you and your wife were not co-habiting. Mr Hardy, did you find Mrs Enderby attractive?

KH: What's that supposed to mean?"

McFadzean got up to object to Briscoe's line of questioning and was knocked back by the Judge.

It was obvious that I was going to get zero protection from Slagdon-Pryk. No matter what I answered, Briscoe would try to turn it into a murder motive for the accused.

"Judge: (After mutterings about obstruction) Witness will address Counsel with due respect. *(Exactly)* The Court has endured persistent obstruction. Answer the question.

KH: *(OK matey)* My Lord, Counsel is trying to imply that on his arrival, the accused, Christopher Berry was caused to suspect that something was going on between myself and Mrs Enderby. That is a contemptible proposal in support of which he has not a shred of evidence. He is trying to impute a murder motive to the accused based on nothing more than his own sniggering schoolboy innuendo." *(That's done it, Hardy – six months for contempt and six years for losing your temper).*

Uproar in court, protest from Fatty Briscoe, counter-protest from McFadzean, Gaulby QC on his feet *(shouldn't have left this one to a learner, should he?)*, roars from the Court Usher and squawks from the Judge *(what's this doing for his hangover?)*, hero register determination, crowd yell and put their backs into it. Witness was removed under guard to a cell, the jury went for a tea break, and the gallery was pacified. Judge and barristers retired to Chambers for a private punch-up over legal points arising.

It didn't take long to settle. All protagonists came back looking smug *(except one)* and the jury filed in brushing down biscuit crumbs. Judge Slagdon-Pryce lectured the gallery on their behaviour. He then delivered a severe and well-phrased rebuke to witness, reminding me of his powers, and offering a night, alternatively several years in the cells. I apologised *(my short career as an investigator was already disfigured with untruths, so why not another?)*. Briscoe sat looking fatly sullen whilst his leader rose to ask a couple of calming questions to which he got polite answers. It was terribly English – no unpleasantness – boring. McFadzean requested permission for further questions.

"McF: Did Mrs Enderby give you the impression that she was about to abandon her marriage?

KH: Yes. She said that her marriage was finished.

McF: After discussing the position with you, what did you conclude was her intention?

KH: To tell Christopher Berry that she was ready to move in immediately and live with him.

McF: Was she aware of their arrangements for that evening?

KH: She told me that they were going to Preston to attend a teachers' group discussion meeting. Afterwards they were going to call on a Mr Benson so that Berry could show him the designs for his proposed website.

McF: And the meeting with Benson was to be at the house called Fellbeck?

KH: She said it was near Coldedge, she couldn't recall the house name. As they were leaving Chris Berry confirmed that it was Fellbeck.

McF: No further questions, M'lud."

That was the end of my evidence. Judge Slagdon-Pryce lost interest in having me hung, drawn and quartered, stood me down instead and offered me a free ticket for the gallery. The court moved on to an examination of technical issues surrounding the forensic evidence. NCF had a lovely time rubbishing the conclusions of the police forensics team regarding the disappeared murder weapons, Caroline's Paisley scarf, access problems to the house, the key or keys. Unfortunately they had found no microscopic traces of blood spray. The vital evidence regarding the fire ash fell flat because the police witnesses had denied the existence of a fire at any time that evening. The jury slept sound as a 1960s nightshift.

Tom offered me a lift back. Once safely inside his motor, he was in no hurry to drive off. 'That was a bit of a shambles,' he said.

'Slagdon was letting young buggerlugs get away with questions like "do you deny that you're in denial?" He was trying to invent a murder motive out of nothing; it could have gone on all afternoon. Haven't wrecked the defence case, have I?'

Tom tried a grin with moderate success, 'by the time his Lordship comes to his summing up,' he reassured me, 'your courtroom spat will be ancient history. You might have done us a favour. Kick the table over and see what lands face up.'

'I think the Judge was on the same errand.'

Tom did not comment, he got into first gear and grunted, or perhaps the gearbox did, before steering out into the traffic. 'What was wrong with the Judge?' I asked, 'is he always like that?' Tom conceded that Slagdon had seemed a touch off-form. 'Looked like a downer to me. I once had a machine operator that came back from his lunch break just like that – sweating, flushed, irritable, pupils dilated.'

'What did you do?'

'I accused him of snorting not wisely but too well and handed him into a taxi clutching his P45 and his holiday pay.'

Tom steered round a baby which was conducting its pram dangerously on the highway. 'I believe Slagdon-Pryce suffers badly from tree pollen allergy at this time of year.'

'What about the dilated pupils?'

'Eye drops to relieve the irritation.'

I rejected the idea of a Get Well card. 'What was Briscoe up to?' I demanded. 'He was back to crime of passion; we've already shown that won't wash. I thought the prosecution's main chance was using the deleted text on Chris's PC, to claim that he'd been planning to murder her since August. How did Chris get on in the box with that?'

'We'll know by the weekend.'

Coupled with the sight of the slumped figure in the dock, that settled any doubts regarding my next action.

52

I decided to move things on with Martyn Enderby. There was no reply from the house in the evening; I got to him the following morning. 'Martyn! I've read the reports about you in court. Congratulations!'

He attempted the upper crust off-hand manner, 'Rahlly?' His acting talent was not quite up to the job – he was lapping it up – 'were you thah?'

I decided that it was a waste of time concealing my involvement with the defence. He was certain to find out so I told him, 'No, until I was called I was stuck in the witness room.'

'Oh Kin, what a bore.'

I was able to agree, 'I don't see what help they expected from me. I was wanted as a character witness because his flat happens to be above mine, but we weren't close.'

He confirmed that he had not witnessed my appearance, 'but I did have a spy.' That was exactly what I'd been afraid of. Enderby rattled on, 'She phoned me yesterday evening, said you were "brilliant". Said you appeared for the defence and sank Berry without trace! "The perfect double agent", she called you.' *(She must be nuts!)*

I took a deep breath, and said I hoped it boded well for Walpurgisnacht.

'Absolutely! I hear the prosecution are looking to have their verdict in at the weekend.'

'Or at least, it'll be a foregone conclusion by then.'

'Either way, our Walpurga's Eve vigil is going to be a real party!'

'Martyn, I want to drive forward with the matter we discussed. How did things work out with Sir Ed'ard?'

'Splindid! Super lunch! I *think* he's on board.'

'He's not,' said the tenner in my back pocket. Sir Edward had downloaded his free lunch and kept his chequebook safely hutched.

'Good. This is how things stand with me: I'm planning a cheque for 25k, now. I'll be in funds for the balance of £75,000 by the second week of September when the contract on my company sale goes to completion; Scott McIver can confirm.'

'Kin, this is really excellent nee-yus, thank you *so* much.'

'I'll post it today, *(Second class stamp, Hardy)* but a word of warning: I'll need to post-date by a couple of weeks to give time for investments to clear.'

Martyn was up to speed with the habits of the rich: big house, big investments, big debts, no cash, 'Of course, of course – *no problem.*'

'No reason,' I said, 'why you shouldn't include me on your list of donors? I mean straightaway, *pour encourager les autres.*' That went down pretty well, I thought, even in my industrial French. I assumed a tentative note, 'Martyn, about Walpurgis Night, next Sunday 30th isn't it? It sounds absolutely inspiring (pause)... I suppose, there's no chance...?'

Enderby was there like a shot: spiritual, sensitive, but firm, 'Ken, *desolée*. This time, it has to be "The Inner Circle"'. In other words, I thought, the gang of three. 'It really wouldn't be safe for anyone who isn't a fully qualified adept. But for next time, November, *(he must mean Halloween)*, we'll have you up to speed.'

I was brave about it, 'I do understand Martyn, but I thought there was no harm...' He was anxious to reassure me – no harm at all. I brightened up, 'I'll be with you in spirit, I thought a candle – if that's appropriate?'

He thought that sounded "brilliant". 'We arrive at the sacred spot at 11.30 and light candles. So make it 11.30 pm Sunday eve, the ceremony proper begins at midnight.'

'Finishes when? I'm thinking candle size here.'

'Cock crow. I don't know exactly what secular time that is. Join us in spirit, you'll be one of a multitude, world-wide.' *(Multitude of one, Hardy?)*. I couldn't take more of this crap. I promised to join the multitude on Walpurga's Eve and rang off. That was a date: Enderby, Benson and Mrs Watts. I wondered whether little fat Sam would be one of them. Furious breath or not, I hoped not: I didn't want to see Sam sent down for life.

I mentioned my scheme to Ethel. She was alarmed, 'I don't like the sound of this. Promise you'll be careful, you won't be on your own will you?'

'I'll need someone else as a witness.'

'I was talking about protection.'

'Protection? Come on Ethel, it's not a citizen's arrest; I'm after evidence.'

'There could be more of them and even if there are only three, they've already committed one murder at Fellbeck. Once possessed, there's no knowing what a demoniac can do.'

'That's why I have to be there.'

I phoned the Army Staff College outside Swindon. The switchboard found the Mess Secretary for me, who undertook to pass my message to Major Wilson. I got a return call at 12.30, 'Mike Wilson,' it said, 'what can I do for you?'

'It's about the murder of Caroline, your sister.'

Wilson's tone hardened, 'Yes. The trial's on at the moment.'

'They're in danger of convicting the wrong man. I've been investigating on behalf of the the defence. There's new evidence, but I need to explain. Could we meet this evening?' Wilson agreed; we met at the Flying Duck outside Swindon.

Even in casual civvies, Wilson cut an impressive figure, he was well over six foot and muscular. He was a good listener

– I explained the problem well under the hour. After that I moved on to my proposed plan of action. We had another pint of southern bitter. Clearly he liked it – the plan, not the beer of course. 'I'm due a weekend 48.'

'The event we want to witness kicks off at 2330 on Sunday . It finishes officially at cock crow on Monday morning.'

'Shit!' said the Major, then, 'no, wait, Monday's a bank holiday, a study day, nothing happening because the civilians have the day off.'

'In my day it was only the Norwegians that stood down for weekends and holidays.'

'Peacetime army,' said Mike, 'but if the French make a move, we have plenty of keen lads on standby.'

I gave him my address. 'See you about 1930 on Saturday,' I said, 'don't stop to eat on the way. Early start on Sunday morning.'

'By the way, when did you last see Caroline?'

'I stayed with her for a few days last August. I fitted it in between Sierra Leone and my posting to the Staff College.'

'Was Martyn there?'

'If Enderby had been there I wouldn't have been.'

'Why haven't the defence called you as a witness?'

'Because of my circumstances. They said that a sworn statement giving the dates of my visit would suffice.' *(That's how Briggs knew).*

★

First thing on Saturday morning, Jason came to me like a fluttered bird. I couldn't determine what sort of bird he was like but he was fluttered all right. I sat him down and gave him a mug of tea. 'It's Mrs Potts,' he said and pulled out a sheet of paper on which he'd drawn a family tree, 'her great grandfather was called Charles Benson.' The signet-ring used for sealing the

Benson envelopes: "CB" stands for Charles Benson, not Chris Berry.

'Does Niall know you've been doing this?' He said 'no'. I told Jason what a clever lad he was and asked him to lay off Virginia's genealogy until the case was put to bed.

'I've developed a taste for digging around in old documents,' he confided, 'I've rather gone off the idea of a career in the law: they all seem to be crooks, don't they? I'm thinking of switching to history.'

The master detective was not enthusiastic when I floated my scheme for Sunday night.. 'I'm not right suited with this, Ken. Get it wrong and our man's down for a twenty…'

'Never mind twenty, our man won't last a year in Strangeways.' I made an offer, 'I'll phone you on Sunday morning, say 10 o'clock. If the job's on it'll give you twelve hours to make your arrangements and get the right side of the border.' That was not enough, Reginald demanded that I whisper in his lughole the real identities of "Benson" and "Mrs Watts". Hairy experience though it was, I complied.'

'Bloody Norah,' said Briggs, 'you'd better be right.'

We went into court for the conclusion of the defence evidence. It lasted into Saturday afternoon. The closing speeches and the Judge's summing up remained. It was clear that we weren't going to get a verdict just yet.

At 3.25 pm, Sir Arnold Gaulby QC rose for the prosecution whilst in the gallery K Hardy settled down to be disgusted. I did not expect Sir Arnold to present a balanced account of the case, not his job. He did not disappoint.

He opened with a *tour d'horizon* of selected bits of evidence, followed by a detailed analysis ignoring all inconvenient facts. Having dismantled the defence case to his own complete satisfaction, he turned on the *hwyl* during which passage we heard at length about the innocence and beauty of the victim torn away from her devoted and heartbroken husband in the flowering of their life together (*not much of which was true*) by the wicked and bestial seducer (*and none of that was*). By 16.30 he was sobbing out his peroration pinched from Marshall Hall and much favoured by mountebanks ever since, 'Ladies and gentlemen of the jury in the name of justice I do not beg, I do not request, I *demand* from you the only possible verdict. *GUILTY!!!'*

Dramatically, Gaulby gathered his gown about him and sat to a great silence. A routine idiot in the gallery clapped, then another and another. Then the shouts started 'yeah!' The shouts merged to a roar. A crowd of student-age persons at the front of the gallery stood up and started whooping and screaming like a reality TV audience. The air was getting a hard time from small fists. I recognised several from the Ditchfield Sceptics event. A chant began of 'guilty (clap, clap, clap), guilty (clap, clap, clap), and was taken up by others in the gallery, guilty (clap, clap, clap), *GUILTY*!'. With the crowd in front on its feet in front of me I could not see Chris's face. I didn't want to.

Roars of 'silence in court' arrived too late and with nil result until after a minute or two the noise began to subside through exhaustion. Seeing that danger was past, half a dozen uniformed PCs entered dauntlessly and took up ambiguous positions making it uncertain whether the intention was to defend the judge or arrest the jury. Eventually, the gallery sat down.

Judge Slagdon-Pryce read the riot act. He was disgusted by this unwarranted and disgraceful outburst the like of which he had rarely heard in an English court of law. For a disgusted judge, he looked quite pleased. I gathered that Slagdon was well-cogniscent of the TV convention that reality judges plump for the popular choice regardless of merit. In the circumstances, he said, the court would rise now and resume on Monday 1st May at 10 am no matter that this was the Bank Holiday, (*so there!*). Slagdon-Pryce then drew stumps and buggered off.

'What chance of a "not guilty" now?' I asked Briggsie. He

374

did not respond. There was a crowd outside the court building, nasty-looking and growing. In an early kick-off, Ditchfield United had lost again at home. Their supporters felt that they were due a public hanging in lieu of three points for a win. 'I'll phone you at 10 on Sunday morning,' I said. He nodded.

At the flat, I switched on the evening news and taped the local stuff. It was as bad as I had expected. The film clip began with press photographers running alongside the prison van trying to take flash photographs through the blacked-out windows. Meantime the BBC film crew went through their own stupid routine of filming the press photographers being stupid. Once the van was out in the street, the crowd surged forward to hammer on the sides: 'guilty, guilty, guilty', (bang, bang, bang). It seemed there was as much chance of an acquital as of Ditchfield remaining in the Premiership. Wilson would be interested, I thought. I started fixing supper for two.

53

On Sunday morning, Major Wilson was up with coffee on the go by the time I appeared. I suggested we take his car, which would not be recognised. By 7.30 we were parked by the New Preston Road. From the bridge, I pointed out where Jason had found the bogus knife. We crossed the road; Mike vaulted the gate and waited politely while I climbed over. We walked across the field to the yard gate. The sun was climbing above the eastern ridge; a bright morning, too bright to last, Fellbeck looked as grim as ever.

I was sure that the house was empty but Wilson volunteered to carry out a quick recce as far as the front of the house. He set off like an Impi scout, bending low behind the stone wall and was back in half a minute, 'nothing doing.' I removed my padlock from the back door and pocketed it. We stood for a moment – silence.

''This is the scullery,' I said, trying not to whisper, 'it connects to the main kitchen area, and this door here opens on the main corridor leading to the front door. If you hear loud thumps, six or eight of them, that seem to be progressing up the passage, don't be alarmed: it's only the resident spirit.'

The sitting room door was standing half-open.

'Is this it?' Mike walked two paces into the murder room and stopped. I stayed by the door. 'Perhaps you'd like a couple of minutes to yourself,' I said, 'I'll keep an eye on things; make sure we're not disturbed.' I closed the door and went to keep watch at the front.

I gave him time and then returned. He was standing

looking at the wall above the fireplace. 'That's where old Ezra Dawson's picture used to hang,' I said. I pointed out the carved fireplace bosses, 'I took a photo of them and gave a copy to a friend of mine. He showed it to his parish priest and nearly got excommunicated. The carving stands for "666", the mark of the beast.'

'Is this how the room was?'

'No, they've moved things around – setting up for tonight.' The fireplace had been reset with fresh kindling and logs for a fire. In front of the hearth one of Enderby's bronze candlesticks was standing. Alongside lay a knife. It was twice the weight and far more wicked-looking than the blade Jason had rescued from the beck. It was also sharp. Wilson picked up the weapon and said something I didn't catch.

On the boards in front of the fireplace, a black cloth about six feet by four was nailed down where the hearthrug had been. The fireside chairs had been moved away to the side walls. The settee now stood across the far corner of the room. 'They've cleared the main space for action,' I said, 'and this is new.' The wall facing the beck was hung ceiling to floor in red cloth.

Mike was gazing at a crude oil painting about six feet by eight. The canvas was pinned to the red backcloth in front of the middle window. 'The Goat of Mendes', he said, 'I've met him before.'

Thinking of Mike's last posting, I imagined a witch doctor's hut in a jungle village and suggested, 'In Sierra Leone?'

'No, Croatia. It's the western Satanist image: the horned goat with a straggling beard and eyes of fire. African images are different.'

So that was what Enderby's spiritual claptrap amounted to – medieval devil worship and murder? 'They're pretty confident,' Mike said, 'leaving all this evidence lying about.'

'Confident that Chris is going down tomorrow or the day after? Hopefully it'll make them careless. Now, have a look at this,' I said and led him into the adjoining room, 'it's hard to tell what this room was intended for.'

'What about church council meetings?' Mike suggested, 'didn't you say Ezra was a church elder?'

'Also a councillor and a magistrate who hated his eldest son and most likely murdered his sick wife.' I showed him the way out through the kitchens to the back door. 'The advantage for us is that you don't have to go out into the main passage. We can lock the scullery door and then, if we do have to leg it, we lock both these doors behind us and we're clear.'

'Sensible tactics,' Mike said, 'but I'm not thinking in terms of retreat.'

We went back to the murder room for a last look. We drew the curtains to let the light in and I took a dozen photographs. 'There's no power in this place. I reckon the action is going to be between the fireplace and the painting opposite with the rest of the room quite dark. Firelight, candles, oil lamps, that's the ambience they want. You don't summon up the devil with arc lights.'

'That means we can watch from the shadows,' said the soldier, 'where's our observation post going to be?' We checked out some possible sight lines. As we left Fellbeck the morning brightness had clouded over and it was starting to rain. 'Welcome to a wet Sunday in North East Lancs,' I said.

When we got back to the flat, Mike set about making breakfast whilst I phoned Reginald. 'It's happening alright, they've left the murder room set up for a Witches' Sabbath.' Reginald was still doubtful until we had talked through the implications. 'I'll be there with Kath for seven. Meantime I'll put together some surveillance bits and bats,' he promised and rang off.

'Can you think of anything else we could do between now and this evening? We could write a risk assessment.'

Mike had a better idea, 'We should write a plan of action.'

I gave him a pen and several sheets of paper. 'What is our objective?'

'To collect sufficient evidence to get the trial stopped and bring murder charges against the enemy.'

'What are the enemy intentions?'

'Hang on,' I got up and made a short telephone call. 'We're going to bum a coffee off the fair Aethelflaed, I'll explain on the way.'

'Since you're concerned about my health and safety, I decided to call in the army,' I told Ethel, 'this is Major Mike Wilson, Royal Engineers and Caroline's brother.' The officer bowed over her hand. 'Will he do?'

She threatened to drop bowlegged, 'Can I keep him?'

I restored order, 'We're here for a technical consultation, Ms Deedes,' I said sternly, 'Forget the courts of love, the clock's ticking in the courts of law.'

My consultant rallied, 'Emmeline's got a brew on the go.'

I did a recap of what we had found at Fellbeck and our objectives for that night's operation. 'What's your take on the enemy intentions? They've gone to some trouble to set the stage up. It seems reckless to leave all that evidence lying around. What are they up to?'

'They're in the grip of a possession,' Ethel said. 'They may imagine that the site is protected by a force field to keep out intruders.'

'It didn't keep us out.'

'Given the date – Walpurgis eve – and the location plus the fact that it's on the exact spot of Caroline's murder, I agree they're planning a Witches' Sabbath. I would expect them to re-enact the murder.'

'What actually goes on at these Witches' Sabbaths?' I asked.

'Impossible to say,' said Ethel, 'satanism isn't a formal religion, you can expect candles, stinks, noises, chanting, dancing possibly naked and all working up to some sort of frenzy that might well be sexual.'

'Enderby said it was going to be a real party.'

'If that's Martyn's idea of a party they're probably hoping to induce materialisation of the devil – routine demoniac behaviour.'

'Demoniac?' Mike wanted to know.

'A person possessed by a demon. The witch makes a pact with Satan to cause the demon to enter and take over a person or persons. The witch possesses the coven so they become demoniacs. In that state they'll probably believe that the devil has materialised before their eyes.'

'Supposing we get evidence against them,' asked Mike, 'does that alter the legal situation? I mean murder is still murder isn't it?'

'Until the end of the 17th century,' said Ethel, 'demoniacs would claim not to remember anything about their actions, so were not charged with any crime. The witch carried the can for colluding with the devil.'

'But not any longer?'

Ethel laughed, 'The law can be pretty daft but I don't expect it to be as daft as that. Ken, who are you expecting for this party?'

'Enderby, the main man, I think he was the killer behind the door, Benson, who lured them to Fellbeck and Mrs Watts who was responsible for taking Caroline into the sitting room.'

'Who are Watts and Benson, do you think?'

'Virginia and probably, Niall Potts. Benson is the one I'm least sure of. I'm not convinced Niall could do the voice.

'Voice isn't a problem,' said Ethel, 'when demoniacs are in a state of possession the voice can change and sometimes their appearance as well.'

'*Dr Jekyll and Mr Hyde?*' Mike suggested.

'That's exactly right,' said Ethel, 'Stevenson knew what

he was writing about – change of voice and appearance. What about Mrs Watts?'

You've seen Virginia. I'm sure she persuaded Enderby that Fellbeck has a spirit presence making it suitable for his spiritual terrorism training centre. In January, she tried to convince me that the place is haunted. Later, at the end of a long phone call, I asked what she thought was behind Caroline's murder and she said "Spirit Possession". Then she tried to cover up by saying that could be anyone who had been exposed to Fellbeck. *(Like me! Thanks Ethel!)* It's the only real clue I picked up from the murder gang. My betting's on her: Mrs Watts, resident witch.'

Ethel corrected me, 'that's Adam and Eve stuff, "not my fault vicar, the wicked woman seduced me". As a matter of fact, most of the possession cases, in France especially, were pinned on male witches. Whole convents full of nuns possessed by renegade priests in league with Satan.' She stopped, 'just a moment…' and shot off.

'I'm finding this difficult to accept,' said Mike.

Ethel was back, triumphant, 'found it first time,' she said, 'Morzine, a small town in the Savoy region of France; the last recorded instance of a mass possession in Europe happened there in 1850. I'll bet Pascal's real family name was Threnadie, later he added "de Morzine" to impress the Engleesh.'

'If he was looking for an upgrade, why pick on a dead and alive hole in the back of beyond?'

'Because he was banking on no one having been there,' said Mike.

On the drive back Wilson went quiet then said, 'Never underestimate the power of surprise. Why not arrange a shock tactic in reserve?'

'Such as?'

'I've got an idea,' Mike said, 'have you got any cardboard, fairly strong but not too thick?'

'Anything else?'

'Paint: not much, mainly black and some white and red as well, if possible, and a thin brush.'

'It's Easter Sunday, but I know a place.' I left the Major at the flat with cardboard, scotch tape and scissors and drove to the maintenance department at the works. 'I've got what you wanted from the factory,' I said on my return, 'unlike HM Armed Forces we work 24/7 except Christmas; we can't risk the nation running short of polythene bags... Santa supplies his own.'

We left the paint to dry and took a late, large and (almost) alcohol-free lunch at the Duke. The landlord was scandalised.

★

Over coffee, 'I don't like to drag things up that you'd rather let lie, but last time you saw her, did Caroline tell you about Chris Berry?'

'No. Her love life was always off the agenda. Look, if the trial goes the wrong way there'll be a second chance at appeal?'

'As far as I know but it's got to be pretty blatant to have a chance. I don't want Chris let out on appeal. Mud sticks, I want Enderby and friends locked up for murder. My problem all along has been to see Martyn as a killer.'

'Unless he's mad? Or as Ethel would put it: a demoniac.'

'Meaning he's mad when he's under the influence, otherwise more or less normal. Tonight's my last chance. If this doesn't work, Chris is on his way to a life sentence.'

'We'll do our damnedest,' Wilson promised, 'don't forget I've got an even stronger motive than you.'

When we got back to the flat Mike said, 'the paint should be dry by now, let's give it a try.' He reappeared a few minutes later wearing black overalls buttoned up to the throat. 'The army issues these for night operations. Stay here until I call out then come through to the kitchen and close the door.'

I did that. The kitchen was dark and seemed to be empty until I heard a hollow groan from the far corner and a light flickered on a grotesque face.

'What do you think?' asked the devil.

'I don't know whether it'll worry them but it scares me.'

'Timing,' Mike said, 'if they've worked themselves up into a frenzy they'll believe anything – for thirty seconds – hit them hard and fast before the shock wears off.'

54

Mike drew up in the back yard of Fellbeck at seven that evening. 'They won't come round the back,' I said, 'they know they can't get in because the padlock's been changed.' I unlocked and pocketed the padlock. Five minutes later Briggs turned up with Kath and parked alongside. I introduced Major Wilson to the other two. Kath opened the boot and dragged out a black canvas holdall.

We walked through to the murder room. 'Remember to leave the door half open,' I said, 'that's how we found it.' Mike suggested the gang left it that way for Satan.

'The devil won't come down the chimney, any road,' Briggs said, 'get his bum toasted.' That summed up Reginald's level of spirituality.

Kath unpacked two tape recorders, a camcorder, a couple of cameras with flash attachments and four powerful-looking torches. 'Shine these straight in their faces and they won't be able to see a thing,' Briggs said.

The master detective surveyed the available sight lines, 'not ideal,' he pronounced, 'but we'll make a do.' We agreed on Kath's post behind the settee in the corner with one tape recorder and a camera. She also had the camcorder; 'You'll likely not get to use it,' said her uncle 'not enough light.'

Kath taped the other recorder to the massive cast iron radiator behind the devil painting. 'The tape machines are practically silent in recording mode,' Briggs said, 'they've got new batteries and enough tape for four hours. Kath will set them both running as soon as we see the suspects arriving.'

There was one more item in Kath's bag of tricks. 'It's a portable strobe light,' she explained, 'guaranteed to cause maximum disorientation, it flattens the battery in two minutes, so it's only to be used once.' She demonstrated.

'Where's the command post?' Mike Wilson asked.

'Behind the dining room door,' Briggs said. 'We'll crack it open an inch to begin with. If one of them doesn't close it before they begin then they haven't noticed so we can risk inching it open a bit more when they get busy. It gives us a view of the fireplace area where Ken expects most of the action.'

'And the word of command to move in and apprehend the murderers?' asked Mike.

'Ken will do that, this is his party. Ken will pick his moment then shout "go, go, go", and we get in there sharp... approach the suspects...'

'Yelling like banshees,' Mike said.

... 'and invite them to line up in front of the fireplace where we can see them. I'll have the second camera and we'll get a few flash photographs off. So what with the surprise, the shouting, the torches and the flashes going off they'll be pretty confused.' Briggsie made it sound like routine, which to him, I guessed it was. I was beginning to feel a bit liquid in the bread basket area.

'Now,' said Briggs, you and me, Ken will man the command post and observe as best we can. Major Wilson, will you start with us until they're all in the sitting room and ready to kick off? When we're reasonably sure that the action is taking place in there, go and stand by in the passage outside the murder room door. I'll leave it to you to judge.'

Mike explained his surprise package, 'it's all about timing, they have to be well worked up before we spring it.'

'Right,' said Briggsie, 'a practice run. How easy is that window to open from the outside – the one behind the painting?'

Mike did two tests, 'That isn't going to work,' he said,

'it's impossible to open silently. If they hear me it'll wreck everything.'

'Could we have the window open in advance?' asked Kath.

We tried that but the breeze was stirring the hangings. Mike said, 'Satan will have to come in through the door like a gentleman.'

'Just a few notes by way of briefing,' Briggs said, 'these Satanist parties generally turn into orgies. With a bit of luck this'll get wild enough for Ken to get his evidence. Keep your ears open because we'll need witness statements. We can't just rely on the recorders because they're difficult to interpret in a noisy situation.'

'Have you met Satanists in Halifax, Reginald?'

'Certainly,' Briggs said, 'one right nasty coven took to kidnapping dogs and cats and tearing them limb from limb. Keep calm and think on: no losing your rag – whatever.'

By 10.30 it was dark in the valley bottom. Kath went to stand by the front window where she could see the headlights approaching. We stopped talking and waited. The house started running its ancient building repertoire of creaks, groans and squeals as the temperature dropped. At times the sounds seemed to join up and organise. It was easy to imagine distant voices too faint to catch what was said. I found myself listening for fleeing footsteps and the terrified scream of a victim. It was an evil place.

I shook myself... *(shut up you, frightening yourself with shapes like a kid)*. It was twenty past eleven; I tried to breathe slow and shallow. I checked my pulse – over 80. My watch crawled to 11.25. Enderby's sussed, they're not coming, he's been tipped off by a spirit entity. My bladder started talking. I told Reginald, 'I'm off out the back for a pee, two minutes maximum,' and went. Job done, I stepped back into the scullery where the door opening onto the main passage was ajar, I heard someone close the front door and turn a key. (The one supplied by Hindley?). Voices – they had beaten me to it.

I walked the kitchens route from the scullery to our command post. Reg was standing with his eye to the crack; I touched him on the shoulder. 'They're round the fireplace,' he said from behind his hand, 'lighting the fire. They've got a lantern each, old-fashioned sort with a candle inside, that suits us.' Shortly, the fire was burning up and adding a flickering light to the gloom, 'they've split up now, each carrying a bundle. One of the men, I reckon Enderby, has gone to the chair at the far side. I can't see the others; I think the woman is at the settee and the other man must be at the chair on this side. What's Enderby doing? Bloody hell, he's stripping off – promising is this.'

When the coven collected again in front of the fire, Mike went to take post outside the murder room door. Reginald bent down enough to allow me to see over the top of his head. Whilst enjoying the aroma of Halifax hair-oil it was convenient for whispering in his ear. All three seemed to be wearing dominoes and nothing else. That meant big ankle length cloaks, tied at the throat and black highwayman masks. Enderby's cloak was red, the second man's black, Mrs Watts was a slim figure in green. Another girl in green – another victim? She appeared relaxed about it – perhaps she hadn't cottoned on. The men's feet in short socks and modern shoes looked odd below the sweeping fancy dress cloaks.

They had set the three candle lanterns in a row on the mantel. These cast a dim light on the black cloth on the floor and just a few feet beyond. The door behind which Briggs and I lurked was practically in darkness. The men formed up behind Mrs Watts; all three carried one red and one green candle in simple double branched candlesticks. They faced the devil painting hanging on the curtain opposite.

I thought they were about to light the candles but instead the coven set up a rhythmic chant: *kyoh-riinghi-m'yoho-nam*. Mrs Watts stood in the centre while the two men circled her slowly. 'They're warming up,' said Briggs, 'she's putting the spell on them.' Suddenly the circling stopped in a wild yell. 'That's it,' Briggs whispered, 'now they'll get down to business.'

The coven formed a line facing half right: Mrs Watts leading, Enderby at the rear. Then, resuming their meaningless chant they began pacing slowly forward.

'Bloody hell! They're coming this way,' I told Briggs.

'No panic, move slowly into the far corners, backs turned and then as soon as they come through the door, freeze'. They were approaching deliberately, one pace for each repeat of the chant and with Mrs Watts stepping short in front we had time to get to the far end of the dining room.

'What if we're seen?' I whispered, trying to sound calm.

'Yell "go!"', said Briggs, 'switch your torch on, grab Enderby, we'll drag them back to the fireplace.' We stood there in the dark. I heard Mrs Watts' hand on the door handle and froze. She didn't seem to realise that the door was already open a crack. The chant went on and on, dreary, meaningless. Then it stopped – silence. I thought, 'sod it they've seen us,' my heart rate went up ten notches and sweat trickled down my back.

Nothing, it seemed for ever, then a sharp scraping sound, repeated, followed by the flare of a match. That explained the blobs of red and green candle wax that I'd found behind the door. They'd come into this room to light the candles. Why? I couldn't guess. The whole plan would be wrecked in moments. Once they had the candles lit…one of the three was forced to spot us… We'd never get to the truth… tomorrow, the prison van to Strangeways… my friend on his way to a living hell.

The chant started up again…faded… they were going. We moved back to the door. It had been left a foot open. Never mind scaring me shitless, they'd improved our field of view. We now had a sight line to the area forward of the painting. 'Can't think how they missed seeing us,' I whispered.

'I can,' said Briggs, 'they were holding the candles at eye level. If you do that you can't see past the flame.'

The coven had lined up before the goat, still chanting. Enderby was in the centre now, the chant stopped. Then it started up with a new theme: *amen, ever and ever for, glory the and power the...*

'Lord's prayer backwards,' I said.

'They chant everything backwards, the first chant was Buddhist.' This was not the first satanist party that Briggs had gate-crashed. They repeated their mantra three times and fell silent. Benson and Watts, on the wings, knelt and held up their candlesticks, Enderby stood standing. Then he spoke, loud and clear, in his own voice, unmistakeable – perhaps Satan was ex-Eton.

'Lord of all, master of the Universe, master of the True Path, master of the Left Hand Way, your servants come to worship and sacrifice (*sacrifice?*). Reveal yourself to your humble disciples, apostles, acolytes and adepts. Guide and command us we implore you.'

They went through the whole routine twice more then stood their candlesticks side by side in front of the painting. Enderby produced a thick black candle from a pocket inside his cloak, lit it and set it on the floor centrally in front of the candlesticks. A new chant started up, louder and more insistent than before. It was hypnotic; I could make no sense of the words. Briggs could, 'it's Latin,' he whispered, 'it's the Catholic ritual for the exorcism of an evil spirit. They're trying to do the opposite; they're trying to summon the evil spirit, so they chant the words in reverse order.' It had seemed almost comic at first; now it began to generate a feeling of contempt.

I concentrated on the voices. Enderby was taking the solo parts acting as the priest – no mistaking his voice; the other two did the responses. Mrs Watts was quite high pitched the man's voice had a grating quality. Benson!

The aroma from Enderby's black candle began to drift towards us: human excrement, rotting flesh and burning rubber combined was the best description I could manage. I hadn't experienced a stink to rival it since the Blitz when a blazing Junkers 88 crashed on the sewage works up our road. It was hard to breathe without retching. I picked up my heavy mallet. The chant died. 'It could put the mockers on the party if they do all this and bugger-all materialises. Suppose I wait until they start up again and then nip upstairs on the quiet and see if I can liven things up with this?'

'Can't do any harm,' Briggs agreed, 'take care.'

I went out into the corridor and walked towards the murder room door. There was no risk of being heard because the Satanists were giving it plenty inside. Nor would they see me passing the half open door because they were facing the goat painting. I tapped Mike on the shoulder and whispered to tell him what I was up to. 'What if they come out to see where the sound is coming from?' he asked. He had a point; I was for chancing it.

'If the devil is going to materialise they'll expect him to come out of the painting, that's why they're facing that way. Why not get your mask on so if they do make a move for the door you can confront them.'

Enderby's party was hotting up to performance level, *'Interitum sempiterum in perdat at mactet furetur destinatas coronam gloriae aeternae ad animasque...'* I edged my up the wooden staircase sticking close to the wall; even so, every other step let out a creaking protest as my weight went on it. The chanting from below was gibberish but as I worked my way upstairs it seemed to grow louder, closing round me so I grew progressively more uneasy. I tried to throw off the hypnotic effect by gripping the handle of my mallet. My intention was to walk along the first floor corridor to the far end then walk back, giving the floor six or eight solid thumps with the mallet as I came. The voices grew louder and louder. My legs were trembling; I broke into a sweat. I was forced to crouch and lean on the wall. I was losing it.

The chanting stopped. Silence.

Now! Don't keep them waiting, only two or three steps to go. I crept as far as the top step, raised my head to look along the corridor, and froze. At the far end of the passage was a figure. It stood at the window, looking out over the yard. Light streamed in turning the figure into a silhouette. Was real moonlight ever that bright? It was a man; I could make him out clearly. He wore a black frock coat, breeches with gaiters down to his boots and a low-crowned black bowler. I didn't need to see his face – I didn't want to. I was terrified that he would turn round and meet me face to face. I knew him. It was Ezra Dawson. Ezra Dawson – builder of Fellbeck, wife murderer, destroyer of lives, died February 1891, rotting in Coldedge graveyard and standing at the end of the passage.

The urge to run back down the stairs was almost irresistible. *(It's not real, stand still.)* I reached for the banister rail. Suddenly a roaring sound started in the distance steadily getting louder. It was the sound that Chris had heard when Caroline was murdered. He had taken it for low flying RAF Tornado jets but it wasn't. It was a tornado of another sort and it was coming fast up the valley – on a cool breezy night in May?

It wasn't a twister, either. It was something evil – Satan, attended by his host, flying on his hellish business. The boards shook, I could feel them vibrating. The Ezra thing was still standing at the window, unmoving, staring out, staring at what? Suddenly, silence – nothing. The window was black, the passage was black. Silence. Was Ezra still there? Then I heard the slow march to hell that I'd intended to imitate with my puny hammer. Nearer and nearer, louder and louder, like the stamp of heavy hobnailed boots, farmer's boots on the bare boards three... four... five... funeral march bearing a corpse six... seven ... eight ... to where I hung on, cowering, clinging to the banister ... It stopped. Was it standing in front of me? Suddenly a woman's voice – a shriek of terror – something soft touched my face as if I had been brushed by the wing of a giant night-flying moth. Silence. Pitch black darkness. Nothing.

Shaking so I could hardly support myself against the banister, I fumbled my way down the stairs. *(Don't rush, don't miss the step, don't look behind. There's nothing there).* I reached the foot of the stairs and stepped into the hall letting go of the handrail and instantly losing my balance, staggering, almost falling until I touched the wall and began to re-orientate. I stood there to recover, afraid that the murder gang had heard me stumbling in the hall, afraid to use my torch in case the light was seen through the gap where the soldier stood at the door. I found the wood panelled wall of the passage and worked my way along.

If the Satanists inside had heard me it would have only increased their frenzy. The noise in the murder room was louder than before: not an ordered Latin chant but a confusion of screams and shouts. I took a chance and slipped past the door. I could hear their feet pounding the boards it sounded as though they were doing a manic dance. As I arrived, Mike whispered, 'Brilliant Ken, that's stirred them up.'

The shouting began to organise into a new chant; in plain English now: 'bitch, bitch, bitch … whore, whore, whore … kill, kill, kill, … blood, blood, blood.' I walked on down the passage and in through the dining room door. Dimly, I could make out the reassuring shape of Briggs standing at our command post; I was myself again. Reginald had moved to the other side of the doorway to get a sight line to the fireplace area. I crossed the room to his side, came up the outside wall and touched him on the shoulder. He didn't react or turn his head, 'Now then,' he said.

The murderers were back in a tight screaming group on the black cloth in front of the fire. They fell silent, standing in line to face the painting. Enderby, in the middle turned and raised both arms to address the Goat of Mendes. 'Welcome, welcome amongst us, Lord and master. Accept now our sacrifice, accept the destruction of the profane, accept the slaughter of the whore, accept our sacrifice. We consecrate this house, this place in your name. We dedicate ourselves and all who come here seeking enlightenment to your holy and invincible purpose.' That made everything plain enough. All three sank to their knees and chanted the Lord's Prayer three times backwards.

'They really think they're in the presence of Satan,' I said, 'he's invisible but they think he's there.' The coven rose. Enderby picked up something that flashed dully in the firelight, held it up high and then dropped it, clattering, on the hearth. It was the knife. All three shouted together, 'thus, *thus*, *THUS*!' The group broke up. Enderby went to the chair where he had left his clothes. The others went to their robing stations disappearing from our view. In the dim light we could make out that Enderby was fumbling for something underneath his pile of clothes, which he then drew onto his head. He swung the red cloak around his shoulders and walked back to the fireplace chanting slowly enough for me to pick out the words: *saecula in eum superexaltate et laudate Domino opera omnia...* As he returned to the arc of firelight, I could see what was on his head: it was the goat's head devil mask that I'd tried on in his study. The cloak fell open. Underneath he was naked.

'Look at that,' I whispered to Briggs, 'how's that for an erection?'

Reginald put me right, 'Is it buggery,' he said, 'it's a strap-on dildo. There's a sex shop keeps them in Halifax.'

The other two had joined their leader on the black cloth. Benson in his grey wig and highwayman mask was naked beneath his domino. Mrs Watts, standing between the two men was wearing her green hooded cloak and mask as before. The chanting started again, grew louder and faster and became unintelligible. Benson reached forward, pulled the cloak from Watts' shoulders leaving her naked apart from a scarf knotted loosely round her neck. None too gently, he forced her down on the black cloth and held her shoulders down on the floor.

'*Interitum sempiterum in perdat at mactet furetur destinatas coronam gloriae aeternae ad animasque…*'

I whispered in Reginald's ear, 'Mike's in the wrong place, I'm going to swap with him.'

Briggs agreed, 'Quick sharp.'

I moved fast to Mike's station. 'Change of plan,' I told him, 'they're at this end. I'll take over here. Do your devil entrance through the command post door; try to time it so you're in front of the painting before they spot you. I've briefed Reg.'

'*Interitum sempiterum in perdat at mactet furetur destinatas coronam gloriae aeternae ad animasque…*'

The chanting ran on for a couple of minutes and stopped. I took a risk, put my back against the door and inched it further open so I could just make out the group in front of the fire. Enderby was crouching between Mrs Watts' legs with the ridiculous dildo lying on her stomach. He reached down, made an adjustment, perhaps he entered her, I couldn't tell. He started to plunge forward and back. Watts began to moan and then to shriek and writhe as if she was having an orgasm. Benson held her down, reached to grab the knife from the hearth, held it high in the firelight, pushed her head over to face the fire, then with a grating moan of '*the knife*, the *knife*, the *knife*!' drew it across the throat of Mrs Watts, threw the slaughter knife back down on the hearth, rocked back on his heels and stood. His "victim" lay at his feet.

Then all three were in line, on their knees, naked and triumphant, backs to the fire facing the goat. Mrs Watts took the scarf from her neck and held it high. Enderby began a high pitched rant, 'Master, accept, we pray our sacrifice of the whore, bless and consecrate this place to your cause, in token of which we commit to the flames, the blood of the *Bitch*!' All three crouched kneeling, foreheads on the floor. All three joined the chant, 'Master! Master! Master!' Again and again. At last, in front of the painting, Satan materialised.

Horrific, outlined in intense blue light, horns, white eyes, red mouth, bared teeth, the devil figure glared at them. The light behind him pulsed slowly on and off causing Satan to disappear, only to reappear, this time with arms partly raised. On and on, in a menacing sequence, the arms rose higher, clawed fingers extended, threatening. A step towards them and another; were they about to be rent in pieces?

Triumph turned to abject terror; hopelessly dazzled and disoriented all three covered their eyes, crouched and started to scream. Satan roared a command, 'Stop!' Instant silence; there was no time to recover. 'Wretches! Liars! Traitors!' The adepts began a keening whine. 'The witch with the relic lay it before me. Now! Now!' Mrs Watts laid the scarf at the devil's feet. 'The club! The knife!' The bronze candlestick and the slaughterman's knife joined the scarf before him.

There was more, 'Enderby! I know you.' Mike's voice was muffled by the devil mask; a shocked Enderby did not return the compliment. 'You who called himself Benson. It was you with the knife.'

A grating, trembling reply, 'Master it was.'

I was concentrating on the silk scarf, it was light coloured, green patterned, but it was stiff, caked, heavily stained with something dark red-brown almost black in the dim light. Suddenly, Mrs Watts was the first to recover her wits. She snatched up the scarf, and scrambled to her feet screaming to the men, 'It's not real. It's a trap.' She had the vital evidence… she was going to set it alight.

I shoved my door fully open so it hit the wall with a bang and shouted, 'Go, Go, Go! Mike, get that scarf, the scarf, *Get* the bloody thing! The *SCARF*!' Mrs Watts had to run back to the fireplace, Major Wilson, aka Satan, charged after her. The rest of us swarmed in, focussing our torches, flashing cameras and yelling like Chelsea casuals. The male Satanists caught kneeling, scrambled to their feet. Enderby cringing with his hands in front of his eyes. Benson grabbed the knife as if to confront the charging soldier, received Mike's hand-off in his chest and fell backwards. Mrs Watts threw the silk scarf at the flames. It flew, fluttering and fell short, half in and half out of the fire. She was too late. Mike Wilson dived forward and plucked the scarf out of the fire. It was starting to burn at one corner; he crushed the flame out between gloved hands and passed the scarf to me. 'Is this what you wanted?'

I opened out the crumpled silk. It was Caroline's paisley patterned scarf, last seen by me knotted round her neck at 5.30 pm on 23rd November and missing from the scene of crime five hours later. Two thirds of it was covered in what looked like dried blood. We had our evidence. I bagged it and handed it to Briggs.

Reginald took charge, he handed a police radio to Kath, and asked her to go outside, 'and call for backup'.

Mike switched off the strobe light and closed down both the tape recorders, 'This is Mike Wilson terminating the recording at 12.29 am Monday 1st May 2000' and stopped the camcorder.

Briggs lined up his suspects and photographed them. He told them to remove masks and wigs and photographed them again. They stood, naked, shocked, shivering and dejected: Martyn Enderby, author, lecturer, spiritualist intellectual and country gent; Dr Pascal Threnadie de Morzine, international authority on Oriental philosophy and university lecturer; Virginia Potts, lawyer's wife, mother and medium.

Pascal lodged a protest, 'Zis is a disgraice. 'Ow dare you? We 'ave rahts!' The spell was broken, Benson's grating tone had gone, the left bank was back.

Briggs did not reply. He told the murder gang to get their clothes on sit down in their respective places, touch nothing and say nothing. Meantime, I photographed the goat portrait with the candles burning before it.

Kath came in, 'backup in ten,' she told her uncle. 'Mind taking charge of your ex brother-in-law?' Briggs asked Mike, 'if he opens his gob you have my personal permission.' Kath went to sit with Virginia. I took several shots of the fireplace area then went to stand close to a silent Pascal. The doorbell clanged, Kath went to open the door and brought back the key – shiny and new just as it had left Hindley's workshop – another item for evidence bagging.

Two young uniformed cops came in, said nothing, and stood at the door. Reginald went out, closing the door behind him. Another wait, Virginia wept quietly. I made it seven more minutes before Briggs opened the door and said quietly, 'Ken, could you come outside?' He looked at the two uniforms 'keep an eye on that one,' meaning Pascal. I went out into the hall.

Reginald made to introduce me to a tall, thin, sharp featured plain clothes officer, 'It's alright,' I said, 'I know DCI Kent. Good morning Nigel, if you think it's good.'

'There does seem to be a problem…'

'Right, but your lot have caused it and we've cleared it up for you.' Kent did not consider that a mere civilian should be speaking to a senior police officer in that fashion, in fact he said so. That did not improve my temper, but there was no point in starting a row with Kent. 'Look Nigel, what's needed here is get this so-called trial stopped before something worse happens. Else, it's heading for a world-class miscarriage of justice and a seriously vexed judge. What's needed here is a confession by at least one of our suspects by breakfast time. Mr Briggs has put you in possession of the evidence, so it'll be easy.'

Kent was prepared to be magnanimous, 'As this is a private conversation, I'm prepared to overlook your remarks, Mr Hardy and attribute them to tiredness and stress.'

'Balls.' I went back to the scene of crime. 'Sorry about the hanging around,' I said to Mike, 'I had to straighten the DCI's jacket for him.'

Kent took in all three on suspicion of conspiracy. Pascal was detailed to the police car with Briggs for light conversation. Kent asked Mike to use his own car to drive Enderby and himself. Kath and self would wait with Virginia for a female crew to collect her and then follow in Reginald's vehicle to Ditchfield police station. 'Cartwright,' Kent said to the second PC, 'you will remain here and secure the scene of crime until relieved.'

On the way out Enderby glared at me, 'traitor, Hardy,' he hissed.

'Sorry about that, wife-killer,' I told him.

'How come you're on first name terms with DCI Kent?' Briggs asked.

'Twenty-odd years ago we had an incident at the works and DC Nigel Kent came to take statements. It was his first serious detective job. Seeing he was wet behind the lugs, I helped him with tips like getting the facts before jumping to conclusions. I kick-started his career, he's hated me ever since.'

When the others had gone, Kath secured her surveillance gear and went to the window to watch for the escorts arriving.

The remaining PC took post at the door. I had a quiet word, 'You're the PC Cartwright that arrived with Tace at the scene of crime?' He was. 'You realise there'll be questions about the police evidence in the Berry trial? I suspect you were under pressure from on high.' An unhappy nod, 'My advice is to think about your own position.'

I sat next to Virginia on the settee. She had stopped crying and was sitting white faced and red eyed staring towards the dying fire. 'Virginia,' I said, 'this is serious. It'll take a few days to confirm the forensic results then if it's Caroline's blood on the scarf, you're on a murder charge. You need to make a full confession the minute you get to the station. Don't think about letting the other two down, they're goners, both of them. Think about Niall and the children. Confess now and as an accomplice, you'll get away with a shorter sentence. So...' Kath called out that the escort were coming up the track. A large woman police sergeant took over, handcuffed Virginia and bundled her without ceremony into the backseat of the car. Somehow, I thought that was a mistake but there was no point in interfering.

I wished PC Cartwright goodnight. 'If you hear strange noises from upstairs, take no notice, it's the roof timbers shifting.'

The lad raised a grin, 'It'll be reight, Mr Hardy. I'll stand at the front door. My mate'll be back directly.'

We went out through the back door and I snapped the padlock behind us. We climbed into Briggsie's car and I navigated Kath to Ditchfield police station. We didn't talk – Kath was not a conversationalist – but there was a relaxed 'job's a good 'un' feeling abroad. I sat back and savoured it.

'I've advised Virginia to confess,' I told Briggs at the station, 'It's her only chance of quality time with the children before they grow up.'

'I've roused Harrison. He's on his way,' said Reginald.

55

Chris Berry was half in and half out of my kitchen door. 'Welcome home,' I said, 'come in'. Nothing moved except his eyes. They flickered round the room: microwave to table, to fridge, to sitting room door – everywhere except at me.

'I was just putting the kettle on.' Washing machine, television, chair, 'Chris, I'm talking to you, look at me.' He did, now he was looking at nothing else, staring straight at me, which was worse, 'do you want tea?'

'I'm back.'

'Bloody hell, it talks.' Probably not the recommended response but I confided that any exchange was better than none. I switched the kettle on, and put a pair of mugs on the table. It made something for him to watch.

He fumbled in his pocket, brought out a crumpled packet of cigarettes.

'When did you take up smoking?'

He looked up at the ceiling, 'Moving things around.'

'I know. I heard you. The police searched your flat and left it like a tip. I went in after them and tidied up. I probably put some things in the wrong places, I expect you'll find them.' I had in mind the Caroline-in-love photograph that I'd liberated before the police arrived. I did not think this the best time to return it. Let him assume the cops had taken it with the rest of their "evidence". I also had his Jack the Ripper books.

Chris was stood standing at the half open door. He examined the lighted cigarette in his hand as though it was a new discovery. He licked the thumb and finger of his free hand, quickly pinched out the burning end and shoved the unsmoked remains into his pocket. 'I know who did it.'

'Who told you?'

'I heard.' That wasn't an answer. Chris started taking deep breaths, I thought he was about to come over hyper. 'Air. Need air,' he said, turned and walked out. I heard him tramping down the stairs and out into the street.

I saw Tom late that afternoon. He had gone 48 hours without proper sleep and he looked like it. 'Chris's trial is adjourned for a week until next Monday,' he said, 'for legal reasons.'

'What does that mean?'

'New evidence: waiting for forensic results mainly. At least we got bail for Chris.'

'I know, he turned up at my door, we had a non-conversation. He didn't seem to be taking anything in. Do you think he's all right?'

'The medical opinion is the same – depression. If he seems worse now it's because he's been suppressing it for five months. He needs time.'

'He claims to know who did it. Does he?'

'He's guessing,' Tom was confident, 'no names have been leaked. The police clamped down on that. They're in enough bother already.'

'What about Enderby and friends?'

'Bailed. No confessions.'

I left him to catch up on some sleep.

Next morning Chris breezed in, no knocking, no lurking on the threshold. 'Morning Ken!' Today's cheery version was no less unnerving.

'That's the style, walk do you good?'

He wandered around the kitchen touching things. I got him to sit down.

'Coffee time, want one?' He sat, legs stretched straight out, ankles crossed, hands in pockets leaning back, smiling like a bad actor doing "relaxed". 'How are things?'

'Fine.'

'What's changed since yesterday?'

He shot me an irritated glance then went on smiling, 'Nothing, it's fine.'

No point being negative, at least he was cheerful. 'Sounds good.'

A flash of suspicion followed by another sunny smile, 'Making plans...back to work.'

'Won't there be a problem, won't there be difficulties?'

That sent Chris to the verge of anger, 'Why?' Then he changed tack and smiled. It was a sly sideways smile, more troubling than the anger. 'I can go back any time. Tomorrow if I want to.' I sat and looked at him. The smile faded, 'What's the matter Ken, why not?'

'You mean go back to... where? St Cuthbert's?'

He jumped up, upsetting his coffee mug. It rolled off the table and broke. He ignored it. 'That place? Never! Worst mistake I ever made!'

I mopped the floor, binned the remains of the mug and sat him down again with a replacement. 'You mean the old job? But you gave up on electronics.'

He leant forward and switched on the smile – confidential this time, 'Yes Ken, but things have changed. I was in engineering – no future in hardware – it's all going to Singapore, South Korea and before you know it, China: low-wage workers with twelve tiny fingers. Our future's in software, dedicated programs, applications. I'm into "C" already.'

'You've never said.'

A fleeting, cunning look, then the unnerving smile. 'Ken, I've had months with nothing to do.' But where had he got his resources from, his learning materials? 'Prisons are funny places. Once you find the way around... ' He was on his feet again, excited, 'Why bother? I've got a few things to sort out.' He paused at the door, 'Sorry about the mug.'

Had he forgotten that the trial was only suspended, not abandoned?

56

Tom said, 'As a matter of interest, how do you reckon it was done?

'Exactly as described in Chris's statement.'

'Not quite what I meant – who invented the murder plot?'

'The lovely Virginia: lawyer's wife and mother, part-time medium and faith healer. Niall was completely under his wife's spell. He told me that Virginia was a "white witch". He got the colour wrong. When he came across the Benson document in the archives he thought Virginia might be interested. As a secretly practising Satanist witch she certainly was. There was also her long-standing infatuation with Martyn Enderby.

'I think Masham had left a "spare" Fellbeck key attached to the Benson document. Niall came across it, Virginia used it, visited, possibly several times and was convinced that the house was haunted by a spirit presence. She fed Martyn the idea of buying Fellbeck to use as an AGROW training centre: deserted, remote and haunted. Martyn arranged for the AGROW steering group to survey the house, went for it big and afterwards was rewarded on the Fellbeck hearthrug. Sam Waters implied all that without realising what it meant.

'Martyn was now ripe for possession by the resident spirit. After that she could put him under the influence whenever she wanted to.

'A few months after meeting Chris, Caroline ended her affair with Hans Meyer. Angry at being superseded by a new and unwelcome member of his staff, Meyer tipped Martyn off about Caroline's affair with Chris. That was the extent of his involvement but it provided the opening for Virginia to convince Martyn that Caroline had to go and how better than as a sacrificial victim to consecrate Fellbeck to their purposes?

'The Benson document gave Martyn the idea for luring Chris and Caroline to Fellbeck. Virginia went on to bewitch Pascal de Morzine to complete the coven of three needed to carry out the murder. Pascal's left bank accent misled me into thinking that he couldn't play the Benson role – I suspected Niall. But when we observed Martyn's Walpurgis vigil we heard Pascal speaking in his Benson voice until we charged in and broke the spell. Martyn was the murderer behind the door who bashed Caroline with a sacred bronze statuette. I don't believe he could have done anything of the sort without being possessed of the demon. Pascal performed the butchery on Caroline to provide the sacrificial blood.'

Tom had heard enough, 'How long have you known all this?'

'Having talked to Caroline on the night she was murdered, I suspected some sort of delusion. Then Virginia asked me to take her to Fellbeck and tried to convince me that the place was haunted, to deter me from poking around. Later, after the funeral, she let slip the idea that the murder was down to "spirit possession". That was my only real clue until I bribed Enderby into revealing his plans for Walpurgis Night.'

'Can you prove all this? I don't fancy McFadzean putting this occult stuff to the judge.'

'She won't have to. Once forensic identify Caroline's blood on her scarf, backed up by our recorded evidence and witness statements from Walpurgis Night, it's done and dusted.'

'Unless they faked the scarf with animal blood just to spice up the ceremony,' Tom suggested with his usual boundless optimism.

'Right daft, that would be. What's Satan going to say when he finds out that Enderby and friends have conned him with pig's blood?'

I moved on before he thought up more objections, 'Tom, I'm sorry to flog this but Chris showed up again this morning: complete turnaround, high as a kite, full of plans: no more teaching, back to electronics – then he was up and out. He's been out several times today, "going for a walk" in the rain. He said there were "a couple of things" to sort out. He also said that he "heard" who murdered Caroline. Does he mean "voices"? I don't like that.'

'Don't worry – he's limited by the bail conditions. His car's in the police pound and he hasn't much cash... all the same,' Tom picked up his phone, asked for Dr Calderwood and spoke for five minutes. 'He says normal people can exhibit short term schizoid-like symptoms after prolonged stress. He's adamant that Chris is harmless, not schizophrenic, but temporarily overactive. He's agreed to have a chat with him in the morning – a mild sedative.'

'He doesn't mean to talk to him at the prison?'

'No, Calderwood's private surgery, I'll drop Chris off at ten tomorrow.'

'That's a relief, thanks.'

I was climbing the stairs back to the flat when Chris appeared coming down at speed. I flattened myself against the wall as he tore past. I shouted after him, 'Tom's got a message...' No answer. He disappeared into the street.

★

The radio alarm clock was showing five minutes to five when I woke. It was warm for early May, I was too hot. I went to the window and pulled up the sash. There was a car standing at the kerb below with the engine ticking over, perhaps that was what woke me. Then I heard the front door of the building close, a man's voice, too low to make out the words, followed by the slam of the car door. I put my head out as the vehicle pulled away fast down the street. I spotted the illuminated sign, "Taxi", on its roof.

Where the hell was Chris going in a taxi at five o'clock in the morning? I phoned Tom. He asked, 'Did you get the name of the taxi firm?'

'I didn't see a name. It was a white Mondeo with a local registration but I didn't get the number. Tom, is he planning something stupid, if so where?'

'If he's blaming himself over Caroline I'd say Fellbeck,' Tom suggested.

'Right, suppose the taxi drops him at the bridge he'll have a distance to walk to the house. I can just catch him.'

'I'm coming,' said Tom.

'No, stay there and be the control centre. It could be nothing. I'd rather you didn't call the police. If Kent's finest turn up at Fellbeck with sirens going full blast while he's contemplating the noose it could push him over the edge.'

'I'll have to tell them pretty soon...'

I didn't discuss that – I rang off and threw on some clothes.

The sun was well up as I drove at fifty up a deserted Coldedge high street and turned left at the top. It was still dusk in the valley foot as I drove from the bridge alongside the beck until the grim frontage of Fellbeck reared up in the headlights. I continued along the side of the house to the yard and parked with my headlights shining full beam into the barn. Nervous as hell, I got out for a shuddering inspection. The barn contained a pallet load of animal feed, half a dozen empty crates and a long stepladder: nothing else. There was nothing in the sheds. I walked round the house checking for a forced or broken window – nothing, doors secure back and front. Relieved, I drove back towards Coldedge until the mobile signal came up then stopped and reported.

'I've rung the 24-hour taxi firms,' Tom said, 'none of them

had a fare to pick up from this address. He may have booked one of the freelance operators. That's a job for the police. I've asked them to trace the taxi.'

I said, 'Good, see you at the office.' I set off down the main road to Ditchfield. Two minutes later I changed my mind. The sign on my right said "Brookford": the village a mile from the Enderby place. If not suicide at Fellbeck, was it revenge at Heywood? I took the Brookford turn. I drove up to Heywood Place at a few minutes before six. The courtyard in front of the house was empty. I stopped and tried the front door. It was locked. I walked quietly round to the back. Enderby's black 4x4 stood in the yard, locked. I gave its owner credit for learning one simple precaution and tried the radiator – cold. The back door was also locked. There were no signs of a forced entry. The house stood silent. My gut feeling was that Martyn Enderby had endured a sleepless night only to slip into an exhausted coma at dawn. Alternatively, he was sleeping like a baby lulled by the conviction that he had done his master's will. More likely still, the house was empty; with its classy owner, as the media like to put it, "staying with friends".

Tom greeted my news with short-lived enthusiasm. He had other things on his plate, like keeping the business going without Niall.

★

For once, Reginald Briggs looked on the bright side. 'Your friend Nigel isn't happy – blaming it on you,' he said.

'When will the forensic result on Caroline's scarf come through?'

'Later today,' unsurprisingly Briggsie had a source at the lab, 'the blood on the scarf is human. They're working to confirm whether it's Caroline's.'

I was for celebrating, 'We've done it, Reginald, we've won.

408

Along with the other evidence from Walpurgis Night this'll convict all three of the buggers. We've got the motive as well. They couldn't use Caroline's body to consecrate Fellbeck so they settled for killing her on site and using her bloodsoaked scarf for a token at the ceremony.'

That ended Briggsie's bright period. 'Hold your horses, Ken,' the master detective warned, 'Enderby's defence are claiming that Caroline's scarf was "mislaid" at the scene. The gang found it last Saturday while shifting furniture for their witches' Sabbath. On the spur of the moment they wrote the scarf into the script. We've proved trespass on private property and distasteful dabbling in the occult but not murder. We need something else.'

There was more, 'Did you know Pascal de Morzine has done a runner?'

I didn't, 'He won't get far. He had to surrender his passport to get bail, so he must still be in the country?'

'Depends how many passports he has,' said Reginald, 'my guess is he took the London train on Tuesday, collected passport B, caught the Falmouth express, hitched a lift overnight with a French trawler skipper, landed Cherbourg or wherever *et voila,* two fingers to *les anglais!' (Briggs speaks French?)*

'So where is he now? Can't the French police pick him up?'

'Don't hold your breath, Ken, we don't know the name on passport B. Any road, it could be too late. I'm betting he's on a trans-Sahara bus, Algiers to Lomé. Good a place as any if you're a French colonial on the run.'

I was not for giving up, 'But look, the very fact that Pascal has done a runner, isn't that a classic admission of guilt?'

'It's suspicious but, for a poor devil of a French citizen in the grip of the British police, it's a reasonable precaution.'

★

I was about to start supper when there was a familiar pounding on the stairs. I got to my door in time to intercept Chris on the landing. 'Where the bloody hell have you been?' He was wearing a grin of the style favoured by cats of an adjoining county. The effect was irritating.

'I told you yesterday, *(hinted, more like)* I've been up to London for a chat with my old boss.'

I reminded him of his bail terms, 'You've had every police force in England out looking for you. You'd better get on the phone this minute, and see what Tom advises. He might be able to get you excused fetters.' To save further messing around I picked up the phone, dialled Tom's home number and handed Chris the receiver. I then picked up my supper and took it through to the lounge, closing the door behind me.

Fifteen minutes later, a deflated Christopher joined me, 'He's spoken to the station sergeant. I'm to report to DI Evans at 0900 tomorrow. Mr Harrison *(not "Tom" – he really is deflated)* hopes they'll take a lenient view.'

'You could be lucky there. Pascal de Morzine has gone on the run. Perhaps Evans will be relieved to get at least one of his lost sheep back.'

Chris gave me a feeble attempt at a smile and left for on an early night. At least he was showing signs of getting a grip on reality.

57

Briggs phoned on Friday. He sounded cheery for him, 'Information from the lab, the blood on the scarf is Caroline's – definite.'

'But they might wriggle out of that. You said that yesterday.'

'But there's more, they've found microscopic traces of blood spray on Enderby's devil mask and the front of his cloak. Enderby was our murderer behind the door. He clubbed Caroline from behind and the blood spray shot over him. That's why our forensic didn't find blood traces. It wasn't sprayed on the door or the wall, it was on Enderby.'

I was more cautious this time, 'Is the blood spray a match for Caroline's blood on the scarf?'

'We don't know; they've only got microscopic traces to work with, but it's human blood, not ketchup. They're trying to identify the person it came from but they're working on the outside edge of the technology, it'll take them a week at least. At finish, it might be impossible to get a conclusive result.'

'Even if they can't, how can he explain human traces? If it wasn't Caroline's whose head did Martyn Enderby bash in whilst wearing fancy dress? Where does this leave Chris?' No comment was the stern reply.

★

'Back on remand,' Tom said, 'he's been a silly lad so they cancelled his bail. He'll be inside over the weekend.'

'What about the trial?' I wanted to know.

411

'That's up to the trial judge,' Tom said, 'he can't go on adjourning indefinitely. If he directs the jury to acquit Chris Berry on Monday, that's the end of it. They can't get a retrial because of double jeopardy rules.'

I said, 'If the forensic evidence *is* decisive they'll set about prosecuting the Enderby gang. One murder, two paydays. Whacko!'

Tom deplored my mode of expression whilst conceding that I might be correct, 'Court proceedings resume at ten on Monday morning.'

I tried to get Mike Wilson for an update but got no reply. It could wait.

*

On Monday I was on the point of leaving for the court when the phone rang. It was Reginald, clearly disappointed, 'Match abandoned,' he announced. 'Enderby's had a right busy weekend. Farmer found him hanging in the barn at Fellbeck – crack of dawn this morning. Pathologist estimates he'd been dead 48 hours, meaning it happened on Friday night or small hours of Saturday.'

'You mean suicide?'

'Well Berry didn't murder him. He had motive but zero opportunity being locked up on remand from Friday morning until Monday. Any road, pending the inquest verdict, if I know owt it's suicide – certainly – and with Pascal de Morzine absconding. It's all over bar shouting. See you in court.'

What followed was a cracking anti-climax. Judge Slagdon-Pryce blew the final whistle: trial abandoned; all charges dropped, and legged it, looking as though he was glad to see the back of Ditchfield.

Chris Berry found Reginald Briggs and self taking a modest celebration lunch at the Duke. He addressed the master detective, 'I just wanted to thank you for all you've done, Mr Briggs. Without you, I really don't know how this might have ended.' They exchanged a handshake. 'See you around, Ken.'

Reginald preened ever so slightly, 'That were nice,' he observed, 'I don't bank on "thank you" cards from Slagdon and the prossy QC but I've done them some fucking service and they know't.' He decided on a second brandy.

When I returned to the flat Chris was gone.

58

I attended the Enderby inquest. After hearing the evidence the jury promptly brought in a verdict of suicide. The coroner then closed the entertainment with well chosen words on the dangers to the balance of the mind of dabbling in the occult. The regrettable matter of the deceased's involvement in Caroline's murder was not mentioned. In short, as McIver would have described it, an English snow job.

'That's it and all about it,' said Briggs. He took a large pull from his glass that demolished the remains of his pint in one and set it down on the bar with a meaningful look in the direction of my wallet.

I fought back, 'Granted that we've seen the last of Pascal de Morzine there's still Virginia.'

Reginald Briggs delivered a Halifax shrug, less suave than the Gallic variety, but more decisive, 'Happen.'

Again, the master detective was proved right. Virginia's brief did some nifty plea bargaining. He was on a winner. After the embarrassments of the Berry case, nobody: police, judiciary or CPS was looking for further revelations. With de Morzine safely out of the way, it was time, in the slippery syntax of the new politics, to "learn the lessons and move on".

Virginia consented to plead guilty to a lesser charge, arrived in court looking heartbreakingly lovely, wept into a tiny hanky, received a six year sentence promptly reduced to three for family reasons, fainted prettily but recovered when the judge suspended the sentence on condition that she undertook not to plot any more murders during the time in question. The media rejoiced like they do if the accused is guilty as hell but pretty: "Scapegoated Beauty Walks Free!" (*Who cares about the beauty she murdered?*)

At the end of July I organised a farewell pint with Mike Wilson at the Flying Duck. His command course was drawing to a close and he was awaiting his posting. 'Looking like back to West Africa, I'm brushing up my Yoruba.'

'You know Mike, there are a few things about Enderby's suicide that I never got my head round. I thought happen you could help.'

I got a pretty straight look by way of reply. 'Just between you and me,' I added, 'scout's honour and as a retired RE.' *(Come off it, Hardy – National Service corporal).'*

'Go on.'

'The inquest found that Martyn, having unhinged his mind by over-indulging in the occult, equipped himself with a rope from the stables, drove to Fellbeck and hanged himself.'

'A nice tidy verdict?'

'A bit too tidy to be true. Sometime on the Friday, he heard from his brief about the blood spray evidence. He was banking on the blood soaked scarf not proving decisive, but how was he to explain the microscopic traces on his devil mask and cloak?'

The Major was getting restive, 'All right, but isn't this academic? Either way, the verdict is still suicide. Isn't that good enough?'

'Not if it was murder.' I got the farmer that uses the Fellbeck barn to show me how he discovered the body early the following Monday morning. I do not see how Martyn could have done it on his own.'

'Why not?'

'Apart from the question of whether he'd got the guts, and I'm not sure he had, the body was hanging at the back of the barn where it would have been pitch dark. The car was parked nose into the barn so he could have used the lights but John Bolton said when he found the body the keys were in the ignition and the lights were switched off. He lit a couple of candles one red and one green – which would only make sense to someone who knew about the Fellbeck party. The stepladder was a wobbly affair standing on an uneven floor and he would have to balance on the top step while he got the rope round the beam. He then came down the steps, switched off the car lights (why?), climbed back up, put the noose round his neck and jumped. All alone in the dark, do you believe he had the skill or the courage?'

The soldier grinned, 'Sounds tricky if he was unaided. Who have we got that would like to see Enderby out of the way?'

'Chris Berry but he was in the prison hospital sleeping off a massive dose of sedative. Pascal de Morzine had skipped – probably already out of the country.'

'So who's left?'

'You and me; let's suppose it was me. Fellbeck is about 12 miles from Ditchfield and about the same from Heywood. I would have driven to the Enderby place, taken Martyn by surprise, strangled him with a nylon stocking, loaded the body into the 4x4, driven to Fellbeck, got him up the steps and hanged him, carefully adjusting the noose to cover any strangulation marks.'

'Then,' said Mike, 'you leg it 12 miles back to Heywood to collect your own car. How would you feel about that?'

'Considering that I'm 65, under-exercised, overweight and exhibiting hypertension, I couldn't have done it,' I admitted, 'but you could. You're familiar with Heywood. You know where to find the keys for the stables and for the car. Martyn was a non-violent pacifist, you're a trained killer.'

Wilson grinned, 'Have it your way Ken, but there is a problem: a seven day tactical exercise against a terrorist group impersonated by the SAS.'

'Where, Salisbury plain?'

'No, a blasted heath in Eastern Europe, location unknown. After Walpurgis I drove back to Aldershot to resume the course. On Thursday, we got a couple of hours notice before being flown out.'

'While Martyn was playing silly buggers in the barn you were abroad with 15 colleagues and the SAS?'

'So,' said Mike, 'how was it done?'

'It wasn't,' I said, 'it was suicide. When Enderby heard about the blood spray evidence he realised there was no way out. That night he got Virginia to put the spell on him, probably over the phone, drove to Fellbeck and did the job.' I didn't quite believe it, but what the hell?

'Remember what Ethel said?' Asked the Major, 'No knowing what a demoniac will do when under the influence.'

Finally, I asked Mike what he would do if he came across Pascal in the jungle. 'Proceed in accordance with local custom – that's British army practice,' he said. There was no call to enquire further, I wished him luck.

★

I picked a sunny afternoon, put the tools in the boot, drove out to Fellbeck and unlocked the back door. This really was the last time.

I climbed the three flights to the attic, worked my way past a hundred years-worth of old carpets and discarded furniture to the gable end. There was some light from the muck-slarted window, but not enough to work by. I lit the Tilley lamp and stood it on an empty box There was the steel chest with the ugly cast iron safe sitting on top. I hung my block and tackle on a roof timber and winched the safe up clear of the chest. I slid the chest out from under, found a couple of lengths of timber to stand the safe on and lowered it.

Energetic work with the hacksaw soon disposed of the

padlock on the chest. I stuck the jemmy under the lid, my legs were shaking *(Now then Hardy, all bullies are cowards).* I held my breathe to shut out the expected stench and leaned on the jemmy. The lid came up with a loud crack. I forced it all the way open, switched on my torch and shone it inside: blankets, old grey, moth eaten ex-WD blankets – Italian POWs for the use of. But what was underneath them? *(Get it over with Hardy!)* I started pulling the blankets out and dropping them alongside, fast, faster, any moment now.

The smell was wrong – not rotting flesh, just musty old blankets. There was also a faint oily aroma that gradually strengthened as I worked my way down the pile. Then it was over, the last blanket – no decomposing corpse at the bottom of the chest. Andrew Masham had not murdered his wife – she really had walked out and disappeared. I flashed my torch at the heap of bedding. The Italians had been too scared to come back for their blankets.

There was something at the bottom of the chest. I thought it was linoleum until I got it out. It was a roll of canvas. As soon as I began unrolling I recognised it – the portrait of Ezra Dawson that I had seen on Nathaniel Ostrick's sitting room wall. My 1992 visit was not a dream. 'You bastard!' I told Ezra's likeness.

I flung the blankets any old how back into the chest, crammed down the lid, lowered the safe back on top and unhooked my lifting tackle. I carted my gear out of the loft and, with relief, shut the trapdoor behind me. Encumbered with lifting tackle, tools and Tilley lamp, plus the rolled up painting, I was tired and sweating. Then I realised there was a shorter way: the back stairs would bring me out near the back door.

Not so clever, the stairs were narrow and dark. I worked my way down to the first floor landing where I put down the lifting tackle and the lamp and took a breather. Then I saw what was waiting for me in the shadows. There was a ragged patch of light on the dark wall opposite the foot of the stairs. I stood and stared. I could not make out where the light was coming from. As I watched, the patch began to resolve into a human face. Then the features started to appear; it was Ezra Dawson, grinning at me, daring me to come down. My legs were shaking under me. I was on the point of falling downstairs when the spectre opened its mouth to speak.

In that instant I understood what I had witnessed on Walpurgis night. Ezra really had murdered his wife. He had snatched her from her sick bed, carried her to the top of the main stairs and thrown her, screaming, to land with a broken neck at the bottom. The something I felt against my face had been the hem of her nightdress.

It was too much, I thought of Caroline and Jenny and I lost my temper. 'Well you can fuck off for a start,' I told Ezra, 'it's over, you're finished, get out of here and bloody-well burn where you belong.' That was not all. I don't recall in detail what I shouted at the spectral features but it was personal, filthy, comprehensive and was followed by the rolled-up painting which flew Exocet-like straight through that evil cake-hole and hit the wall behind with a thump. The tool bag and the block and tackle followed. I staggered, shaking, down the stairs with the remainder. There was no apparition there to meet me.

I collected up my impedimenta and carried it out to the car. I came back with my can of emergency petrol from the boot, collected Ezra's picture and walked up the main passage.

The murder room was brighter than I had seen it before. The evidence of Enderby's devil worship had gone, the furniture was back in place. I stacked the firewood that Enderby had laid in to warm his all-night vigil in the grate. I took the roll of canvas to the fireplace and stood it upright on top of the logs with the top end poking up the chimney. Ezra was destined for a bonfire, not the municipal art gallery. I soaked the timber and the canvas with petrol, stood back and threw in a lighted match. It went up with an explosive whoomph! and settled down to burn. I stood and watched. When it was finished I walked out, padlocked the back door and drove to the front door.

The courtyard was in full sunshine. I stopped the car, walked to the side of the beck and threw my illegal padlock key far out into the water. I was not coming back. I stood a moment looking over the Fell Beck. It was summer, the water was low, cheerfully chattering over the stony riverbed and the sunlight was glancing off the ripples. On the opposite bank a mob of sparrows was debating in a tree. Downstream a pair of ducks was messing about, up-tailing for weed. I walked back to the car and stood looking out down the farm track.

A hundred yards from where I stood, were three figures, three women, walking away from me side by side. They were not dressed for a warm day: one long skirted with a winter coat, one caped, one in a waterproof that reflected the sunlight. They stopped, turned and looked back at me. I couldn't make out their faces but they were young. I waved but they made no reply. Then they turned and walked on out of sight beyond the bend. I stood for a minute taking in the peaceful surroundings then got into the car and drove slowly out of the courtyard and up the track. When I rounded the bend the way ahead was empty. I hadn't seen their faces but three girls in green – I knew who they were.

I drove on towards home. Slowly the euphoria wore off. *Who are you kidding, Hardy? You exorcised the evil spirit of Fellbeck with assorted missiles accompanied by remarks that you must have picked up in the street?* There was no spirit presence at Fellbeck. Some people believed there was and after my call in November '92 I half believed it too. It was my own delusion that I had expelled. There were others who imagined themselves possessed of the demon and murdered Caroline to flatter their fantasy. I did not regret burning Ezra's likeness. He was an evil man and best forgotten.

Stefan's takeover of Ditchfield Packaging completed, I banked my cheque, shook hands with McIver and left for my tour of duty in Cape Town. Would I complete it? Old Dick Barber had said, "If she turns round and looks at you, you'll be dead in a twelvemonth". That was six years back. I'm still getting away with it.